THE THREE RITES OF CHRISTMAS

A Holding Files Novel

Ethan M. Strowd

For Brett

Always the center of my story.

TABLE OF CONTENTS

PART ONE

TUESDAY, DECEMBER 20TH

"There is no enemy as deadly as ignorance. Our purpose is to study and to learn, to observe and to experiment. On the dark day our knowledge is ever needed, it must be complete and it must be authoritative."

The Holding Associate's Handbook

Chapter One

As the son of a psychic, Nathan Cole tried to always keep two minds about things.

The Holding wouldn't want it any other way.

Mother Sable would have preferred I keep a few more than two.

Currently, he was trying to decide if this stranded bus was ever going to move.

It had felt like hours and the bus still hadn't gone anywhere. It was still sitting in the same gas station parking lot outside of the same small-town repair shop. He pulled the headphones out of his ears by the wires, silencing Enya in the middle of a dreamy ballad. He fidgeted with the silver ring on his index finger. He was alone on the bus. Everyone else, he supposed, had already abandoned ship.

Nathan yawned, shook his hands out, and had a long drink from the water he'd purchased when the bus had last stopped somewhere with a vending machine. Where had that been? St. Louis? Somewhere along an Illinois highway? *Thanks for Visiting Timber's Edge, Est. 1806*, the low white sign outside read. Nathan's window was fogged with condensation, but he could still make out a small banner hung beneath the sign.

The home of angels, Nathan read to himself. *Charming.*

He ran his hands through his shaggy blond hair and rubbed the tiredness from his eyes. The cold was beginning to bleed through the floor, and Nathan decided that the lady who had ridden next to him had the right of it. There was no point staying here. Everything had its place, and Nathan Cole's place wasn't sitting still. Not when there was a new town outside, even if it was past midnight and below freezing.

The door cracked open and a blast of chilly air pushed into the bus. The driver, an old white man who wore a short sleeve button up regardless of the cold, heaved on board. On his sleeve was a logo, three curling vertical lines, that reminded Nathan of smoke. The name Ronny was stitched into a patch on the shirt, and Nathan thought the name hung on him like an ill-fitting shirt. It just didn't fit. Nathan grinned inwardly.

Like I'm one to talk.

The driver fished in his front pocket for a pack of cigarettes and packed them against his hand. With a creased forehead, he looked down the aisle at Nathan, and tossed them on the dash before scooping up the PA handset.

"Alright folks," Ronny's voice crackled over the bus PA. He seemed to notice then that Nathan was the only passenger. With a grunt, he tossed the PA handset back down. "This is as far as we can go tonight. I got a call from the company. They're going to put you up here for the night, or at least until we get a new part sent over. There's an inn just down the street. You-ah should be able to walk to it."

In silent reply, Nathan cocked his head at the driver.

"Well, up and at 'em." The driver's scratched his chin with a long finger and looked like he was about to say more. Apparently he thought better of it because then he turned on his heel and bustled back outside.

Nathan found himself amused. As a frequent rider of the bus lines, breakdowns happened, but he had never been offered to be put up for a night in an inn in some charming town.

And in the home of angels, no less. Lucky me. At least I'll have something to do.

He felt the familiar itch at the tip of his fingers, the one that made him fidget with his ring.

Let's not get ahead of ourselves, Nate.

It remained to be seen if Timber's Edge had any Trace at all. But the itch was there, like a static charge, and Nathan had learned to listen to it. The corners of his mouth twitched upwards as he retrieved his burgundy woolen overcoat and worn leather duffel bag from its spot above his row. Timber's Edge might be an amusing diversion after all.

Outside the bus, Ronny was waiting for him. "You want to go that way," He pointed down the road. "It's not too far. You won't miss it. At this time, it'll be the only place with lights on." He barked a laugh at that, but Nathan couldn't understand the joke. "You got any luggage?"

Nathan hefted the bag. "Just this."

"Ah. You travel light huh?"

"I try. You're not coming with?"

Ronny rapped his knuckles against the bus. "Gotta lock her down."

Nathan suddenly swelled with pity for the driver. "I can wait. You've got to sleep too, don't you? I insist."

Ronny chewed his lip, then shrugged. "Sure it'll only take a minute. If you don't mind freezing out here, that is."

✳

It was a cold walk to the inn. After only a few minutes, Nathan's ears were frozen. It was simply the worst feeling; it felt like the cold sapped his mind right out through his ears. He needed a new hat. Where had he lost the last one, the gray knitted cap? The memory came after a few crunching footfalls. Just north of Nashville. He'd left it at that old motel and never went back. Not that there had been any time to go back. That had been a day.

More importantly, that had been a hat. I wonder where it ended up. Hopefully keeping someone else's ears warm.

Stretching his legs felt good after so long on the road. Fresh air breaks were well and good, but there was nothing like the stretch that came at the end of the day. Knowing that he was headed towards a warm bed was enough to give Nathan goosebumps.

Mother Sable had never cared to take breaks back when they traveled together, not when there was so much to see and too many people to help. Nathan traveled much the same now that he was alone. Every now and then, though, the road would catch up to him. Sleeping in train terminals or cooped up against the window of a bus took their toll and eventually muddied his thoughts. He'd been on a tear these last six months and his thoughts were good and muddied; there was no question about that. He could probably count on his hands how many times he'd slept in an actual bed in that time, and he was looking forward to adding a finger to that count.

On their way to the inn, Ronny led Nathan down a wide sidewalk lined with cedar trees, tidy hedges, and a low stone wall. The limestone bricks, flecked with pale frost, had shifted with time until they had become comfortably cracked and uneven. Lanterns hung from the doors of several buildings. In the black night, their meager flames cast dancing shadows, giving the buildings the impression of melting into shadow. Each lantern was a slightly different size, but each was made from the same black cast iron.

The same, but different.

After about half-a-mile, they came to a cozy two-story brick building. A sign out front called it *The Inn at Timber's Edge*. Handsome cottage windows looked out over the front lawn and, even from outside, Nathan could see the flickering of firelight in a front room. Already it was making him sleepy, but the small parking area, crammed full of cars, didn't give him much confidence.

The dream of a bed just took a step away.

At the entrance, Ronny stopped him just before he could cross over the threshold.

"Oh hey," Ronny said. He fished around in his front pocket, and Nathan half expected him to offer a cigarette. Instead, he held out a glossy piece of paper. *TransAmerica Bus Voucher*, it read. *Valid for one free trip on any TransAmerica bus ride (Limited to 1000 miles)*. On the back was Ronny's scrawled initial, a QR code, several paragraphs of terms and conditions, and the route number: 621416. Nathan's name was stamped neatly on the front. "Just in case I miss ya. Your ticket's got an insurance."

Nathan tucked the ticket in his coat's inside pocket, and asked, "When do you think we'll be headed out?"

"Love our service that much do ya? Hah. Replacement part should be installed tomorrow, so I expect we'll be able to head out the day after." Ronny nodded as if he was trying to remind himself of something.

The driver pulled the pack of cigarettes from his front pocket. Under his coat, he was still wearing his short sleeve shirt despite it being below freezing outside. If he was uncomfortable, the old driver didn't show any signs.

"Just relax," he said. "Enjoy the town. It's beautiful. Yessir, you won't want to leave, but there's not much I can do about that. We only got a day." Ronny had coaxed a cigarette into his hand.

"You're not coming?"

Ronny waved a hand. "Got more important business out here," he said as he lit up the cigarette. He licked at his lower lip and looked like he was watching a horse race. "Besides. It's Christmas. There's always room at the inn."

✳

The entrance foyer was neat with thick carpet and a wall of pictures of random, happy people. Nathan assumed they were previous guests. Most importantly, the inn was warm.

He desperately hoped that there was a bed for him, but the full parking lot tempered his expectations. Ahead of him were a family of four; the two young girls were fast asleep in their parents' arms. Behind them was a sour-faced man with slicked-back graying hair. Judging from the face of the parents and the sour-faced man in front of him, they had completed a similar calculation. Nathan's green eyes met the sour man's pale browns.

Please, Nathan thought. *Don't make us share.*

A short, happily plump woman was standing behind a desk at the end of the hallway. She was humming what sounded like "O Come, All Ye Faithful." A pot of poinsettias sat on the desk, large enough to obscure almost her entire face besides her frizzy white hair.

One by one, Nathan watched as the woman gave out heavy looking keys—two to the young family, one to the sour-faced man who smirked as if she'd given him a fist of solid gold. Finally, it was Nathan's turn at the desk. When her black eyes darted down to the paper and settled back on him, he knew it was bad news.

"You're Mr. Cole I take it?"

"That's me," Nathan replied.

"Marie Richards," she said briskly and stuck out a hand. Marie barely came up to his shoulder, but at that moment, she dwarfed him. Her black eyes crackled like coal and her hair seemed to carry an electric current. He took her hand in his; it was callused and rougher than he expected.

"I'm sorry. I wasn't expecting so many tonight. I already had to send some down to the Timber Lodge. That family's having to squeeze into three twins. With Mr. DeMarco and that dear Ronny, I'm all full now," Marie said.

Ronny. That bastard stole the last room. No wonder he had time for a smoke.

She clucked her tongue and flipped over the appointment book, as if something in the book would cause her inn to grow an extra room. "The roads didn't give you any trouble?"

"Gave the bus plenty of trouble," Nathan replied.

"I guess you're right there. Gave our other visitors plenty of trouble too," Marie chuckled. "They're not too bad yet, but they can get worse after the First Snow on Tuesday." Her eyes darted up to the clock. "Hah. Look at that. Today, that is."

First Snow on Tuesday. Quite the specific forecast, Nathan mused.

"Sometimes you'd be lucky to get up and over the mountain on Wednesday morning. I'm normally full for the season. Those other lost lambs, they're lucky I even had space."

"It's very fortunate," Nathan said. "For them."

Marie picked up a phone handset. She dialed a number.

"We'll see what the Timber Angel has to say about it, shall we? Yes, Paul? Sorry to bother you so late." Marie said after a moment of waiting. She put her hand up to silence Nathan's question. "Is your guest house free?"

Nathan could hear another voice, a man's gruff voice, on the other side of the line. *The Timber Angel has a phone number?*

"Oh I see. No I don't think he'd mind. It should only be for a few days, that's what the driver says." Marie described the bus break down, taking pains to make it sound like such a miserable circumstance that even Nathan was feeling badly for himself. "Oh, excellent. Alex is such a dear." Marie hung up the phone and her eyes crackled up at Nathan.

"Looks like you're in luck. The Ashfords are going to let you use their guest house for a few days. They're connected behind the Inn. Follow the path out front round back. Follow it through the yard and over the creek. You'll see the guest house right there at the bottom of the Ashford property. And, don't mind the ghost. He's harmless."

Nathan didn't like the sound of that, but before he could ask, she had pushed on.

"We do breakfast here. It's normally wrapped up by ten, but you look like an early riser." Marie chimed in.

Early to rise. Late to bed. Way too many thoughts in my head. Nathan massaged a cramp at the base of his neck. He needed sleep.

"There's also the restaurant down past Calbot Square. Then there's the roadhouse at the end of Main." She checked her watch. "It's late, but I'll rustle you up some sandwiches to take with you."

"That's alright," Nathan began, but Marie waved him off before bustling into a kitchen behind the staircase.

After Marie pushed a plate of wrapped sandwiches into his hands, Nathan was halfway down the hallway when he saw something sitting on the front door's molding. It was staring into the room, staring down at him, with two hands folded in its chest.

It was a small wooden figurine carved into the shape of an angel.

There's no need to look so smug, Nathan thought at it. *But thanks for the room.*

✳

Outside, Ronny was still standing by the stairs. A cigarette hung out of his mouth and another sat crushed by his foot. When he breathed, his breath fogged in front of him in a cloud of mist mixed with cigarette smoke. He looked at Nathan like he hadn't seen him before. "What are you doing out here?"

"Guess you were wrong. No room at the Inn," Nathan replied cheerfully.

A frown crossed Ronny's face. "You didn't get a room?"

"Guess they're busier than they thought," Nathan replied evenly. "That lady, Marie, she found somewhere for me."

After a moment, Ronny's face cracked into a smile, and he playfully clapped Nathan's shoulder. "Well, 'ain't that lucky. I would've hated for us to have to share."

You and me both, Nathan thought.

"Very lucky," Nathan agreed. Ronny still didn't move. "Would you mind letting me pass?"

"Sure, sure," the driver said. Ronny stepped to the side and took another drag on his cigarette. Through a cloud of smoke, he said, "Guess I'll see you at breakfast."

Nathan agreed, then, eager to put distance between himself and the driver, bid the older man a good night. Ronny's response hung with him for a few steps. What did he have to frown over? He had a bed.

He found the stone path Marie had mentioned and followed it to the side of the inn. It wound under an oak tree that spanned the distance from the road to the path. The path was icy and Nathan almost slipped as he crossed around the back of the building. There was a handsome patio with sets of tables and chairs organized around a fire-pit. An outdoor kitchen sat at the other end of the patio, but it looked like it had seen several weeks since it had last been used. The patio opened onto a lawn where a tidy wooden fence marked the property's boundary. From there, there was a gulf of blackness until Nathan could make out a rectangular structure. It looked every bit the guest house of a bus traveler's dreams.

Behind the guest house, up a slightly sloping yard, sat a larger family house, but Nathan's focus was on the guest house.

Just a shower. Maybe even a bed. That's all I need.

Hitching his duffel bag over his shoulder, Nathan crossed the stepping stones through the inn's yard. Between the fence and the guest house, a trickling creek burbled and bubbled alongside a thin walking trail. An arched stone footbridge waited for him, so he unlatched the gate and crossed down the trail.

As he approached the bridge, he slowed as he saw a stone statue take shape out of the darkness. It was small, about the size of a bowling ball, and sat on top of a pedestal. A single, glowing electric light, placed above the pedestal, threw strange shadows around the trail.

Nathan drew closer, but stopped once he could make out the elegant carving.

"Timber's Edge's, you've got specific taste," he remarked out loud.

It was a ghostly robed statue of death. And it was wearing a Santa hat.

In its hand, the statue held a chain, at the end of which dangled a faintly glowing lantern. Like the others in town, this one was also made from cast iron. Nathan poked it, and it swayed gently in the night, creaking on its chain. Nathan had half-expected an electric shock.

Too long on the road, Nate.

When nothing happened, Nathan smiled and shook his head. "Alright, Timber's Edge," he said. "You've almost got my attention."

On his way up to the guest house, Nathan wondered whether there would be an angel figurine inside.

Angels inside, death outside. Was that it?

More likely, Nathan considered as he turned his ring on his finger, they were both angels. Not all angels brought life, after all.

Plenty of them brought death.

*

Through the guest house's large front windows, Nathan could see someone crouched over the fireplace. It was a young guy, maybe mid twenties by the look of him.

Alex Ashford, if Nathan remembered the name Marie said correctly.

Snowmen flanked the front door and a cheery wreath hung in its center. Being on the road the last five years meant Nathan had spent his Christmases at a Courtyard or a Holiday Inn. If the last five years had been bland, at least Mother Sable had made up for that when he was younger. No year had been the same. She could've been on a job for The Holding all the way up to December 24th, but she would still be ready with a plan for Christmas Day.

After Nathan knocked, it took only a few seconds for the door to open. Alex was wearing a red zip-up hoodie over a blue shirt along with a pair of jeans. A mop of black hair covered his forehead and just brushed in front of his dark gray eyes.

As Nathan had guessed, Alex looked around his age. Judging from his lean face, his host seemed fit, but it was the easy shift in his weight when he lifted his arm that confirmed it. It wasn't something everyone would've noticed, but it was the small tells that were so important in Nathan's line of work.

"You're Nathan?" Alex asked in a higher voice than Nathan expected; a twinge of a Virginian drawl landed on the end of his question. He pointed to Nathan as if it was necessary to single him out.

It's not like there's a crowd outside. Nathan must have made some sort of face because Alex's cheeks turned scarlet, an effect made all the more dramatic by his pale complexion.

"Nathan Cole. Stranded bus passenger," he lifted a hand. "Pleased to meet you."

Alex gave him a sheepish grin that showed off a neat smile save for a few uneven teeth. He gave Nathan a strong handshake, then welcomed him inside.

"I'll show you around right quick," Alex said. "Sorry, it wasn't quite ready for guests. I was uhh actually living here until ten minutes ago."

Nathan surged with guilt. "Oh shit," he said. "That lady, Marie, she didn't say anything."

"Don't worry about it," Alex said. "It's normally reserved for guests through the season, but my dad pulled it off for the season this year." With a glance at Nathan, he added, "And, it was all mine. I can take those." Alex grabbed the sandwiches and placed them on the counter.

"Lucky for me, I guess," Nathan said.

"It was lucky for me too. Until you showed up." Alex grinned at him, the smile not quite reaching his eyes, before showing him a small kitchen with a fridge, stove, and dishwasher. The remnants of what must have been Alex's dinner lay in the sink, but, aside from that, the kitchen was spotless. "There are plates, bowls, and stuff in the drawers. I'm sure you'll find everything. There's room in the fridge if you need to store anything." He opened the fridge and gestured to a six-pack of craft beers. "Don't touch those, but everything else is fair game. How long are you supposed to be staying?"

"Not sure," Nathan said. "The driver said we'd be on our way day after tomorrow, but I have my doubts. He seems ready to winter here."

Alex let out a surprised laugh. "No offense, I hope you're not here that long. I'd like my fortress back."

"Your fortress?"

Alex gestured around the room. "So you'll see the First Snow then?"

There was that First Snow again, and the weight, the reverence, with which he said it. "I guess I will be here to see it. Whatever it is."

"It's a big deal for the town. It's the official start of our Christmas festival, and we take the holidays seriously here."

Nathan twisted his ring around its finger. "And does the Timber Angel have anything to do with it?"

"Ah," Alex said, a wistful smile pulling at the corners of his mouth. "You know about them already? Funny, some people never pick up on that."

"Kinda hard to miss," Nathan remarked.

Thinking of.

He scanned the room, taking care to check each of the door frames.

Alex laughed. "It's not a secret. And there isn't one in here. I can't stand them staring at me."

Nathan stopped looking, but, when his attention returned to Alex, the question must have been written on his face.

"If you must know, the Timber Angel only shows up on certain years, and it only makes itself known during the Angel Week—that's what we call First Snow up until Christmas Day. That's when it shares its magic. Tomorrow, the Angel will make it snow."

"If it shows up," Nathan said.

"Right," Alex replied. "But, if it does at exactly three in the afternoon, it will snow."

Alex was showing him a family bathroom done in blue and white tile. A pocket window looked out on inky blackness, but Nathan could see distant squares of light sprinkled over the dark landscape.

To Nathan, the description suggested a real power. A dangerous one. Power was typically proportionate to the size of the thing one was trying to change. Being able to affect the weather for an entire town, well that was pulling on something awfully large. Which meant the town itself was either saturated in Trace or something was playing with a well of power that it couldn't possibility control.

Power like that never comes free.

"Sounds like a nice story."

Alex chuckled. "A nonbeliever, huh? Don't let Marie hear you say that, she won't feed you breakfast." He pointed down a short hallway which ended in a closed door. "Down there is the master, but that's still got all my stuff, so you can leave that."

Nathan's eyes must have asked another question.

Alex added. "The sofa pulls out." Alex led him back to the main room and then retrieved a stack of bedding from a hall closet. He put the bundle next to the couch then gestured to the fireplace where a pile of charred logs sat. "I, uhh, tried to make a fire, but it's not my strong suit. It shouldn't get too cold, but if it does, there are some extra blankets in that closet."

"You live in Christmas town and can't make a fire?" Nathan asked. When Alex's eyes narrowed at him, Nathan raised his hands in a peaceful gesture. "No offense."

"We have gas in the main house," Alex said. Judging by the way his face drooped afterwards, it was not the defense he had hoped for. "Oh I almost forgot." Alex crossed back into the hallway and pulled something out of the closet. It was a basket, wrapped in plastic. "Since you're an official guest, you get the welcome wagon," he explained. Nathan could make out a bag of local jerky, a can of nuts, and what looked like a local jar of red jam.

"Festive," Nathan said.

"There's a local channel on the TV you can watch, if you like game shows. But that's about it," Alex stopped as Nathan frowned. "What?"

"Well, it's just..." Nathan trailed off then let out an exhausted sigh. He was used to a bit more friction. "You're all very trusting around here, aren't you?"

Alex shrugged and his face crossed into an impish grin. "It's a Timber's Edge thing," he said. "It's one hell of an adjustment when you come back from Philly on school break. Besides, it's not like *I'm* sleeping here. *You* might be a crazy person."

Nathan smiled. "I get that a lot."

✳

After Alex left, Nathan completed a private inspection of the guest house. It was well-stocked with snacks and, more importantly, had a coffee machine and grounds. He was tempted by one of Alex's beers for no other reason than he was told not to take one, but he was already tired.

And that wouldn't make me a very good house guest.

On the side table next to the sofa, he noticed a graphic novel that he figured Alex had been reading. *Collected X-Men.*

Officially, Nathan hadn't been allowed to read comics as a boy. By The Holding's standards, they weren't considered good nutrition for a growing mind. It was one of the few things The Holding and Mother Sable actually agreed on. She'd insisted that Nathan pore through Hawthorne, Dickens, and Shakespeare, alongside wading knee-deep into every major religious text available. Nathan had spent plenty of summer afternoons in the library while Mother Sable was looking into something particularly dangerous. When he knew she wasn't looking, he got to know the X-Men and The Avengers while hiding among the stacks.

Well, once she gave me my first silver, at least. It became a lot easier to hide it then.

He clicked on the TV and chuckled when a black-and-white image of three panelists appeared. *What's Your Line? Sweet.* He changed the channel, but all he could find was static. For someone who lived in and out of the roadside hotels across the country, Nathan was well acquainted with basic cable, and he'd never been saddled with a single local channel stuck in the 50s. It was a good thing he hadn't seen the episode.

After finishing the episode, convinced he could've won even without the hints they annoyingly flashed onto the screen, Nathan finally stood, took off his coat, and slung it over a barstool at the kitchen counter. He retrieved the three stones from his jacket pocket along with his scuffed iPod and headphones. The iPod he placed next to the X-Men comic, but the stones he took to the kitchen table.

Where had these come from? North Carolina, maybe.

They gleamed with the polish that could only have come from years under a churning river. With a gentle push from his finger, he spun one of the stones around the table; as he focused his mind on it, the stone began to float a few inches above the table. The other two joined it in the air. He felt a small strain on his mind, right in his temples, but it was a familiar friend.

As Nathan sat at the table, the three river stones hovering around his hand, he cast his mind to the Timber Angel, and the so-called First Snow. His two minds were still debating whether or not it was real, but he had time to kill, and Nathan Cole was nothing if not curious.

Alex had mentioned an Angel Week. If the snow is only first, what comes next?

In the back of his mind though, the uncomfortable thought lingered, and he remembered his X-Men more closely —particularly, Storm, the mutant who could change the weather. If the Timber Angel was real, and it could indeed change the weather at will, it could be one of the most powerful beings he'd ever encountered.

And that was just its opening act.

Chapter Two

The next morning, Alex Ashford rose two hours earlier than usual. With the First Snow looming, he hadn't been able to sleep much. At least, if he had, he couldn't remember any dreams. All he could remember was a fitful tossing and turning until the black night had turned to a dull gray morning. That was sign enough for him to give up, pull on his sweatshirt, and head out for a long run.

The guest house looked quiet, but there was a light on in one of the rooms. Nathan Cole, it seemed, was an early riser as well. Maybe he'd caught the town's enthusiasm and was soaked in anticipation for the First Snow.

Like a string of fresh lights, the town's fervor was especially vibrant this year. Alex wondered why everyone was so sure that this was an Angel Year—but that was in Alex's head. There was no way they would know any more than last year. It was just an excuse for some fun. It was just a nice tradition.

At least, that's what he told himself.

Once he got through the town square and across the bridge, he opened up his pace. At the treeline, the noise from the town fell away, and Alex was left alone with the pounding of his feet and the rhythm of his music. At this time—and on this particular day— there was no traffic on the trail, a blessing Alex was determined to enjoy. He followed the trail as it inclined towards the mountains and began to feel the burn in his calves and quads. The trail came to a fork. The left route led farther up the mountain while the right looped deeper into the woods and around the old farms. The air in his lungs was crisp and the scent of pine invigorated him. Today, Alex took the left. Today, Alex felt like he might have wanted to keep running forever.

The trail wound up the mountain in switchbacks. After a while, it opened into an overlook called Iron Shoe Point. There was a stone bench at the far side of the clearing and, from here, the entire valley was visible, including Timber's Edge. A small crystal lake separated the bench from a gazebo carved from similar stone. The trail kept going, but Alex normally stopped here to rest before heading back. Farther along, the trail straightened out. Eventually, it would climb again and keep climbing until it summited the mountain.

Today, Alex was tempted to keep going, but the sun was already above the horizon, and this was a big day for the town. Like it or not, this year, he had a responsibility to tradition—he was also curious, though he'd never admit it.

Timber's Edge had woken up by the time Alex had returned to town. Cars swam through the streets, and the sidewalks were lined with families grabbing their breakfasts. The diner already had a cluster of customers waiting at the door. Alex made his way to the walkway that ran behind the neat row of cottages that flanked the Inn. As he crossed past the guest house, he noticed something in the window that looked on into the kitchen.

Nathan sat at the table in a black tank-top, a steaming mug in front of him, deeply focused on something. Alex hadn't noticed his guest's build last night, but he could make out the shape of Nathan's arm—it was a brawler's arm, thick and roped with muscle.

Nathan's hand was next to his face, and he was turning a finger in slow circles. Even from here, Alex could make out the glint from his silver ring.

Suddenly, Nathan glanced at him, so Alex, not wanting to invade his privacy, waved and moved on. But, up at the main house, he stopped and looked back. Was he imagining it? No, he was sure he had seen something. Three dark shapes, like omens, had been floating around Nathan's hand.

I could go back, Alex thought, but he dismissed the thought. There was enough going on today without him worrying about Nathan Cole.

Even so, Alex made himself a promise. If the First Snow happened today and if he saw those shapes again, then he'd confront the muscular bus passenger, invade his privacy, and demand answers to questions that he had no business asking.

After all, in Timber's Edge, Christmas magic came first. Any other variety of weird immediately came second.

*

Nathan had to hand it to the Ashfords. They didn't spare any expense when it came to a sofa bed. He'd expected the worst, but by the time his blissful body would let him get up, it was already past eight in the morning.

A good night's sleep for once. I might have to retire here.

Tucking his iPod back into his bag, Nathan pushed himself out of bed. He changed in the bathroom into his workout gear and put on a pair of sneakers. He caught a look at himself in the mirror. As always, the first thing he saw was his tattoo. It consisted of three groups of symbols, stenciled in black: ξς ια κδ. He lingered on them for a moment, just to make sure they hadn't changed.

The shaggy blond hair needed to be trimmed back, and he'd have to find a razor to tame the stubble. But his eyes, the color of a freshly-mowed lawn, they looked sharper. It was always like that, Nathan found. Waking up for the first time in a new place. It set something off in him. Especially when Nathan had questions and the town wanted to talk.

Timber's Edge wanted to talk.

I can feel it.

He found a space in the living room and started a basic body-weight workout. It felt good to move his body again, but his chest and legs were stiff. His arms wobbled during his push-ups, and his abs screamed at him during his sit-ups. Never again. Never would he spend so long away from a bed again. When it came time to stretch, Nathan had to push himself through a brief routine which he didn't remember being nearly as difficult when he had done it before.

He would stop. He had to stop, at least for a little while. He'd promised himself. He had promised Mother Sable as well. It just hadn't felt like time yet.

Every now and then, she had said. Stop and see the world. Breathe it in.

Sorry Mother, but it's not that easy to do for all of us. Not when home is so far away.

One day, he would get back to The Holding. He dreamed about it, on the rare days he slept more than a few hours.

It wasn't much like this, Nathan could recall. For one, it was haunted by the spirit of a logger. It also lurked in an evergreen forest with views overlooking the coast. When he tried, Nathan could smell the sea salt, hear the crying of the birds, taste the crash of the surf. What he couldn't do was see it, The Holding itself. It had been so long now. All he could remember were fragments of rooms and fuzzy recollections of faces.

One room, one face, haunted him more than any other —

No. Not here. Not today.

He started floating his stones, banishing the thoughts from his mind.

From his place at the kitchen table, Nathan took in the morning view. He could see why they built the guest house facing the inn. The historic brick building was framed by small cottages on either side. The stepping stone path invited Nathan back down to the inn, and, beyond that, into the town. From the other side of the bridge he'd crossed last night, the ghostly statue watched him.

Something's changed, Nathan thought. Was it the lantern? No, that was still hanging freely. The Santa hat was still, somehow, sitting cheerily askew. It took him a moment, but once he saw it, he couldn't unsee it. *It's the angle.* The statue had been ever so slightly rotated on its pedestal.

Before coming to the guest house last night, the statue had been standing such that those crossing the bridge would face it directly. But now, it looked like the statue had rotated so that it had a view of the guest house window, just enough so that it could watch it out of the corner of its eye.

Or you just couldn't see it last night and now you're finding precisely what you're setting out to find. Let's stick to evidence, shall we?

Outside, a red sweatshirt crossed down the foot lane and over the bridge. Alex followed the same footpath Nathan had around the house. His flushed face and damp hair suggested he'd been running or hiking.

Alex stopped in the middle of the yard. Concern knotted into his face while the stones still floated around Nathan's hand. Their eyes met, and Alex offered a small wave before moving on.

A smile crept into Nathan's face and he guided the stones back to the table.

See something interesting Alex? Would you admit it even if you did?

After he'd showered, Nathan retrieved a small glass vial and a bronze dish from his duffel bag. The vial's contents were a clear liquid, about the viscosity of oil. He poured a small amount into the dish, then he twisted off his ring and swirled the liquid over it a few times before letting it sit.

From one of the duffel bag's inside pockets, he retrieved a long silver chain. Hanging off of the chain were several small charms.

Among them were the moon of Islam, a silver Christian cross, the Star of David, and others that only a historian might be able to identify. With a frown, he studied the second cross from the chain. This one was wooden and half of it was scorched black.

Promises to keep.

He placed the chain on the kitchen table, then sorted through the inside of the bag, passing aside a beaten-up copy of the King James Bible, a short, wickedly pointed knife in a black sheath, and an old used tablet. To most, he may have seemed a Luddite, but even Nathan saw the occasional use for the Internet, despite The Holding's tenets on the subject. Besides, it wouldn't do to carry every copy of every book he'd need. Besides, the digital version of *Ancient Symbols and Rituals* was actually pretty good.

Once he changed into a black quarter-zip pull-over and khakis, he wrapped his chain carefully around his left wrist, tying it so it wouldn't fall off. Then he dried off his ring and replaced it on his index finger. He didn't expect to need it, but it never hurt to be careful.

Especially when there might be a Timber Angel around.

He pulled on his overcoat, slipped his stones into their place in his right pocket, then headed outside into the cold morning and down to find breakfast.

The statue hadn't moved. That was good.

It did take on a different look in the morning light. Now that it was morning, the lines of the sculpture were sharper, cleaner. The robes billowed out behind the statue as if the ghostly figure was caught in a windstorm, and, the skin of the outstretched hand was mottled with patches of darker gray stone that looked like scars. Nathan hadn't noticed it last night, but it made him even more eager to put the statue behind him.

Do they include it in the Timber's Edge postcard?

Through the patio door, Nathan could see into the dining room where he recognized at least a few faces from the night before. He ignored the back entrance and returned through the front door where Marie was waiting at the reception desk.

"There you are," she said. "Breakfast is through the way, in the dining room."

Nathan followed the hall, past more photos of old guests. They were a stream of passing years, with each subsequent picture showing more crisp clarity until eventually Marie appeared in the final picture.

The floorboard creaked as he stepped into the dining room, a long rectangular room that ran parallel to the Ashford guest house. It extended farther than Nathan would've thought, large enough to house a massive twelve-person table. A smaller round table sat in an adjacent alcove while a hot buffet station, piled high with eggs, bacon, and hash browns, was set up along the wall that separated the two rooms. Two baskets, one full of breads and one full of pastries, sat at either end of the buffet while a coffee pot sang to Nathan from a square table that faced the street.

Ronny was at the head of the table, his plate more bacon than anything else. He wasn't wearing his driver's uniform. Instead, the old man wore a bright green and red cardigan. The young couple from last night sat next to each other at the other end, and the balding man and his family sat together in the middle.

One of their kids, a little girl her mother called Lisa, was scooping cereal from a bowl and engaged in animated conversation with another, older girl Nathan didn't recognize. She had dark, straight hair, and a wide smile that hadn't decided which teeth to keep yet.

Next to them was DeMarco, the sour-faced man. He'd slicked back his graying hair and put on a wrinkled button-down shirt. As the kids continued to talk, DeMarco kept shaking his head until finally he simply stared blankly ahead at his coffee cup.

"And that's when it's going to snow," the girl said confidently.

"Really?" Lisa asked. "Dad, did you hear? Are we going to be able to see it?"

The question was answered by a snicker from their father who wore the rimmed glasses of an accountant. "We'll see," he said.

"After that," the girl continued. "The tree comes. My dad drives it down from our farm. Then we hang our ornaments and it lights up!" The girl's hands made a dramatic, exploding gesture.

"Dad!" Lisa's cried. "Can we stay for that?"

"Lisa Brenner," her mother warned. "Not so loud. There are other people here."

DeMarco scoffed, and every adult glared at him in unison. The children didn't realize.

"Sorry," Lisa replied. She turned to her mother. "Mom?"

The decision making authority has changed, Nathan thought with an inward smile.

"It depends on the car, though," Lisa's mother replied. The Brenners' car had broken down. It was out front in the parking lot, having been towed there, or so Nathan had gathered.

Their son, who looked to be between eight and nine, the same as the local girl, seemed content to stay quiet, but he was watching intently.

"You shouldn't have much trouble," Ronny interrupted. "Let's see. If the shop can get the bus up and running before they close for the festival today, they should be fine for your car the day after." The bus driver dove back into a piece of bacon.

DeMarco's mouth turned into an incredulous sneer. "I can't believe it," he said. "Two days? For car trouble?"

Ronny glanced at him.

"What kind of way is that to run a business?" The sour-faced man asked the room.

Nathan couldn't disagree with the question, but it was launched like a crossbow bolt dipped in acid.

What about your car Mr. DeMarco?

Nathan cast his eye around the room. At least half the parties around the table hadn't chosen to be here. A small knot began to form in his stomach. It was a coincidence, yes, but not necessarily magical.

Though the line between the two can get a bit blurred.

"When I was running my business," DeMarco was saying. "I would never have allowed it."

"You can feel free to march down there," Ronny replied, waving a slice of bacon. "Whip everyone into shape. Yessir, I'm sure that'd be a nice Christmas bonus." He grinned, but the sour-faced man didn't look amused. "If you don't want to wait, feel free to leave with us." He pointed his bacon at Nathan. "We'll be out of here as soon as the bus is back up, isn't that right?"

Ronny's a slippery fish.

"That's the plan," Nathan replied while he was scooping some eggs and bacon onto a plate.

Ronny barked a laugh. "You see? That's the attitude." Nathan hovered over a pastry dusted with powdered sugar. It wasn't normally something he would eat, but it was some sort of flaky hand-spun dessert, something between a croissant and a tart. A layer of chocolate filling peeked out of the end.

"Winter horns," Marie said brightly from his side. "I made them fresh this morning."

Nathan was tempted, but his workout was fresh in his brain, so he left them alone.

"Not going to have one?"

One wouldn't hurt.

Nathan silenced the thought. "Not this time," Nathan replied. He poured himself a cup of coffee and left it black.

Scared of a pastry Nate?

When Nathan turned to leave back out the front door, Marie put a small hand in his back and pushed him towards the table. "Plenty of room right here." She guided him to a seat directly across from the two girls—Lisa and the local.

"Hey mister," the local girl greeted him with a toothy grin. Her interruption pulled his attention from the bus driver. "You're staying at the inn too?"

"That's right. Well, mostly right. I'm inn-adjacent," Nathan replied.

The girl's eyes lit up. "Oh! That means you're staying in our guest house."

Now Nathan saw it, the similar complexion, the same thin mouth, and the similar round eyes. Although where Alex's eyes had been the color of a thundercloud, his sister's were a vivid, icy blue.

"That's why Alex has been acting so weird this morning," the girl said.

Over a minor psychic showcase? Maybe this Timber Angel won't be so impressive after all.

"You're his sister?" Nathan asked, chuckling. Now, he was looking forward to seeing Alex again, if only to have some fun.

"How'd you know that?" The answer didn't seem to matter. The girl had already moved on before Nathan could open his mouth. "My name's Maddie. What's yours?" She kicked her feet under the table and wiggled on her seat.

"Nathan Cole," he said.

"What's that?" Maddie asked.

"What's what?"

She pointed at his wrist. Nathan swallowed his bite of bacon then lifted his arm. The silver chain rattled. "They're just charms. Between you and I, they're a tiny bit magic."

I thought we hated that word.

"Really?" Her eyes widened. From across the table, Nathan noticed Ronny and Lisa's dad looking curiously at them. He covered his wrist back up.

"Really," he replied solemnly. "Magic isn't something I'd lie about."

Well…

Maddie looked a bit suspicious. "Can I see?"

"I suppose that depends on this Christmas festival of yours." When Maddie's face scrunched in confusion, Nathan added, "My charms need magic to do their magic. It sounds like your festival has a bunch of it."

She brightened, her train of thought jumping a track. "Are you going to the festival today?"

Nathan grinned. "I wouldn't miss it. You're going with your brother I take it?"

The girl laughed and shook her head. "Cool! I'll see you there. I'm going with my dad," she said. "Alex can't come with us this year. He's gonna be with Jules."

Jules? Julie? Ah young love. Still, choosing a girl over his sister? I didn't get that sense from him.

Nathan found himself disappointed, dismissing the feeling as soon as it appeared. It wasn't his business. Besides, disappointment wasn't objective, disappointment wasn't impartial.

He wanted to change the subject. "It snows?" He added in a conspiratorial whisper that made Maddie laugh. "Between us, really?"

"Not every year," she whispered back. "But this year it will."

"You sound sure."

"I am," she said with a smile that electrified her blue eyes. "Angels never ever break promises."

Chapter Three

By the time Nathan had finished his breakfast and left the guest house, he could hear Timber's Edge alive in the throes of a busy morning. An icy chill still clung to the air, so Nathan buttoned his coat. After a few minutes, the tops of his ears began to sting. What he really needed was a hat. As he walked, he kept his hand in the pocket with his river stones.

Two-story shops lined Main Street. Occasionally, these were intersected by large evergreen pines, but Nathan couldn't be sure if they'd planted the pines or built the shops around the trees. It was an eclectic mix of retail offerings—within the same five-minute stretch, he walked by an antique shop, a store that offered handmade leather souvenirs, and a small general store. The Timber's Edge Outfitters seemed busy, and, through the store front window, Nathan saw that every customer had a pair of gloves in their hand.

Perfect.

When he emerged a few minutes later, he wore a gray knitted cap, complete with *Timber's Edge: Home of the Timber Angel* stitched into the top in bright white letters.

Outside the grocery store, a display of multi-colored snowball molds tempted any young child walking by. Another shop sold kits for making snowmen, snow shovels, gloves, and even a plastic snowball thrower.

And yet, not a trace of snow on the ground. Not even slush or ice.

Narrow alleyways cut between the buildings here and there, curling this way and that. Nathan wondered what lay behind them. They looked like they had been there for a long time, small channels slashed through the town's design for necessity or convenience. The stone accents and the clustered streets gave Nathan the impression of an English village—at least the idea of one.

He may have been to almost every state, but Nathan Cole had yet to cross an ocean. *Too dark, too deep.* His stomach churned whenever he crossed too large a bridge. Timber's Edge had a few big bridges of its own; the stone arches crossed the clear, wide river at several points. Eventually, Nathan would have to cross them too.

He sighed. *Such is the life.*

Eventually the line of shops on the far side of the street broke into Calbot Square, a manicured square lawn framed and surrounded by neat gravel paths. A building rose at one side of the square; opposite this was a squat octagonal tower made from bright white stone. A large clock was set into the tower's surface.

Nathan spotted a brass bell at the top of the tower, but he couldn't recall having heard it chime. Plenty of hours had passed since he'd arrived in Timber's Edge. Nathan checked his watch then glanced at the tower's clock.

At least it can keep the time, even if it does keep it to itself.

Calbot Square itself was a hive of activity. People bustled the various colorful tents that had been set up for the festival. Most of the tents were themed for the holidays, and many of them were decorated for Christmas. There were others, though, including one themed after Native American holiday traditions and another one staffed for Kwanza. A small cluster on the river-fronting side of the square was decorated with blue and silver.

Is that…is that really a Hanukkah garden?

He checked his charms, but they were silent, including the Star of David. Even in the presence of all of this, they were silent. *Now, that is curious.* Nathan felt a small smile play at his lips. *Very curious.*

In the center of the square, a blank space had been roped off. At first, he wasn't sure what it was for until he remembered what Maddie had said at breakfast. The square was missing its Christmas tree. If Maddie Ashford had been right, it would find one before long.

Strange though, that they wouldn't put one up before the 20th.

He walked on but didn't get very far before he came across something that should have made his charms sing.

A lantern stood between the blank space and a monstrous building at the end of the square. Nathan felt it draw him. It sat atop a square plinth of stone and, even in the daylight, managed to glow. The lantern had been sculpted out of pitch-black metal, polished to a great shine. The panels were made of stained glass that depicted scenes of happy town life: one of a carnival, another of a busy craft market. The third panel displayed some sort of festive gathering of people around long tables.

The last panel brought a frown to Nathan's face. The scene showed a large Christmas tree, surrounded by a crowd of people. It towered over them and was covered in a carpet-bombing of decorations.

They do take their Christmas seriously here, he observed, but it unsettled him nonetheless. Mostly because his charms remained silent. Against something like this, they were never silent.

At the far end of the square, across the lawn, stood some sort of architectural mutation. It looked like someone had spliced two different buildings together, one from the past and one from the present.

At first, Nathan thought it was two buildings, but then he saw that they were connected. One half of it looked to be some sort of historical building, all worn and faded brick with cast iron window frames and sculpted eaves. By comparison, the other half looked as if it had been constructed by aliens. It wore a face of sleek metal and glass, and, on its black sloped roof, solar panels sat in three tidy rows.

Gray letters ran like a raised eyebrow along the modern half of the building, spelling out *Timber's Edge Town Hall*. The other half of the building—*the old maid*—was left with a plain blue sign sitting near its door. According to that sign, the older section of the building was the Timber's Edge Library.

It was an easy choice.

At the library door, Nathan glanced up at the sky, and there wasn't a cloud in sight.

✳

The library was a dark cave compared to the bright morning outside and smelled like dust. Nathan could hear several different voices whispering in a hushed conversation, but when his eyes adjusted, he saw that there was only one other person in the spacious room, a boy reading at a table alone. He looked to be between seven and ten and had short, dark hair. The dim lighting made shadows dance among the numerous stacks. It was a well-appointed library for being abandoned.

Nathan listened again for the whispers, but the room was silent. The boy at the table wasn't even whispering to himself, just flipping quietly through pages. Nathan was sure he had heard something. Positive, in fact.

The circulation desk was a round oval in the center of the room. Behind it lay bright tables, decorated with comic book characters and surrounded by shorter stacks stocked with colorful covers. Here, the boy flipped through a comic while eating a PB&J. Having been a library child whenever Mother Sable had to investigate something too dangerous for him to tag along, Nathan would've loved spending an afternoon here.

A woman surprised him by calling out from a low, wide hallway at the left of the room, her calm voice echoing around the room.

"Sorry, I didn't think anyone else would be in today, so I snuck away to deliver some reports to the mayor." The woman's flowing shawl made her appear to float as she moved behind the circulation desk. She removed a pair of glasses, letting them hang from the chain around her neck. Her long arms and thin body reminded Nathan of a stick insect. "We're closing early for the festival. El," she called to the boy. He looked up from his sandwich. "You hear that? You don't want to miss anything."

"I won't, ma'am. My mom will be here soon," the boy replied.

How late was it? Nathan checked his watch. It was almost one in the afternoon. *Had he slept that late?* He had just checked his watch outside, but couldn't recall the actual time, only that it had matched the clock tower.

She turned back to Nathan, replacing the glasses. "How can I help you?"

The name tag pinned to the left side of her jade shawl identified her as *Denise, Librarian*. "I was just killing time," Nathan said slowly, carefully. Nathan noticed the boy glance at him before returning to his book. "Before the festival starts."

Denise brightened a bit, her glasses magnifying her eyes. "Oh, then you've come to the right place. We actually have a small museum. An archive, actually. It's been around for a while. It's got all kinds of memorabilia about the town and the festival as well."

"And where is that?" Nathan asked with an excited smile.

"Just down there," she gestured behind to another hallway, different than the one she had entered from. "Our," she said, after searching for the right word, "volunteer is getting ready to close, but he'll let you in."

"If he doesn't," Nathan replied with a smile. "I'll say you sent me."

Denise laughed. "Don't make trouble for me. I'm new here. Just started." A curious look crossed her face, as if she wasn't sure if she should have disclosed the information. "I will say that the mayor has told all of us here—" Nathan stole a glance around the empty room—"that we should do whatever we can to support the town. I'm sure she wouldn't be pleased if one of our visitors wasn't allowed to see the museum."

A familiar feeling of disquiet lingered in his stomach. He knew a warning when he heard one, and he was glad it wasn't directed at him. "I'll keep that in mind," he said.

The Angel Archive was little more than a single rectangular room, but it was stuffed. It reminded Nathan of a science lab. High tables ran around the room's perimeter, paired with equally high stools made for work stations. There were stacks of newspapers, labeled cabinets, and even labeled drawers for microfilm. A simple wall clock hung on the far side of the room while two friendly corkboards full of candid photographs framed a single window that looked on to a corner of the square.

The centerpiece of the room, though, had to be the display that dominated the center.

Now we're getting somewhere.

It consisted of six snow globes, each one sitting atop a hand of brass and each one a carefully constructed display of a different holiday scene. The workmanship was precise and full of detail. Engraved into some of the brass hands were two letters.

Nathan wondered if they were the initials of previous angels. Maybe the power transferred, and it wasn't just one being. That made the First Snow even less likely. A power like that should be old, should be deep. It wasn't the sort of thing that could be easily passed around, not without help. Power grew with Memory and Memory grew with time, Nathan recalled from his time at The Holding.

The room appeared empty. No sign of the volunteer that Denise had mentioned.

I'll behave, I promise.

Nathan pulled up his left sleeve, letting the charm chain was hanging freely. In a careful motion, he waved his wrist over the top of one of the globes. This one depicted a fair, complete with a carousel decorated with Nativity scenes.

The charms didn't respond.

Nothing? It didn't seem possible. *No, it didn't just seem impossible. It was impossible.* He was staring straight at an item that must have some of the Trace, in the middle of a room that should have been saturated in it. Nathan repeated the process over each of the snow globes, but the result didn't change.

A frown wove itself into his forehead as he examined the wall displays. One in particular caught his eye. Engraved into a golden plaque was some sort of poem. It was called *The Three Rites of Christmas*. Nathan read it once, and then again.

> *At the Angel's Call,*
> *First there will be Snow,*
> *With the Angel's Touch,*
> *Second there will be Light,*
> *From the Angel's Flame,*
> *On Christmas Morn, Finally there will be Joy.*
> *And Forever will the Angel's Memory*
> *Remain with Timber's Edge.*

How delightfully vague. Nathan stepped closer to the case, and studied the plaque more closely. Next to the second, fourth, and fifth lines were dates: December 20th, December 23rd, and, finally, December 25th.

Next to the plaque, inside a glass case, hung a brass hand bell. It wore a coat of tarnish and the leather strap was frayed and cracked. He waved his charms over the display, but, like they had with the snow globes, they offered him only silence. An inscription on the bell's surface was faded, but not impossible to read. It was simple, only a few words: *I sing for Angels*.

A familiar voice broke into the room and drew his attention. "What are you doing here?"

Alex Ashford now stood in the back of the room, a frown clouding his storm gray eyes. Since his run, Alex had changed into a navy blue long-sleeved shirt and a pair of dark jeans. They fit well, showing off his athletic build—if he had to guess, Nathan would've put Alex on a swim team in high school. *Lacrosse, maybe.*

"The librarian," Nathan said, confused at how he had missed Alex when he came into the archive. "She told me I could come back here." He crossed over to Alex where he saw the room broke into a ninety degree turn. Tucked into the hidden alcove was a small workstation and an office chair.

Alex's eyes darted to the bell, and the frown deepened. "Did you touch that?"

"The bell inside the glass case?" Nathan asked. "No, I did not."

"Oh, right." The storm in his eyes cleared. "Nice hat."

"I've got 'a face for hats and a knack for trouble,'" Nathan replied cheerfully. "That's what my mother always said."

"So, what do you think?"

"That she's right about the hats, but I try to stay out of trouble."

Lies.

Alex glowered. "No. About all this?"

"It seems your Angel's been busy." Nathan waved his charms again over another snow globe in the display, this one featuring a miniature train puttering around a winter village. Again, nothing.

"What are you doing?" Alex asked. "What are those?"

Nathan shot him a sly grin. "Magic magnets, in a sense."

Alex's frown returned, but it wasn't able to mask the flicker of recognition that crossed his eyes. "What? I mean, are you serious?"

Nathan shrugged. "You tell me." He grinned, then went about waving his charms over the other displays.

Not one of them responded, but when he reached the rack of old newspapers, Alex spoke again. "What are you looking for?"

"A reaction," Nathan said simply.

"To what?"

Nathan looked up from the newspapers. "To a memory. Now, pick a year. Somewhere between 1950 and, uh, 1991."

Alex rolled his eyes. "1950."

Nathan found the paper, then snorted.

"Not a good year?" Alex asked. His voice dripped with sarcasm and frustration.

"Not really. No sign of snow on the 20th. Just a boring Tuesday."

Recognition returned to Alex's eyes. "That's not how it works."

"How's it work then?"

"Well, the Angel decides what year it will—wait, you first. What are you doing here? Just who are you?"

"Nathan Cole, I told you."

"Don't bullshit me. You know what I mean."

You asked for it.

Nathan dipped his hand into his pocket and retrieved his river stones. He concentrated on them and, after a moment, they floated in a neat circle above his hand. "Good enough?"

Alex stepped backwards. "What the f—"

"Now, now, it's not that serious," Nathan chided with a laugh.

"Just who are you?" Alex asked again. "Are you psychic or something?"

Nathan grinned. "Afraid not. My mother was, but not me. I'm just passing through. I suppose you can think of me as a problem solver for issues of the abnormal variety."

"So, you're, what, a magic detective?"

"If you like," Nathan replied with another shrug. "Although I don't care for that word. It's not very precise."

The stones floated back into his pocket with a comfortable clack. He resumed waving his charms over the remaining exhibits.

Alex stepped cautiously forward. "And what are you doing now?"

"Looking for Trace," Nathan replied. "Magic—"

"I thought you didn't like that word."

"Magic, for lack of a better word," Nathan continued with a grin, "happens to leave fingerprints. We call it Trace. Other objects can resonate with that Trace, but only if they share communal Memory."

He held his charms up, so that Alex could see them more clearly.

"Think of it like a magnet, except where a magnet has only two polarities, objects can carry more. Many, many more."

"So, you take that cross into, say, The Vatican…"

"And it will come very much alive," Nathan finished.

Alex furrowed his brow. "They're not doing anything now."

"It's a problem," Nathan admitted, "because they should be registering some Trace."

"Maybe you're full of shit," Alex suggested. He was still frowning, but the corners of his mouth wanted to smile.

"Oh never doubt that I'm certainly full of shit," Nathan replied. "But not about this. Never about this. The price can be too high to pay."

Alex's eyebrows tightened.

Nathan continued, "it's curious, though, that someone who works in this—"

"Volunteers," Alex interrupted.

"—Someone who volunteers in this Angel Archive would doubt me. We should be trading notes and swapping stories." Nathan grinned again. "Unless you don't even believe in all this?"

"I believe in the Angel," Alex replied carefully. "But that doesn't make what you're saying true, either."

"Very good," Nathan said.

"He said condescendingly," Alex shot back.

Maybe a little bit.

Nathan ignored the barb. "But it is true. About magic, that is." He peeked outside the window and saw the crowd outside beginning to build. Nathan pointed a finger to the window. It was time to get going, especially since lunch had snuck up on him. "I imagine I'll see you there."

"I'll be there," Alex said.

With Julie, apparently. Nathan managed to keep the thought to himself.

"I have it on good authority that this is one of those years," Nathan said. "An Angel year. What do you say to that?"

Alex stared at him for a few seconds before he finally spoke. "I'd say you're well informed Mr. Cole."

Nathan clapped him on the shoulder. "You'll be surprised what you hear around the breakfast table Alex, and there's no better source for information than an excited kid." He retreated back to the entrance, and, when he turned back, Alex's cheeks were flushed.

Oh Alex, Nathan thought, *I do hope you're not a poker player.*

✳

After the library, Nathan still had some time to kill before the festival began in earnest. The diner down from Main Street caught his eye. It was the only place in town with a neon sign—*Gloria's Place*, it read. However, that wasn't the sign that drew Nathan inside. It was the second sign. The wooden one, with a white coffee cup filled with deep black coffee. *Always Fresh! Always Hot! Coffee!* it declared in the capital letters of the caffeinated.

Inside, it was a sprawling space that couldn't seem to make up its mind about what it wanted to be. To the right hand side, there was a coffee shop, complete with a bakery case and squashy armchairs. In the center of the room, there was a dining room where tables and chairs looked as if they had been stolen from that familiar American institution: an old Denny's. Finally, a line of vinyl booths ran along the left side of the building, all the way back to an open kitchen and eat-in counter. Pictures lined the walls, some large and some small. Most hung at slight angles.

Apparently the local hardware store doesn't carry spirit levels.

Everyone in the dining room had clearly still been in the mood for breakfast. Gloria's Place was alive with chatter and the clinking sounds of forks spearing eggs and fat sausage links. A four-inch-tall, hand-carved wooden angel greeted him from its perch atop the host stand, and Nathan eyed it like he might a predator.

Over the course of the morning, he'd seen at least a dozen of them. Most of the shops had the wooden angels lurking above a door, as in the style of the Timber's Edge Inn, but not everyone in town followed suit. The Timber's Edge Outfitters had theirs sitting on top of their cash register while Lost Then Found Antiques had taken the egregious step of allowing a six-foot tall angelic monstrosity stand right at their entryway to glare at each customer that walked in.

A raspy cackle came from the kitchen, breaking Nathan's concentration. A loud bang followed it, the sound of something hitting metal. In the open kitchen, a Black woman in chef's whites marched up and down the line of burners. There was only one other cook back there with her, a muscular Black man who towered over her. They both laughed at something. It was a joyful laugh, and it made Nathan smile. She waved a wooden spoon in her hand, and, every few minutes, she would slap one of the counters with it.

There were several open seats along the counter. *Is that because of fear?* When she spotted Nathan, the spoon banged again.

"Well, you are a new face, aren't you? Come on up here. I don't bite."

The hell you don't Nathan thought, but he sat. By now, he must have partaken in most of the diners still running across the United States, and he knew —and loved—her type. Mother Sable used to tell him, "There is no-one better to tell you the truth than an old cook. They're too old to care about lying and too proud to give it to you anything but straight."

This, he decided, *must be Gloria*. Up close, Gloria's deep wrinkles were clear to see, and she had a curious way of licking her lips before speaking. Nathan soon realized this was her way of clicking the safety off her weapon.

"You are a tall glass, aren't you? Well, not that tall, but a good drink all the same." She said after slipping her black-rimmed glasses on.

Two slippery fish in one day.

"Take a seat. Coffee?"

"Please. Black."

Gloria grinned at him. "Special day. I'll get you a cup. Back in a minute." She slapped a menu down in front of the seat up against the wall, Nathan's assigned seat. She then marched through the restaurant and checked the other diners' plates. A few of them looked up from their plates, surprised at something.

"Thank you ma'am," Nathan said when she'd returned to the counter with the coffee.

The chef sniped a glare at him. "None of that 'ma'am' stuff here. I won't be called that in my place. Call me Gloria." She appraised him before rotating the menu and studying it, as if she was seeing it for the first time. Finally, she made a noise, something between a cough and a sniff. "Meatloaf," she declared at last.

"I like meatloaf."

Gloria nodded. "Green beans. Mash." It wasn't a question.

"Okay," Nathan replied.

"You here for the festival?" she asked as she wrote the check, passing it to the kitchen without looking.

"Not by choice," Nathan replied. "My bus got stranded."

"Well, you got here just in time. We're about to close." The restaurant was full, was bustling, and Nathan peered at her with the question plainly on his face. "They'll be done eating in time," she said with authority. "They always are." Gloria winked at him before disappearing behind the pass.

After she left, Nathan watched the restaurant dining room. It was slowing down, that was clear. Diners paid their checks, filtered out into the street, and the tables were left empty.

"Here you go," Gloria said, sliding a plate in front of him. She filled his coffee as well. The moment he saw the thick slice of meatloaf, the mound of mashed potatoes, and the handful of green beans, Nathan knew he wouldn't leave a scrap. Gloria was looking at him expectantly. "Well?" she asked.

I can't say I'm used to eating under observation. Nathan obliged her, and at the first bite, it was clear Gloria had made the right choice.

She didn't wait for him to answer. "Glad you like it," was all she said before she returned behind the food pass.

That's an understatement, Nathan thought as he shoveled down another savory bite.

Halfway through his plate, Nathan tried to stop, but he failed. He would leave the plate for a few seconds before his hand would find the fork again. He took some comfort in knowing he had been able to resist the winter horns that morning, but the meatloaf had worn down his resolve.

"Any idea what to expect today?" Nathan asked as Gloria made another round. "I hear it's going to snow."

"That's what they say," Gloria agreed.

"You have your doubts?" *You'd be the first.*

Gloria considered the question. "Yeah, I think I do. But then I doubt anyone who doesn't let me feed 'em. Angels included."

Chapter Four

When Nathan returned, Calbot Square was filling rapidly. It felt like the town was inhaling, drawing all of the people inside the square.

The Angel Festival had brought vendors from all over the area, it seemed. Nathan was unfamiliar with many of the names he saw. There was a coffee roaster from Blue Pine, a couple selling roasted nuts from a farm outside of town, and Christmas trees from what sounded like every farm within fifty miles. Timber's Edge proper had some representation, however. Gloria herself was manning a tent and spooning free samples of pot roast into the hands of a crowd four-deep. How she managed to close up shop and make it out here was something Nathan hadn't the answer to. The smell of roasted nuts stole three dollars from him, and the fresh roaster got another two.

A line of cars snaked slowly down Main Street. After the conversation at breakfast, it was good to see some cars still working. Nathan eyed their queue which went all the way up over the mountain. A few more were still heading into town, and Nathan wondered if they were going to be able to find parking. There were no cars leaving. *No one wants to miss the show*, he observed.

Snow or no snow, it was clear that the crowd was here to enjoy themselves. He could see it on the bright faces of the people as they visited booth to booth. *How many of them come here every year?* They moved around the festival like regulars, but then any alienation Nathan himself might have felt dissolved with each crunch down the gravel paths.

The blank patch in the square was still empty, but the lantern beyond was shining brighter. The lantern's light made the stained-glass panels cast colorful shadows around the ground. Most everyone who passed it clicked a photo, normally with a disposable camera, but some families had more hobbyist gear with them. Nathan saw the Brenners in a line, ready to take their pictures. Lisa had a camera already in her hands.

There was a rhythm to it. The conversation would die down, then a click from the camera, then the chatting would pick back up. Nathan watched for a few minutes, mesmerized.

Click. Click. Click.

There were no phones, he noticed after a moment.

Click. Click. Click.

No cell-phones? Not a single one? He cast his gaze around the crowd. No streamers walking with their phone in their face, no selfie-sticks sticking up into the sky. He fidgeted with his ring, trying to place why he found the sight so troubling. Had he missed some sort of local law?

Timber's Edge. Home of angels, but hell-scape for cell-service?

He listened again for his charms. They refused to make any sign at all, and it didn't make him feel any better.

It doesn't make sense. Nathan could feel it. There was Trace here. Plenty of it.

Timber's Edge isn't following the rules.

The thought bit his lip, and then he turned the stones over in his pocket. There were two kinds of people who broke the rules, in his experience. The ones who didn't know them, and the ones who didn't care about them.

As he passed in front of the lantern, he overheard customers buying trees from a stand declaring that these trees were from the farms surrounding the town. It didn't get more local than that,

Nathan figured. But it didn't explain the line. By the 20th, most of these people should have already had their trees up. It had been some time since Nathan had enjoyed a traditional family Christmas —*Have we ever actually had a traditional Christmas Nate?*—but, from what he understood, the trees were up far longer than five days.

A towering man stood by the tent, and his voice boomed across the square. He wore a flannel shirt along with a heavy beard. Nathan was reminded of Paul Bunyan on the day he forgot his axe at home.

"Oh that's a nice one," he said. "Jonesy here will load it for you." He gestured to a tall farmhand at his side.

"And the town tree?" The heavyset man damn near beamed as the farmhand took the tree and marched it towards a truck.

"We've got a great one this year. Cutting it tomorrow so it's fresh as can be for the big day." the farmer promised.

The customer left, and then Nathan watched the next customer, a short man in a heavy coat, shake the farmer's hand. "Another Blue Spruce this year?" The short man bowed his head, as if in prayer.

Nathan moved on, stunned at the reverence these people placed on Christmas trees. Mother Sable, a stickler for tradition, had always insisted on a real Christmas tree. That much Nathan could remember clearly. Even though they had lived on the road most of the time, that hadn't stopped Mother Sable. She would simply drive to the nearest lot and take in the smallest, most shriveled thing she could find, then set it up in the space that passed for her camper's living room. Nathan could remember the sound it had as she'd driven, the ornaments jangling with every quick turn and needles spraying the floor with every punchy stop.

When Nathan had grown into his own camper, she would inevitably sneak one into his as well, although he'd never managed to catch her. One year, when Nathan had asked about it, Mother Sable had wrinkled her forehead and said simply: *It's not as if you would have gotten one for yourself.*

At the end of the square, he bumped into Ronny, who was walking with the young couple from the inn. The two thirty-somethings wore the same nervous expression.

"Ah. Mr. Cole," Ronny said. "This is quite fine, isn't it?"

"Quite fine," Nathan replied pleasantly.

"And look at you," the bus driver added. "Getting yourself a souvenir. You can't help but join 'em. You two need to get some souvenirs as well. Before you leave." He let the young couple walk on, their pace increasing after a few steps. After they'd left earshot, Ronny turned to Nathan. "Those two were good enough to let me tag along with 'em."

Nathan spotted Maddie at a stall further ahead and turned to break away, but Ronny grabbed his arm. "You're ready to go tomorrow, aren't you? We need to hit the road nice and early. Got to beat the traffic and make up all that ground."

Nathan looked at the road out of town. Not a single car was leaving. "All packed," Nathan said.

"Good man," Ronny replied.

He turned to see where Maddie had got to, but he'd lost the younger girl in the crowd.

An impeccably dressed woman joined them. She was perhaps in her mid-forties, and her dark suit was pressed and tailored. A sprig of holly was pinned in her lapel. Her eyes, a blue so deep it was almost a shade of purple, studied their faces. Darting quickly, they reminded Nathan of a hawk. "Excuse my interruption. I'm always on the lookout for our new faces. I'm Mayor Benneteau." She offered a hand to them. "Are you enjoying yourselves?"

"Oh, most certainly Mrs. Mayor," Ronny said. "This sure is a treat."

"And I have it on good authority we're in for a show," Nathan agreed.

The mayor's eyes narrowed at Nathan. "Is this a friend of yours?"

Ronny barked a laugh. "He's a friend of mine, but I can't speak to the other way 'round, seeing as I'm the one who stranded him here, I'll leave it to him to decide that. Me? I try to be friends with everyone. Things are easier that way, dontcha think?"

The mayor was nodding. "Absolutely."

Something caught Ronny's eye over at the other side of the square. It was DeMarco, and to Nathan's surprise, he wore a camera around his neck. "Well, would you look at that?" The driver said, half to himself. "If you'll excuse me, I'll go make sure our regular sour puss is getting along."

After Ronny left, Mayor Benneteau took notice of the roasted nuts bag in Nathan's hand. "Enjoying yourself?"

"Christmastime," Nathan replied with a good-natured smile. "What's not to enjoy?" Thinking about what he'd seen earlier, he continued. "No phones around here."

She nodded. "There's no law against it, if that's what you mean. People just tend to forget them. They stay in the moment. It's how we like it. Some of them take lots of pictures and contribute them to our little archive."

"You mean the Angel Archive? That's right, the picture boards." Nathan said. He tried to remember how many pictures had been on the wall. There had been dozens. "How long have they been doing that?"

"Oh for years," The mayor straightened the front of her suit. "You've seen our little museum then? You're quite thorough."

"I try," Nathan replied. His eyes darted back to the Brenners. Their son was now examining a candle-dipping tent.

The mayor regarded him a moment longer before saying, "If you'll excuse me, I need to start the festivities." She left, and Nathan followed her with his eyes. She crossed the square and climbed the steps to Town Hall where Alex was waiting.

Now what are you doing there Alex? And where is Julie?

Someone handed the mayor a megaphone to address the crowd.

"Timber's Edge," she called. The crowd clapped politely. "Here we are again for another Christmas Festival. This might be my first year as your mayor, but I can say with certainty that this will be one of the greatest festivals we've ever had. Don't forget we have an entire week of fun planned. We have our tree lighting in two days, then of course, the grand finale, our gift fair!" The crowd's applause grew.

The Brenners were clapping along heartily. Lisa Brenner, in particular, was cheering.

The mayor was continuing to talk, but Nathan's attention fell to Alex. Where the mayor was drinking in the crowd, the younger guy's eyes kept darting to the mountain ridge. He looked preoccupied.

"We're only a few minutes away," the mayor finished, then she gestured for Alex to step forward.

You've been holding out on me Alex. What's your part in this?

"Now, as you know, we have another little tradition for our Christmas Festival. I like to think of it as our version of Punxsutawney's groundhog ceremony." A titter of laughs broke out among the crowd.

The mayor flashed a flawless smile. "For those visiting us, here, in Timber's Edge, the town of Angels, we have been fortunate to be visited by the Timber Angel over the years. On those special years where the Timber Angel visits, on those Angel Years, it's up to us to celebrate as hard as we can, with as much joy we can muster, and to savor the gifts the Angel bestows upon us. Now, we're just moments away from finding out if the Timber Angel is going to give the first of those gifts. The First Snow." The crowd clapped kindly.

Even from his place in the crowd, Nathan could make out the red creeping into Alex's cheeks. When he made eye contact with Nathan, Nathan shot him a sarcastic wave. Alex turned an even deeper shade of red.

Nathan glanced at his watch. Only a few minutes to go, yet there still wasn't a cloud in the sky.

At three o'clock, however, one thing happened that Nathan didn't expect.

He had expected a snow machine to spit foam over the crowd.

By this point, he'd even expected perhaps real snow summoned by the Timber Angel.

But he hadn't expected this:

Absolutely nothing happened.

*

The crowd deflated in one breath. The mayor turned to Alex, a question in her eyes. Then Nathan heard something from far away, down the other end of the square.

It sounded like the tolling of a bell.

He turned towards the source of the noise, towards the old clock tower. The bell wasn't moving. He could see it from here.

The sound of the bell grew louder. Soon, it flooded the square. No one in the crowd noticed, or, if they noticed, they didn't seem to care. Nathan scanned their faces. They all wore the same expectant look, all of them waiting for the mayor to continue speaking. The bell sang across the square, the town's deep baritone voice.

Only one other face stared towards the tower. Alex Ashford met Nathan's gaze again, then his eyes widened in a signature look of surprise. Alex leaned over to the mayor and whispered something in her ear.

Evidently, it was good news. A grin erupted on the mayor's face before she returned to the megaphone. "Everyone look to the sky! The Timber Angel needs to hear you!"

Now that is a neat trick, Nathan thought.

The crowd clapped again before a wave of cheering started. Even

Alex had swapped his glare for a sheepish smile. The crowd continued to cheer louder and louder until it matched the bell tolling in Nathan's head. With each cheer, the lantern in the center of the square brightened. *It's like the town is sending a message.* It didn't take long for Nathan to realize who the message was for.

It was for the sky. For that clear blue sky.

And the sky, it had a response.

That's not possible.

Before his eyes, the sky changed. A swarm of gray clouds hovered above the mountain ridge. They were moving quickly; they would be on top of the town within seconds. Before Nathan's eyes, they seemed to stop.

This is impossible.

He watched, almost in a trance, as the pale gray clouds swelled, darkening into black. It was like watching a weather report on fast forward.

Nathan's stomach pitched and he blinked. The clouds were moving again. In fact, they were already above the town square.

Maybe they had always been there. Nathan couldn't quite remember the sky being clear. *It had been gray all morning, hadn't it?*

A voice called from the other side of his head. *No, it hadn't been. It had been clear.*

The clouds opened then, precisely on time. Only a few flakes appeared at first, but they quickly gathered into thousands that carpeted the town square. Nathan heard the children cheer but wasn't sure the noise was real until the adults began singing. They sang in a chorus: *O, come all ye faithful, joyful and triumphant.*

✳

John DeMarco watched the first flakes float into the air from a bench out of sight behind the ornament stands. Already, it was giving the town a good dusting, the way a snow globe did after a healthy shake. He wasn't a weather man, but it had seemed like it was going to snow all day, so he wasn't too surprised. He wasn't sure what everyone was getting into such a fuss about. It was just snow.

Although it was pretty, he had to admit. For a moment, the view almost made him forget about his car. Almost. He almost forgot about the whole damn business, but it came back hot and angry. How could it take so long to fix a car? That mechanic wanted to screw him.

John snapped a photo with the disposable camera he'd found in his room's welcome basket. He had thought it was a foolish expense for the Inn to give them to their guests, considering everyone has cell-phones nowadays. But, when he had left to walk around town, he had taken it anyway. John didn't like to waste anything, and, if he had already paid for it, then he was damn sure going to use it.

There were five pictures left and he was looking forward to having them developed. The silly thing reminded him of being a kid. He used to be a shutterbug, especially around the holidays. Being able to get some pictures developed. Properly developed. That was a rare treat.

John made himself a small vow. He'd get back his camera and start taking more pictures. Once a week, he could hit the trails and try find some good shots.

A smile snapped to his face when he pictured himself stomping around the cold, muddy trails with his camera around his neck. He may not have been going to the gym as often as he should, but he could always start. It couldn't be that hard.

"Well, look who's having a nice time," a familiar voice said.

The smile melted off of John's face.

Ronny, that damn mechanic, was standing over him and grinning. The snow swirled around him, catching in his white hair and against his face. "You see, it's not that bad that you got stuck, is it?"

John shifted his weight. "It certainly isn't a good thing," he said. By now, the roofs of the buildings had all fully put on their jackets of fresh snow. It really was a nice sight. But, it was just weather. It wasn't worth him missing all of his appointments, and John DeMarco had no shortage of appointments.

Ronny leaned into the bench beside him. "You see, that's your problem. Everyone else is having a nice time, but you're still complaining."

John felt himself beginning to boil. "I just want to be on my way."

Ronny smacked his lips. "Yup. I understand that, but that doesn't mean you have to kill the vibe." He shook his head then rested a meaty hand on John's shoulder.

"Excuse me?"

"Everyone else is having a nice time. And you're sort of ruining it."

John let out a bitter laugh. "I'll act however I like." John decided it was time to leave. "Ex—"

He didn't finish the statement. An icy hand clapped his forehead. John was aware of two fingers pressing into his temples, and then an obscene pressure. It felt like a vice had been placed where the fingers had touched, and now it had immediately closed. No build-up, no gradual increase. There was nothing and then there was a crushing weight in his head.

John wanted to scream, tried to scream. But he couldn't even make his mouth move. New thoughts wouldn't come. They died before they could even form, strangled right in the crib of his own mind.

"Well," Ronny's voice said from somewhere far away. "Would you look at that?"

The waves of pressure pressed down, taking John's vision and swimming it far away. As his sight faded into black, the last thing John saw were white specks.

They looked like snowflakes.

Chapter Five

"It's your go," young Madeline Ashford said. After a cup of coffee at the Inn, Nathan had been tempted to return to the guest house, but when Alex's sister had thrust the Sorry! board in his face, he'd buckled under the unrelenting pressure of a child with a want.

"So it is," Nathan replied. He rolled the dice, got a four, and moved one of his green tokens forward. It was his last one on the board. Maddie had a single blue one left as well, but Lisa Brenner only had two of her yellow tokens back home, so he was liking his chances.

"How are you doing that?" Maddie demanded. Her face was creased in concentration. There were worse ways to spend an evening, Nathan decided. Marie had prepared hot chocolate for them all. A bright fire was dancing in the grate. The wind gusted outside, and the snow pecked the window.

"Doing what?"

"You're never getting the bad squares."

"Tactics," Nathan replied. He heard a snicker from across the room, and looked up to see Lisa's dad watching them.

"What's *tactics*?"

"It's planning. Thinking about my next move."

"But the dice tells you where to go."

"That's part of it," Nathan admitted. "But I think about what number I need before I roll. That's the key."

"That works?" Lisa asked.

"It has so far," Nathan shrugged.

On her next roll, Lisa took the dice, screwed her eyes shut, and then tossed it onto the table. It came up as a six, exactly what she needed to bring one of her pieces home. She cheered when it came home, and Nathan rolled his eyes.

It won't be enough to save her.

One precise roll from Alex's sister got her last piece within one square. Nathan still had five squares to go to secure his.

No problem. With a dramatic sigh, he dropped the dice and allowed it to hit a three. *Coward.*

Maddie gave an excited cheer when her last piece made it home. "I won!"

"A strategic loss," Nathan said. "That's all."

"What's that?"

Lisa's dad chimed in. "He's saying he lost on purpose," he said with a chuckle.

Maddie's face became mocking. "Aww. You're a sore loser."

Nathan laughed. "Never doubt it."

"It's okay. My brother is too."

Alex. Nathan hadn't seen him since the snow began, and he had a lot of questions. Starting with the bell. His eyes darted to the window where the snow continued to pile.

Yes. I've got a lot of questions.

✱

So, it actually snowed.

Nathan was still turning it over. It didn't seem possible. The three smooth stones floated above him, rotating with the subtle movement from his right hand. There was a time when this simple exercise would demand all of his focus, when it would make his temples ache and his forehead sweat, but now it was as easy as walking. And concentrating, of course.

Little more than a parlor trick next to real snow. On demand. As easy as streaming a movie. And it wasn't as if it was just a few flakes. Altering the weather for a whole town? That's real power.

"It could be dangerous," Nathan whispered aloud.

There's no could be about it. The power was definitely dangerous, but that all depended on who was wielding it. A frail, old man could be dangerous if he happened to be ex-special forces, Nathan observed. *Especially if he's properly motivated.* The thought tightened the knot that had been forming in Nathan's stomach. Anything he'd seen that afternoon had just been turned on its head. Everything had its place, after all, so what was this Angel's place? What was its motive? Why did it do what it did?

An entity capable of making it snow does so for no other reason than Christmas joy? Hard to believe.

He lay on the sofa bed, stared up at the rotating stones, and turned the thoughts over in his head. Occasionally, he stole a look out of the window. Night had fully fallen outside, but there was enough light still for him to see the flakes flowing down in complex spirals. It wasn't a particularly heavy snowfall; it was nowhere near a blizzard. Nathan doubted it would give any of the cars around here trouble. If he had to pick a word to describe it, Nathan had settled on "comfortable." A comfortable snowfall, the sort that belonged to a Christmas Eve stroll down a waterfront. *A perfect snowfall.*

Perfect. The word lingered in Nathan's head and tightened the knot even more. It was true. There was an intention behind it. A design. It wasn't just a storm; Nathan could feel the hand behind it, shaping it. "The hand of an angel," he muttered.

The corners of his mouth twitched into a small smile. He cast his mind once again to the town square and sank into the details. He smelled the roasting nuts again, heard the cheering of the children, saw the snowflakes appear in the clear morning sky. The so-called

Timber Angel was there as well.

And somehow, you missed it.

The stones wobbled. Nathan tried, but his mind couldn't stabilize them again. Eventually they drifted apart, farther and farther, until they finally dropped to the floor with three successive thuds.

Nathan remained on his back for a few more minutes, then sighed, and pushed himself up and out of the sofa bed. He collected the stones from the floor and put them on the side table where they joined his iPod and the silver chain of charms.

He went to his leather duffel bag and retrieved a velvet pouch from one of the hidden interior pockets. Inside the pouch was an unremarkable piece of polished glass, framed by a rough white material that might have been bone. Inside the mirror, he saw his own face staring back at him. The strain and stretching from days of travel still lingered, but the green eyes looked anything but tired. After a moment, the reflection faded from the mirror and was replaced by the image of a door at the end of a simple corridor.

Nathan let go of the mirror, but it didn't fall to the floor. Instead, it simply hovered. He stared at the door, feeling the familiar vertigo as the door drew closer. There was a pulling sensation and then Nathan was standing in the corridor before the door. It was silent. Still.

Don't look up.

"Never look up," he said. In the silence, the words were as loud as a scream. The door wasn't locked. It never was. At his touch, the door swung inwards.

The pulling sensation returned, stronger than before. Nathan blinked and was no longer in the silent corridor. Now he stood in the entryway of what looked like a massive Swiss chalet. A wall of glass towered opposite him, opening onto a vista of snow-capped mountains and alpine lakes.

Nice view, Nathan thought. *Certainly better than it was the last time I came.*

It was late afternoon, but the sun was still peeking out from behind the rocky peaks. A large, heavy set of curtains sat on either side of the wall, ready to be used later.

After hanging his coat on one of the hooks that lined the wall, Nathan stepped forward into a comfortable lounge, stuffed with leather armchairs and sofas. The walls and floors were all rounded logs; somewhere and some-when a forest must have died for the materials. A fire roared in the stone hearth and the smell of wood and cinnamon hung in the air. A grand staircase led up to a second floor.

The room appeared empty, but at this time that wasn't unexpected. Corridors branched off the lounge in different directions. One, Nathan knew, would lead to the staff area. He checked behind him. Even from the wall where he'd entered, there were three corridors. He had come from the center corridor… or had he?

Things, after all, were subject to change.

The door at the end of the corridor was green, three sconces lined the hallway, and then, of course, there was his coat. *That should be enough of an anchor. I hope.*

It wouldn't do if he could never find his way out.

Something scratched at the far end of the room. The sound had come from one of the wingback armchairs that faced the view.

Nathan stepped forward carefully. "Anslem?"

It would've been a nice surprise if the Aegyl didn't keep him waiting for once. As Nathan drew closer, he heard the sound of sobbing, and it deflated him.

Not Anslem then. An Aegyl doesn't cry.

In the wingback chair sat a man. He wore a loose shirt and pants, both made from plain white muslin. He was of average build and appeared to be in his late sixties, although that meant very little in

Anslem's thread of the Weave. In his callused hands, he cradled a plain brass tuning fork. The man gave a wet sniffle. Clearly, he'd been crying.

That wasn't entirely unexpected, either.

Nathan felt neither pity nor disdain for the man. Everyone bore the Choice differently. It was a weighty thing, after all, and the Price couldn't ever truly be understood until it was faced.

He was about to retreat and to leave the man to his consideration when the other man gave a start. He looked at Nathan, looked through him, as if he wasn't really standing there. "It doesn't seem fair," he said. "It just—it's just not fair."

"Fair is for playing games," Nathan replied. "Decisions aren't fair. There's only the choice and then there are the consequences."

"I can't do it."

"You can," Nathan said. "But if you do, you won't be the same."

A smooth voice spoke from behind Nathan. "That's rather the point."

Nathan faced the Aegyl. It wore its chosen form, that of a young man in a midnight blue suit. The skin was the color of rich, terracotta and his short hair was in tight curls. Where there were supposed to be eyes, there were instead cobalt ink wells. Inside, stars swirled in spirals. "Wouldn't you agree Nathan Cole of The Holding?"

*

The man made his choice, and the Aegyl took him to his room. When he reappeared at the top of the staircase, Anslem had changed forms. He now looked like a mass of whirling fire. The hue of the flames shifted from pale yellow to deep red. He was in a vaguely human shape and, where the arms might have been, there were bronze rings of metal. A larger ring of metal ran around its middle, and another sat atop the Aegyl's head like a tarnished crown. The eyes were the same inky pools.

Anslem appraised Nathan from the top of the staircase before vanishing into a cloud of sparks. Nathan grinned when the sparks appeared next to him.

Anslem walked out of them as easily as crossing the room. He elected to switch again to his preferred form, complete with the midnight blue suit. The form was tall and roped with lean muscle. Nathan had always wondered exactly where Anslem had gotten it, but the Aegyl had never said.

If you're going to choose how you look, Nathan thought, *you could do a lot worse than an Olympian swimmer.*

To maintain his own body, Nathan had to exercise when he could, and, when the mornings felt very early, he sometimes thought of Anslem and his ability to grow abdominal muscles the way a worm might grow its body.

"How long has it been?" Anslem asked in his familiar smooth voice. Nathan was accustomed to the being's controlled voice. Meteors could fall from the sky and Anslem wouldn't be phased.

Nathan might have been a questioner, but Anslem was primarily a listener. Only his eyes hinted at something else. Whenever he spoke to Nathan, the swirling stars twinkled with bemused curiosity, and, not for the first time, Nathan felt very much like an ant next to a god. *Still, it was nice to have friends.*

"About three months," Nathan replied. "Maybe four."

The stars spiraled. "Ah, your linear time never ceases to amaze," Anslem replied in an even voice. "There is something different about you. An air of purpose, perhaps? We are not in harmony with The Lady this evening. The rotation differs."

"I'm not here to see Her," Nathan said quickly.

"That is well," Anslem said with an incline of his head. "What then brings you to this strand of the Weave, my friend?"

Nathan recounted the story of Timber's Edge, of the Gift festival, and of the First Snow. The Aegyl listened without interruption and, as the story went on, began to go about his business of straightening up the lounge. *Everything in its place.* Nathan was content to follow Anslem around the room as he spoke. When he'd finished, Anslem was carefully placing another log into the hearth with his bare hands. If the roaring flames bothered him, he showed no outward sign.

"So," Nathan ended. "Could it be one of yours?"

Anslem turned away from the fire and faced Nathan. "An Aegyl?"

"You're the only being I've ever encountered that could do that. And it might be changing its face, I didn't mention that. I suppose I want to know what I'm getting myself into."

"As always, your limited experience flatters me," the Aegyl replied. As a senior associate of The Holding, Nathan Cole was perhaps one of the world's five greatest paranormal investigators. Even asleep, he was at least in the top ten. Next to Anslem, though, that didn't count for much.

It certainly does keep the ego in check.

"To answer your question," Anslem continued, "I am uncertain. It is entirely possible. My kin have spread widely throughout the Weave. Some have even visited your plane. A few, perhaps, even your world. Some have even been known to mate with the lesser species."

"Wait," Nathan interrupted. "Really? You never told me that." It wasn't often Anslem talked about his kind.

Anslem's head twitched in a slight motion. For the Aegyl, it was tantamount to throwing something. "Because it is abhorrent," he said.

"That's nice," Nathan replied.

"We are of the Divine Spark," Anslem said. "You are little more than apes."

"What kind of child would even come from such a union?" Nathan was distracted now. It was even more rare for the Aegyl to air dirty laundry.

Anslem waved a hand. "Something like you, I suppose."

"A what?"

"As I told you when you first arrived: a unique soul."

Nathan scoffed. He remembered the conversation well. "Aberration. You called me an aberration."

The stars swirled again. "As you say. My meaning carries." The Aegyl changed the subject. "I am hard-pressed, though, to believe one of my kind would be content to relegate themselves to participation in a barbaric celebration of a solstice."

"Barbaric celebration? You mean Christmas?"

The stars in Anslem's eyes danced. "Quite so."

"It's not barbaric. It's a sacred day for my kind. For some of them, at least. It's all good will and joyful tidings. You'd like it."

"Curious, the weight you place on single days when there are so many that have come before and so many that are yet to come," the Aegyl replied. He fell quiet for a moment before speaking again. "This Angel visits every one of your, what was it, years?"

Nathan shook his head. "Whenever it feels like it, apparently. Like you, it seems to keep its own time," he replied.

Anslem drifted around the room, moving an item here and there. "And how many times has this Angel visited?"

Nathan thought back to the Angel Archive and the snow globe display case. "Six, at my best guess."

The answer pulled Anslem's attention from his tidying. He stared out of the window, out over the mountains. The sun had almost disappeared under the horizon. It wouldn't be long until the lounge was full of visitors. "So this would be the seventh visit? A powerful number, seven. Although I have always found it lacking compared to nine. But what it lacks in wisdom, it makes up for in drama, wouldn't you agree?"

"Seven's a bit of a drama queen, sure," Nathan replied. "It beats five though. Five's a real piece of work."

"You shouldn't be so crude," Anslem chided gently. "Five has a noble soul."

"Sorry."

"It is quite alright," Anslem said. The form of the young man exhaled deeply. "Find the Angel and bring it here," he said at last. "If it is one of my kind, I would very much like to speak with it."

"What if they, the Angel, what if they lie?"

The stars swirled again. "I will know it as one of my kin on sight. There will be no need for dishonesty."

"And if it refuses to come with me?"

"There could be some need for persuasion," Anslem admitted with a slight bow of his head.

"Terrific," Nathan replied. "It only has the power to shred me down to my atoms." *It'll just need some convincing, that's all. Then a gentle push into a floating mirror.* He tapped his finger to his upper lip. "And if it isn't an Aegyl after all?"

The Aegyl favored him with a long look. "Then we shall, as you say, cross that bridge when we come to it. But, I can assure you, Nate, if it is not an Aegyl and it means ill to you, then it will not trouble you." The stars vanished from the eyes and Nathan felt like he was staring into a black hole. "Friends look after one another, is that not so?"

"Quite so Anslem," Nathan replied. "Quite so."

From somewhere among the floors above there came a strangled sound. It was something like crying. But here, Nathan knew, it could have been something much more like a scream.

Part Two

Wednesday, December 21st - Thursday, December 22nd

"The best thing is to return any unstable Memory to The Holding. When this is impossible, destruction may be the only realistic alternative."

The Holding Associate's Handbook

Chapter Six

The bus rattled along the highway, but it didn't sound right. It was a gentle sound, like the one Christmas ornaments made when the blast of air from the heater hit them just right—not at all the heaving lurch that came from a cross-country bus. A few of the reading lights flickered. Outside, the snow was falling in thick sheets, and Nathan wondered how long it would be before they had to stop. He could barely see the street lights down the center of the road, and it felt as if they had been driving nonstop for days. How long had it been? Nathan couldn't say for sure.

One thing for sure was that he needed to use the bathroom. He pushed himself up out of his seat, gently past the woman sleeping next to him. The bus swayed on the road, and Nathan lost his footing and stumbled into the aisle. The woman didn't wake up, but someone tutted him from behind. Nathan spun, rounding on the sound, but all of the seats behind him were empty. He looked the other way, down towards the front of the bus, but there was no one looking at him.

Right there in the aisle, his legs were stuck in quicksand. *The sound had come from somewhere.*

The bathroom forgotten for now, he stepped gingerly towards the front of the bus. The next few rows of seats were empty as well. Nathan couldn't remember if anyone had even been sitting there. He made it to a row where the reading lights were turned on.

Even there, the seats were empty.

The bus rattled again. Now Nathan was running up the aisle. He had to check on the driver. It must have been a mile to the front of the bus. By the time he reached the driver's seat, his lungs burnt and his legs ached.

There was no driver.

The bus swayed, and Nathan saw through the windshield, a thick layer of snow building despite the wiper's best efforts.

"Not to worry," a voice called from behind him. He turned, and there she was, a short, older woman with coal black eyes. She wore the uniform of a bus driver.

He knew her name: Marie.

She walked briskly up the aisle, and Nathan could smell the fake tropical fruit of her shampoo as she pushed him aside to get to the driver's seat. Once she was settled, she turned to Nathan. She cracked a wide grin and remarked to him.

"It's really coming down out there. I love driving on nights like these. It feels like we're the only thing on the road. Don't you think?"

Nathan didn't get to answer, because there it was again. The gentle, familiar rattling of metal on metal. Something scratched at Nathan's wrist, so he pulled his sleeve back.

It was the charms. And they were dancing. All of them, together, straining at the end of their chain. The cross, the moon, the hammer, the star, the book, the ankh, all of them.

Nathan untied the chain. He had to see where they were going, what they had to show him.

The chain fell off of his wrist, but the charms didn't fall. For a moment, Nathan expected them to fire off, but they simply hovered in place until, at last, they began to change. As each one slipped off of the silver chain, they began to spiral in the air as if they were planets revolving around an invisible sun.

Nathan reached out for the cross. At the first touch, the charm fell and struck the floor with a clunk that belonged to a much heavier object. One at a time, the other charms fell. The book. Clunk. The moon. Clunk. The star, the hammer, the ankh. Clunk. Clunk. Clunk.

Before he could move, a bright light appeared on the road ahead.

"Better hold on," Marie the driver said in a casual voice. "This part's never fun." But there was nothing to hold.

The light grew brighter, blinding, burning Nathan's eyes. He couldn't bear to look at it, but there was nowhere else to turn. The light flooded into the bus from all sides, from all the windows.

Finally came the sound of breaking glass and crunching metal.

Chapter Seven

Nathan woke in a terrible sweat, tearing the headphones out of his ears. He kicked himself up and rolled off the sofa bed, and his iPod clattered to the floor. He sucked in deep breaths of air and tried to steady his heart.

"This place is getting in my head," Nathan said out loud. *There are never dreams after visiting Anslem, not normally.*

Anslem's mirror still sat on the bedside table. He considered using it, just for relief. *It doesn't hurt that his nightly party is probably in full swing by now.* Instead, he shook out his trembling hands, and picked his iPod back off of the floor. He started his playlist again, right from the beginning, and tried again to sleep.

Even after listening to an entire Enya album, Nathan still couldn't fall asleep, so he gave up and went in to the living room. It was just past two in the morning, and the darkness in the guest house seemed thicker than usual. The strange local channel on the TV was playing some sort of Christmas movie. Nathan kept the volume low, too low for him to hear the words. He just wanted the noise.

There was no tea in the guest house, but there were pouches of instant hot cocoa. *That won't work.* Nathan spotted Alex's forbidden beers in the fridge and, without a hint of hesitation, popped the top off of one. *I'll owe him.*

The beer was soothing. Nathan finished it before leaving the kitchen. At the bottom of the bottle, his hand finally stopped trembling. Nathan sipped a second while watching the black and white shapes on the screen.

When he finished it, he got up to grab a third—*they're not so bad*—but stopped when something moved outside of the windows beside the front door. Outside, the snow continued to come down in a soothing sheet. The night had grown colder than he'd expected, and moisture hung in the air. His eyes caught the movement again, a small shadow scampering in the darkness, just outside of the porch light. For a moment, Nathan wondered if he had truly woken up. *It wouldn't be the first time I've fallen for that particular trick.* He didn't have to wonder long. The shadow moved again, and this time, drew close enough for Nathan to see it.

It was an orange cat. As soon as he noticed it, the cat sat down at the boundary between the pitch black and yellow porch light and seemed content simply to stare back at him.

"Why do I get the feeling you're used to scoring freebies?" Nathan asked it. The cat did nothing to respond. It looked clean and well fed, a green collar hanging on its neck. It probably lived nearby. "Wait there friend," he said. Nathan left the door ajar, and retrieved some of the jerky from the welcome basket Alex had left. He picked out a few pieces of beef and returned to the door. The cat hadn't moved, but it did cock its head when Nathan returned.

"Jerky," Nathan said, tossing the beef into the snow. Again, the cat didn't move. Nathan took a bite of another piece from the bag.

Not poison, see?

Still, the cat refused to move, save for licking its paw. "No? Take it up with the management. That's all I've got." Eventually, the cat stepped towards the meat, snapped up the chunks, and gave Nathan a final stare before darting back into the dark. *Hopefully, back towards its home.* Just as its bushy tail faded from view, Nathan called out, "You're welcome."

As he watched it leave, Nathan cast his eyes across the stone bridge. There was the robed statue, and it seemed to be glowing. Pulling his boots over his bare feet, Nathan stepped out into the cold and headed down the path. As he approached the bridge, Nathan slowed. There were no lights on, not up at the guest house nor at the Inn. Everyone was already in bed, but the snow continued to fall. When he crossed the bridge and came face-to-face with the statue, he stopped as surely as if he'd stepped into cement.

The statue wore a shawl of snow on its shoulders, but that wasn't the change that had frozen him. Though it still wore its Santa hat, the statue's face was no longer covered. The hood, despite its being made of stone, had been pulled back. In its place was the face of a woman. It had a sharp nose, angular cheekbones, and its mouth was set in a straight line. Its eyes were made from some sort of black glass, and they glinted in the light cast from the lamp above.

The lantern in her hand was fully alive now, flickering with a reddish flame that threw dancing shadows around the ground and through the falling snow.

He stepped in a careful semi-circle, never taking his eyes off of the statue. The charms were silent, despite the clear impossibility in front of him. This, more than anything, made him cautious. Some reflection of Memory was right there, clear as day, and, whatever it was, apparently didn't resonate at all.

Impossible.

Nathan thought of Anslem's words. *And how precisely am I supposed to get a statue back to Anchor?* Nathan knew it probably wouldn't matter. He doubted that the statue was the Angel itself. After all, someone would have noticed a statue walking around during the First Snow.

And Alex apparently had a hand in that. At the very least, he was troubled by it.

Turning his ring with his thumb, Nathan finally stepped forward until he was able to see all the grains of the stone. He reached out; he touched its face.

There was no response from the statue. "Trying to send me a message?" he asked it. "I prefer the direct approach."

Still, the statue didn't respond.

"Guess I'll see you around," Nathan said. "But, if you're trying to hurt them, best if you quit now."

He turned his back on it, half expecting to feel a stone hand grasp his throat, but nothing came. Only when he turned back, did he see something that brought a grim smile to his face.

The statue had changed again. Where before its mouth had been a straight, emotionless line, now the edges of its lips curled upwards into the suggestion of a cruel smile.

Nathan lingered a moment longer, smiled despite himself, then headed back across the bridge.

You want me to stay? Have it your way.

*

It was still snowing in the morning. Over the night, snow piles had appeared around the base of the windows and a clear white blanket covered the Ashford lawn. Any sign of the cat had been swept away, but there were two lines of footprints, one coming, one going. They brought a small smile to Nathan's face. *Alex got an early start.* When he checked his own watch, the smile vanished.

It's not Alex. It's me. It was almost nine, far later than he usually slept. *Far later than the dreams normally let me.* Across the bridge, the statue was back to how it had been, hood and all.

Breakfast at the Inn was a busy affair; some of the faces around the table Nathan hadn't met yet. There was talk of nothing but the Angel Festival and the amazing First Snow. While the adults gushed about the different stands and stalls they had seen, the four children, led by one Madeline Ashford, talked only about the snow.

"It was up to our knees so fast!"

Or, "The snowman I built's gonna be there 'til Christmas Day!"

Ronny was sitting at his usual place at the head of the table, his plate weighed down by no fewer than a dozen slices of thick bacon. The rest of the adults crowded around the table, choosing to give their spots to the children. There was a difference in the air this morning. After he'd filled his coffee cup, Nathan realized what it was. Ronny, for once, was silent. His flinty voice and booming laugh were absent, and, in their place, was a comparatively solemn expression. He still watched the room, and his eyes lingered on Nathan for a few long seconds, but he didn't seem to have any comments.

DeMarco was missing as well. *That's a shame.* Nathan was looking for some speculation, and DeMarco was sure to have plenty. After waiting a few minutes for a seat, Nathan decided to take his plate to the guest house. He could do many things, but eating eggs standing up while balancing a mug of coffee was apparently beyond him.

"You're not eating alone are you?" Marie called out.

"Just a bit too loud," Nathan replied.

A bit too festive would be more accurate.

"Of course, of course," Marie said brightly. "You can eat in the kitchen through here." Nathan had no chance to refuse as the short innkeeper bustled him into a small eat-in kitchen. The kitchen was still a hive of food in various stages of preparation. There were jugs of milk and cereal, open boxes of teabags, and jars of every breakfast condiment Nathan could imagine. There was even a small jar of Vegemite. "For the more exotic guests," Marie confided when he pointed it out. "It lasts forever because it was rancid the day it was made. You can have some if you like."

"You didn't sleep well?" she asked.

"Hmm?" Nathan asked. He had heard the question, but his mind had already moved on. *There's a lot of ground to cover, and I need a room.* His thumb began rubbing against his silver ring.

"Or maybe it's you don't like our little town?" Marie mused.

"On the contrary, I find it quite charming," Nathan responded.

"You wouldn't think it to look at your face," Marie said. "Well, you look quite shitty, if I'm being honest." The egg-laden fork on its way to his mouth froze in midair.

"Finally," Nathan said. "Something to put on my Yelp review."

Marie chuckled and waved a hand. "Oh the Inn isn't online. We're strictly a word-of-mouth business."

Nathan barked a short laugh, then took a bite of eggs before diving into a slice of a fluffy pancake.

"I thought I might stick around," he said after swallowing. "See the rest of the festival. If there's room for me."

Maybe hunt down an Angel. You know, keep it casual.

"So you *were* impressed?" Marie asked with a laugh.

Nathan took another bite and waved his fork like a conductor's rod. "You sure can cook," he said through a mouthful of pancake.

"You know how to charm."

"Just calling it like I see it," Nathan said. "When Alex kicks me out, think you have a room for me?"

Marie shrugged. "Who knows? I wouldn't worry. I'm sure we can find something. Especially once everyone else is on their way. Although..." she let the thought drop away.

"Although?"

"That makes two of you wanting to stay."

Nathan sipped his coffee. It was doing wonders to send the dream to the back of his mind. "Really? Who else?"

"That man, DeMarco." *Now that's a surprise. Seemed no one wanted out of here more than him.*

"Who figured?"

"You're telling me," Marie agreed. "My two sourpusses are the two cats that don't want to leave."

*

"Well, we're not going anywhere," Ronny announced to the dining room, even though Nathan was his only charge. He was wearing his uniform again, the one with the smoke logo. His face looked like he'd just bitten into a lemon. "She's still not wanting to start."

"That's convenient. I've decided to stay," Nathan said.

"What happened to 'all packed?'" Ronny asked.

"I unpacked," Nathan said.

Ronny put his hands on his hip and blew out his mouth. Then he shrugged. "Well, I guess it don't matter. Bus ain't running. Besides, it is quite fine here, and this was my last route 'til after Christmas anyways." Nathan glared at him and Ronny grinned back. "Not sure where you're going to stay though, son. The Ashfords put you up on charity, as I recall."

"I'm working on it," Nathan replied. *I'd been planning on your room after a deep scrub you crusty old lobster.*

Two more joined them from the patio door. Alex and a tall, wide man Nathan recognized. It was the tree farmer from yesterday. Marie found the older man across the room. After a moment, she beckoned Nathan over.

"Nathan, this is Paul Ashford."

He pulled Nathan into a hearty handshake. "Everything alright with the house?"

"Perfect," Nathan said. "Thanks for the hospitality. I won't forget it." Nathan meant every word. He would've been impressed with a lumpy couch, but he had hit the jackpot for stranded passengers.

"Glad to hear it," Paul replied. "You lucked out. It's normally booked for the season—for this week especially. But we're happy to help those in need."

"That's what I wanted to talk to you about," Marie said. Alex looked like someone had told him Christmas was canceled. When Marie was explaining the situation to Paul, Alex pulled Nathan aside.

"I thought you were leaving," he said with a whisper. Nathan overheard her haggling with Paul on a rate. She was a vicious negotiator. "Take the Inn," Alex said. It almost sounded like pleading. "Stay here instead."

"I'd never dream of it," Nathan replied.

Paul apparently overheard. With a laugh, he clapped Alex's shoulder. "You'll survive a week with family. It's the holidays. Show some spirit," Paul said with a sideways smile. "Once they leave the nest, they never want to come back, I guess."

"From experience, it's not always that easy for the birds," Nathan said. A pair of Maddie's icy blue eyes looked down at him.

"'Spose so. So Marie says you want the house for the week."

"Until the day after Christmas, the end of the festival. Would that be a problem?"

Paul shrugged. "Not for me, but you're going to have to pay this time." he said with a laugh.

Alex let out an exasperated sigh.

To his son, Paul added. "You said you wanted to help. You got your first customer Alex, and remember: five-star service, son."

Alex's smile was as thin as a razor. "I'm thrilled."

Nathan grinned then ran a hand through his hair. "I'm sure. Don't worry, I'm easy to please."

Paul nodded. "Good, I want my stars."

Ronny's voice cut in. "Found a room huh? Out back in the stable?" His voice was like a rifle shot. It was surprising to see the intensity from him.

"Afraid so."

Ronny's laugh was short and absent a note of humor. "Well ain't that a Christmas miracle," he said. He made a sucking sound with his lips. "Yessir. I'll head out for a nice walk then."

He passed Nathan on his way back out to the bus. In a low voice, he asked. "You sure you want to stick around? There's still time to get on the road. I'm sure we can figure it out, get her up and running."

"It's a nice town," Nathan replied.

Ronny nodded. "Sure is. But it's not where you were headed right? Quite the detour you're taking."

"What's it to you?"

"Ah, nothing really. Guess I feel a bit responsible. I was why you got stuck here in the first place, after all." He licked his lips again before dropping his voice. "And, it isn't where you were headed."

Where was I headed? The memory took a moment to dislodge. *Chicago. To return the cross. Then…then I'm not sure.*

"Ah," Ronny continued. "I don't mean to pry. But I see it all the time. People drop off the road, and get stuck somewhere they didn't mean to be. Sometimes they even get lost and can't find their way back."

Chapter Eight

Two hours later, Nathan wasn't surprised to hear the door knock. He also wasn't surprised to find Alex outside. The other guy had changed from his running gear. Now, he wore a pair of light jeans and a dark gray hoodie the same shade as his eyes. There came that sheepish smile again, but then his eyes darted for a brief second.

What was he nervous about?

"Hey," Alex said. "How's everything?"

"Fine," Nathan replied.

"Good. Uhh…" Alex trailed off. *Agh. If I could only pull it out of him!* He stepped halfway inside, and Nathan raised a calm hand.

"One normally asks," he deadpanned. Alex smirked and his eyes blinked into his forehead.

"May I come in Mr. Cole? To inspect the premises."

"Certainly." Nathan dropped his hand and stepped to the side.

"Thanks," Alex said. Inside, he pointed at the fireplace. Which, Nathan was pleased to say, was crackling merrily. "Oh, you got it working."

"I did." There was a way, after all, to do things. Nathan watched as Alex's eyes scanned the room. Normally, he might have said something. But, in this case, Nathan found himself curious. Especially, when Alex's eyes landed on the three empty bottles. He grinned and pointed in mock accusation. "Oh," he tutted.

"Hospitality fee, I think the paperwork in the welcome basket said. Since I'm paying it now…"

"Fair enough," Alex said.

"Fifteen percent, I may add, is kind of outrageous."

"I don't set the prices."

"I mean, I'm staying a whole week—"

"Okay!"

"I should have a six-pack a day. You wouldn't happen to have another basket would you?"

Alex's eyes darted upwards again. "You're so annoying."

Nathan laughed, and he offered Alex one of the remaining beers. Alex weighed the option before shrugging and accepting the bottle. Despite the hour, Nathan took one as well.

It is the holidays, after all.

"What can I do for you?"

Alex popped off the cap against the kitchen counter.

Someone's been to a frat party. I just can't picture it. Nathan too had been to his share but never as a willing participant. Not many places had more toxic Memory than a Greek life house.

"I came to pack," Alex said, and Nathan raised an eyebrow. "You kicked me out, remember?"

"Ah," Nathan replied. "I suppose I did."

Twenty minutes later, Alex returned with both a backpack and a scowl he didn't bother to hide. He had scooped up all of his belongings from the guest house bedroom; considering he'd only been there for a few weeks, he'd made himself quite at home.

"All set," Alex announced. His eyes darted to the TV where *Miracle on 34th Street* had started. Again. "You should know, there's a Blu-Ray player in the bedroom."

"Civilization," Nathan declared to Alex. "Where do you keep the movies?"

"Library," Alex replied, sighing. "Why couldn't you stay at the Inn?" Alex asked. "This was going to be a perfect holiday. Now everything..."

Everything, what's happened to everything?

Alex sighed again. "I'm in my old room for the rest of the season."

"It can't be all that bad," Nathan said mildly. "Time with family. During the holidays. During a magical Christmas season?"

Alex glowered at him.

"It's…loud…up there, and it's a twin bed," he said.

Nathan himself stood at six-feet and Alex had a half a head on him. The guilt, however, was only momentary.

"Sofa bed's all yours," Nathan replied. He injected as much sarcasm as he could, but, for a moment, Alex seemed to consider it.

"Hah," Alex said at last. "You're hard to read. I can never tell if you're being serious."

Nathan, who had slept on floors, on rattling buses, and on plastic train station seats, wouldn't have hesitated. So long as he had his playlist, he could sleep almost anywhere. At least, for a few hours.

"So," Alex asked. "Why uhh exactly did you decide to stay?"

"Curiosity," Nathan replied. He caught a glimpse of the snow falling outside the window. It covered the ground in fresh white powder. The stone bridge looked like a postcard, albeit one featuring a hooded figure that looked like Death. "Your Timber Angel," Nathan continued, choosing his words carefully. "It's worth looking into."

Especially if it decides to turn the heat up on this snowstorm. A blizzard would strangle this town.

"So you're a believer, then?" Alex asked. "In the Angel?"

It was Nathan's turn to laugh. "I've always been fertile soil for a new idea." Nathan leveled a stare at Alex. "But belief, disbelief? Those aren't facts. They're interpretations, little more than dressed-up opinions. In my work, they're like—like weeds in a garden of facts. If you let them, they'll twist themselves into the evidence, distort it. A fact is a fact regardless of if you choose to believe it. It's our job—it's my job, that is, to separate the superstition from the facts. In our case, the Timber Angel either exists or it doesn't."

Alex was staring out the window, watching the snow.

Nathan could tell he was no longer listening. "Are you scared it's going to stop? Or scared that it won't?"

The question got his attention. "Sorry?" Alex asked.

"The snow."

He watched it a moment longer before turning and grinning at Nathan. "Just thinking. You didn't answer my question. Not really. Why'd you stay?"

Sometimes, Nathan would lie when someone would ask that. But, Alex's gray eyes were as serious as a thunderhead. Nathan tapped his ring with his thumb.

How much to explain? Sometimes, this life is like hunting. I spend all my time trying not to spook the deer.

"You remember what I told you yesterday? About these?" He pulled up his sleeve to show the charms.

Alex looked dubious. "Hard to forget."

"I told you they respond to Trace, to Memory, right?"

Alex nodded.

"Consider a tree," Nathan continued. "A big, old tree that's been around for a while. It saw towns rise and fall. Now imagine that old tree was cut down. It didn't go easy. It was the sort with deep roots and a broad trunk. But, technology and manpower can overcome many things. From there, what happened to it?"

"I guess it was put to use."

Nathan nodded. "Right. It was turned into logs or planks or paper or those little carved Christmas ornaments. The Memory of the tree, of all its history, would live on in those things. You follow? Those things would inherit that Memory."

"I guess."

"Well what happens if that tree was used for lynching? Or hanging witches? That Memory is not always good. And, if the

Memory is bad enough and strong enough, then now it spreads to all those things."

"And you think the Angel is some sort of bad Memory?"

Nathan shook his head. "Honestly? I don't know. I hope it isn't. But I think there's a chance it might be, and, if there's even the slimmest chance, then leaving now would be like walking away from a fire starting in the woods—it's asking for trouble."

"And you actually believe all this?"

"There's that word again," Nathan said. "Faith is only needed in the absence of proof. Your impossible snow is already evidence enough that there's something happening. Your canary in the coal mine is already singing."

"I guess so," Alex murmured back. He paced around the kitchen.

"Your turn. Why'd you really come here?" Nathan asked.

Alex's stare was somewhere a thousand miles away.

"It wasn't just to pack," Nathan suggested.

"Yeah?"

"You're packed, but you're still here. And, if I'm not mistaken, you've not gotten quite what you came for."

Alex frowned again at the snow, but didn't reply for a moment. Eventually, he said, "I just wanted to tell you that there's nothing to worry about. Everything's fine. The Timber Angel, they're here to help."

"Are you the Angel Alex?" Nathan asked. The words hung in the guest house.

Alex's eyes widened at the question, but he quickly recovered. "Not me, sorry."

"Alright," Nathan said, the disappointment creeping into his voice. "But, if for some reason everything's not fine..."

Alex was already heading for the door. "Then I know right where to find you."

It's about time we pushed a bit harder. Walls, after all, rarely fall on their own.

✱

After Alex left, Nathan inspected the bedroom. By the look of it, Alex had changed all the bedding and even took a pass at wiping down the ensuite. The job was a little rough around the edges, and the kind of thing that a DeMarco would chomp at the bit to complain about. For Nathan, however, it was downright indulgent.

The room faced the Ashford backyard, and Nathan watched for a moment as Alex crossed into the main house. He entered through a farm door at the back of the house and vanished from sight. Nathan tried to guess where his room was based on the windows when a light clicked on the left side of the house.

Nathan rubbed a hand over his chin as he turned over what Alex had told him. Yesterday's stubble had grown thick enough to be annoying. *I suppose if we're going to do this, we should do it properly.*

Fifteen minutes and a brisk walk later, Nathan stepped into the general store, Marley's. All things considered, it was well stocked, better stocked than Nathan had expected.

"Mornin'," an older man called out when he entered.

"Would that make you Mr. Scrooge or Mr. Marley?" Nathan asked.

"You feelin' alright son?"

"It was funnier in my head," Nathan admitted. *No. I don't think it was.* "Sorry, I'll be out of your hair in a minute."

"You take your time," the older man said.

A model train ran the perimeter of the store, disappearing up into a second level at the back of the shop. Nathan followed it through the aisles. Some of the snack brands he didn't recognize. Others he did. He was particularly taken by a box of cereal: Cocoa Rocks. A cartoon T-Rex was on the box greedily digging into a bowl. The cartoon was familiar and comforting. The first year he was old enough to go on the road with Mother Sable, she had made sure the camper was stocked with it. It had been one of the few cereals Nathan would eat. He ran a finger over the box. The cartoon was almost precisely as he remembered it, almost as if it had leaped out of his memory and straight onto Marley's shelf.

Several aisles of the store were dedicated to souvenirs and toys. There were recreations of the clock tower, several different variations of the lantern in the center of town, and a row of train engines. They were crimson and die-cast in heavy metal, the sort that a child would pull back and release. *The Christmas Express* was stamped across each one. Before he could think about it, Nathan grabbed one. *Many pokers in many fires.*

By the time he approached the check-out line, he had collected the toy along with two boxes of the cereal, some more bags of jerky, a pack of disposable razors, a small bottle of laundry detergent, and a six-pack of beers. At the end of the line, the middle-aged clerk checked the tag on each and typed each price into the manual cash register.

"You're here for the Festival?"

"That's me, red-handed," Nathan replied.

The clerk nodded. "Good year for it, that's for sure." He was a heavyset man with meaty hands and a broad smile. At the cereal and beer, he stopped. "Interesting diet, Mr…"

"Cole," Nathan replied. "But call me Nathan." He held out a hand. It was one of the things he liked about traveling the country. In small towns, people tended to have names instead of just being faces.

"Jake Marley," the clerk said, replying with a rough handshake of his own. "I run the place."

"I'll remember," Nathan replied.

Marley grunted then resumed pecking the prices into the register.

"What's with the toys?" Nathan asked, curious at the level of detail on them.

"I make 'em," Marley replied. "A bit of an old hobby. Something my grandfather passed on. Helps with the Mondays, y'know?"

"Nice to have something to look forward to," Nathan agreed.

"You're at thirteen dollars," Marley said.

That's it? If this angel isn't psychotic, I might definitely retire here.

A hook full of bags of cat treats caught his eye and Nathan tossed a bag on the belt.

"Fourteen dollars."

Nathan pulled out his cash and counted out bills.

Marley tapped the treats. "You got a friend out there then?"

"I'm not sure yet," Nathan replied. Marley deposited the money and then passed back a single. "The plan, however, is to find out."

✳

Alex Ashford's throat was beginning to grow sore. He had just finished explaining the story of the Timber Angel to another group of travelers. He'd come to think of them as strange pilgrims, summoned by the confirmation of the First Snow—Timber's Edge's very own coal-loving canary as Nathan Cole had put it. Alex couldn't disagree with him, especially as another group drifted into the museum to admire the snow globes and the other exhibits. Most of the groups wanted to see the snow globes, of course.

Ever since the First Snow had begun, each of the snow globes had started to snow as well. It was as if a hand was gently shaking each one at the same time.

It was part of the ritual, Alex knew. Part of the First Rite.

He was already growing tired of answering the same questions.

"How are you doing that?"

"The Angel is doing it."

"What will this year's gift be?"
   "Only the Angel knows that."

"Who is the Angel?"
   "The Angel never reveals themselves."

"How long will it snow for?"
   "Until the Angel gives their gift."

And the worst question of all, normally asked in a hushed whisper and answered in a thin smile:
   "Do you really believe all this?"
   "I believe my eyes. Don't you?"

Alex was just about to leave for lunch when he heard the telltale sound of heels clicking down the library hallway. The trip from town hall wasn't one the mayor took very often, and Alex was already wishing she hadn't chosen today for one. He knew what she wanted, knew the questions she'd ask, and knew that he had no answers for her. He cast an eye over the room. There were still a few groups left. Enough, he hoped, to keep the mayor from being, well, too much like the mayor.

Each step sounded like a knife into the worn wooden floors. He already knew she wouldn't be happy. He had nothing up his sleeves for that. As soon as Mayor Benneteau stepped into the room, her face creased, and, again, Alex felt like a prophet.

"How's it going?" the mayor asked. As she drew closer, he could smell the lavender and honey in her expensive perfume. The suit was similarly expensive, but it fit well and wouldn't be out of place at the White House. The mayor knew it too.

"Coming along," Alex replied. He tried to keep his tone mild. The remaining groups floated out of the museum; the last sound Alex heard was them laughing about where they were going to find lunch. Alex wished he could've joined them.

Once she was sure the room was empty, she asked, "It's an Angel Year. Just like you wanted. Why are you so worried?"

"Because it's not happening like it should," Alex said with a bit more bite than he intended. He was tired of this conversation.

The mayor's hawkish eyes pierced him, but she said nothing. They were both trying, it seemed.

He took another look around the room to make absolutely sure it was empty. "Nothing is happening like it should. The snow started on its own."

"And the—" the mayor's face turned dark. "The Angel? It's no help?"

"They're not talking to me," Alex replied.

She stared into his face, sending heat rushing to his cheeks.

"It's not me, Julianna. I didn't ring it. No one could have. It was locked up."

"And the bell?" she asked.

"Still ringing," Alex said. Always ringing. He thought it might drive him mad before the week was over.

"But the legend. It's clear," Her mouth turned into a thin line as she cast her eyes over the room. "What that means—it's written right there."

Alex glared at her. "I know what it says. It's not up to me Julianna."

"I don't understand," the mayor said. "Maybe there's some step, something missing. The Angel is supposed to ring the bell themselves. It's part of the Rite. That's what you said."

Alex gave a bitter laugh. "That's not what *I* said. That's what the *legend* says. It's right there." He pointed to the plaque on the wall where the Three Rites were imprinted.

Just then, another familiar voice spoke from the door. "The Three Rites of Christmas. Precisely what I'm looking for." Nathan Cole said.

Alex flushed. How long had he been standing there? The green eyes lit up when they met Alex's and a quick smile crossed his face when he noticed the mayor's scowl.

Nathan stepped all the way into the room, faced the legend and solemnly intoned:

"At the Angel's Call,
First there will be Snow,
With the Angel's Touch,
Second there will be Light,
From the Angel's Flame,
On Christmas Morn, Finally there will be Joy.
And Forever will the Angel's Memory
Remain in Timber's Edge.

Very dramatic. If, a bit vague." Nathan's thoughts appeared distracted by the wall of self-shaking snow globes, and his voice dropped to a mutter. "Now, that is quite interesting."

Alex could see the question on his face, but he didn't get a chance to ask.

"Who exactly are you?" the mayor asked.

Nathan pulled himself away from the snow globes. His eyes seemed to laugh at a joke only he could hear. "Oh I wouldn't worry about me. I'm just passing through." As if to himself, he added, "There's no mention anywhere of what happens if the Angel doesn't deliver. I suppose Christmas gets canceled."

The mayor's glare deepened. "What did you say? *If* the Angel doesn't deliver? Why would that ever happen?"

"Not sure," Nathan replied. "Car accident? Called back to on-high? As I said, it's all a bit vague, isn't it?"

Alex tried to stop the smirk crossing his face, but he couldn't quite contain it. A flicker from Julianna's eyes told him that it hadn't escaped her either.

"So, what do we think?" Nathan asked.

"The legen—" Alex began.

"Nothing happens," Julianna interrupted. "There are more non-Angel Years than there are Angel Years Mr—"

"This is Nathan Cole." Alex said.

"Guilty," Nathan replied. To the mayor, he held out a hand. "Now I'm at the disadvantage."

The mayor stared at the outstretched hand as if unsure what to do with it. Finally, she reached out with one of her own and gave him a whisper of a handshake that rattled her expensive bracelets, "Julianna Benneteau," she said. "As I was saying, Mr. Cole, nothing happens. Aside from the fact that a lot of hard work from our volunteers gets celebrated, and everyone in town celebrates the season."

"Let me ask it another way," Nathan said. "Has it ever happened where an Angel Year starts but doesn't complete?"

"It doesn't happen," the mayor replied.

"Fascinating," Nathan said.

To the mayor, Alex added. "Nathan—he got stranded when his bus broke down."

The mayor's mouth stretched into a smile that didn't come within a football field of her hawkish eyes. Somewhere behind her eyes, a light turned on. "Oh of course. We met yesterday. I thought I recognized you."

"That's me." Nathan grinned before his attention returned to the snow globes. The visitor began humming quietly to himself. Alex recognized the song. It was "O Come, All Ye Faithful"—the Angel's prayer.

The mayor glared at Alex.

"He's staying in the guest house," Alex explained quietly.

"And just extended my stay as well," Nathan added.

Considering how intently he'd been looking at the snow globes, Alex was surprised that Nathan had been listening at all. At each snow globe, the visitor was waving his chain carefully in front of them. If they were moving, Alex couldn't detect it. Again he thought that Nathan Cole was quite full of shit. But then, he could make those stones fly without touching them.

So casual Nathan had been about it, Alex had almost forgotten it had happened. Actual magic, in front of his face, and not just connected to the Timber Angel either. It should have sent him running for the hills, but Nathan's comfortable manner had made it seem so normal.

But it wasn't normal, Alex reminded himself. None of this was.

Julianna called to him. "What exactly are you looking for? Sorry, what is it you're doing?"

"Research," Nathan replied casually. He frowned at the globes, pulled his sleeve back down, then resumed circling the room. He gestured excitedly around the room. "I hear it's been some time since a—what do you call it—an Angel Year, happens. I'm looking forward to seeing everything."

Just what the hell is he doing? Alex wasn't sure if Nathan remembered the conversation from earlier, or if he even cared. That wasn't right. Alex was almost entirely sure that he remembered, just that Nathan Cole did whatever he pleased.

Nathan began picking through the newspaper racks. "Give me a year," he said. "One of you. Please?"

The mayor's lips thinned to an almost invisible line. "Again?" Alex asked. Nathan was now opening drawers.

"Microfilm," he said. "Not your everyday find in a small town museum." He looked around. "Is there a viewer?"

"No," Alex replied, his mouth thinning. "At least, nowhere I've seen."

"Ah," Nathan said. He closed the drawer then glanced up at them. "A year? Between 19—"

"For crying out loud, the newspapers again?" Alex said.

"Who says 'for crying out loud'?" Nathan shot back.

Alex glared at him. "'86," he said.

Nathan gave the rack a sideways glance and ran a finger down the newspapers. When his eyes narrowed, Alex interrupted him. "Did you find something?"

Nathan grinned again but didn't answer. "How about you Madam Mayor? Do you have a year in mind?"

"'70," she said after a moment.

Nathan flipped through the newspapers again. This time, now that he was looking for it, Alex caught the flicker of a frown. It made Alex's stomach tighten. Had Nathan found something that quickly?

"I'm sorry Mr. Cole, but the library is closing," Julianna said. The mayor's smile returned, and she made a move towards the door. "You feel free to come back any time. Any time we're open, that is."

From his place at the newspaper racks, Nathan looked back over at them. His eyes darted between Alex and the mayor, then he shot them a familiar, wide smile. "Just lost track of time," he said. "All the little details, they can be so interesting, sometimes I lose track." He said his goodbyes but stopped at the door. He appraised the mayor then addressed her directly. "You have a very beautiful town," was all he said before disappearing into the hallway.

The mayor turned to Alex. "He's strange," she said.

Alex snorted. "That's an understatement." Still, he walked over to the newspapers and examined them himself. There was nothing on either of them that Alex could see as interesting. Neither year was an Angel Year, so the papers simply described the lack of snow.

"Anything?" Julianna asked.

"No, nothing."

"Just strange," she repeated. When Alex didn't reply, she spoke again. "I don't like the look on your face. And what was that back there?"

This time, Alex faced her. "What was what?"

"Alex…" Julianna replied.

"It's nothing," he said. "It's just things aren't happening like they should."

Julianna's lips tightened.

"For the last time, it's not me!" Alex said hotly. As his temper rose, he felt a dreadful cold in his shoes. Not again, he thought.

"I know you're worried," she said. "But whatever for? Even if this, this glitch, happened, it's not like the town gets wiped off the map. The festival will be the same as it always is." Julianna continued. "Yes, people will be disappointed, but life will go on. The best thing we can do is relax and enjoy ourselves. It's Christmas."

Alex considered telling her everything Nathan had told him, but dismissed that idea out of hand. All it would do is convince her that Nathan Cole was, indeed, strange; it didn't help that a large part of Alex agreed.

"I thought maybe he could help," Alex suggested.

"Don't let yourself get hurt Alex," Julianna said. "You don't know him." She exhaled. "Now, I thought it would be nice for us to all have dinner tonight."

A polite, quiet dinner was the last thing he wanted to sit through, especially considering the cold feeling was climbing up his legs.

"That's alright," Alex replied, struggling to keep his voice level. "I've got plans."

Julianna winced. "You need space from this Alex."

He bristled. "I'm fine."

"Leave the archive alone. Don't come back for the week."

Screw that. Alex's mouth opened in protest, ready to fight.

"I mean it," Julianna said, raising a hand. "Spend time with Maddie and your father. Don't waste your holidays with this. Not everything can be controlled, and not every problem can be fixed." She pointed to *The Three Rites of Christmas* hanging on the wall. "Some things are best left to fate."

When Alex didn't answer, the mayor sighed then left him alone in the Archive; the first thing he did was lock the door after her. The cold feeling was growing, climbing into his chest. He had first felt the strange coldness the night before, just after the bell began to toll. There hadn't been anything he'd been able to do to stop it. That feeling, the one he'd now come to know as the Cold Place, ran down his arm and collected in curled fist. It felt as if he were holding a fistful of ice cubes, but it didn't hurt. He was aware of the temperature, aware of the cold, but it caused no pain.

Finally, something released, and, around him, the air became full of snowflakes.

*

Alex was still flushed as he stormed through the library. He was still shaking even as he pushed outside. Even the frosty air wasn't doing much to calm him down.

"Alex," a voice called. Alex's heart sank and then jumped. It was Nathan.

Alex wasn't in the mood to talk. "You were waiting for me?"

"Maybe a little bit." Those green eyes were studying him. He took a few steps closer, and Alex tried to ignore the increase in his heart rate. Nathan's next words were quieter. "Everything alright?"

What Alex needed was time to think. "Fine," he replied. "Everything's fine."

"You say that a lot," Nathan observed, shooting him a wide, knowing smile. "Far be it from me to disagree, but you're not wearing an 'everything's fine' face."

Alex couldn't help but laugh. It was choppy and full of bitterness. Part of him wanted to tell the visitor to go find someone else to harass, to leave him alone. But, at the same time, it was Nathan he had been thinking of in the museum when the Cold Place struck. Nathan Cole and his weird charms. Nathan Cole and his talk of magic and memory. Nathan Cole and all his impossibility. Julianna was right about one thing. He didn't know Nathan. But that problem was easy to fix.

Eventually, Alex simply sighed. "What are you doing for dinner?"

Nathan didn't even have the courtesy to look taken aback. In fact, he looked liked he had been planning for the exact thing. Jesus Christ, Alex thought, am I that transparent? Alex was used to being the one who could tell what someone was thinking, but Nathan seemed to be able to read him at a glance. In return, Alex couldn't even guess what was going through Nathan's mind.

"Funny you should ask," replied Nathan. "I've got just the place in mind."

"Before, though," Alex said. "What did you see on the newspapers?"

Nathan raised an eyebrow. "Just old weather reports. Nothing too interesting."

The answer helped Alex get to know Nathan a bit better.

He now knew that Nathan Cole could lie with the best of them.

Chapter Nine

Standing opposite the mechanic's shop and an ancient two-pump gas station was the roadhouse. The building probably hadn't been renovated in a decade. It had a low rectangular frame, paneled wood doors, and a simple sign above the door that simply read The Pit Stop. There was no wooden angel taking up a position in front of The Pit Stop, and the owners had apparently forgotten to hang their lantern as well.

I bet they're popular at the town meetings. Nathan smiled, happy to find somewhere outside of the Timber Angel's grip

Inside, The Pit Stop was much as Nathan suspected it would be. It smelled of fried food, stale beer, and no-filter cigarettes. *Like Mother Sable's version of a Happy Meal.* There were a handful of customers in the dark rectangular room, and most of them were shooting pool at one of the two tables towards the bar's rear. At the bar itself, two men chatted about something, and, judging by their roars of laughter, it was something funny. Nathan slid into a seat at the end of the bar, away from the other two men and where he could see the door. A twenty-something bartender with a tired smile asked him what he wanted. She wore a pair of black pants along with a simple white t-shirt.

"I'll take a bourbon, please. Neat," he replied.

The bartender shook her head. "Sorry," she said. "We don't have any bourbons. Owner doesn't like them."

"Vodka soda?"

She brightened. "That I can do. Lime?"

"Always love a lime."

She finished the drink and put it and his tab on the bar. "If you need anything else, shout for Tanya." As she walked away, Nathan smiled to himself.

Nathan checked his watch. He was early, but he always tried to be. He was surprised Alex had asked to meet him, but it presented an opportunity. Halfway through his drink, the door to the bar opened, and Alex Ashford entered. Even though they had made plans to meet here only a few hours ago, Nathan was still surprised that he actually showed. He scanned the room from the door before spotting Nathan. He hesitated for a moment. *Last chance to back out.*

"Hey," Alex said, taking the seat next to Nathan's. He pointed at the drink. "What're you having?"

"Not bourbon," Nathan replied.

Alex exhaled, rolling his eyes. "I don't understand you half the time."

"Vodka soda," Nathan said. When Tanya came for his order, Alex chose some local beer that Nathan had never heard of. "Between you and me, I'm surprised there's a place like this in Timber's Edge."

"Oh?"

"The town just seems so squeaky clean and Christmas-y. Then here's The Pit Stop. No Angels, no lanterns, and not a health inspection report in sight."

Alex chuckled, but the laugh did nothing to lighten the weight his eyes were carrying. When his pint arrived, he promptly drained half the glass.

"No toast?" Nathan asked.

Alex shrugged. "Bad luck without a full glass," he said after wiping his lips. "Besides, I'm just catching up."

Nathan studied Alex for a moment. There was something about him, riding a bar stool at The Pit Stop, that gave Nathan pause.

Perhaps there was more to him than Nathan had first thought.

"What? Something on my face?"

Nathan shook his head. "Nothing. Just wondering how exactly someone like you ended up somewhere like this."

Alex looked amused. "In a bar?"

"That's not what I meant."

"Someone like me?"

It was Nathan's turn to work on his vodka. *I'm not the only one on a fishing expedition.* He knew he should be careful, that Alex was very possibly the Timber Angel. Hell, that was part of what he was here to figure out. While, in Nathan's estimation, it was growing less likely, it was still possible that Alex was an Aegyl.

Pissing one off wouldn't be too smart Nate.

But it would be efficient. "I wasn't referring to your predilection for the male form if that's what you mean."

Alex gave him a long sideways look. "My what—no."

Whoops. Hell if I'm wrong though.

"It means—"

Let's not make it worse.

"—I know what it means, dick. And no that's not what I was talking about."

"And, for the record," Nathan said, "I did notice, several times actually."

Way worse, Nate. Way worse.

Alex laughed. This time, it sounded full and joyful. "You are so annoying. If you must know, it's not a secret."

Knew it.

Alex drained the rest of his beer and a distant look crossed his face. "What did you mean then? Someone like me somewhere like this?"

Nathan ran a finger along his ring. "You seem out of place. I put you at twenty-four. Maybe twenty-five—"

"Let's see," Alex said. "Twenty-five, completed my undergrad at UPenn in biology. Just finished my Master's in sports medicine. Now, I'm fixing to move out west."

Bless your heart, Alex. You did try to get rid of it, didn't you?

"—Twenty-five, two degrees, and you're here," Nathan said. He swirled his glass, allowing the ice to clink together. "Volunteering at a small town museum in the middle of nowhere. Over a Christmas week that's watched over by a legendary Angel. It's an odd sequence of events."

"Says the self-described magical detective who's in the same small town over the same Christmas week."

Nathan finished his drink then signaled Tanya for another. It didn't escape his notice that Alex ordered a second round as well. "At least I can hide behind professional obligation," Nathan said at last.

"Professional," Alex snorted.

Nathan wanted to laugh as well. He really did, but he all he was able to do was rattle his ice glass.

He's got you there. Professionals don't get people killed.

"Sorry," Alex said. "I didn't mean anything by it." Their drinks arrived, and this time Alex raised his glass in a toast. "To an Angel free night. May she stay far away for a few hours."

Nathan almost missed it, but then he raised his own glass and a wide smile crossed his face. *Even if Alex really wasn't the Angel, then Anslem would be able to see the touch.*

After they'd drank, Alex studied him for a minute. "Are you dangerous?" he asked.

Nathan coughed in his drink, surprised at the direct question. "Me? I'm your run of the mill bus-loving hardened felon. Wanted in eight states along with the great province of Alberta."

"Cagey," Alex noted.

You bet it is, Nathan thought. He had no desire to talk about his life story, not today, so he tried to change the subject.

"So it's a Friday night," Nathan said. "You're sitting here drinking with a stranded bus passenger and potential felon. Is the Timber's Edge party scene so dead?"

"We get by," Alex said. "And it's not even nine yet. By ten, these streets will be alive. Just you wait."

"I'm sure."

"Hey, this place isn't so bad."

Nathan shot him a long look. "Come on Alex, it's a dive."

"It's not a dive! I had my first beer here!" Alex replied. His smile had returned.

"Are those pool tables in the back?" Nathan asked, grinning. "And, is that a karaoke machine? Let me guess, performances start after nine?"

Alex said nothing.

Nathan pointed a finger to the bar. "It's a dive my friend. But there's nothing wrong with a dive. Sometimes the best places are dives."

"You think so?"

"No one bothers you at a dive. Best place for a quiet drink. Hands down."

Alex tapped the bar. "Well aside from the drunk people singing."

"No, that's not it. Quiet is a state of mind," Nathan explained. "It's a state of minding your own business. I was at a restaurant once. A Mexican place. Somewhere in Georgia I think. They had some sort of karaoke machine set up and a two-for-one drink special—a misguided combination, if you ask me—and do you know what the tipsy interstate superstars would do when it was their turn?"

"Sing?"

Nathan scoffed. "Oh, they would sing. They marched down the aisles, tugging that stupid little microphone with the cable behind them, all around the tables, belting out Journey and hitting one note in a dozen. I've never seen anything like it." Nathan shuddered. "Some of them would try get the people eating to join in. Have you ever seen someone try to hide behind a plate of fajitas?"

"Can't say I have," Alex said. His smile had come back, and Nathan felt spurred on.

"Do you have any idea how many times I heard *Livin' on a Prayer, Pour Some Sugar,* and *Don't Stop Believin'* butchered that night? By the time they were done, it was like a graveyard filled with 80s songs."

Good God. I can still hear it.

"Did they try get you to join in?" Alex asked with a laugh.

Nathan said nothing for a moment, and fixed Alex with a stony stare. "Maybe."

"And?"

Nathan said nothing.

"Oh come on. You gotta tell me what happened."

Nathan sighed. "A brave woman tried. Once." Nathan lifted his hands. "She may have left with the idea that the microphone would've been left violently…inert…if it came near my face again."

Not my proudest moment perhaps. But I stand by it. I was one-hundred percent justified.

"Oh jeez. They didn't throw you out?"

"Quite the contrary, she came back later. Apparently she thought I was flirting with her."

Alex covered his face and laughed again. His pale cheeks flushed pink as he tried to contain his laugh.

Nathan continued with a smile. "And this is my point. At a dive bar, you tell a drunk woman to beat it, the world continues to turn, hurt feelings notwithstanding. At a regular restaurant? You get propositioned with a topless haircut in a middle-aged woman's apartment later that night."

Sometimes, the road not taken is paved with the stuff of nightmares. Nathan ran a hand through his hair and wondered why it was that story he had decided to share.

"Karaoke can be dangerous," Alex said. "I tried it once."

That was a surprise. Nathan chuckled at the image of buttoned-up Alex Ashford belting something out. "What was your poison? You look like a *Every Rose Has Its Thorns* type to me."

The red in his cheeks deepened. "It was Seal, if you must know."

"Oh Alex, not *Kiss From a Rose?*"

"*Love's Divine,*" Alex admitted, hiding a rueful smile behind his glass.

"That's a tough one. I'm scared to ask this but, uh, how'd you do?"

"It was like hooking up with a girl in college," Alex said with a grin. "The second it started, I knew I'd made a terrible mistake."

*

When their next round of drinks were little more than a rattle of ice cubes and a ring of light foam, Nathan checked his watch. Once again, he was surprised by the time. *Time flies when you're having fun, as they say. It's time to move this along.* He was enjoying the conversation, but the hook was well-baited. It was time to see if he could reel something in.

"It's getting late," Nathan said, waving Tanya for his tab.

Alex glanced over. "Somewhere you got to be?"

"As a matter of fact, I promised to meet a friend."

It's not technically a lie…But it might be missing a few key details.

"You've got friends here?" Alex whistled. "I'm shocked." Nathan raised his eyebrows, and Alex tapped his chest. "Not counting me."

"Present company excluded," Nathan chuckled. "And he's not just a friend. He's my best friend."

Alex frowned. "And he's like you?"

"Nope. Can't say that he is." Nathan said. "He's about as impossible a being as you'll ever encounter. And about as noble, though I'd never tell him that."

"I can't believe half of what you tell me."

Nathan tapped the side of his glass with his ring. "I can show you if you like. Easy to believe then."

He checked his tab then carefully placed some bills on the bar. Alex stared at his glass before waving for his own tab and pulling out his credit card.

Outside, they headed back into town at a steady pace. This far out of town, it was quiet and still except for the light flurries that still swirled in the air. Night had fully fallen, bringing with it a crisp chill that bordered on bitter. Nathan pulled his overcoat tighter and was glad he'd bought his hat.

"Too cold?" Alex asked, his first words since leaving The Pit Stop.

"I was in Memphis before this," Nathan replied. He remembered watching a blues band at a juke on Beale Street. It felt like months ago now.

Before this what? Before the bus? Before this town? Why is the sequence so difficult to remember? Nathan pushed the thought away, but it left a shadow of doubt creeping in the back of his mind.

When they crossed around the cemetery behind Calbot Square, the sounds of the crowd floated over the graves. It was a joyful chatter, ringing clearly with the laughter of children. As they rounded the corner, they saw a healthy snowball fight taking place around the merrily glowing lantern.

Nathan shook his head and smiled. "Back into the Christmas of it all, it would seem. It was a nice reprieve."

Alex laughed.

Nathan pointed at a boy in a blue jacket sprinting and sliding and shouting. "I imagine that was you, back when you were eight?"

"More or less," Alex replied. He knocked a fist against his chest. "Proud veteran of the snowball wars."

They watched for a moment more. The snowballs were rifled like bullets across the square. Several exploded against the lantern and sent powder through the air. Even some of the parents were involved in their own private skirmish.

Before Alex could get any ideas, Nathan said, "We should get a move on. My friend, he can be very particular about time. Or, at least, that's what he says."

"Where exactly are you taking me?" Alex asked when they crossed away from the square and back towards the Inn.

"We have to stop by the guest house," Nathan explained. "I need to pick something up." *And then, with any luck, we go through the looking glass.*

Nathan left Alex in the main room of the guest house as he retreated back into the bedroom. He pulled the mirror out of its place in his duffel bag. *It feels heavier than normal.* Nathan dismissed the thought with a flick of his head. He found his reflection staring back at him.

Are we sure about this? You're playing with his sanity.

The reflection grimaced. This was where the evidence had led. There was a cost, yes, but Alex could take it, and he was holding back. Nathan felt confident about that. Besides, he had to know what he was dealing with. If it was an Aegyl, he had to be sure.

Alex himself had confirmed it tonight. *She,* he'd said. *May she stay away.* Not it. To Alex, the Timber Angel was a person. Despite his charms remaining silent, Nathan could still play a hunch. Especially if there was a chance that lives were at stake.

✳

Alex was concerned. The object on the table was small, barely larger than the palm of his hand. The surface cast a reflection of light against the ceiling. Alex still hadn't looked into it, despite Nathan's offer to do so. The other guy was sitting on the couch, turning one of his shiny stones through his hands. Nathan Cole wasn't particularly tall. Alex had almost a full head on him. But for what Nathan lacked in height, he made up for in density with his thick arms and broad chest. Those items were becoming increasingly hard for him not to notice. The thought stung Alex like a reproachful needle.

Now, leaning back on the couch, Nathan seemed as if no force on earth could move him if he didn't choose to be moved, and, for the time being, he seemed content to simply watch and wait for Alex to make up his mind.

So much for his friend being particular about time, Alex thought. When Nathan had shown him the mirror, Alex thought he'd been just screwing with him, but a minute under Nathan's serious gaze had evaporated that thought.

"What will happen?" Alex asked at last.

Nathan considered the question. "It's complicated to explain in those terms," he replied. "But it will take you to see my friend. And I'll be there the entire time. You'll be safe. Protected."

"And who is your friend?"

"He's complicated as well," Nathan said. "But just as impossible as your town raining snow on its own or your Angel bringing joy. If it helps, consider it this way: your town is complicated, but you know the rules. For all I know, this place is a giant death trap. You tell me everything is safe. I'm trusting you."

Nathan leaned forward and continued, "I'm here because I'm curious. You wouldn't be here, in this room, if you weren't curious as well. Curious about the mirror. Curious about magic." Nathan grinned. "Curious about me."

He's got me there, Alex thought. It was unnerving. Alex normally had such a good read on people, especially when it counted. Now, when he needed that instinct the most, it was gone.

"The mirror is complicated. The place it leads is even more

complicated," Nathan continued. "But I know the rules. Better than any man alive, if it helps. And I can say that with absolute certainty. I won't be forcing you to go Alex, but I will be forcing you to decide." Nathan's eyes flicked down to his watch, but then they were back on Alex, more earnest than before. What's it going to be? they seemed to ask.

All Alex could do in response was nod and whisper, "Okay."

"You're going to want to sit down," Nathan said as he scooped up the mirror.

"Why?"

"Helps with the bruising."

Alex sat, and Nathan held the mirror up as if it were a phone and he were taking a selfie. At first, Alex was underwhelmed. There was nothing strange about the reflection in the small mirror. However when Nathan released it, the mirror remained suspended in the air before them. The reflection then began to change. It no longer showed the guest room and the couch. Instead, a simple corridor took its place. Alex and Nathan, or rather, the reflections of them, stood in the corridor, staring back at them seated on the couch.

Alex felt like he was staring down from the edge of a cliff. It was like he was staring at two images at once. The first was from the perspective of sitting on the couch, but the second was from the corridor staring into another mirror where he could see himself sitting on the guest room couch. He felt a terrible cramp in his stomach and thought he was going to refund his light beers right then and there. But would he hurl in the corridor? Or in the guest house?

"Steady," Nathan's voice said from beside him. From both sides of him. As the word drifted into silence, Alex's vision blurred and he lost any sense of where he was. There was the feeling of falling, then, in a sudden snap, his vision cleared and he was standing in the corridor; whole and complete but contending with an image his mind simply couldn't process.

He was staring at a full length mirror hanging from a concrete wall. The guest house was inside the mirror along with the couch. Suddenly, Alex realized why Nathan had told him to sit. For, on the couch, he could see copies of himself and Nathan, both heads all the way back and both clearly asleep.

Something grabbed his shoulder, and Alex jumped up against the wall.

"You're alright," Nathan said softly. "You're still you."

"I'm what?" The question came out shakily.

"Just relax. You're in sort of a shock. It's the first time you've done this—consciously at least. Your mind is taking a second. Just don't look up."

Of course, that was the first thing Alex started to do, but Nathan wrenched his shoulders and cupped a hand behind his neck.

"Don't. Look. Up," he said again.

His green eyes were like emerald fire, intense and focused. Alex stared at them and finally felt his pulse slow and his breathing steady. Eventually he nodded and Nathan let him go.

"I'm good," Alex said. "I think. A warning might've been nice."

Nathan grinned and clapped him on the shoulder. "Come on. It's just through this door."

"What about us?" Alex followed him down the short hallway, careful to follow Nathan's instruction. I'm quickly becoming a believer, he thought. Either that, or he drugged me. "Nathan. Are we dead?"

Nathan laughed. "We're not dead. But we're out of the house for a moment. Not to worry. You've got plenty of natural defenses to keep everything running. And we'll be back before long." They came to a simple wooden door which opened at Nathan's touch. It revealed a gently flapping brightly patterned cloth. From beyond the cloth, Alex could smell heat. He could hear voices as well. Lots of them, all chattering and bickering. And loud music. At this, Nathan cocked his head. "Hmm. We're later than I thought."

"What is?"

"Not to matter," Nathan replied, but he turned to face Alex. "I was just hoping to introduce you gradually. Still, it'll be an experience."

That wasn't what Alex wanted to hear. "And if I'm not in the mood for an experience?"

Nathan shrugged. "Mirror's right there. It'll let you back." It was just then, Alex realized Nathan was wearing his jacket again, the one the color of red wine, despite never having put it on before picking up the mirror.

For himself, Alex was wearing a simple black t-shirt and jeans. He looked behind to check the mirror. Sure enough, the Alex in Timber's Edge was still wearing his gray sweatshirt. He'd never taken it off.

When he asked Nathan about it, the green eyes widened by a fraction. If Alex didn't know any better, he could've sworn Nathan Cole was surprised. "It's a quirk of Projection which is what Slipping—what we just did with the mirror—is in its simplest form. With the mirror as a guide, you've projected your consciousness, for lack of a better word, to this place. It's curious. You must have a strong mind. Most people when they first Slip, they wind up naked."

Of all the answers Alex was expecting, that wasn't it. "Wait, naked?"

Nathan shrugged, then, apparently thinking the answer was satisfactory, turned back to the cloth.

"So I'm in another place?" Alex asked.

Nathan turned back around, his face creasing. "Well obviously you're in another place."

"I mean, like, if I walked out of here, I could get back to Timber's Edge and—"

Nathan checked his watch again. "No. Not that kind of place. A better way to think about it is that you're on another, separate, layer. At least, your essence is." Nathan pulled his stones out of his pocket and floated them in a vertical column. With his index finger, he pointed to the stone in the middle. "Presume this is Timber's Edge, our home plane." He floated the bottom stone down towards the floor. "Our *essences* are now here. Our substance. All of our memories, our feelings, our spirit. It's here now." He pointed at the middle stone again. "All that's left here, back through the mirror, is, more or less, meat."

"But I have a body. I have clothes."

"Formed from your Projection, yes. Keep in mind you don't really exist here. Not fully. You're more like a temporary resident. Bound by the rules of the plane, able to exist within the plane, but not *of* the plane. And, without the mirror, it would take an extraordinary level of power to keep a Projection like ours stable this far from home."

Alex was struggling to keep up. "This can't be real. I mean, you can't be serious. You're saying I'm a ghost."

Nathan shrugged again. "Interpret your experience however you wish. But, for the record, a ghost is more like a virulent presence, bound to specific Memory. That's why they're almost always localized."

Alex decided to let that batch of questions go. For now, at least. "But I can't be Projecting myself. Or Slipping. Whatever you call it."

Nathan raised a finger and his silver ring caught the light. "Ah. Key distinction. Projection is just the act. Slipping is when you Project consciously. On purpose."

The emphasis chilled Alex. "What do you mean, on purpose?"

The green eyes lit up again. "You dream, don't you Alex?"

Alex nodded.

"You ever have a dream so vivid, you can still remember every detail? Like it was a real memory?"

Alex nodded again and felt his face flush. One in particular stood out. One he tried to never revisit.

"Congratulations. You've projected."

"No," Alex said, "I can't believe it. I'm not sure I do believe it."

Nathan shrugged again.

A horrible question occurred to Alex. "Wait, what happens if we never go back? If we get trapped here or something? Can that happen?"

Nathan nodded. "It can happen. And, to answer your question as to what happens, it's quite simple. It's what happens when all meat's left out," Nathan's eyes turned wide and excited and his mouth broke into a toothy smile. "Eventually, it rots."

Nathan was about to push aside the flap of cloth, but then something made him stop.

"What is it?" Alex asked, half-hoping, half-dreading Nathan was going to send them back through that mirror of his.

"It's your first time. You should go first."

Alex felt the blood drain from his face. "I should what?"

"Go first. Take it in, as they say. After all, you never forget your first."

Nathan gestured for Alex to join him before stepping back. With one hand touching, feeling the cloth, able to hear the music more clearly, able to hear some sort of meat sizzling, sent electricity charging through his body. "This is very stupid isn't it? I should turn around and walk straight back to that mirror."

"Very stupid," Nathan agreed. "And that is precisely what any reasonable person in your position would do. So, what're you waiting for?"

With a deep breath and with no idea of what he was about to walk into, Alex pushed the cloth aside and took a large step forward.

What he saw was unlike anything he could've imagined; Nathan could've painted him a picture, could've shown him a photograph, and it still wouldn't have been able to capture the sensation.

From his side, he heard an exhale. "Well," Nathan Cole said, impressed. "That is certainly not what I expected."

Chapter Ten

Anslem's been busy again. The chalet was gone, monstrous fireplace and all. Nathan had figured that much as soon as he'd opened the door. However, that didn't prepare him for what had replaced it. The mountainside house had been replaced by a bustling desert camp, set beside a lush oasis. At the center of the camp stood an enormous circular tent, its entrance marked by colorful banners. Music flooded from out of the tent, and the glow of a fire within cast dancing shadows on the outside of the canvas. *The party, it seems, is in full swing.* Nathan chided himself for being late, but, when it came to Anchor, it was difficult indeed to know what the right time was.

Besides, he should have set more time aside for questions.

For now, Alex stood silently at Nathan's side, his eyes wide, desperately scanning this way and that. They were standing at the perimeter of the camp, their door having placed them just outside another, far smaller tent flanked by green banners. At the boundary, Nathan dropped an old charm the shape of a silver cross from his pocket.

A circle of these tents lined the camp's edge. Beyond lay only darkness, and above them a blanket of stars stretched well into the distance. Several larger structures flanked the larger tent. One, Nathan judged from the smoke rising from its center, was the cookhouse. Which meant, another one would likely be the residence. *Whichever one it was,* Nathan thought, *it would be the one with all the screaming.*

Across the camp, a group of three individuals came out of another one of the perimeter tents. They wore bright blue, flowing clothes, and Nathan recognized their kind, if not the individuals.

This should be telling.

When Alex noticed them, he became entranced by them. It might have been the fact that each of them had a set of twin tails protruding from their lower backs.

"Are you seeing that?" Alex asked.

Curious, Nathan thought to himself. He was becoming more certain by the moment that Alex Ashford was no Aegyl. *Still, we can't give away the game.*

"It's not polite to stare," Nathan remarked. "They're Vael."

Alex faced him. "Sorry, but they have tails."

As they approached the tent, Nathan could make out their finer details. Two of the individuals had twin black tails. The last, and oldest, carried a single black tail along with a white tail. This one, Nathan knew, was likely the oldest of the group. Alex had failed to notice other more subtle differences, including their reverse ankle joints and pointed ears.

As for their teeth, let's be glad we're far enough away, shall we?

"I think they're aware of that," Nathan said. "Do you have a problem with it?"

"No," he replied quickly. "I just, wasn't...you could've warned me."

"I could have," Nathan admitted. "But it's a lot more fun this way."

Alex sighed and then laughed. "You are a dick."

They made their way across the smooth sand and approached the entrance to the central tent. Before they entered, Nathan stopped Alex and said, "Be careful inside. Stay in the main area, in the lobby. Do not, under any circumstances, go through any doors. Understand?"

Alex looked confused. "I understand. I think."

"This is me warning you," Nathan said. "Here, doors aren't always doors. They could be portals. And portals can lead anywhere. Like you've already seen. Go through the wrong one, and you might get lost. That would be bad."

"No doors. Got it."

"Oh, and try not to embarrass me," Nathan said.

A look of concern crossed Alex's face.

"What is it?" Nathan asked. "I was only joking."

"Which tent was ours?" There were dozens of tents spread over the perimeter of the camp, and each one looked the same. *No wonder he's confused.*

"Don't worry," Nathan said. "I've marked it. One of the first rules of Slipping: always know where you parked. Sometimes you have to leave in a hurry."

Inside the tent somehow seemed even larger than the structure outside. Like the outside, however, it was laid out like a circle. There were no chairs. Where tables and chairs might have been, thick rugs instead lined the floors flanked by fat cushions and comfortable day beds. Dozens of people, including the twin-tailed Vael, congregated around a buffet in the center of the room. More were spread around the space engaged in conversation or gambling. At the far end of the space, a thick curtain formed a boundary for the section that had been reserved for a stocked bar and a dance floor. While they were close enough to hear the music Nathan knew was thumping inside, all they could hear was the faint echo of the sound. It was as if they were standing a mile away instead of only a few feet.

One of my better ideas, Nathan remarked to himself. *Though it still astounds me that I was able to get Anslem to go along with it.*

"What is this place?" Alex asked.

A voice from Alex's left answered, "This is Anchor." Anslem materialized in a shower of sparks next to them.

Alex shot sideways in alarm.

Anslem wore flowing beige robes, but otherwise his form was still that of the young Black man. The stars in his eyes spiraled as he appraised Alex. "It is a place of harbor for those who need refuge. A place of rest for those who are weary. A place of stillness for those who cannot act. A strand of safety within the Astral Weave." To Nathan, Anslem added. "It is good to see you again my dear friend."

"Alex," Nathan said. "This is Anslem. My truest friend."

Anslem inclined his head in a small bow. His eyes flicked over to Nathan and that single instant told Nathan everything.

So, Alex is no Aegyl. That made things less complicated. But also potentially more dangerous.

Alex, who was still nursing his shock, stammered, "Nice to meet you."

Anslem said nothing. Instead, he studied Alex the way a cat might study a tuna can. "Will he be staying with us?"

"Not today," Nathan said quickly. "Just passing through."

"Staying?" Alex asked.

"A pity," Anslem replied. He looked once again over Alex. "A pity," he said again. "Please, join us and be at peace. But beware, when the sun rises, you must either pay for shelter or return to the storm." A sadness crept into the Aegyl's voice. "Such is the cost of peace."

Alex stepped back, away from the Aegyl.

"We will be gone before the sun rises," Nathan assured Anslem.

Anslem gave another small tilt of his head. "Then be welcome." To Nathan, he added, "Come, Nate, we have some things to discuss."

Anslem glided deeper into the tent, and Nathan made after him. Over his shoulder to Alex, he said, "I'll find you in a bit. Go. Get a drink. Mingle. Remember, no doors." As he walked away, he caught a bewildered look on Alex's face and grinned in reply. He turned away before he could make out the full obscenity Alex mouthed back, but he did catch the middle finger.

"Your companion seems displeased," Anslem remarked once Nathan reached the Aegyl's side. As far as Nathan could tell, Anslem had no way to see Alex's gestures. *But when has that ever stopped him knowing everything that goes on here?*

"He'll be fine," Nathan said. "I've come to think he's a unique soul."

"Quite so," Anslem said. They cut through the crowd, and Anslem spent a few moments leading Nathan around this version of Anchor.

When they passed the group of Vael sniffing at bowls of some sort of porridge, Nathan remarked, "Unusual to see them here."

"They have been more frequent guests as of late. They have been particularly feisty." Anslem took Nathan to the buffet where he proceeded to precisely arrange each serving utensil. "He is not of my kind," the Aegyl said at last.

"I've come to suspect as much. Is there any Trace?"

"None. He is the Angel of which you spoke?"

"My chief suspect, yes," Nathan replied. "He insists he isn't, but there's something he knows. If it isn't him, then he's wrapped up in it somehow."

Anslem nodded, examining a series of hanging square lanterns, each one a different, vivid color. "Then it would seem there is another force behind your Angel. Whatever it is, it is not the work of an Aegyl. It is curious, however."

"What's curious?"

"Do you recall when you came to see me about this Angel?"

"Of course."

"I told you that there was a difference about you."

"An air of purpose as I recall."

"Quite so," Anslem said. "It is difficult to describe. It is almost like an aura or an energy. It curls off of you."

"What does it mean?"

"That, I do not know," Anslem replied. "But it curls off of this Alex Ashford as well. I would suggest you be cautious. Whatever is at work has you both."

Both of us? What sort of energy could it be? Nathan ran his head through the different spells or rituals he'd encountered, but nothing seemed to describe what Anslem was seeing. He knew the Aegyl wasn't lying, but he had no idea what to do with the information.

"You know me," Nathan replied with a confidence he no longer felt. "I'm always careful. Do you still have my box?" *Whatever power was behind the Timber Angel was enough to make Anslem warn us. That counts for a lot. That counts for more than a lot.*

"You know that I do," Anslem said. "You think you will need it?"

"Alex might," Nathan replied. "And I might need an insurance policy."

Anslem's eyes skipped a beat.

Nathan shrugged, "You're the one who told me to be cautious."

✳

Anslem moved the lanterns a fraction here and a tiny amount there. Though they weren't black iron, they still reminded Nathan of the lantern in the center of Calbot Square and of the one hanging from the statue's grasp across the bridge from the Ashford house. Then there was the ones hanging from some of the other buildings around town.

The lanterns had bothered Nathan from the beginning. Timber's Edge was a town of Angels, after all, not a town of Lanterns. Now, looking at Anslem's arrangement casting light of different colors and shades, Nathan understood why. The lights that the Timber's Edge lanterns cast were all different as well. He considered the lantern in the park. When he'd first arrived, it had been lit, but only dimly. By the time of the First Snow, it was glowing considerably more. Even more so when he saw it an hour ago with Alex.

Then there was the statue's lantern. That one never changed. The more he thought about it, the more convinced he became that the lanterns mattered. The more he thought about the lanterns, the more convinced he became that Timber's Edge was starting to feel like a trap.

But a trap for what purpose? If it is a trap, it's hardly doing a very good job.

It was only after a moment that he noticed Anslem watching him. It looked as if the Aegyl was expecting Nathan to say something. There was something curious about him. He was standing taller, at his full height, and the stars in his eyes were sparkling.

Is he preening?

"I've meant to say," Nathan ventured. "Anchor looks rather… different."

The eyes began to twinkle, and, though Anslem's voice barely fluctuated, Nathan knew he was pleased. "Yes, I decided a change to this particular reflection was in order. One inspired by you Nathan Cole."

"Me?"

Anslem gave a small nod then began to rearrange the banners. "You seemed very taken by this celebration. It was important, you said."

"Are you talking about Christmas?"

When he finished with the banners, Anslem lit a series of incense burners and the heavy perfume coated the air. "Christmas. That was the name. It had escaped me. When some souls from your plane found their way here, I asked them. All about celebrations of good will and joyful tidings—that was how you had described it. Desert travelers, they said they were."

Has he gone insane? Anslem has never really cared about the lesser planes.

Anslem continued, "It took some time, but eventually they told me of this celebration. It intrigues me. I can understand why it appeals to you."

Nathan looked around the tent. *Not a Christmas tree in sight. Not even a shred of tinsel. No Monopoly being played.*

"When, exactly, were these souls from?"

Anslem seemed unconcerned. "Is it relevant?"

"I think it might just be. Many of these things, from my plane, they change with the passage of time."

The stars in the Aegyl's eyes halted. "Your plane's linear time again."

"I'm afraid so."

"This would be your past then?"

Nathan grinned. "Not mine, personally."

Anslem nodded. "I understand. Tell me everything then of your current celebration. Of your present Christmas."

"Uhh—"

The stars began to move again. "You may begin. I will stop you should I have questions."

✳

Alex wasn't sure what was in the heavy crystal glass. It was some sort of sweet, acid green liquid, and it definitely had a kick. He wandered around Anchor, careful to avoid the things—the people? —with the tails. Thankfully most of the other people here looked more or less like, well, people. Still, he hadn't drummed up the courage to actually talk to any of them.

What was he going to say? *I'm Alex. From a town called Timber's Edge. We're working on trying to keep Christmas alive.* Would any of them even know what Christmas was?

He was in another plane for crying out loud! The thought still amazed him even though he didn't really comprehend what it meant. He caught Nathan following his strange friend, Anslem, around the place. They had been talking for a while—about, what, Alex couldn't say, but Nathan was starting to look a bit flummoxed. There was a certain sense of satisfaction to that, Alex had to admit.

He drifted through the curtain that led to the dance floor, and was amazed at the change in volume, in energy. Before the curtain, the tent was full of bustling conversation, behind the curtain, it was like stepping into a night club. All of the bodies merged together in one hot mass. Alex saw a few horns within the crowd along with several other tails. The twin-tailed creatures were here as well, but whether they were the same individuals as before, Alex couldn't tell.

When a blue-skinned girl jostled him by accident, Alex almost spilled his drink. He stepped back, towards the edge of the floor, and simply watched. He felt like he was in college again, attending his first fraternity party. Standing on the edge, drink in hand, unable to remove himself from the wall. Unable to see how exactly he fit in. It was like the crowd was speaking a foreign language. Some of them, he supposed, had to be, unless blue-skinned people spoke English.

By the time he finished his drink, he began to get a handle on the music's beat. It was a strange song, made from instruments that reminded him of a particularly aggressive violin. Some sort of alien drum provided the rapid beat. Whatever this music was, it sure seemed popular. A pleasant buzz had set up shop in his head, and he thanked the green drink for it.

He wasn't sure for how long he'd been standing off to the side when he finally drifted onto the floor itself. Alex found the beat easily enough, and, before long, was moving his body in time with the other dancers. He and the blue-skinned girl eventually came face-to-face and then danced together. A wordless intuition had taken over.

Thanks to the blue-skinned girl, he was able to work out how to act, even when they merged together with another group. It was hot on the floor, and when the music got faster and faster, it got hotter and hotter. The songs changed one after another without any break. With each song change, Alex felt a bit more comfortable. At one point, he tried to speak to the blue-skinned girl, to introduce himself, to mingle as Nathan had said, but there was no point. The noise was too loud to possibly hear a word.

It was like being transported to those first college parties. Eventually, he had gotten a sense for it, a sense for what he was supposed to do, how he was supposed to move, and for what was expected from him. That was where he had met Patrick. A sophomore when Alex had been a freshman, Patrick had introduced Alex to the world of adulthood, and, like the blue-skinned girl, most of the time he had never had to say a word. He had known what classes to pick, what professors to avoid, the best places to study, and, most of all, who could be trusted. Alex had been able to read him, to understand him, almost without thinking. And, when they finally became more than friends, Patrick became a constant presence in his mind. For years, Alex came to crave him, to need him, and Patrick was there—

Until he wasn't. Until that part of his mind that craved him starved and withered, a gaping mouth impossible to feed.

The thought hit Alex like a surprise blow to the back of the head. Distracted, he stumbled and almost fell while dancing. The blue-skinned girl grinned at him, her mouth full of too many pointed white teeth.

What was he doing?

It took him a moment to realize where he was. Sweat slicked his skin, and his stomach threatened to turn. It was enough mingling for one day, he decided. He drifted out of the dance floor and found his way back behind the curtain.

Compared to the dance floor, it was blissfully silent. Alex's ears still rang with the music and the beat still throbbed in his head. He crossed the tent, but it was only after a few steps that he realized something had changed. Most of the crowd had cleared away, leaving the tent mostly empty. Of the few people left, some were having quiet conversations in the corner. He spotted Nathan and Anslem still talking. Nathan was covering his eyes and laughing, but Alex couldn't tell what he found funny.

Maybe he was laughing about me, Alex thought.

He dismissed the idea almost immediately, disgusted it had surfaced in the first place. When it came to Nathan, all that intuition he had come to possess turned to dust. When it came to Nathan, all Alex could come to feel was a dreadful uncertainty. That, and a dangerous curiosity. Part of him wanted to head over to them, to join their conversation, but he wasn't sure he'd be welcome. There it was again. That uncertainty.

He turned away from Nathan and Anslem, and saw that while he had been watching them, someone else had been watching him. It was a young girl. She looked to be about fourteen, and she was sitting alone amid a circle of cushions. Take that back, Alex thought. She wasn't alone. There were dolls of all kinds seated around her, carefully arranged. Some wore dresses of different colors, others looked to be more simple carvings. A few wore intricate, flowing garments. He did, however, recognize one, a knitted girl with buttons for eyes. Maddie had one just like it.

The girl herself had reddish-brown skin and wore an ornate pearly white dress. When she raised a hand in a gentle gesture, Alex considered ignoring her. But Nathan did say to mingle.

Up close, she appeared more alien than he had thought. Her eyes were the color of black oil. They seemed wet and almost bubbled. Alex thought that she might be blind, but when she looked clearly up at him, he got the distinct sense she was studying him.

"I didn't think you would come say hello," she said. "But I'm glad you did."

Alex couldn't think of something to say. He was sure Nathan would know. At the thought, blood ran to his cheeks.

"Please, sit. You can move Miriel there. She doesn't mind sharing."

The girl gestured at a doll wearing a periwinkle dress seated directly across from her.

Before he touched it, Alex asked, "Are they alive?"

"They are to me," she said. "But then, don't all precious things take on a life of their own? You tell me, are they alive to you?"

Feeling his throat turn a bit dry, Alex studied the doll she had called Miriel. It was made from porcelain and while it had eyes that followed him, it didn't seem any different from the dolls he had seen at his grandmother's house. "No, she doesn't seem to be alive to me." Still, he lifted Miriel carefully and placed her gently on the next cushion. Then, he sat and crossed his legs. "What can I call you?"

"I am the Keeper," she said.

"And what exactly do you keep?"

At the question, the girl smiled. Her mouth was full of perfectly even teeth that could have been porcelain. "I keep my Lady informed. So many things can change, and sometimes She can lose track." Before Alex could say anything, she continued, "You arrived here with Nathaniel." Nathaniel?

It wasn't a question. "That's right. You know him then?"

"Very well," The girl replied.

Alex felt a nervous thread pull at the pit of his stomach. He was in over his head.

"In a sense, we are family, though he chose to leave us some time ago."

Was she talking about Anchor? Nathan did call Anslem his truest friend, but he never called him family. Alex knew how complicated family could be.

"I don't know if I should believe you," Alex said. The uncertainty was becoming too much to bear, but his intuition told him that she was telling the truth. The words simply didn't sound like a lie.

"Tell me, what would be the point of lying to someone like you?" the girl replied with another even smile. The oil-pit eyes began to unnerve him. "Some of us come to accept the Price," the girl said. "For some, the Price is too heavy a burden."

"And which is Nathan?"

The girl picked a doll up from next to her and began to brush its hair. "Dear Nathaniel is neither," she said at last. "He paid his Price, completed his service, then left that life behind him—our life behind him." Her stare lifted from the doll and set onto Alex. "More or less, that is."

A desire to stand, to walk slowly away, came to Alex's mind, but sheer curiosity was in control now. His voice shook when he asked, "And, what—what was his Price?"

The girl, the Keeper, began to answer, but another voice came from behind Alex. "I served," Nathan said. The Aegyl stood at Nathan's side. Nathan didn't look at Alex, and instead stared at the diminutive Keeper the way one might watch a hornet. His fists were clenched, and his jaw was set.

The girl resumed brushing the doll's hair, unconcerned. "Dear Nathaniel," she said. "It's been too long. Our Lady has been asking after her Black Thorn. And Brother Flame, he says it's a fine day for a ma—"

"She's not Our Lady any longer," Nathan interrupted in a lash of anger. "I'm not interested. I don't care how fine the day is. It can be pretty fine. Mighty fine. You know damn well I'm not interested." He checked his watch again. "Anslem, can you take care of Alex? We have to be leaving soon."

"Of course," Anslem replied. To Alex, he said. "Come. You need something for your strength."

Alex stood, and gave the little girl a final look.

Before he could turn his back, she said to him, "It was nice to meet you Alex Ashford."

It wasn't until he was halfway back across Anchor that he remembered that he never told her his name.

*

Anslem scooped some of the white porridge into a ceramic bowl and handed Alex a spoon. "I'm not hungry," Alex said.

"Eat," Anslem replied. "It will help with your return. Unless you would rather stay." Alex took a slow bite; realizing that he was, in fact, very hungry, he kept going. Anslem paid him little attention, instead focusing on Nathan and the girl.

"Who is she?" Alex asked.

"The Keeper? Her mistress cannot directly intercede here. The Keeper is her voice, her conduit to this and other places. In a way, she serves The Lady similar to how I serve my own superiors," Anslem said.

Alex was surprised. "You have superiors?"

Anslem's gaze landed on Alex. "It surprises you?" he asked in his almost robotic voice.

"I just thought. Since you're so, well, powerful..."

"Power is merely a currency Alex Ashford. And, like any currency, there will always be those with more and those with less. I do what I can with the power afforded to me, but freedom is a gift I have yet to receive. It is a rare soul indeed who serves no master but their own design. Even for an Aegyl." While speaking, Anslem's gaze shifted back to Nathan. Alex didn't know the Aegyl well, but he got the sense that Anslem was concerned.

"Will Nathan be alright? That girl, she seemed to know him."

"You wish to help him?" Anslem asked. "Do not trouble yourself."

"What does she want?"

"That is not my story to tell," Anslem admitted. "But I will tell you this. Above all else, Nathan abhors violence. He will avoid it whenever he can, however he can. Even when it is necessary. The Lady does not; violence is a large part of Her currency. And She will spend freely when it suits Her."

Alex was going to reply when he saw Nathan turn his back on the Keeper and cross his way back to them. When he saw the bowl in Alex's hands, the easy smile returned. "Good," he said. "You're eating."

"All is well?" Anslem asked.

"As well as could be expected," Nathan replied. He scooped porridge into his own bowl and devoured it. When he'd finished, he checked his watch again. "Far too late," he muttered. "Alex, it's time to go."

He pushed quickly to his feet. Together they walked back to the entrance to the tent and pushed outside. The stars in the sky had vanished, replaced by the purple haze of morning. A sunrise threatened the horizon, and Alex remembered what Anslem had said. *When the sun rises, you must pay for shelter or return to the storm.* Alex wondered if that was the same Price the Keeper had referred to. The price that Nathan had paid.

"I look forward to your return," Anslem told them at the boundary to their tent. "And remember, Nathan Cole of The Holding, should you ever need shelter, I will always pay the price for you."

"And I would for you, my friend," Nathan replied. "Time and time again."

The Aegyl inclined his head, then appraised them both. His impossible eyes lingered on Alex. "Safe journey, both of you. Do what you can with the power afforded to you." With that, Anslem turned and strode back into the desert. He made it halfway to the tent before his form began to spark and fracture. One orange spark became a storm and then Anslem was gone, leaving only an incomplete set of footprints in his wake.

Chapter Eleven

Alex broke the silence that had settled over the living room since they Slipped back. There was the momentary disorientation followed by the thoughts becoming sharper, more focused. Finally, the memories all came flooding back, almost at once. Like a section of the brain was plugged into power.

"It's not even two yet," Alex said. "I swear we were there all night."

"We were," Nathan replied. "A night Slipped there isn't as long as our night here. Still," he checked his watch. "I expected us to be back earlier." *It should've been closer to midnight. Unless my calculations were wrong. Am I getting that careless?*

"Okay," Alex said, "I have to ask."

Nathan shot him a look.

"The watch. You said it doesn't tell time in Anchor."

"Is that what I said?" Nathan asked.

"You said the hands don't move."

"They don't." Nathan grinned. "It doesn't mean that the watch doesn't tell time."

Alex rubbed the bridge of his nose.

Nathan continued, "The hands don't move. At least, in no way that I can observe. But if I can still tell time..."

"Then the face is changing?"

"Correct," Nathan replied, his smile fading a bit. "It's another quirk of Projection. Have you ever tried to turn on a light switch in a dream? It barely ever works. The connection of cause and effect starts to get a bit murky when you Project. Similarly, my watch face changes, but the hands never move. I simply look down and it's another time. But, if I were to watch it, really carefully, you know what would happen?"

Alex rubbed the space between his eyes.

"Nothing. In Anchor, if I stared at my watch for ten minutes, no time would pass. It would start at 2:00 PM and end at 2:00 PM. Now, if I set an invisible timer for ten minutes, and then came back to my watch, time would pass. The hands would not be where they started."

"Okay —"

"You're confused," Nathan said. "But it gets a lot worse, I'm afraid this holds true even if I have another frame of reference. The hands also won't advance the full ten minutes. They could advance more. It could end up as 2:15 PM or even 4:00 PM. That part really got me when it first happened. Anslem had to walk me through that."

"I'm totally lost." Alex rubbed his temples with his hands.

"Yeah," Nathan agreed. "I was as well, but I've had a lot of time to get used to it. It comes down to observation and perception. What you observe, what you perceive, can form your reality. Especially in places rooted in Memory, like Anchor. Let me ask you this, why do you think Anchor had no windows?"

Alex chewed on the question before his face lit up in a flash of excited lightning. "It's to do with the sun."

"Not bad," Nathan remarked. *Someone pays attention.* "If someone goes outside, or within observable distance of the sky, they may think that it's been too long, that the sun should be up. Just by thinking such a thing, perceiving that sky, observing the sun is what can make the passage of time advance. Especially if multiple beings observe the same thing together. Together, their perception can change Anchor."

Alex looked troubled by something.

Well he probably needs a minute. It's been a big night for him.

"What happens if someone never goes outside?" Alex asked.

Now that is a good question. "You tell me," Nathan replied. His voice had chilled a few degrees. He could see where this was going.

Alex took on that familiar inward look, the one he got when he was thinking about something. It was something Nathan liked about him. Alex tended to consider problems; in Nathan's experience, it was a rare trait. "The night would last forever. Or until something messed with it."

Nathan inclined his head. *Impressive.*

"That's impossible," Alex stammered.

"Is it? In Anchor, a place about as deep within the Weave as can be, the power of observation and perception are multiplied—they're more obvious—but you can see it all the time whenever you Project. Let's go back to our dream example. It's not like a dream progresses neatly from one event to another. It jumps around. Like a rabbit with places to be. In many respects, there isn't much to mark the passage of time. Not without a reference."

"Your light switch."

Nathan nodded. *He's got a natural grasp of it, that's for sure.*

"But you said you remember every moment in Anchor. 'With perfect clarity.'"

"That's right," Nathan replied.

As perception grows more powerful, so too does the impact. All of the days in Anchor unfolded before him. The scale of them gave Nathan vertigo and he was glad to be sitting down. *So many memories. What had She said, all that time ago? Too many for any one mind to bear.*

Alex gave him a long look before speaking. "Then you must have seen some long nights. I guess I'm wondering how many."

None I'd care to recall. A particularly brutal night under the humid twin moons hammered back into his mind. Nathan could feel the blows. The cracked rib that made each breath feel like being stabbed. The broken fingers that finally gave way after too much punishment. *Too late.* Nathan smiled at Alex and suddenly he felt every day of those memories.

Nathan's shoulders slumped forward. "Ask your question Alex," he said gently. "It's alright."

Alex choked back his words. "How—how long have you spent there?"

Nathan stood, and pulled the collar of his shirt to reveal a tattoo that sat just above his heart. The black stenciled symbols were clear as day: ξϛ ια κδ.

"They're Greek," Nathan explained. With a finger, he moved between the three sets. "Years, months, days. Sixty-six years, eleven months, twenty-four days. Give or take."

There it is. Out in the open now. Nathan was curious how he'd respond. Alex was standing across the room from him, and his eyes darted towards the door. *One step too far, Alex?*

Nathan tapped his ring with his thumb and considered his next words carefully. "Is it that hard to believe? You're living the impossible in this town. Right now."

Alex started. "It's just...crazy. I'm sorry." He lifted his arms. "Actually I'm not. Sorry that is. I just don't know what else to call it. That would make you..."

"Going on a hundred?" Nathan cracked a quick smile. "Not looking too bad either eh?"

Alex rolled his eyes.

Nathan stepped closer. "I didn't take you to Anchor for no reason Alex," he said carefully. "It's because I needed you to see, to believe me, that I know what I'm talking about. I know what I'm talking about when I tell you that something might be very wrong here."

"Look—" Alex started.

"You know something," Nathan said. "You were surprised when

the bell rang. I saw it on your face."

The blood seeped out of Alex's face. He opened his mouth, but no words came out.

"Yes. I can hear it as well. Lives might be at stake. Please."

"I told you," Alex said with a sharp bite. "Everything's fine. The Timber Angel isn't some evil thing. It's important to everyone here. It's important to the town."

"Is somebody making you say that?" Nathan asked. Immediately, he knew the question was a mistake.

Alex backed up a step, his eyes two hard stones.

We've lost him. We're going to need another plan. Nathan exhaled and ran a hand through his hair.

"It's late," Alex said. "Sorry. I've got to go. Enjoy the house." With that, Alex pulled open the door and stormed into the night. He dragged the door shut behind him, leaving Nathan standing alone in the middle of the guest house. The TV had switched to a showing of the black-and-white *A Christmas Carol,* and Nathan overheard Scrooge talking with Marley's Ghost.

"Ah you don't know the weight and length of strong chain you bear yourself," Marley's Ghost was saying.

Nathan glared at the TV.

I'm working on it. Honest, I am.

Aloud, he sighed and whispered, "Let me help you Alex. Before it's too late."

*

The streetcar rattled again as it wound its way down the icy San Francisco hills. Bells chimed in a chorus of passengers demanding their stops, but there were too many chimes for the amount of passengers. Outside, a blizzard raged, dumping snow and ice across the hills. More than once, the streetcar's wheels slipped and there was a brief, horrible moment of sliding. None of the other passengers seemed bothered.

But Nathan was. He stumbled down the aisle, just as he had on the bus before. He was expecting to see Marie at the wheel, but she wasn't there. Not this time. Instead, Ronny sat behind the wheel. The old bus driver glared at him and his face was thick with disgust. The logo that had once been on his arm was now a flickering flame, sending acrid smoke curling into the cabin.

"I told you to leave son," he growled. "This is on you now."

The blizzard cleared for a moment, enough time for Nathan to see that San Francisco was gone. In its place, the streetcar was hurtling down mountain curves. There wasn't a town or a stop in sight, but that didn't stop the passengers from ringing the bell. Down one curve, the streetcar toppled precariously to the right.

"Whoa, boy," Ronny said.

"That was close," Nathan finished. He said the words in a daze. He knew these roads. And he knew what came next.

The streetcar roared around another curve.

"Shit!" Ronny shouted.

In the streetcar's path, in the middle of the road, was a man. He wore a red sweatshirt and jeans. *Alex!* Ronny threw the brakes and the metal screamed. There was a terrible crash, and the streetcar tipped again. This time it went all the way over and hurtled towards the edge of the road.

Nathan shut his eyes just in time, but there was nothing he could do to prevent the invasion of weightlessness that came with free-fall. It was now only a question of when. The horrible anticipation hung in his mind and each second stretched longer and longer until Nathan was no longer sure that he was falling.

But in these sorts of times, gravity won't long be denied.

The question's answer came in an explosion of steel and wood.

Nathan felt himself hurl forward, and then he knew no more.

*

Alex felt a pit in his stomach that the hot coffee could do nothing to fill. Leaving the bar last night, he'd felt like things were looking better. The time spent with Nathan had made him believe, believe that he might still be able to salvage this mess. Now, it seemed things were worse than ever.

The Second Rite was due to be performed tomorrow night, and Alex still had no idea how these things were happening. The First Rite shouldn't have been possible to perform, but, now that it had, the town was already preparing for the Timber Angel to light the tree. He didn't know what would happen if it wasn't performed. No one seemed to think that there could be any consequences, but Alex had a different idea. Any time he tried to talk to Julianna, she brushed him aside.

A thought came with a bitter shake of his head. Nathan had posed that exact question to the both of them in the archive yesterday. Of course he'd already thought of it.

Last night, he had thought it was right to leave. Nathan—or was it Nathaniel?—said such crazy things. He's almost one-hundred. Spent sixty years in whatever the actual fuck Anchor was. And I'd been checking him out. The blond hair, the green eyes, and the thick arms; for crying out loud, I'm only human.

It was the mind that was the worst. Alex was used to feeling on top of conversations, but Nathan always seemed one step ahead of him. Who was he kidding? Half of the time, he seemed a full lap ahead.

When Alex had first—what was the word—Slipped back, he'd thought Nathan might have drugged him. But then, after a few minutes, he realized it had all been real. He tried not to linger too long on the overall concept of real. It made his head hurt. As Nathan might say, it was complicated. But what he knew was that he had been there. He'd met Anslem. Danced with the blue lady. Talked with that strange girl.

The sound of a door opening upstairs broke his concentration. Soon, the stairs creaked under the familiar sound of Paul Ashford's footsteps. His father looked surprised to see Alex at the table. "Late start for you isn't it?"

Alex raised his coffee and smiled weakly. "Running on half batteries. There's a pot if you want some."

"Damn right I do," Paul said. "Thanks." The kitchen chair groaned as he sat on it. "It's going to be another long day," he said.

"Farm busy?" Alex asked. He was only half listening. The other half of him was thinking about the disappointment on Nathan's face when he'd left. For crying out loud, Alex.

"I didn't know so many people lived around here," his father replied. "We can barely keep up with it all. Speaking of, do you have thirty minutes today?"

Julianna did tell me to leave the Archive alone, Alex thought. Insisted on it, in fact.

"What do you need?"

"Just some help moving some trees down from the farm. Jonesy will load them up. Just need your truck is all."

"Eleven?"

"That'll work," Paul replied. "Then, do you think you can cut one for us?"

Alex winced at the thought of them not cutting the tree together. It used to be his mother who picked it out. Another thing that's changed.

"Jules, Julianna, she wants to keep it all a surprise for Maddie, so do you mind keeping her at Gloria's for a few hours? She's got her puzzle mat, so she'll be fine."

Alex considered challenging him, but he could tell his father's mind was made up. "Like catnip for nine-year-olds. Who knew?"

"You're telling me. It's been a Godsend what with th—everything else going on."

"I didn't even know she was into puzzles. At least, not like this."

Paul scratched his beard. "Sure you did. I told you six months ago. And you saw her during summer break. She was making that one with all the kittens."

Sure enough, across the room, Alex noticed the glued and framed puzzle hanging on the wall. It showed a wicker basket stuffed with kittens of all colors.

Alex took a long gulp of coffee. He could remember the conversation now. "Guess it slipped my mind."

Paul's hands opened. "You've got a lot on your plate. What with finishing school, planning your move, and—"

"Everything else?"

His dad smiled. "Yeah. Everything else." Across the table, Paul Ashford studied him. For a moment, his father was no longer Paul Ashford, Christmas Tree Farmer. He was Professor Ashford, tenured lecturer of English Literature. "You sure everything is alright? You look off."

Alex shrugged. "It'll all work out. I just, uh, might have done something stupid last night."

Professor Ashford groaned like he'd just received a particularly poor essay. "Does that stupid night involve someone staying in our guest house? I know I said I wanted my five stars, but there's a line, son."

Alex had to laugh. "It's not quite like that." He met his father's level stare. "It's this Angel stuff. Julianna's telling me to stop worrying about it."

"She's not wrong."

"No," Alex admitted. "She isn't. But even though the legend isn't happening like it should, she's still apparently willing to leave it to faith," He sneered at the word, and Paul Ashford chuckled. "Our house-guest—Nathan—thinks something else might be behind it."

His dad cocked his head, considered the words, considered the problem. Alex admired a lot about his father, not least of all his ability to analyze even in the absence of all of the facts. All he needed was a few scraps and he could piece the story together. Over many years, father and son had mastered the art of talking around difficult subjects. And for almost twenty years, it had held together quite well. "And what do you think?" he asked at last.

"I think the legend might be wrong," Alex replied. "Maybe the Angel doesn't have much to do with it at all. It's snowing, right?"

"It is," his father agreed.

"So maybe the Timber Angel is just a face for something that happens on its own. And it will all just work out," Alex suggested. It felt hopeful to say it out loud. "But I can't help but ask myself…what if Nathan's right? What if there is something I more I can do?"

Paul Ashford cocked his head again. "You know, there's never enough time at the holidays. They take forever to get here and then they're gone before you can blink," his father said at last. "Everyone's always wanting something or you're needing to be somewhere or there's some event to go to. Look at us. We've got the farm. The tree. You've taken on this Angel business. And that's before, you know, the normal Christmas stuff.

"Your mother and I, we'd talk about this a lot. Especially when you were younger. When I didn't know what to do, she'd ask me, 'Where can you make the most change? Where can you do the most good? Who can help you?'" Paul scratched his beard again. "Drop what you don't need. Or what can wait. Work on the most pressing things first." His eyes glinted with mischief, and Professor Ashford was back on sabbatical. "And, anyone who doesn't get that, well they can pound sand. Angel or not. Right now, is there anything you can actually do about this Angel stuff?"

"I'm stuck, and I don't want to mess it up."

"And what about Nathan? Anything he can do about it?" His

father staggered around the question.

"Well he might blow the whole thing up." While Alex chewed on his next sentence, he was surprised when Paul gave a deep chuckle. "He thinks it might be dangerous Dad." Saying it out loud made Alex feel foolish, but his father's laugh cut off. Alex felt the change from across the table. "He's kind of an expert on this...stuff."

"You believe him?"

"Yeah. He's, uh, made a convincing case." To put it lightly.

Alex already had a sense of what his father was going to say, so he simply nodded.

Paul nodded slowly. "There's another thing your mother used to say," he said. " 'Don't fear the truth. It will always come out eventually.' Son, what if he's right? What if it is dangerous?"

"But it's not," Alex insisted. There was nothing he wanted more than for Maddie to experience an Angel Year before it was too late, but this wasn't turning out anything like he'd hoped. "I know it's not. I just can't prove it."

"Then maybe you need to let him prove it. It's what he does, right?"

It was good advice, Alex reflected as he changed for his run. He pulled on a steel-blue sweatshirt over an athletic shirt, grabbed a pair of briefs, and pulled a pair of joggers over them. He'd find Nathan later, tell him what he knew, then wash his hands of it. Julianna was right. If he wasn't the Angel, then it wasn't his responsibility. And his father was right as well. There were other things he could be doing with his holiday.

Outside, the morning air was brisk, just like Alex liked it. For once, the sun was already peeking over the trees, so the morning's gray cloak looked to be hiding a lantern. As he made his way down the lawn, Alex did some kicks to unfreeze the blood in his legs.

There were no lights on in the guest house, and Alex relaxed as he drew closer. Nathan would probably be in town by now. He was an early riser as well. That was good. Alex wasn't ready to face him yet; he had no idea what he would say, how he might explain. When he passed the front door, he noticed it was ajar, and Nathan was standing in profile. His heart leaped into his throat.

He only wore a pair of gym shorts and a beat up pair of sneakers. It was the first time Alex had seen him without a shirt. Judging from his matted hair and heavy breathing, he'd clearly been exercising. His arms were crossed in front of his bare chest. They were working arms, responsible for more than just lifting weights in a gym. He turned and the toned chest and smooth stomach told the same story. There was the tattoo, the same as the night before, with all that it stood for. A suggestion of abs lingered around the top and bottom of his navel, and a line of golden hair ran down into his shorts.

Nathan noticed him then. A look of surprise crossed his face, and Alex felt his cheeks flush. Only human, Alex reminded himself, but he started his run right there and then; there wasn't much choice, for it wouldn't take long until the blood found other places to go.

✱

Marie had a particularly strong pot of coffee ready the next morning, and Nathan was happy to see it. The dream of the streetcar still hung over him along with his last conversation with Alex. *He could barely look at you earlier as well.*

"Late start for you today," she said as she poured him a cup.

"Thanks," Nathan said.

"Everyone else is already gone. DeMarco didn't even eat breakfast, can you imagine that?"

"Is that right?" Nathan wasn't paying particular attention to John DeMarco, not when Alex Ashford was forefront in his mind. *What had gone wrong?* It was a setback, that was for sure. He needed Alex on his side. *We pushed too hard.* Nathan didn't have a true psychic's talent for mind reading, but he knew when someone was holding something back, and Alex had been holding back from the second they'd met. He had thought, honestly thought, that Anchor would've shaken some of the truth loose, but all it seemed to have done was close Alex up more.

"Don't worry. It's not poison," she said, gesturing at Nathan's untouched coffee. She shook her wrist, rattling her collection of beads. "I'm not angry with you for picking the house. Of course, you didn't even give my Inn a chance."

"Sorry," Nathan said sheepishly and sipped the coffee.

"Cable TV. Claw foot tubs in each room. Local masseuse on call."

"Impressive. Do I sense the touch of an Angel?"

"Are you accusing me? Already?" Marie asked with a laugh. "Come on, it's no secret you're looking."

"Gotta start somewhere." *Not to be a stickler, but I started two days ago.* Nathan hadn't actually intended to make an accusation. *But I could use a new suspect.*

"I suppose so. Still, I was hoping for a bit more flash. Like setting me up for a trap or something where I would reveal my magical powers. Instead you come right out and ask." She waved her hands for dramatic effect, then shrugged. "No snow. No ice. No Christmas magic here. Sorry kid, I'm just a fan."

At this Nathan laughed. "Yeah, my mother would've been as well. Not all magics are a curse, she used to say."

"You don't agree?"

Nathan's gaze dropped to his cup. So few understood. So few would ever understand. Straddling the line between normal and arcane for as long as he had, it did make it hard to know what to say. How Mother Sable had lasted so long, Nathan didn't think he'd ever understand.

But she'd had The Holding's backing. My situation's different.

"In my experience," Nathan said quietly, "it's the bad Memories that talk loud enough to garner attention. All they ever do is grow louder. Eventually, they start to shout." He met her eyes over the mug. "And that's when people get hurt."

"And you suspect the Angel Rites are bad magic?" Marie asked.

Nathan smiled. "Nothing would make me happier than to let it go, confident that everything will be fine. But experience can be a hard teacher to defy. Problem is, the town's mysterious benefactor doesn't want to be found."

"It might be for the best," Marie suggested.

Nathan nodded and said, "That's true enough, but all I want to do is talk. To see for myself."

Marie frowned. "You have that right? To barge in on their business?"

"When it comes to matters of the arcane," Nathan said, "it's like meddling with uranium in your backyard. We all hope that you know what you're doing, but, if for some reason you don't, then you need to be stopped. The risks of getting it wrong...they're too great."

Whether it was his solemn voice or his stony gaze, Nathan wasn't sure, but something changed Marie's tone. "You asked Alex?" she asked.

"Yes, I've asked him. A few different times. He either doesn't know who the Angel is or he's not telling." *Just my luck to be saddled with the most stubborn person in town.* His mind darted back to something she'd said earlier. "Wait, you said everyone was already gone. Where'd they go?"

Marie looked at him like he'd lost his mind. "Out on the town of course," she said. "Where else would they be? They're all enjoying the snow, drinking hot chocolate, and admiring all the preparations for tomorrow."

Ah, the Second Rite.

Nathan gave her a sharp look, and the thorn threatened to come out. "What did you say?"

"That everyone's outside?"

Nathan drummed his fingers on the counter. "No. That's not it. Tomorrow." To himself, he muttered. His mind began to race. He had spent so long focused on the Timber Angel that he hadn't spent nearly enough time on the Rites themselves. *I can be so blind. So blind!* All of a sudden, he had leads to spare, starting with that Angel Archive. It had started with that bell, the one Alex said was locked away. *I should've demanded to see it! To hold it! Dammit, Nate!*

It was only when Marie put a cold hand on his wrist did he pay attention. "Slow down. I'll fix you a thermos. I can already see you're not here any more." She poured what was left of his coffee into a thermos and then topped it up from the pot. When she placed it in front of him, Nathan didn't take it. "What is it now?"

The truth was, he wasn't sure. He was struck by the setting, by the simple kindness. The thermos in front of him, the smell of the coffee, even the evergreen candle burning by the sink. Together, they acted like a tuning fork, resonating with the frequency of his mind. He couldn't quite grasp it, and the thought slipped through his fingers. Nathan could only hope it would return, for it had been a nice thought. He was sure of it.

He stepped away from the counter and fixed the old innkeeper with a long stare. "Why are you still here? You can't just be waiting to fix my coffee." *Come to think of it, she wasn't at the Angel Festival either.*

Marie waved her hands in front of her like she was casting a protective spell. "Oh no, much too busy out there for me. Don't give me that look either." She brought a hand to one of her plump cheeks. "I just—well—it's like you said. Experience can be a hard teacher to defy."

"Yeah," he agreed. "He can be a tricky son of a bitch when he wants to be."

He thanked her again for the coffee before heading down the entryway and back out into Timber's Edge. As he passed under the front door, he caught a look at the angel figurine staring down at him.

If he didn't know any better, he could've sworn it was staring back, the once-gentle smile on its face now feeling like a threat. Come, find me then, it seemed to say.

I'm working on it, Nathan thought again. *Honest, I am.*

Chapter Twelve

Nathan hadn't gone inside Town Hall during his first visit to the strange mutant building. He'd been more taken with the library. Inside the metal and glass building was a two-story atrium. There was a reception desk, but there was no one there. There was, however, a sign that read: No town business due to Angel Year! See you after Christmas!

God forbid someone wants a zoning permit during the holidays.

Sure enough, at the top of the stairs, there was a closed and locked door that looked to lead into a row of dark offices. There was a glimmer of light coming from somewhere within, and Nathan was willing to bet that it belonged to the mayor's office. From what he'd seen of her so far, he doubted very much that the mayor took a week off, Angel Year or not.

The landing at the top of the stairs featured four paintings that caught Nathan's eye. Each showed the same scene, that of a man and a woman standing on a mountainside, looking down into a valley. Each picture showed the valley in a different season, beginning with a young spring, a summer full of wildflower, and then a fall coated in a blanket of orange and yellow. In the first painting, the valley was blank, but in summer some tents and lean-to structures had appeared. By fall, there were what looked like boarding houses and even a tavern. Only in the last painting, a view of the valley coated in white powder, was there a town. Nathan could see the general layout matching Timber's Edge. The tableau was called Calbot's

Dream.

He crossed over to the library. Denise the Librarian was behind the circulation desk. She gave Nathan a friendly wave. "Back again?" she asked, her face wearing a serene smile.

"Back again," Nathan replied, heading back towards the Archive.

El, the same boy as before, sat at the kids' table, but this time he was reading a different comic. Nathan recognized the X-Men on the cover, including Professor X and Jean Grey. "That's a good one," he said quietly when he passed.

The kid's gray eyes flicked up, and checked the front of the book before he said, "Yeah. I've read it a bunch of times. They're my favorite."

"Good choice," Nathan said. He'd spent plenty of afternoons with them as well, but never when there was a winter wonderland outside. "Don't like the cold?"

El gave a smile that was still missing some of its permanent teeth. "Just waiting for my mom to get off of work."

Ah. So Timber's Edge is like other towns in that respect. "I've been there kid." Nathan was about to walk on when a question came to his mind. "Say, do you believe in the Timber Angel?"

The boy blinked a few times, as if confused by the question. "I guess," he said at last.

Nathan nodded. "Me too. At least, I think I do. I'm trying to work something out though."

"Oh yeah?"

"Yeah," Nathan said. "Where do you think it lives?"

El screwed his face up in concentration. He flipped his comic closed, holding his place with a finger, and then squinted up at Nathan. "Isn't it obvious? Angels, they live in the sky."

✴

There were two groups inside the Angel Archive. A single family of five and two women. Alex was nowhere to be seen; Nathan even checked the little workstation in the back. Still, he had hoped…*hoped that Alex would be here. Hoped that I'd be able to reach him somehow.* When he came to the locked case that held the brass hand bell, he frowned. *Hoped that I'd be able to convince him to unlock this for me.* It would take him a long time to pick it psychically, but he could always break the glass. *Desperation is the mother of invention as they say.*

"Not sure they say that," Nathan whispered to himself. "And I'm not quite that desperate yet." He tried his charms against the case, but their silence was no longer a surprise to him. A family was browsing through the snow globe display, the charming "Shake One! (but carefully!)" label being dutifully followed. *Although, I have to question the purpose of shaking a snow globe that was already snowing.* Nathan let the family finish shaking each one in turn, and turned his attention back to the other side of the room. The bell was hung in a case next to the Three Rites themselves. Nathan read it again, this time more freely than he'd been able to with the mayor breathing down his neck.

At the Angel's Call,
First there will be Snow,
With the Angel's Touch,
Second there will be Light,
From the Angel's Flame,
On Christmas Morn, Finally there will be Joy.
And Forever will the Angel's Memory
Remain in Timber's Edge.

With a grim smile, he turned to the bell. He read the inscription again.

"If you sing for angels," Nathan whispered, "why can I hear you as well?"

Curious, Nathan cleared his mind, as he had before, and waited.

It took a moment, but there it was, the gentle tolling of a bell. The note was low, resonating as if it were a recording that had been made in some grand chapel. *No way this little guy is making that noise.* He peeked out the window and saw the octagonal bell tower across the square. Even from this distance, he could make out the much larger bell on top. *That one, on the other hand. It might stand a chance.*

Presuming, of course, that size made any difference at all to the note of a phantom bell.

He was about to turn away when he noticed something right at the top of the hand strap. It was a discoloration, almost like a stain. *Now, where did you come from?* It hadn't been there yesterday, Nathan was sure of it. He chided himself then smiled. *A change in perspective can be a wonderful thing.*

The family examining the snow globes left out of the double doors, leaving Nathan alone with two women, a cheery brunette and a powerful older woman. Judging by the similar shape of the mouth and the same round jaw, he assumed they were related, probably mother and daughter. They were going through all the displays, pointing and chuckling. In her hands, the older woman held a gray knit cap, the spitting image of the one on Nathan's head. *Great minds,* he decided, *tend to think alike.*

By the time they'd left him alone in the room, Nathan had completed his own circuit. He'd shaken each of the snow globes in turn. Sure enough, there wasn't anything to be gained from shaking an already snowing snow globe, but it seemed the professional thing to do.

He studied each one carefully, starting with the first. It contained what looked like a long feasting table, heavily decorated with red ribbon and lengths of miniature green garland. Mimicries of roasted turkeys dotted the table, along with rustic breads and bowls of vegetables. Small figurines were seated at the table, the group displaying the full spectrum of races. *Guess it is a small world after all,* Nathan thought. He turned it over in his hands, stopping at the plate at the base of the brass hand. This one was scratched and had no letters.

The second snow globe contained the carousel along with what looked like Santa's workshop. It dominated the globe, all life-size toys and presents. As the snow continued falling, the carousel turned. Although he was sure he was imagining it, Nathan thought he could hear the twinkling notes from the calliope in the globe. Absently, Nathan's thumb found his silver ring. He turned this one over again, and, again saw a plate. This one, however, wasn't scratched, and two letters were engraved: J. M.

Globes three and four contained a European-style winter market and a full gingerbread village respectively. The winter market looked alive with the sounds of bartering and carols while the smell of fresh gingerbread hung around the fourth globe. The nameplates on both were completely faded.

The fifth globe contained something curious. It was a town, and the layout was familiar enough for Nathan to recognize it as Timber's Edge, albeit limited to Calbot Square and the surrounding buildings. Thankfully, the grotesque Town Hall was absent. *Presumably, it wasn't built yet.* This one also bore a name: J. C.

The final snow globe had a faded nameplate, but Nathan could make out the imprints of old letters. A.P. Within, there was only a Christmas tree, surrounded by piles of brightly colored presents. Snow from the globe coated the tree and the presents, wrapping them all in an extra layer of powder. Nathan watched it. The snow continued to swirl around the globe. Some stuck to the tree while the rest stayed suspended. Once again, he felt the pull of an invisible hand, gently shaking each of the globes, all at once.

A woman's iron voice interrupted him, "I hope you're taking care with our treasures Mr. Cole." Mayor Julianna Benneteau was standing in the doorway, watching him. Her face did nothing to hide her disapproval.

"Showing nothing but respect Madam Mayor," Nathan replied

cheerfully. He turned to face her and she stepped all the way into the room.

Deliberately, she closed the double doors fully behind her.

"Intimate," he noted.

A small smile crossed her face, and the mayor stepped up to the long table in the middle of the room. She tapped one of her immaculate black acrylic nails against the closest snow globe, the one that showed the Christmas tree. "I'm curious," she said. "What do you make of it?"

Nathan stepped around the table so they were on opposite sides of the snow globes. "The snowing?"

"That's right. Impossible snow. You seem like a man with opinions."

Can't argue there.

"You'll have to be more specific," Nathan said. "Outside snow, or inside?"

"Would you really tell me your thoughts on either?"

"No," he admitted. "I don't share theories with suspects."

"Suspect?" The mayor laughed. "Is that what I am?"

"Everyone's a suspect until they've been eliminated," Nathan said simply.

"Like a murder mystery," she said, her voice thick with condescension. "And how exactly do you eliminate a suspect, Mr. Cole? Do you have an interrogation room nearby? Or perhaps thumbscrews?"

"I left them at home," he replied. "But this room is quiet if you want to answer some questions."

The mayor moved down the table. "Funny, I thought I was asking you the questions."

Nathan shrugged. "How about I give you some trust on credit? We trade questions. You ask, I ask." He raised a warning finger. "But no lying."

A dangerous game if she's the Angel. But, if she's not, she's one of the likeliest people to know who the Angel really is.

Julianna Benneteau crossed her arms and her Hermès bracelet rattled against what Nathan thought was a Rolex watch. "Why not? I have a few minutes."

"Champion," Nathan said in a dry tone. "I'll even let you go first."

"I already did go first Mr. Cole, and the question still stands."

"What do I make of it?" Nathan repeated. "Vague, but that's alright. My answer's rather vague as well, I'm afraid. Truth be told, I haven't made much of it yet. The First Rite, as you call it, bears some similarities to other things I've seen."

Her eyes narrowed. "What similar things?"

Nathan smiled. "Oh you'd be surprised. I told Alex that the source of most of what people think of as magic comes from Memory, and that Memory can be carried in items. Or, more accurately, items can carry Memory. Like my charms. Or your bell, passed down from Angel to Angel. Your Angel's power is driven by the items, that much is clear. But it must have some inherent power without them as well. At least, I've not encountered a being that is not able to use so-called magical items without having some sort of inherent power, even if it's latent. My working assumption is that the items are acting like foci, sort of like a repository for its power."

Julianna glared. "What, you can't stop there."

"I certainly can. I gave you an answer. And an honest one." Nathan brought his hands behind his back. "I believe it's my turn."

The mayor gave a curt nod.

"Who are you to Alex? You're someone close to him; I've gotten that much. Someone familiar as well. But how familiar?"

The mayor rolled her eyes. "We're not having an affair, if that's what you're implying. I'm not exactly his type."

Nathan laughed. "Well aware of that, Madam Mayor. So, who are you to him?"

She examined one of her long black nails, and then said, "Alex has a tendency to act against his best interests. He just completed his studies, and he's already talking about moving back here to help with his father's farm. It's about as far from sports medicine as you can get. Paul doesn't need the help. Alex knows better. Who am I Mr. Cole? I'm one of the only people who will protect him and tell him what he needs to hear, especially since his own mother passed away."

The words slapped Nathan. Hard. He had guessed as much, but the confirmation still stung. *I'm sorry Alex.* "How did she die?" The question came out sharp, more of a thorn than he'd intended.

The mayor knew she had his attention. The widening of her eyes confirmed that.

Come on Nate, play it a little better than that.

"One question," she said, her thin lips pulling into a smile. "That was the rule, wasn't it?"

"It was," Nathan agreed.

"You said the power was similar to something you've seen before," Julianna said. "What power? Be precise."

Nathan shrugged. "Witchcraft, if you must know."

The answer clearly wasn't what she'd expected. "A witch," she repeated.

"I'm not fully convinced yet," Nathan pointed out. "I'm merely suggesting that there are witch-like tendencies in your Angel's powers, albeit with a bit more festive cheer than I'm used to."

"Seems to be it could just as easily be a wizard. Or some other made up nonsense."

"A wizard is something different entirely," Nathan replied. "Good job dodging a question, by the way."

The mayor's smile was cold.

Nathan continued, "But, I never did say it was a witch. Just witch-like. Their powers tend to stem from the natural world, like the Angel's. Linked to locations and places of power, like the Angel and the town. They're regular users of foci, like this bell. But that's where the similarities end. Witches are keyed to their foci and very protective over them. Their items can even carry their life-force. Because of that, the items are normally heavily warded. The Angel's are passed down, kept in a simple locked case. No witch would ever be so careless. At least two people have touched it. One—Alex— declares he isn't an Angel. Both did so without any apparent ill effects. If anyone had done that to a regular witch's item without first attuning to it, they'd probably still be in a coma."

"You believe him then?" The mayor asked. "Alex, that is."

Nathan raised a finger.

Julianna scoffed. "Fine."

"Your town must have records," Nathan said carefully. He tapped a finger over each snow globe in turn. "And these are apparently the work of prior Angels." *Individualized foci. One for each Angel.*

"Is there a question in there Mr. Cole?"

"None of them have dates. And only some of them have letters which I'm guessing are initials. What do you know about them?"

Julianna raised her hands in a gesture of surrender. "I'm sorry you've wasted a question Mr. Cole. I really don't know much. Beyond that they are, as you say, related to previous Angel Years—" Nathan's heart skipped. *Well, that is a thought.* " —I'm not sure anyone in town knows much more. Perhaps the Timber Angel does. Alex's working theory, at least as far as he's told me, is that he thinks each one shows that year's Third Rite."

"And 'Finally, there will be Joy.'"

"That's what he says. As for how he knows that or why, you'd have to ask him." Nathan scoffed, and Julianna chuckled; the laugh was a pleasant surprise. "I see he's as closed to you as he is to me."

"So that's why you suspect him. Not a question by the way, just a statement."

Julianna nodded. "And you?"

Nathan shrugged. *It wasn't hard to guess.* "Of course I did. Part of me still does. He hasn't been forthright about everything though. All I want is to help, but without all the variables, it can become difficult to solve the equation."

"Presuming there is a solution."

"There's always a solution Madam Mayor. Even if the outcome is undefined. It's still an outcome."

The mayor nodded then began to step towards the door. "Thank you, Mr. Cole. For the conversation." As she strode past him, a cloud of Chanel perfume hung in her wake.

"Aren't you forgetting something?"

Julianna turned with a smirk.

Clearly not. "How long has Alex lived here?"

Whatever question she'd been expecting, that wasn't it. She frowned and chewed at her bottom lip. Finally, she said, "He's always been here Mr. Cole. He's lived in Timber's Edge his entire life."

After she'd left, Nathan took another pass around the room. Through the window, activity in Calbot Square drew his attention. Alex, wearing a long-sleeved black shirt with a Christmas tree logo, was there, helping unload bundled Christmas trees from the back of a black pickup truck. Pat's Tree Farm was written across the side of the truck; a slogan underneath read: Best Trees in the West. *Curious,* Nathan thought, *the West of what?* The question picked at something in the back of his head. Something else he'd spotted.

Perhaps it was time to get ahead of this thing. He shot another look at the bell and was tempted to break the glass, but it wouldn't take the mayor long to track it back to him. What he needed was something less noticeable. A quick glance at the wall clock told him it was just about noon.

Time sure flies when you're having fun. There was that thought again too, picking again at him.

Dismissing it, Nathan stuck his head outside the door and checked the hallway. It was clear, so he silently shut the door before casually clicking the lock. He checked outside the window. Alex had finished offloading the trees, but he'd left the truck parked. He was headed towards Gloria's. *And it's almost time for a lunch break.*

Nathan's work didn't take him long. The clock showed 12:05 when Nathan Cole strode out of the Archive. His hands were in his pockets.

One contained his river stones.

The other held three small microfilm cases.

Chapter Thirteen

The cat was waiting for him outside of the guest house by the time Nathan returned with the microfilm cases. It watched him while he opened the front door, and meowed when Nathan grabbed the bag of cat treats he'd purchased from Marley's.

You know what this bag is, I see," he told the cat. He tossed it a few treats, careful to keep them a good distance away from his legs so that he didn't spook the little guy.

The cat stretched its way across the grass, sniffed at one of the treats, then scooped it into its mouth. Nathan tossed it a few more, then returned the bag inside. After finishing the treats, the orange cat stared at Nathan with eyes that were just a shade away from his own.

"Can you keep secrets?" he asked, then smiled to himself. "Something I'm asking myself too, come to think of it."

The cat meowed again, then turned tail and padded its way over the bridge, past the Angel statue, and out of sight.

Nathan hid the plastic cases at the bottom of a desk drawer in the bedroom. It wasn't likely they would be found even if he just left them on the coffee table; Timber's Edge wasn't exactly a place where anyone locked their doors. He'd look through them later. *Preferably with a temporal assist from Anslem, if it comes to that. There were some advantages to Slipping.* For now, he wanted to find Alex.

Is that all you want Nate?

Of course it wasn't. There wasn't even a problem here that he

152

really needed to fix. Only suggestions of one. Suppositions of a problem. He opened his hands then closed them into fists, repeating the motion a few times. Stealing the microfilm was an escalation; he couldn't escape that. It was a necessary risk, especially if the mayor was going to be hanging around every time he visited the Archive. He'd considered the other possibilities, even the ones the mayor and the bell both suggested, and still he had decided it was the best way to find the real Timber Angel.

It's the best way to satiate your curiosity as well Nate. Let's not forget that.

"I know," he whispered. It was a dangerous game, meddling with a ritual he didn't understand. And that was precisely what he was doing, for he was becoming more and more convinced that Alex, that everyone in Timber's Edge, needed help. Ever since his first visit with Anslem, a pit had been forming in his stomach. It had been growing day by day, with each curious coincidence, with each small strange step.

Lemmings, Nathan thought, reminded of the old video game he would play in Mother Sable's trailer. When the road wasn't safe enough, he would spend hours leading those little pixel men, trying to save as many as he could. *It's like we're all being played.* There was no cosmic entity hovering overhead, no demon changing faces, no Unending raining fire down upon them. Instead, it was like they were walking, slowly and surely, towards some terrible fate.

It was more than intuition. There were threads he seemed unable to fully grasp; pulling the wrong one too hard could tear the entire tapestry apart. *Knowing there's a pattern and being unable to see it: it's infuriating.* It all felt so very fragile, like he was walking at the edge of a cliff in a pitch black night. One wrong step was all it would take.

But, one thing was for sure, something was at work.

The town was growing busier day by day, yet the roads leading in and out remained empty.

The lanterns flickering all over town, outside some houses, but not others.

There was his sense that the Angel figurines and statues were watching him, studying him.

And then, the statue of death, apparently able to change its shape at will.

Outside the window, the snow continued to fall. It had slowed since the first few days. Now, it was a gentle flake, barely replacing that which melted away in the sun.

The snow globes snowing on their own, the bell. They were impossible items, but without any actual purpose. Why did the Angel exist in the first place? The Three Rites didn't say.

Then there was Alex. Incongruity curled off of him like smoke. His slight accent for one. His knowledge of the Angel. He had Slipped without any difficulty, and even Anslem said there was some power surrounding him. Nathan was moving on from him being dangerous. Alex simply didn't seem to have the steel for it. *That's no defect*, he thought.

Too many strange steps for there to be nothing, but there was nothing overt enough to alert anyone to a danger.

Maybe the right course is to leave, Nathan thought. He snorted in disgust.

But, Nathan knew a horrible truth, one he'd lived himself, one that had sustained him through sixty-six years, eleven months, and twenty-four days in servitude.

It was one that was true for all forms of life—magical or otherwise—that he'd ever encountered: there was nothing more dangerous than a cornered animal.

It was true for Angels as well as people, Nathan reasoned. Maybe his staying increased the chances of turning a potentially minor danger into a major one.

If left to its own devices, maybe the Angel would take a life. Maybe a few. Wasn't that better than risking them all? He could leave. Ask Ronny for the next bus and never think about Timber's

Edge again. The town had survived for centuries.

What right do we have to judge? To interfere?

"They need me," Nathan said out loud. "And if they don't yet, then they will. And when they do, I had better be ready."

Besides, Nathan told himself, there was no harm in idle curiosity.

Pretty sure there's a saying about that Nate. Go ask the cat.

Maddie was working on a puzzle at the diner table. It was a thousand pieces, and the sort of thing that Alex didn't have the patience for. She'd been working on it since Alex had left her there that morning and was still working on it when he'd returned. It was about halfway finished, and the picture of an ice castle was taking shape in the center of the table. The radio was on, playing a Christmas song that Alex didn't recognize. There were Christmas songs he didn't recognize? That didn't feel right. Maddie recognized it; she was humming to herself and kicking her feet beneath the table.

A pot of coffee was on the warmer, and Alex poured himself a cup (Gloria would've killed him if he had asked first) before sitting next to Maddie at the table. "Want some help?"

Her eyes shot him a surprised glance. "Sure," she said. She scooped a handful of pieces and put them in front of him. "You've got to find where these ones go."

The pieces were all random, and most of them were simply black and blue. He looked at the picture of the box. Of course, the ice castle was set against a pitch black night sky. That wasn't encouraging. He spotted one that looked like a good fit to the top left of the castle, and tried fitting it onto the picture. It wasn't a great fit, but looked close enough. Maddie's stern frown sent the piece back to Alex's pile.

After twenty minutes, Maddie had found homes for at least thirty pieces. Alex still struggled with his first. *When had she become so good at this?* She'd been interested in puzzles and games for a few years now, and, when he'd returned for summer break, she was putting the finishing touches on the five hundred-piece kitten puzzle hanging in the living room. She'd finished it sometime after he left, and their dad had poured puzzle glue on it and framed it for her. It hung in the living room. In her room there were others: a butterfly and a roller coaster that Alex didn't even remember seeing her work on.

Before long, Gloria came out from the back of the house. In her hands, she held two plates of food. "Before you ask," she said to Alex. "These aren't for you. How fares the war?" she asked.

"Good," Maddie replied. "Alex kind of sucks."

"Hey—"

"Language," Gloria warned with a cackle.

Maddie grinned at Alex, then plucked one of his pieces to fit it neatly into the picture. "He's not very good," she amended.

"Better," Alex said.

Gloria ran the food, then returned to the booth. She took a seat next to Maddie, sighing heavily.

"Everything okay?" Alex asked.

"Busy busy busy. Every day seems we're just getting busier." It was true. The restaurant wasn't quite packed, but it was full, just as it had been for breakfast. She pointed to the pass where Alex could see her massive son working the line, "Even Christopher's starting to sweat if you can believe that. Says it reminds him of cooking for the Marines." In a low whisper, she added, "Between us friends, I think he likes it."

"We can leave. Give you the table back," Alex offered.

Gloria raised an offended hand. "No sir. Not in my place. You come. You stay as long as you like. Even if all you get is a cup of coffee. I'm not trying to turn tables like some Michelin star joint. I did that plenty. Ain't no joy in it. Pride, yes, joy, no. And pride, that'll clip your wings eventually."

She picked through the pieces on the table, found one that looked like it fit, but frowned when it didn't. Maddie gave her the same glare she'd given Alex twenty minutes before.

"You're not very good either," Maddie said.

To Alex's surprise, the old chef laughed. When he was younger, he wasn't sure he'd have the nerve to say that to an adult.

"No, I suppose I'm not," Gloria said. She held up a piece for Maddie. "How about this one?"

Maddie scrunched up her face, then pointed to a spot in the sky.

Gloria tried the piece and it fit. The grin transformed her face and brought a crackle to her eyes. "Well would you look at that," she said with a small whoop.

Alex smiled despite himself.

"Surprised to see you here," Gloria said casually.

Alex tried not to take it as a rebuke. Gloria wasn't one to dress up a difficult conversation, after all.

"Figured you'd be all gung-ho for tomorrow night," she continued.

"Still barking up the wrong tree Gloria," he said.

The chef raised her hands in surrender.

"What tree?" Maddie asked.

"Never mind," he said.

"Is this Angel stuff?"

Gloria raised her eyebrows.

"No, it's a saying," Alex replied. He caught the almost imperceptible shake of the chef's head and made a show of studying his pieces. "My dad asked me for some help and to keep an eye on Mads. I figured I could use the break." And it gives me time to work out what I'm going to say to Nathan. If I say anything to him at all. He tried another piece, but it was an even worse fit than before.

His disgusted sister almost slapped it away. "I don't need you to watch me," Maddie protested.

"She's right there," Gloria added.

From the back of the house, Christopher emerged with a few plates of food. Gloria's son was enormous. He towered over everyone else in the place, and Alex was certain he could probably shift the building's foundation with his bare hands if he needed to. Without a word, the chef walked the food over to their tables. On his way back, he stopped by the booth.

"All good Ma?" he asked in his booming voice. For him, Alex thought, that was probably a whisper.

Gloria laughed and patted her son's arm. "Just resting the old dogs," she said.

He gave her shoulders a quick squeeze. "Take as long as you need. I got this."

Gloria watched him disappear back behind the pass before switching her gaze to Alex. "Ever consider getting some help?"

Alex shook his head. "It's not that easy."

"Sure it is," Gloria replied. "You ask. Simple as pie." She fit another piece into the puzzle.

Maddie nodded her approval and the old chef gave the girl a fist bump.

From behind, Alex heard the chime of the door opening, and Gloria glanced up before flicking her eyes back down.

Maddie was focused on the puzzle.

"Hey Mads," Alex said. He held up a piece. "How about this one?" He floated it near the base of the castle. "Here?"

Maddie covered the spot with her hand. He spotted a place above a turret where it seemed to fit. Maddie considered it before nodding. Sure enough, it fit easily.

"Good job," she said.

Alex grinned.

"High praise from an eight-year-old," Nathan's voice said from the side of the booth.

"I'm nine," Maddie declared.

"My mistake," Nathan replied.

Alex hadn't noticed him walk in, but there he was, wearing his burgundy overcoat and a dark pair of jeans. The gray knitted cap sat atop his head, but his blond hair poked out from the sides and back.

"May I join you?" Nathan asked. "No other room at the inn today."

Alex hesitated before a glare from Gloria sent him sliding over to make room. "Busy morning?" The old chef asked.

"Just some wanton debauchery," Nathan replied. "Same old. Same old."

"What's debauchery?" Maddie asked.

"Something stupid," Alex replied.

Nathan's eyes sparked with mischief. "Did have a nice long talk with the mayor though," he said casually.

Alex had been about to place a piece, but his hand froze in midair. "Wait, what?"

Nathan shrugged, then his gaze flicked up to the counter. He seemed distracted by the back of a kid's head.

Alex didn't recognize him and quickly returned to the puzzle.

"I figured that kid lived in the library," Nathan said.

Gloria turned and looked. "El? Yeah, he comes in all the time. His mom works, so I look out for him. He's a good kid. How about you Nathan? What're you having?"

"Just coffee and a club sandwich, if that's alright." Nathan hesitated.

"Coffee and a club sandwich it is," she said, pushing herself out of the booth.

"What happened to 'You got legs to get your own damn coffee?'" Alex asked.

"He's a guest Alex. You're not." Gloria laughed. "Better get back to it," she said with a wink. To Alex, she said again. "You ask Alex. Easiest thing in the world. Unless it's pride that's keeping you afloat." Gloria returned to the kitchen and before long, Alex heard the bang of her spoon and the cry of her cackling laugh.

"What was that about?" Nathan asked. He picked up a piece, then asked Maddie. "May I?"

She nodded, and he slid a piece into the puzzle neatly. She offered him a fist bump, mimicking Gloria.

Inside, Alex fumed. "Don't worry about it," Alex replied to the first question.

Under Nathan's sideways stare, the blood pounded into Alex's cheeks. There was nothing else for it. He'd spent the morning thinking of what to say, how to explain, and it had become just as Gloria said. Simple as pie.

So, when Maddie got out of the booth to get a piece of pie, Alex finally bit the bullet.

"What if I told you that this is all wrong?" he asked.

Nathan looked up from the puzzle. "This piece fits."

"Not the puzzle. The snow."

"Alex," Nathan's voice became direct. "Are you behind it? Are you the Timber Angel? If something's gone wrong, I can help."

Alex looked away as if he couldn't stand to meet Nathan's gaze. "No," he said. "I'm not. I promise I'm not. I tried ringing it. The bell," Alex said. The confession made his face hot. "Nothing happened. It made no sound."

"I sing for Angels," Nathan repeated.

Alex looked as if he'd swallowed a shot of dishwater. "I locked it up afterwards. In the archive. I put it in the cabinet and locked it up myself. I even hid the key. There was no way—no way—anyone could've touched it. Not without me letting them."

"And if they couldn't ring it..." Recognition flashed across

Nathan's face. "I see."

"They couldn't have started this," Alex replied. "This isn't following the rules. It's not how it's supposed to go."

Those green eyes studied him, dissected him. Maybe this was a mistake. "What about the Second Rite? It's tomorrow, isn't it? 'With the Angel's Touch, Second there will be Light.' You know what it means?"

Alex nodded. "Are you doing anything after this? There's something I want to show you."

Nathan leaned back into the booth, cocked his head sideways, and an excited smile creased dimples into his cheeks.

In that moment, Alex became sure that Nathan had been thinking just as he had.

"Sure," Nathan said. "So long as I can finish my sandwich."

Chapter Fourteen

Pat's Tree Farm was a fifteen minute drive outside of town, the turn-off lying along the two-lane road that headed up out of town, the opposite direction to the Pit Stop. As soon as they'd cleared the town proper, Nathan could spot the farm. It was a massive expanse of trees, a forest in its own right, tucked up against the foothills that led up into the mountains. Those foothills encircled the town, surrounding it with wild forest that extended all the way up the mountains. *There must be miles of trails.* No wonder Alex takes his morning run there.

He was sitting in the front seat of the truck. As they wound up the country roads during their approach, Nathan felt his hands grow clammy. The expansive view was doing little to help. He opened and closed his hands and tried to focus on the horizon. The only problem was that the horizon wasn't staying put, not with the turning roads and Alex's rather relaxed approach to braking.

"Whoa," Alex said as he hit the brakes a bit hard going into a turn. "That one snuck up on me." He glanced over at Nathan. "You okay?"

"Never better," he lied. His stomach was starting to revolt, and, while he had devoured the club sandwich ten minutes ago, he was regretting it now. His mind, on the other hand, was busy picturing the truck rolling off of the road, smashing into the ravine and crashing into a wall of trees. The frown returned to Alex's face. He looked over at Nathan.

Watch the road. Please watch the road.

"Hey, I said I'd take you to see the tree," Alex said.

"The tree, the farm, not the bottom of a ravine," Nathan replied.

"I thought you live on the road."

"Highways and buses, not tight roads and a lack of brakes."

Alex whistled. "Road trips must be a nightmare for you," he said cheerfully. Ever since they'd left the diner, Alex's mood had apparently improved.

"Not with copious application of Dramamine and sleeping pills," Nathan replied. He must have looked queasy.

"Well don't hurl," Alex warned. "It's a lease."

He took another turn, and the road opened to a vista of the town below. *We've climbed that high already?* From their position, Nathan easily spotted Calbot Square, Town Hall, the clock tower, and even the lantern. The bus was still sitting where he'd left it, and the Pit Stop looked busier than it had been when he'd visited with Alex just a few days ago. A rainbow of match box cars inched around the streets, but none made it to a street outside of town.

It's like they're treading water. Lemmings, trapped in a circle.

"Nathan? You listening?"

The thought had been clawing at Nathan's mind, so much so that he hadn't heard the question.

"No, actually," Nathan replied. "I wasn't."

Alex hit the brakes again and adjusted the wheel. Nathan could've sworn half the truck left the road.

"No need to punish," Nathan said through gritted teeth.

"Sorry," Alex said, smiling. "There was a pothole. Like I said, it's a lease."

"What did I miss?"

"I uh was asking about Anchor." Alex scratched his head while his other hand was drumming the steering wheel.

Both hands on the wheel. Please. Both hands on the wheel.

"Yeah?" Nathan could hear the nerves in his own voice.

"That girl, she called you something. Her Black Thorn."

Nathan paled even more. "It's not a title I'm proud of. She wanted to twist a knife."

And she succeeded.

"And Nathaniel?" Alex said.

"My full name. Nathaniel Hawthorne Cole," Nathan replied. "My mother was a fan of the classics. Particularly the American Romantics."

Mother Sable had driven the classics into him, and, though he didn't advertise it, he had become a fan of some. Shakespeare, Dickens, Melville, Dumas, and, yes, Hawthorne. Though, nowadays, it was mostly occult texts, Nathan still found time for the occasional popular novel. In particular, he had come to like romances, though he'd never admit it out loud.

"Mine was too," Alex replied. "She was an English professor, but named me after Alexander the Great. Met my dad while they were working together."

Alex floored the gas casually, and the truck flew up the road.

"Was?" Nathan asked, although he already knew the answer. Against his own desire, he grabbed the window handle to stabilize himself.

Alex laughed when he noticed, then said, "Yeah. She uh passed away. A few years ago now. Wait, almost four years ago. Has it been that long?" He shook his head.

"I'm sorry," Nathan said. "No matter how long, it never goes away."

Alex nodded. "You? You said your mother 'was a fan of the classics'?"

"Five years ago. Car accident," Nathan replied. Unbidden, the smell of burning oil and the sound of screeching metal came to his mind.

"And with your uh Anchor time?" Alex asked. "Sorry, I don't mean to pry—"

"No need to apologize for asking a question," Nathan replied. "Seventy years. Like I said, it never does go away."

✳

The rest of the drive passed in relative silence, partly due to the fact that every time Nathan spoke he ran the risk of throwing club sandwich all over the truck's spotless dashboard. Once Alex parked in front of a large barn, he didn't even get to turn the engine off before Nathan hopped out the truck. He shook the clamminess out of his hands and a few deep breaths of the cold country air made him feel better almost immediately.

Once he was sure he was on solid ground, Nathan finally took stock of his surroundings. He'd visited a few farms in his travels, but none had specialized in Christmas trees. If there was any doubt that's what this one grew, it was quickly dispelled by the sign hung across the barn: Pat's Tree Farm. The sign was too wide for the words, and the letters were painted in an uneven rush. Beneath that, in golden script, was another line of text: Proud Grower of the Timber's Edge Christmas Tree.

Next to the barn was a quaint two-story farmhouse. It was made from white wooden planks that had faded over time. The triangular roof was well-maintained, and the wrap-around porch hosted a number of rocking chairs. Nathan thought it looked like something out of a postcard. But, then again, that was par for the course for Timber's Edge. *The entire place could fill the Christmas card section.*

They were set up for business as well, although, to Nathan's surprise, they were the only ones who seemed to be there. A white pickup sat next to the barn, but there was no other sign of human life. From their position at the edge of the rows, Nathan could see some blank patches, along with trees that hadn't yet reached their full height. There were still several full-grown trees towards the back of the rows, along with some already cut and tied trees by the barn.

"Almost everyone who wanted to cut their own tree has already done it," Alex explained. "But it's not for everyone, so we still run down some for the visitors just arriving."

"Not so many big ones left," Nathan observed.

"Yeah," Alex agreed. "We harvest a chunk of the farm each year, but the other trees still need to finish growing. Tonight, the town tree is cut and then we'll start wrapping everything up. That's when my dad gets to finally kick back. At least until the planting season starts."

Nathan took another deep breath. The scent of pine blanketed the air like yuletide chemical warfare.

Alex retrieved a bow-shaped saw and a coil of rope from the back of the truck and passed the saw to Nathan.

He took it with both hands and comfortably held it like a weapon.

"On second thought," Alex said, "give that back. You look like a walking insurance problem. You can carry the rope."

Nathan let Alex take the lead but was surprised at the tools. "We're cutting down the tree?" he asked.

"We're cutting down *a* tree," Alex explained. "The one I'm taking back home. They're a bitch to carry by themselves, so I figured you wouldn't mind lending a hand."

They crunched their way across the icy gravel. The quiet struck Nathan. He would've expected the farm to be abuzz with activity.

"My grandparents used to live here," Alex explained as they walked. "When Grandpa Pat—everyone in town just called him Pat—passed, my dad took over officially. He always says that he can't believe he gave up academia and ended up a farmer. But, truth be told, he's good at it." The first row barely rose to Nathan's shoulder, and Alex stopped to examine a few of them. "These will come out nice in a few years."

Partway through the neat rows of trees, Alex slowed. Nathan wasn't sure why. Alex examined each tall pine. Or spruce. Or fir. Or Christmasy tree.

Alex looked around. "I suppose this is as good a place as any. These are all spruces anyways."

"Is that important?" Nathan asked.

"Ours has to be a spruce," Alex explained. "That's the rule." He examined the tree next to them. It was perhaps ten feet tall, nowhere near the largest left in the lot, but it was a vibrant shade of green and its branches carried all the way to the tree's crown. "You want to do the honors?" he asked Nathan.

"Not with your family tree," Nathan replied. "But I'd be thrilled to see an old hand at work."

Alex rolled his eyes but set to cutting the tree. He worked, at first, in careful long strokes until the saw had caught and then chewed through the tree with ease. The entire process took only a few minutes and had filled the air with the scent of wood and pine.

Nathan had been right. There was something impressive about the work.

When he was finished, Alex told Nathan, "Get the rope ready to tie it off."

Nathan tried to tie the rope around the felled tree. It wasn't nearly as easy as he would've assumed. The needles kept sticking his hands and the branches refused to be manipulated. When he looked up, Alex was frowning.

"I'm not even sure what to call that," Alex said. With an exaggerated sigh, he stepped forward, took the rope from Nathan, and bundled the tree like he had been doing it all his life.

Which, I suppose, he probably has.

When Alex was finished, he turned to Nathan and said, "You can help carry it, right? Or are those arms just for show?"

*

After several choice expletives between them, they got the great tree settled in the bed of the truck. Nathan wore a fresh cloak of needles and twigs. Alex didn't fare much better; his cheeks were flushed and several needles had caught in his hair and in the collar of his shirt. Finally, it was time for the Angel Tree. Nathan was surprised by how low the sun had fallen. Alex led the way back to the tree line and into the rows where they walked until they came to a row of taller, heavier trees.

"These were planted years ago," Alex explained. "These ones are all for special occasions. You can't buy these." He led them down the row and, as the trees got taller and taller, the spaces between them got larger and larger. Even a Christmas tree novice like Nathan could see that there were different species and varieties. Alex stopped in front of a particularly tall one that looked like the Ashford tree writ large. Its thicker needles were vividly green, and it carried a strong scent of fresh pine.

"And, this," Alex declared, "is the town tree." Around its center, tied like a scarf, was a length of thick red cloth inlaid with flecks of gold and green. The edges were frayed and some of the red had faded to a dark pink. *I wonder if that's another foci. An Angel Ribbon to go with an Angel Bell. If it is, then this tree might carry some Trace.*

"This is what you wanted to show me?" Nathan asked.

"Yeah," Alex said. His voice had become tight and unsure. "I wanted to know if there was anything you could, uh, detect about it."

Nathan glanced at it. "It looks like a tree to me."

Alex exhaled. "I knew this was a mistake."

Nathan stepped around the tree, studying the cloth. "What's with the bow?"

"The ribbon?" Alex asked. "It's just a marker for the town tree. We put it on every year to make sure no one else cuts it."

"It looks old," Nathan noted.

"I suppose so," Alex replied. "It's kept in the mayor's office outside of the holidays. Once we know what tree will be the town tree, it gets put on."

Nathan examined it closely. A script was sewn into the cloth in black thread. *I guide Angels.*

"What does that mean?" he asked.

Alex frowned. "I've never seen that before. I don't know."

Nathan pulled a small branch off of the tree and brought it to his nose. The pine was clear and fresh. *That'll work.* Nathan pulled up his left sleeve and found a loose part of his silver chain. He threaded the chain through the piece of the tree he'd broken off.

"What are you doing? Are you even listening?"

Nathan was, but he was also ignoring him. He let the piece of the Angel Tree fall freely from his wrist, connected to the charms.

"Nath—"

Nathan put up a hand. "Shh." He watched the branch hang and realized he was holding his breath.

Come on.

"I don't see—"

Finally, as if caught by an invisible breeze, the branch began to move. At first, it spun like a wind chime and then, after a few seconds, it began to swing like a pendulum.

Alex stared at it, his mouth half open. The branch finally came to a stop at the peak of its amplitude, and it hung there, straining against the chain.

The branch pointed directly at Alex's chest. With a knowing smile, Nathan turned to Alex.

Alex took a step back, as if he suddenly remembered that Nathan was the same person who'd taken him for an audience with an

Aegyl.

I'm sorry Alex; this isn't going to go the way you had planned. But thank you for bringing me to something with plenty of Trace.

"Let's get the big guy out of the way first, shall we?" Nathan asked. "You are a Timber Angel, and I think it's time you stop lying to me."

✳

A breeze blew a flurry of snow across the farm, but Nathan's stare didn't leave Alex's face. Nathan seemed to be carved from steel, and, if Alex were to turn to run, he wasn't sure if Nathan would even move. Nathan didn't appear angry, didn't appear frustrated or disappointed. He looked at Alex the same way a parent might look at a child he'd just caught stealing a cookie.

It was at that moment that Alex understood. From the first second he'd met Nathaniel Hawthorne Cole, Alex had been manipulated. It made him furious. At Nathan, but mostly at himself.

"I'm not...I'm not what you say," was all Alex could say. It was the truth; as far as he understood it, that was.

Nathan's tone sharpened, "You're still going to lie to me?"

"I'm not lying!" Alex cried out. The emotion surprised him. He took a deep breath and steadied himself before flipping his right hand so that the palm faced towards the sky. The cold feeling came back to his feet, seeping into his boots. "Something's happening to me. It started as soon as I heard the bell. I tried it, I told you, but I couldn't hear anything."

He shivered and concentrated on his hand. He wasn't sure what he was doing, but somewhere instinct took over. He felt the imaginary ice cubes turn to powder and then icy sparkles began to float up out of his hands, like diamond dust. The effort drove an ice-pick into Alex's temples, and he struggled to maintain it.

Nathan's charms began to sing from his wrist, the one he'd made from the Angel Tree struggling against the silver chain, pulling the others with it.

Finally, the effort was too much, and Alex released the strange power. He shivered again, and then was aware of tears in his eyes. He wiped them dry, then faced Nathan. "I don't know what's happening, but I'm no Angel. I'm not lying. I didn't do this. I don't…I don't know what to do. And I'm scared. Of what will happen tomorrow."

"The Second Rite?"

Alex nodded. "The Timber Angel lights the tree with a touch, and I don't know what will happen to me afterwards. I'm changing, and I don't know why." Alex sighed. "I should never have rung that damn bell."

For the first time since he'd met him, Nathan Cole looked concerned. He stepped forward, close enough that Alex could smell the earthy scent of him. Nathan took Alex's upturned hand in one of his own and examined it. He then turned it over and placed his other hand on top of it. The look of concern vanished, replaced by his easy smile. "I'll help you, Alex. I promise you that—we'll get to the bottom of it."

Alex was surprised. He had half-expected Nathan to perform some sort of exorcism or to stab him with a stake. "Why?"

Nathan's easy smile flickered. "I don't need a reason to help, do I?"

✳

They were walking back through the rows when Nathan asked, "You said you rang the bell. Why'd you do it? You wanted to be the Timber Angel?"

Alex hesitated, but then said, "It was for Maddie. She's getting older. Now she's at the age where Christmas isn't what it used to be.

She used to be attached to my mom at the hip during Christmas, like I was at her age."

I can understand that, Nathan thought.

Alex continued, "When the bell didn't work…"

"Who says it didn't work?" Nathan asked. "As far as I can tell, the First Rite went off without a hitch." *Well not exactly. It was late.*

"I told you," Alex said. "I would've heard it."

"Delayed response?" Nathan suggested. *Of course that didn't explain the stain.*

Alex stopped for a moment. "Did you mean that?"

"I did," Nathan replied. "Logically, it makes sense. When did you ring it?"

"Tuesday morning."

"It fits okay," Nathan said. He turned it around in his head. "The alternative is that there's a second Angel. And it was that Angel that rang the bell on the day of the First Rite."

"But I told you—"

"That the bell was locked up, yes. I haven't figured that part out yet. They could've picked the lock I suppose. What I can't figure out is what they'd hope to gain. Anonymity won't last, especially with the Second Rite coming up. So they'd have to have some other motive. Otherwise, I'm stuck at delayed response."

Alex's voice was quiet. "It's the Third Rite. They'd be after that."

"'And Finally there will be Joy.'"

"Right," Alex said. "For the Third Rite, the Angel can create anything in town."

Did I hear that right?

"When you say anything, what are we talking about?"

"I don't know the limits exactly," Alex replied. "I don't think they can create anything living, I know that."

"How?"

"The last time there was an Angel Year, I—I was here," Alex said, sighing again. "At noon on Christmas Day, we went up to the Gift Field in a parade, like every year. It's the big field just outside of town."

Nathan remembered walking briefly near it while exploring the town.

"That year, there was a tree—a huge Christmas tree—and there was a present there, one for each of us. One for every person in town, including the animals too. But no one got puppies or kittens during that Third Rite. Every kid wants a pet for Christmas."

"That's actually… quite impressive reasoning," Nathan said.

Alex rolled his eyes. "He said condescendingly. Again."

"More accurate would be 'with pleasant surprise'."

Alex glanced at him and offered a weak smile.

Nathan stared over the trees and spoke almost to himself. "And what did you get?"

"Same thing everyone did—exactly what I wanted."

Nathan was turning it around in his head. A well of power like that would be a prize indeed. And it could call for a decoy.

"The snow didn't start on time," Nathan said quietly.

"It was a few minutes late," Alex admitted.

Nathan nodded. "Once we heard the bell, that's when the First Rite was completed. Because that's the real power. The Rites must be like mile markers, pointing the way to the Third Rite. The Bell is something like a conduit, connecting you to wherever the real power is stored. It's only temporary, probably just enough to prime the pump. As for the snow, well you just showed me you could do that writ small. I imagine the Angel—the true Angel—, connected with a focus, connected to a well of power enough to do what you describe, had little trouble bringing on the snow."

Nathan felt another piece click into place. *Resonance*. For a reason he didn't yet understand, the word filled him with dread.

"I bet you felt it, didn't you?" Nathan mused, "the force, pulling at you?"

Alex could do little more than nod. "Yeah," he said quietly. "I got cold all over. Like I was dunked in a frozen lake."

Alex exhaled a deep breath.

"What's happening to me?" Alex asked, a crack echoing in his voice. "Do you know?"

"Not yet. Not precisely, that is. You would've felt it if you'd been the direct cause for the snow. It's not something that would just happen. My guess is that, like me, you're naturally attuned to Memory, to magic, if you want to use that word. Like how you were able to Slip so easily when we went to Anchor. I can hear the toll, same as you, but I haven't touched the bell. I suspect if I had, I might also be able to shoot snowflakes out of my hands."

"So I can do the Second Rite?"

"Can and should are two different things. It would be a very bad idea for you to try to perform it, at least until we know more. I'm thinking something is behind this, wanting to stay hidden. I don't know why it's doing this, why it doesn't just perform the Rites out in the open, but I promise you it has a reason. And the last thing you should do is help it."

They reached the truck. Seeing the Ashford Christmas tree tied up in the back brought a small smile to Alex's face. "Wait here," he said. "I forgot to get something."

As Alex walked back towards the rows of trees, he swung the saw gently, to a rhythm only he could hear.

I guess he's got something to think about now. He took Nathan's theory well enough, and, if Nathan could talk to the true Timber Angel, then maybe he'd figure out what precisely was at stake. As he'd said, he had his guesses. *Each one worse than the last, but that's another problem.*

More urgently, what are we going to do about this Second Rite? Two days. Nathan gave a wary glance to the darkening sky. *Scratch that, one night and one day.* The ribbon was bothering him as well. *I guide*

Angels. What did that mean?

Again, the word came back: Resonance. Everything was starting to connect, but it was too tidy. Too designed. Magic—*if we want to call it that*—was many things, but tidy was not one of them. The thought still spun in Nathan's head when he spotted Alex coming out of a row down at the far end of the farm. He was carrying something in his arms and had the bow saw balanced on top. When he got closer, Nathan could make it out. It was a small Christmas tree, the sort of ugly duckling tree that never grew to full height.

When he reached the truck, Alex asked Nathan to take the saw while he dumped the tree into the truck. "There," Alex said. "Now we can go."

"Just tidying up?" Nathan asked. "I guess no one was going to buy it."

Once again, a look of surprise widened Alex's eyes, and his sheepish smile returned. "No," he said. "This one's for the guest house. It's for you. For helping me."

Chapter Fifteen

Nathan grimaced as the truck took another turn. The words stitched into the cloth stomped around his mind. It guided the Angel to the Third Rite, that seemed simple enough. But why? The Second Rite was a public affair, public enough that Alex knew what it was just by virtue of having been here before. The Third Rite, however, seemed more obscure. It must have had something to do with the power at the ritual's core, but Nathan thought there was more to it than that.

"With the Angel's Touch, Second there will be Light." Nathan said as Alex guided the hurtling truck back down the farm road. "Lighting the way," Nathan mused. "If the Bell proves your worth, then the tree shows you the way to the prize. *From the Angel's Flame, Finally there will be Joy.* Any ideas?"

Alex shook his head. "That I don't know."

When the farm road rejoined the highway into town, Alex stopped the truck. Alex was about to turn back towards the town when something occurred to Nathan.

Angels tend to have wings. "Wait," Nathan said, "go the other way."

"Up the mountain?"

"Yeah. Just for a bit. I want to check out the view." *The way a Timber Angel might see it.*

Not a single car passed them on their way out of town. Not one coming into Timber's Edge, and not one leaving. Alex insisted it was normal, but it didn't sit right with Nathan. Now, out in the middle of it, it concerned him. *It doesn't sit right at all.* As they crawled up in elevation, the road began to wind. Eventually, they came to a ridge and a scenic overlook.

Without a word, Alex pulled the truck into a parking spot, then put it into park. "That should do it, right?"

Through the windshield, Nathan could see the other side of the valley. Through his window, he could see the lights of the town.

"This'll do," he said.

The sun was already growing dark in the sky. Nathan still wasn't used to how short the days felt, and it felt like each one was growing shorter. There were some patches of forest, wide acres of farmland, and, beyond them both, the tell-tale black ribbon of an American highway. In the fading light, pairs of lights crawled across the highway in both directions. As far as Nathan was able to see, all the way to the horizon, the highway was full of cars, full of other souls. And not one of them needed to stop in Timber's Edge.

✳

The metal plaque described the local snowdrop, apparently a common species of plant in the area. Nathan read it slowly, trying to absorb the words at the same time he was trying to absorb the cars speeding along the highway below. Could it be that there simply was that little traffic to Timber's Edge? *If that were true, where were all the cars coming from?*

Metal plaques lined the brick boundary of either side of the scenic overlook. Each one described the wildlife, or plants, or the local history of the area. He'd read about half of them, trying to clear his mind, but it was hard to focus on any of the details. Nathan rubbed his hands together. The night was closing in and the temperature was dropping. He wanted to leave before too long. The ride back down would be anxiety-inducing enough. It'd be worse if it was dark and below freezing.

Alex was about twenty feet away, staring off and over Timber's Edge. From here, the town looked even smaller—a cluster of fairy lights with the clear shape of Calbot Square at its center. Once they'd arrived and stepped out of the truck, Alex had fallen strangely quiet. Now, he seemed lost in thought.

Eventually, Nathan made his way to the side of the overlook that looked over Timber's Edge. The plaques didn't tell him anything he didn't already know. The town was formed in 1806, in a valley home to fierce winters. Timber's Edge was kind to the neighboring Native American tribes, outlawed the ownership of slaves, and consistently celebrated Christmas. It was only when he reached the plaque nearest to Alex did he see something that he didn't expect to see, here of all places. This particular plaque carried the likeness of a bald man in a suit and with a pair of metal eyeglasses perched on the end of his nose. Nathan recognized him from the paintings in Town Hall.

John Calbot (1770 - 1825) was the founder of Timber's Edge. In the shadow of the Revolutionary War and wanting to escape the young nation's conflicts with its neighbors, Calbot led his young family and a mixed group of settlers west from New York. They arrived during Christmas 1806. While the early days of the colony were full of hardship, under his leadership, Timber's Edge continued to grow. After the death of his wife in 1824, Calbot left Timber's Edge the next November and was presumed dead. Calbot Square remains named in his honor.

A quote was engraved on a separate plaque beneath the inscription: *We must see the world as we want it to be, and not be simply content with it as it is.*

Alex crossed over to him, noticed the sign Nathan was reading. "Our benefactor."

Nathan glanced at him. "John Calbot's Dream," he muttered, thinking of the snow globes. One of them bore the initials J.C. and Nathan was quite sure he was looking at the likeness those initials belonged to. Something clicked into place. "He was the first Angel," Nathan said. "Whatever power is here, he was the one who found it." *And used it.*

Alex exhaled. "I think you're right. If he hadn't. There would be no Angel Trees. No First Snow. No Third Rite. No Timber Angel."

"If I didn't know any better, I'd say you sounded wistful."

"Wistful?"

"As in wishing something were to happen."

"I know what it means, dick," Alex said, laughing for the first time since he'd made it snow in his hands. "No, I don't wish it had never happened. Despite what you say, I still think the Three Rites are good. I still remember my Angel Year. It was the best Christmas morning."

"Alex," Nathan warned. "I know you want to make this happen for Maddie, but—"

"Don't worry," Alex said. "I'm in your hands. If you tell me not to try, then I won't."

"What did you get?" Nathan asked again. "Exactly what you wanted," Nathan said. "But you never said what it was?"

"Me?" Alex laughed. "Funny you should ask."

He returned to the truck and pulled something from the back seat.

"Here it is. The Angel's Gift," Alex said with a reverence straddling the border between solemn and ludicrous. "I brought it with me. I was trying to work up the courage to level with you."

"Your pièce de résistance?" To Nathan, it simply looked like a book box set, albeit an expensive one. It was clearly some sort of collector's item; the box was made of thick fabric and the books themselves were bound in leather. Alex slipped one of the books out of the case and, carefully, passed it over. Nathan got the sensation that he was the butt of some joke.

"You can't be serious," Nathan said. Alex had handed it over with the book cover up. The cover said:

Amazing X-Men, Volume 1.

✳

Nathan retreated back to the truck and flipped the cab light on. *Of all the things…a comic?* The book felt heavy in his hands; it was definitely some sort of special edition. Where most of the graphic novels and comics he had seen were thin and glossy, this book had thick pages the way an expensive art-book might. He flipped through a few, carefully and gingerly under Alex's watchful eye. While Alex was trying to act relaxed, his fingers were tense and coiled; he'd snatch it out of Nathan's hand at the first sign of trouble, there was no doubt about that.

"Alex, I've handled a mummy's urn before," Nathan finally snapped. "Actual people parts. I'll take care of your book."

Although, that urn did end up in pieces. Lots and lots of pieces.

The finish on the book was impressive. The panels were vivid, bright, and full of clean detail. They looked as if they'd been drawn and inked yesterday. Nathan placed his left hand on the page, and noticed his new charm wriggle. It was a slight motion, but it was there. He turned through a few more panels of Professor X and Storm talking before glancing at Alex.

"This is a book," Nathan said. "It's a nice book, don't get me wrong. There's even some Trace, but it's still just a book." Still, as he said the words and drummed his fingers across the page, Nathan wasn't sure he completely believed it. There was something wrong with it, something off.

Alex pulled the book away from him and began flipping backwards through the pages.

"It's funny," Alex said. "I'd have agreed with you. But, then, I know something you don't."

"I'm all ears Alex," Nathan said. He didn't mean to sound

impatient, but, at the same time, the not-knowing cut into him.

Alex grinned. "Nathan Cole, not knowing. That's got to be painful."

"I can always beat it out of you," Nathan suggested.

"Fair enough," Alex laughed. "Here's what I know that you don't. I know that this is one set of a dozen that came in my Angel Gift. That morning, I went to the Gift Field, along with everyone. For an Angel Year, I told you the town goes up together in a parade. That year, the path up there was covered in Christmas lights and, like always, a big section of the field was roped off. Normally, that's empty, but that year, it was stacked with presents. There was one for everyone in town. Each one had a handwritten card on it."

Alex pulled something out of the front of the book and put it on the dashboard. It was a small, plain white card, but stamped in gold on the front was the hourglass Angel. Inside, written in a neat, precise script, was Alex's name.

"You might say that that's not enough proof," Alex said. "I mean, you can buy a card anywhere, right?"

"Right," Nathan said, but actually he wasn't thinking that at all. He was doing math, rapid math, in his head, and, today, math was refusing to give him even the slightest bit of comfort.

"But the thing about this Gift—"Alex capitalized the word when he spoke "—is that it don't quite exist."

"Come again?" Nathan asked. Alex pointed to the page.

"This series isn't published like this. The binding doesn't exist, the edition doesn't exist. Even the story itself is one of the rarest ones out there."

He pulled another book out of the set. This one wasn't even the X-Men, it was the Green Lantern.

"This one was another one I had always wanted, but was never able to find. Over and over again. Each story in each book. They don't exist anywhere but here. Even if my parents were comic aficionados, which I promise they aren't, how could they ever have known that these titles were all the ones I had never got to read? How could they have gotten them printed? More than that, who arranged for all the other Gifts that day, as well?"

Alex flipped to the front of the book, and spun it back around so Nathan could read the publisher information. While Nathan scanned the page, Alex leaned against the truck, clearly satisfied.

At first glance, the page looked like any other publishing information page, except, as Nathan read, he found obvious errors. If he didn't know better, he'd have called the book a forgery, which, he supposed, it technically was. The ISBN numbers, the publication dates, they were all nonsensical. But, putting aside the cost of custom printing the book for a moment, why would the "forger" even bother faking the publication information?

At the bottom of the page, printed into the book itself, where the publisher's name was supposed to be, was another hourglass symbol. Nathan rubbed his finger over it and could feel the raised ridges of the print work.

"So," Alex said. "Now you know everything I do about the Timber Angel and the Three Rites. What's next?"

Now, we're getting somewhere. Nathan met Alex's eyes, those eyes the color of thunderclouds, and held them for a long time.

"I'd like to see this field," Nathan said, his controlled voice in defiance to the submarine dive his stomach was performing. "Can you arrange that?"

Alex broke into a smile. "Only if we get some supplies right quick. I'm starving."

*

The sun had fully set by the time they'd returned to town. Nathan had turned silent during the drive. *Was it something I said?* When

Alex pulled the truck into one of the spaces on Broad Street, Nathan had almost leaped out of the vehicle. From down the street, Alex could hear the sound of carols being sung. They stopped inside the Chinese restaurant, and, while they were waiting, Nathan acquired a six pack of light beer. Alex wrinkled his nose at them.

"You have terrible taste," Alex said.

Nathan shrugged. "I'm a man on a budget," he replied. "Come to think of it, how did you even pay for that drink in Anchor? I saw you had one."

"I didn't."

Nathan tutted. "I'll be hearing about that." To Alex's concerned face, he added, "Don't worry, Anslem will put it on my tab."

"How would I have even paid?" Alex asked to his back.

"It's complicated," Nathan called back.

"Typical." Alex muttered.

Alex drove them the rest of the way to the field. The smell of his lo mein was making his stomach growl. The Gift Field, as it was called, lay along the Hawke River, and just down beyond the cluster of large houses that made up Timber's Edge's oldest homes.

It was a large field, about the size of two soccer fields placed side by side. A few kids were playing in the snow, and the remnants of several snowmen dotted the ground like old tombstones. They pulled into a parking spot near the field, and, once again, Nathan couldn't seem to wait to get out of the truck.

"Why do you keep doing that?" Alex asked.

Nathan's eyes narrowed. "Doing what?"

"I'm not that bad of a driver," Alex said.

This time, Alex could tell that Nathan knew precisely what the question was about. Nathan started fidgeting with his ring. "I don't do well in cars," he said eventually. "Not since the accident."

"Your mom?"

"Yeah," Nathan said. "The accident—when she died—I was...it

was me driving." He shook his head. "I haven't driven since."

Alex's heart fell into his shoes. "Oh shit. I'm sorry."

Nathan shrugged then that easy smile of his returned. He clapped Alex on the arm and said, "Don't worry about it. You never need to apologize for a question."

This time, however, the smile didn't seem to reach his eyes. Nathan took his food and headed towards a bench that faced the river. For a time, they ate in silence and took long pulls from their beers. Eventually, Nathan broke the silence.

"Don't you, you know, want to be spending time with them? Your family that is." Nathan asked as he speared a piece of beef from his food. "Between the Timber Angel, and now this, you're keeping busy."

"Never enough time during the holidays. That's what my dad says. Besides, there's plenty of time," Alex replied, rolling his shoulders. "If I'm being honest, I don't really have much of a place up there anymore. My dad's girlfriend is up there all the time. Won't be long before she takes over my room."

"You don't get along with her then?"

"She can be a bit much."

"Seems to be in the water here," Nathan said. "That mayor of yours, for exampl—"

He must've noticed Alex's face flush.

"Oh it's the mayor!" Nathan chuckled and then broke into a full laugh. "I'm sorry, but that tracks. Should've caught that. Dammit Nate, not paying attention."

"Nate?" Alex asked.

For the second time that day, a look of concern flashed across Nathan's face.

"Sorry, thought I was talking to myself," Nathan said through a mouthful of broccoli. "Guess I'm distracted."

Alex scooped a web of noodles from his food and chewed them

slowly. Nathan took another long pull from his beer, and the icy river churned in front of them. "What about you? Where were you headed before the bus dropped you here? Back to see family?"

Nathan turned inward and he squinted, as if he was trying to remember. "I don't really have any family," he said. "Not since Mother Sable died." Nathan shrugged. "I was headed north. I have a charm I need to return to my f—friend up there."

He lifted his arm and picked a charm off of the chain. It was a thick, wooden crucifix, but it had been singed and burned.

"She sent it to me for a job," Nathan said. "Overnight expressed it, in fact."

"And, did it help?" Despite living in Timber's Edge, and believing in the Angel Gifts, Alex still couldn't keep the hesitation out of his voice.

"No," Nathan said with a sad shake of his head. "I'm afraid it didn't."

"Sorry," Alex said.

"Never be sorry about a question," Nathan reminded. "To your next one: After this, I don't know. Something might come up. Or I was thinking of heading back west and visiting my mother. Well, her grave at least. It's been a bit too long."

"Yeah, I still go by mine's. Each morning I run, I stop by the cemetery then circle back over the bridge there," he pointed to the stone bridge that crossed the river.

"You go far?"

"On the run? I just go up the trail there to Iron Shoe Point and come back. 'Spose it's three miles or so." Alex followed an estimate of the path with his finger. "It's not nearly as far as I used to go in high school. Back then, They'd make us run all over the place. They had us running so damn much, it's probably why my knee gave out in college."

"You seem alright," Nathan said.

"I got better. The rehab was agony, and my dreams of college athletic glory ended, but it ended up getting me into sports medicine, so there's that," Alex said.

"Your degree," Nathan said, almost as if reminding himself.

"I can wrap an ankle with the best of them," Alex said with a smile. "And don't get me started on my splint work. It's top notch."

Nathan swallowed his current bite. "There's a skill I could use," he said, chuckling.

"It was my mom's idea," Alex admitted. There was a thought that hadn't shown up for a while. Alex had visited, still on his crutches, and absorbed in every scrap of research he could find about fixing his knee. That's when Mom had suggested it. The next semester, Alex switched his major and started looking into Master's programs.

"What was she like, your mother?" Nathan asked. "Tell me about her."

"She was the best, right? You know she was an English professor, a big-time one? She wrote some books too and she would lecture all over the place. She met my dad one day on a lecture tour. He's a professor of English Literature too. My dad stopped lecturing and started to help with the farm. My dad took over the farm when her dad, Grandpa Pat, passed away. Mom kept lecturing and teaching, but eventually..."

"She passed?" Nathan asked.

Alex nodded then took a long sip of beer.

"Oh, she loved Christmas too of course," Alex said. "That's for sure. I used to help her cook a ton around this time of year. Oh yeah, I learned all of the dishes," Alex said, his words sounding too thick for his mouth. "Gingerbread. Snickerdoodles. Yule Log. Roasted turkeys, beef, chicken, and even a sea-bass one year," in a sly aside, he added "Maddie was having a thing about poultry that year. All at Mom's side. Except for the last few years of course, those I had to do solo."

"Nice memories," Nathan said.

Alex smiled. "Yeah."

He took down the rest of his first bottle, and Nathan followed suit. The beer left a tinny quality in his mouth and left a flower of courage in his chest.

"So, since we're trading stories," Alex said, "what was Christmas like on the road? For the son of a psychic?"

Nathan leaned back on the bench. Maybe it was the beer, or maybe it was because Nathan was going to be gone in a few days, but it felt harmless to ask. Alex had nothing to hide, after all. Not anymore. He was surprised when Nathan answered.

"It was just me and my mother most years," Nathan said. "Mother Sable—that's what I called her—she took me in when I was ten. The Holding, the group she was a part of, specialize in, well, stuff like this. Foremost experts on the planet, if you asked them. I was raised in that life. For Christmas, she'd always be wanting to do something different. One year, it was a Denny's. The other year it was a five-star hotel. One year, it was cans of Spaghettios heated up over a campfire in the middle of a Dakota. I couldn't tell you which one."

"Wait, Spaghettios? For Christmas?"

"They did have turkey meatballs in them," Nathan said with a shrug. "The fruitcake—Mother Sable liked her fruit cake warm— didn't survive the fire very well. It came off of the fire a charred block of exploded raisins and burnt sugar. The turkey she made one year was worse. That was the year where the theme was Christmas at home. That poor bird," Nathan shook his head. "It never saw her coming. It didn't stop her eating it, and when I didn't want any, she demanded to know the reason why. You remember when I said I was raised by a psychic? You ever try lie to a psychic Alex Ashford?" Nathan grinned. "It doesn't end well. Especially with that one. Come to think of it, that was the last time I was home. At least until the year she died."

He finished his food, wiped his hands, then stared into the river. Alex got the sense he was traveling back in time.

The vision of Mom in a hospital bed swam in front of Alex's eyes.

"It was cancer for us," Alex said. "Brain cancer. The doctors said it had been there for years, but it only took a few months to go bad, towards the end she wasn't much like herself. She died in January, but just before, her old self came back. Dad, Maddie, and I, we went to her hospital room, gave her one last Christmas…"

Alex smiled, but the memory burned in the back of his throat. As he trailed off, he exhaled deeply.

"Hey," Alex said. "Have you ever thought what you would do if you had ten minutes back? With your mom, that is. Say you can go back in time and relive a memory. What would you pick?"

Alex was staring forward into the river, into the churning water that swallowed each falling snowflake like a greedy mouth.

"I'd do Christmas morning. Of the Angel Gift and walking up here with her. It would mean something more now, I think."

Alex met Nathan's eyes and it felt like seeing him for the first time.

"What'd you pick?" Alex asked. "If you got ten minutes with your mom, where would you go back to?"

Nathan shook his head. He was somewhere else, his mind cast to some foreign place.

"Not ten minutes back," Nathan said, his voice barely a whisper. "But I would take ten minutes more."

Chapter Sixteen

"Great fit," Alex said once they put the shriveled tree in its place in the corner of the guest house living room. It sat near the fireplace, naked and unadorned, and had already lost more than a few needles on its journey in the back of Alex's truck. "Needs some decorations, but it's a start."

Still, the ridiculousness of the tree did seem to bring a smile to Nathan's face. Alex was glad he'd thought of it.

"Thanks," Nathan said. He meant it. Even though Nathan was a hard read, Alex was sure he meant it. A rush of blood flushed into Alex's cheeks.

"Well you're being helpful with all this Angel stuff. Seems only fair."

There was an awkward beat before Alex asked. It's just a question. Never apologize for a question, right?

"I've been wondering. About Anchor."

Nathan turned away from the tree, appraised him with those bright green eyes. "It would be strange if you weren't."

"Anslem, he referred to the, the Weave," Alex said.

"And you want to know what he was talking about?" Nathan asked.

Alex nodded.

"Are you sure? It might change your whole worldview. Certainly more than a comic book."

Alex flushed deeper. "You're such a dick."

Nathan laughed, but he went to the kitchen and rummaged around. He went through the pantry, shelf by shelf, and didn't seem satisfied, but when he went to the fridge, he grunted with approval. Then, he turned, facing Alex with a grin. In his hand, he proudly held an orange.

"Behold," he said. "An approximation of the Astral Weave."

"That's an orange."

"Perspective, Mr. Ashford," Nathan chided as he pulled a cutting board from a drawer and a chef's knife from the block on the counter. He placed the orange in the center of the cutting board. "What shape is this?"

Alex crossed his arms.

"Come on, humor me."

"It's a sphere," Alex replied.

Nathan admired the orange on the board. "Yup. And almost perfect too."

With the knife, Nathan traced a line vertically up the skin of the orange, and another one horizontally around the orange's center. An equator and a prime meridian. Nathan placed the fruit on the cutting board and met Alex's eyes across the counter. He placed his finger at the top of the fruit.

"This is infinity," he said. He placed another finger at the opposite end. "Negative infinity. Each plane exists at another point on our vertical line. There's a one, a two, a negative one, a negative two, all the way to either end."

"Alright," Alex said. "We're at zero?"

Nathan smiled. "Yes we are. So far, so good. Traveling lower, like we do in dreams, like we did to get to Anchor, is called Slipping. These are all negative, relative to us that is."

He put his finger at a point on the orange halfway between the equator and the fruit's top.

Nathan continued, "In Ancient Greek myths, humans weren't

allowed on Mount Olympus. In Norse mythology, the people of Midgard could never enter Asgard. Christians can't just waltz into their Heaven. And so on, and so forth. This similarity, the concept of levels, exists in many mythologies."

"They're the higher levels?" Alex asked. "Like ten."

"Right," Nathan said, with an approving nod. "We can travel negative to us. We will exist in those planes through Projection, like we talked about. We will have bodies, hair, et cetera. Back here, back in our plane, we leave bits of ourselves behind to mind the shop so-to-speak. Not enough to save us if we're killed in those lower levels, that is. But enough to keep us remembering to breathe. It's relatively straightforward, so long as you have a mind capable of sensing those planes."

"Psychics?"

Nathan nodded. "There are different types of psychics, but primarily, yes. But, regular minds can Project as well, just normally not very far. It's what we do when we dream. Every dream we create, after all, is a reality in and of itself. It's just short-lived and indistinct. A psychic mind is able to Project much farther and even bring other minds along for the ride. Psychics also have much more vivid dreams and—" Nathan's face soured. "—their nightmares can be very dangerous. I know this from experience."

"Your mother. You said she was psychic."

"That's right, and I saw the toll some of them took on her," Nathan said.

Nathan stared at the fruit on the counter with a frown. Then, in a moment, the frown was gone, replaced by his easy smile.

"We can't travel positive," Nathan said. "Not without help at least. Take Odin for example. He could come to visit Midgard whenever he pleased."

"He would Project—no, Slip?"

"Right," Nathan said. "He was going from his zero to somewhere beneath him, no offense to us. But, when a mortal had to travel to Asgard, they would need the help of the gods. The Bifrost, a bridge of fire, earth, and air, connects Midgard to Asgard. It's watched over by Heimdell, another god."

"I've seen the movies," Alex said.

Nathan's smile was sardonic. "Then, you know what Heimdell's job was."

"He commanded the bridge. You couldn't travel it without his help," Alex rolled his eyes. "Jesus."

"Olympus couldn't be reached," Nathan continued, "except with intervention. The princess Psyche—more beautiful than Aphrodite—was granted the right to live there by Zeus after she married Eros. So, now I ask, what about the planes beneath us? Our negatives. If they wanted to visit *us*, how do you think that would happen?"

Alex shrugged. "Ghosts?"

Nathan shook his head. "No. Ghosts are fragments of Memory, a different matter entirely." He grimaced. "You said you've seen the movies. Ever seen one called *The Exorcist*?"

"You're not serious."

"Is it that hard to believe? Like the gods inviting us to Olympus, demons are often invited here through rituals; they can't stay without help either. Now, just like how not all gods are kind, not all demons are necessarily evil, but, sure as shit tends to stink, they tend to lean that way. Not all of them are the head-spinning, projectile vomiting kind either, though they—well, let's just say they're out there."

"You've...You've met them?" The question stuck in Alex's throat.

Across the counter, Nathan's eyes suddenly looked worn. "I've met them, and that's all I'll say about it. I won't give them the satisfaction of being remembered." he said, his voice clipped.

Nathan ran his finger up and down the orange's prime meridian. "Anslem described it to me as an axis of morality. The farther down you get, the closer you get to the Infernal Engines. This is where souls are pulped for their raw Memory. In these planes, power is the end goal and it doesn't matter who you hurt and how much you hurt them to get it. There is no Memory as reliably potent as that born from pain."

Alex could vouch for that. He could vouch for that very well.

Nathan moved his finger to the top of the orange. "Here, the higher we go, the closer we get to the Empyrean Choir, the force that keeps the Astral Weave singing, keeps new souls spinning. They cannot function without the Infernal Engines and the Infernal Engines can't run without the souls that the Choir sings into being. They form the two anchor points of the Astral Weave, diametrically opposed, but balanced."

Alex's attention shifted to the equator. "If the vertical line is morality. What's that one?"

Nathan's smile returned, and he began slicing the orange across the prime meridian such that each slice was another disc. From one of the discs, he plucked a seed. This, he showed to Alex.

"This is us," Nathan said. "Our reality. Our universe. All the planets. All the galaxies. From the Big Bang to whatever happens at the end, follow?"

Alex nodded slowly.

Nathan found the disc that contained the equator and placed the seed directly in the center. "This is us in the Weave." He took other seeds and placed them in the disc as well. "These are other universes but they remain on our plane. One theory suggests there is one seed for each different decision we might make."

Alex felt something click in his brain. "You're about talking parallel realities? I've seen that one as well."

Nathan shrugged, pointing at the widest point of the orange with the tip of the knife. "On one end, every choice is the right one. On the other, every choice is the wrong one. This—and this is my speculation—is the axis of entropy. On one end, order so perfect that everyone is happy. On the other, chaos so complete that the universe never formed at all. However, this is just my guess work. The Holding has never confirmed a parallel reality, and certainly never traveled to one."

"Anslem doesn't know?" Alex asked, surprised.

Nathan grinned. "As far as Anslem is concerned, they all happen together. It's the danger, he likes to say, of being touched by the Divine."

✻

Nathan found a box of ornaments and even a few ropes of silver tinsel in one of the guest house closets. Alex had left a few minutes ago to escort his sister and the mayor to the tree's arrival. Having seen the crowd on their drive back through town, Nathan wasn't in a rush to go. So long as he got there just after the tree arrived, he wouldn't miss anything. *At least, nothing we don't care to miss.* The Angel, the real Timber Angel that was, it could do nothing until the tree was in place after all.

Nathan hung a few red ornaments on the scraggly tree Alex had acquired for him. He'd taken the Weave rather well. Again, Nathan was struck by how naturally matters of Memory came to Alex. Not for the first time, he wondered if there was more to Alex than he'd first thought. He considered the possibility that Alex was a full psychic, the way Mother Sable was, but it was unlikely. He would have awoken to his powers years ago.

It was possible that, like Nathan himself, Alex was a psychic-latent with enough of a glimmer to see the influence of Memory. It was more likely, but still far-fetched. He'd have had to have lived a very sheltered life to have not noticed, and Alex had just come back from college. He hadn't been hiding away, and Nathan didn't think he was the type that would've ignored ghostly classmates or visits from other planes. *No, there's something else at work here.*

He strung the tinsel around the tree then ran a rope of lights around the few branches that still survived. After plugging them in, Nathan stepped back and admired his handiwork. The stubby tree was the spitting image of the sort that Mother Sable used to sneak into his camper. Nathan sat on the couch and stared at it for a time, a sad smile crossing his face. Suddenly he was ten years old again, meeting Mother Sable in her attic for the first time.

"Too much isn't making sense. Between you and me, I'm nervous," he told the tree. "I wish you were here Mother. You'd know what to do."

Chapter Seventeen

Spending so much time on the road took its toll. It was hard to stay fit, for one. Hard to stay positive. Hard to stay grounded. But, for all those difficulties, there were physical matters to attend to, even when Timber Angels were lurking around the corner. These were the simple problems, like where to get food, or what shops had good bathrooms, or, as it happened after more than four days, where the laundromat was.

Nathan had searched the guest house for a machine the first night he'd arrived, but that was one amenity the Ashfords had decided not to include. It was one of the first things he kept an eye out for; it was never a bad time to do a wash. He had never come across a town without a laundromat, but there were first times for everything. *Especially here. More first times than I can seem to keep track of.* Besides, wherever it was, it wasn't likely to be full. Not with everyone already milling around the square.

Marie was preparing some sort of mixture in the Inn's kitchen when he walked down the path that ran along the building's back. She caught his eye and waved him over. *Caught.*

Soon, she appeared out of the patio door. She wore an apron over a flowery blue sweater and hugged herself against the cold afternoon.

"Where are you going with that?" Marie asked at the duffel bag he had slung over his shoulder. "You look like you're about to flag down the nearest trucker."

Nathan pulled the pack of laundry pouches out of the top of his bag and waved it at her. "Not quite. Laundry."

"Oh! Machine's in here." She beckoned him over. *Trapped.*

With a sigh, Nathan strode over.

"You've got to remember you're a guest," Marie said. She moved to pat his arm, but then stopped herself. She showed him into a room off the kitchen, and, as they passed through, Nathan caught a whiff of something with ginger and spices. *Another reason why it's hard to stay fit,* he thought. Side-by-side stackable machines sat along the wall and a folding station stood at the opposite side of the cramped room.

He set to work loading his clothes into the first machine.

"I can switch it over for you," Marie said.

"You don't have to do that," Nathan objected.

"Nonsense," Marie said. "When you stay here—or adjacent to here as it happens—you're supposed to feel at home."

"I do my own laundry at home," Nathan protested. *Not that he really had one of those these days.*

"But was it ever as good as when your mother used to do it for you?"

The thought of Mother Sable doing Nathan's laundry was in and of itself laughable. They had always gone to the laundromat together with their own laundry bags. It would've been lucky if she'd even share her detergent.

"I choose not to answer," Nathan replied, but the edges of his mouth couldn't help but twitch.

Marie took the laundry bag out of his hands, and began loading the clothes into the machine. Nathan stepped in to help her, but she slapped his hand away. The woman was a force, there was no doubt about that.

"Besides," she said, "shouldn't you be down at the square? The tree will be coming down any minute. You can either go do that or wait for your drawers to get washed. It's entirely up to you."

She stepped back into the kitchen and examined her mixture. She tipped the bowl around, was apparently dissatisfied, and then started ferociously stirring. "Gotta work those lumps out," Marie said. "Sometimes a thing needs some help to come out alright."

"Is there a message in there for me?"

Marie chuckled. "If you find meaning in lumpy batter, that's your business." She stirred for a bit longer and looked thoughtfully at Nathan's hands and arms. "Can you stay for a few minutes? To help me with the cake. It's at a delicate stage."

Unsure how to say no, Nathan agreed, and Marie passed the spoon to him with a relieved sigh. It was a ginger cake, Marie explained, and that meant he had to stir.

"It's the treacle. It makes it lump up. Come on, harder than that. But not too hard."

Nathan slowed his stir but increased the power.

"There, smooth. Very good. You're a natural."

Nathan continued to stir while Marie tossed in a handful of chopped walnuts. The nuts made the mixture tougher and harder to stir. Eventually, Nathan's wrist began to tire.

"Now, did I forget anything? I always forget something."

She's enjoying herself.

"Not the concrete," Nathan said, "that much I'm sure about."

Marie ignored him and found a square baking pan under the counter.

"Okay, pour it in. That's it."

She picked up the pan and dropped it on the counter a few times.

Nathan saw no visual change, but the application of gravity satisfied Marie for she took the pan and slid it into the wall oven behind them.

"Tea?" She didn't wait for an answer and instead clicked on an electric kettle and tossed two tea bags into cups. "I always have a cup of tea while I wait for a cake to bake," she said.

Nathan watched the water come to a boil. A thought occurred to him,"Why don't you come with me tonight? We can live dangerously and let the laundry sit for a few hours."

Marie waved a hand. "Oh no, not me. It's much too cold for me out there."

Nathan didn't push it.

Marie poured hot water into the cups, then stirred a spoonful of honey in hers. "Honey?"

"Not for me," Nathan replied. He took the cup and felt the warmth sink into his hands. "This is good, thanks."

"I don't mean to pry," Marie said. *But that's not going to stop you.* "But, why'd you pick now to do laundry of all things?"

"Never a bad time for a wash," Nathan replied.

Marie clucked her tongue.

Nathan took a deep breath. "Because experience has taught me to take advantage of the quiet while it's here. Right now, it's like the calm before the storm. I can feel it. To me, it's just in the air. Soon, the clouds will break, and there won't be time for laundry or cakes or tea."

"You make it sound so ominous," Marie observed. "You really think the Angel is dangerous?"

Nathan exhaled like someone finally making a long-awaited confession. "Yes," he said quietly. "I'm almost certain it is. But how or why, I don't quite understand yet." He looked out the window, watched the snowflakes drift against the pitch black sky. "But I'll find out. I can promise you that."

This time, Marie did pat his hand, and Nathan didn't pull it away. "I don't know anything about this magic business. But I for one am glad you're on the lookout."

She got up, beckoning him to follow her into the entryway. From a closet, she retrieved a broom handle. Then, she proceeded to march to the door frame, where the small angel figurine stood guard, and, using the broom, she knocked it down. It fell to the floor with a clatter. "See? If you think it's dangerous, then that's good enough for me."

Nathan laughed at the absurdity of it. "One down," he said. He met the short woman's coal eyes. "You're sure you won't come with me?"

"No. But I can find you some company. I'm sure Mr. DeMarco won't want to miss it."

"Joy to the world," Nathan muttered. He hadn't seen the bitter man and can't say that he'd missed him.

"It's the holidays Nathan," Marie chided. "Everyone deserves a bit of extra grace." She headed up the staircase, calling behind her, "Don't let my cake burn or I'll have you mix me another one."

Nathan watched the cake dutifully. *How long has it been since we've stopped and watched a cake bake? Probably never. We should do it more often. While we're at it, we should eat cake more often.*

When he heard her shuffle into the kitchen behind him, he said, "It's lookin—" He stopped when he saw her pale face. "What is it? What's wrong?"

Marie's voice was barely a ghost of its former self, "I think your storm's arrived."

Marie led him back into the Inn's entryway, and wordlessly they climbed the narrow staircase to a corner landing. The hall was lifeless. There were no cheers from the Brenner children, no excited chatter from the couples getting ready for the evening. All of the other guests were probably already down at the square. They stopped at a door on the left, just before the end of the hall.

"I made sure I didn't touch anything," Marie said, "once I found him."

The room was comfortable enough with a squishy-looking bed, a simple wooden desk, and plenty of late afternoon light streaming through the window. There was a small television on a dresser in the corner of the room; it was playing the same local channel that Nathan had watched on his first night, but now the program was an old *The Price is Right* rerun. John DeMarco was lying flat on his back on top of the flowery comforter. His eyes were closed and he appeared to be sleeping. He was fully-clothed in a wrinkled dress shirt, pants, and even a brown jacket. Shoes remained on his feet, a layer of dirt running around the sole.

Immediately, Nathan moved to DeMarco's bedside. There was a pulse.

"He's alive," Nathan said. DeMarco didn't seem the type of man who would've got into bed fully clothed, even for a nap. He certainly wouldn't have worn shoes with dirt on them. This happened somewhere else, Nathan realized, frowning. He'd been moved here, and somehow no one had noticed.

He examined the man's face. Nathan tried waking him, but DeMarco didn't respond. The man didn't have the blank stare of someone Projecting or Slipping. Nathan tried forcing his eyelids open.

The pupils were there. They reacted, just slightly.

Nathan lay his hand, the one with his ring, on his forehead.

The pupils reacted again, wrenching themselves in the direction of the contact.

Would you look at that?

Nathan's stomach turned. "He's conscious. At least, part of him is."

"What happened to him Nathan?" Marie's voice was high and afraid.

He looked back at her. "I don't know. Honestly, I don't know."

He waved the charms over DeMarco. When the angel charm shook slightly, Nathan winced like he'd been struck. It was like something—no, not something, the Angel—had scrambled the man's brain. Nathan wondered what DeMarco was experiencing. He imagined it to be a prison of sound, of endless sensation, a storm of sensory chaos. *A terrible resonance.* The man's mind had simply been blitzed.

"I'm sorry," Nathan whispered. "I didn't know." *I should've been looking closer.*

Music drifted through the window from outside, and the sun was starting to fall closer to the horizon. Before long, it would be night. Now, there was no way he could miss the tree. And, if the Timber Angel happened to show, he intended to have a word with it.

Nathan turned to Marie. "I need to go." The innkeeper's eyes were still wide with shock. Nathan crossed the room to her, placed his hands firmly on her shoulders. "There's nothing you can do right now. Keep this door shut. Do you—"

"A doctor. He needs a doctor."

"I need you to trust me Marie. No doctor can help him," Nathan said. "The door stays shut until I say otherwise. Say nothing to anyone. This is critical. Do you understand?"

She nodded. "I'll do what you say. But in the morning—"

"I'll explain everything I know," Nathan promised. "The best thing you can do right now is pretend nothing's happened." He tried to smile. "Besides, you've got a cake in the oven."

Marie gave DeMarco's body one last, long look then nodded up at him. "To be honest, I don't have much of an appetite anymore."

If you did, Nathan thought, *then there would be something very wrong.*

When they reached the bottom of the stairs, Nathan headed straight towards the door. He stopped by the angel figurine, still sitting on the floor. He stared down at it then glanced back at Marie.

Despite not being a psychic, she read his mind. "Are you going to be able to stop it?"

"I'm not sure," Nathan replied. "But I certainly intend to try."

Chapter Eighteen

With thoughts of DeMarco's body pushing him on, Nathan strode out of the Inn and joined a crowd heading towards Calbot Square. By the time they reached Calbot Square, it was already swollen and alive with the rest of the procession. Gloria and her son were both out, and Nathan spotted Ronny mingling with the Brenners. A four-piece band had just sang out the last notes of "Jingle Bell Rock" and a cider-making contest had just crowned its winner. Maddie stood proudly next to Julianna. Together, they looked almost like family.

Nathan's hands were balled into fists. Someone had been attacked, right under his nose. Someone was suffering, and he hadn't even noticed. The disgust filled his gut with a hot, fiery anger. Worse, there was nothing he could do about it.

Use it Nate, don't let it control you. Remember Brother Flame's lessons. Don't get sloppy.

He needed a distraction, to reset. More than that, he needed to look like everyone else, enjoying the scene. Nathan found a stand selling heavily spiced cider and bought himself a cup, calories be damned.

When in Rome, I suppose you don't skip the pizza.

He made a circuit around the square, and saw Jake Marley talking with a couple who looked to be visitors. The two women who ran the antiques shop were talking with Old Man Hartford, who ran Hartford Curiosities and apparently managed half the rentals in town. El was sitting on a bench, a book in his hands, and even Denise the Librarian was drifting around the block.

When a loud truck horn blared through the night, the crowd erupted into a cheer. Nathan turned and saw a black pickup approach slowly. It looked like Alex's, but with more mud on its tires and more miles under its hood; it too had Pat's Tree Farm emblazoned across its side. The truck was covered in garland and lights and, standing tall in its bed, was the Angel Tree, its red and gold ribbon fluttering in the breeze. In the reflection of the lights, the tree and ribbon both shone.

The crowd cheered again when the truck parked in a special parking space beside the square. That's when Nathan spotted Paul Ashford and a tall farmhand, in the truck. They hopped out and, together, hauled the tree out of the back of the truck. They carried it through the square, and the crowd seemed desperate to touch the tree, even just for a moment. *Like Springsteen crowd surfing.*

Nathan glanced across Calbot Square and found that Maddie and Julianna had joined Alex up near Town Hall. Alex was watching the tree as well, a massive grin on his face. The doubt and the fear from earlier had apparently been forgotten. Maddie had climbed one of the stone pillars that framed the building, and she was laughing while her brother held her steady.

Each face wore the same expression of cheer, of awe. Each face except Nathan's. If anything, the display disturbed him. It was like someone had set off a chemical bomb of Christmas Cheer in the air, and everyone had become infected. He retrieved the charms from his pocket and retied them to his wrist. He'd expected the angel charm to react almost instantly, but instead the small bough he'd taken from the tree hung limp from his wrist.

Another thing that doesn't quite track, Nathan thought. *I'll add it to the list.*

It was then that Nathan saw another face that didn't seem to be full of joy. It belonged to the TransAmerica bus driver. Ronny met his eyes and, in a moment of mutual understanding, they both headed towards the other.

"Quite the scene," Ronny said. He had to speak directly into Nathan's ear to be heard.

"You don't seem impressed," Nathan replied.

Ronny considered it. "I've been all around, son. Seen lots of things. Fireworks over Boston Harbor on the Fourth, that sort of thing. You know what I remember most about then? About all those nights? The fights. It was so strange to me that people could be fightin' on the Fourth."

Nathan had seen them as a teenager by Mother Sable's side. That had been a party as well, but Ronny was right. There had been more texture to it. Some people were angry at not getting close enough. Others furious at the price of drinks. More variety.

It's all too tidy.

"I guess I'm waiting for the fight to break out," Ronny laughed.

Nathan didn't particularly like the bus driver, but he couldn't help but chuckle with him. "I know the feeling," he said. "Too good to be true normally is."

"Yup," Ronny agreed. "It gets my dander up is what I mean to say. Puts me a bit on edge. Might be the old bouncer in me."

Reflexively, Nathan opened and closed his fists. "Some habits never die," he said quietly.

Try as we might to kill them.

"Well, security. Fightin'. Those are a young man's games," Ronny said. "The road is more peaceful. While the bus is runnin' that is." With a laugh and a clap on Nathan's shoulder, Ronny left him, and Nathan watched as the bus driver exited the square and headed back towards the Inn.

The moment the tree had been placed in the center of the square, the crowd practically exploded with cheers. A rendition of "Oh Christmas Tree" broke out, and it didn't take long for the band to join in. After that came "The Twelve Days of Christmas" and a version of Nat King Cole's "The Christmas Song" followed that. *Sometimes I wonder if he was my namesake*, Nathan thought. Mother Sable had always loved his voice, after all.

Eventually, the band stopped playing, and the crowd, all sung out, began to disperse. It seemed to take hours, but the square quietened. Alex, as he left, met Nathan's eye and raised his hand. Nathan, however, bought a cup of coffee and found a bench that faced the newly positioned Angel Tree while keeping him somewhat hidden from the street. As if in time with each person leaving, the lights on the vendor tents began turning off as they packed up as well. Even the lantern in the center of the square was turned down until it was only a whisper of a flame.

Soon, Nathan was the only one left in the Square. *One day. And the Second Rite will happen right here.* He sipped the coffee. It was hot and strong and the paper cup helped to warm his hands. To him, the next step was obvious. With Alex out of the picture, at some point, the Angel would have to perform the Second Rite. *And this time, there would be nowhere to hide.* And now, he had more than just questions to ask. Whether it was here or somewhere else, the power would eventually find its way to the tree. From there, it should be a relatively simple matter to track the power back with his charm.

Are we really about to stake-out a Christmas tree?

"Looks that way," Nathan muttered, settling into the bench. He retrieved the river stones from his pocket and set to work floating them around his wrist.

All that was left now was the waiting.

✳

Alex dreamed of the town that night. The streets were abandoned, but there was somewhere he needed to be. He pushed down Main Street, the thick snowfall making it hard to keep on the sidewalk. A heavy wind cut across the road, buffeting a wall of snow into his face and shards of ice into his hands. They cut through his gloves and stung his hands, but did nothing to shake his grip on the item he held. He kept pushing forward. There was somewhere he needed to be.

The streetlights were all out, their power slaughtered by the blizzard. Alex could still see his way, thanks to the lanterns hanging outside most of the buildings. They swung wildly in the wind, but their flames didn't go out.

That was important, but he wasn't sure why.

Because they couldn't go out. No matter what, they couldn't go out. Each one carried lives. Each flame was an innocent's flame.

In his hands, he cradled a snow globe. It was one he had taken from the Archive. J. C. The snow globe that showed the town.

He had to take it somewhere. That was where he needed to be.

A sudden jolt of fear pushed Alex into the small alleyway between the ice cream shop and the antiques store. He couldn't be seen. He had forgotten, or maybe he'd never remembered it at all. But he couldn't be seen, not with the snow globe.

After all, he was a thief.

That was right. He had stolen it. From where. The Archive. That was where. Where else?

Once he was certain that no one could see him, Alex braced himself and stepped back into the blizzard. He couldn't tell where he was headed, the wind was too strong, the snow too thick. But he kept moving, sure in his heart that whatever direction he was headed was the one he needed to go.

✳

The night quickly grew cold, and Nathan was glad for the hat he'd purchased. As the time moved on, the temperature continued to drop and the snowfall turned to white sheets. Gossamer moonlight managed to push through the hazy clouds, blanketing the square in pale, ghostly light. With each shift of the minute hand, the shadows appeared to shift as well. At first, the vendor tents built black shapes across the square. These fell, eclipsed by a distorted shape created by the clock tower. Finally, the lantern, with its flame reduced to barely a whisper, threw reflecting motes of light all around itself.

Nathan was tempted to stand, to stretch out his legs, and to pace the square. *But the key to any good stakeout is to stay put.* He didn't know what he was looking for, but he had a feeling he'd know it when he saw it. *The impossible was like that. At least, if you had the wit to recognize it.*

Tomorrow, the tree would be lit, and, if Nathan was right, the Timber Angel would be shown the way to the Third Rite, but the legend was very specific. *Well, it was specific about its lack of specificity.*

There were dates written next to each Rite, but there were no times.

Which meant, now that the tree was here, the Angel could perform the Second Rite at any time starting at midnight. Which, to Nathan, made his place here, on this bench, in this square, until… something…happened. *No one said it was a glamorous life. Or a warm one, for that matter.*

A yawn of wind made Nathan shiver. It brought crystals of set snow across the square, but, aside from that, nothing moved. He checked his watch. It was already approaching midnight. *Time flies when you're having fun. That thought keeps coming back to me. Why is that?* Nathan felt a scratch on his wrist, and he knew what it was before he had even pulled the sleeve of his coat up.

The charms were dancing again. As before, the angel charm was leading the pull. Nathan stood, checked the direction, and saw that it was pulling out of the square, towards the Inn. Something clicked in Nathan's mind. *Alex. It's going after Alex.* Instinctively, he stepped in that direction but then stopped himself. *Bait. It could just be bait. To get me out of the square.*

Nathan sighed. There was nothing for it. And, if there was one thing Nathan Cole couldn't stand, it was being manipulated.

✳

The trees surrounding the Gift Field were all dead. Gray and scarred, they looked as if they'd been burned by a fire that had long since died out. Alex began to run. Time was running out. He had to get. Somewhere. He didn't know. But he had to be somewhere. The memories. They were somewhere. Out there.

A gale of wind, full of sleet and slush and ice, swept across the field, and Alex dropped to his knees. He crawled forward, each meter cutting into his hands and knees. He crawled and stumbled and crawled some more. The field seemed to stretch forever. Finally, Alex forced his head upwards, blocking the wind from his eyes with his arms. The center of the field was just ahead.

The wind died, just for a moment. The giant had taken a breath. The snow cleared enough for Alex to make out a shape in the center of the field.

He didn't understand.

It was an urn. Inside, its stem coated in thorns the color of boiling tar, lay a single white rose.

✳

The charms led him out of Calbot Square and down Main Street, towards the Inn. There were no lights on in any of the windows. Only the moonlight showed his path. He followed the footpath around the Inn, cut through the patio, and went out the gate. There was the stone bridge, and, at its boundary, sat the statue, once again with its hood pulled back.

She had become like no woman he'd ever seen. Gone was the high-blooded beauty, and the softness to the cheek and mouth. There was a cruel, unnatural curl to the lip and a hardness to the eyes that transcended the stone. Though she didn't move, the statue watched him through her stone eyes. Nathan was sure of that.

"Whatever you are," Nathan said aloud, his voice clear and stern, his hands tightly closed. "You've made your first mistake. There's still time for you to make it right."

As if in response, the electric light above the statue exploded into darkness, leaving only the dim glow of its lantern.

Nathan scoffed. *I've never been one to be afraid of the dark.*

Slowly and smoothly, he walked past the statue.

Make your move then. Let's get on with it.

The statue didn't move, however. It made no sign whatsoever that it had heard him. Or that it cared about what he had to say. Across the bridge, Nathan looked back at it. The hood was back how it had been, covering the statue's face. The charms rattled at his wrist, first towards the statue, and then towards the Ashford house. He doubted very much that he'd scared it, but one thing had become clear. The Timber Angel knew who he was, and the Timber Angel wanted to scare him.

He rushed up to the Ashford house. It was a handsome two story dwelling, with cottage windows, clean shutters, and tall trellises. As with the rest of Timber's Edge at two in the morning, the upstairs lights were all off. However, a light still sat on in the living room. *Probably left on by accident.* Nathan considered the trellis nearest Alex's room. *It could hold me. Maybe.* But then what? Knock on his window? Ask to be let in?

He strained his ears, but could hear nothing. Soon, it came to him. The low tolling of the Angel Bell. Nathan considered the direct approach of breaking down the door, but he wasn't even sure Alex was actually in danger. *Don't play the hand too hard.*

Nathan struck the door in three sharp knocks.

A voice boomed from inside the house. "What the he—"

The back door opened, and Paul Ashford stood at the doorway. They stood, staring at each other, Paul in a bathrobe and pajamas, Nathan with his charms straining against their chain. He pulled down his sleeve.

"Mr. Ashford," Nathan said stiffly. "I need to talk to Alex. Just for a minute."

"For crying out loud…you know what time it is?"

Nathan brought himself to his full height. "I think he's in danger. I need you to go find Alex. Can you do that for me?" Nathan hoped the urgency in his voice was clear. For the briefest moment, he was prepared for Paul to block his path.

That won't be pretty for you, Mr. Ashford.

Paul Ashford stepped aside. "Wait inside," he growled, but his icy blue eyes had cultivated an urgent fire.

✳

A woman wearing a white dress trimmed with gray fur appeared from the far side of the field. At his distance, Alex couldn't make out her features. As she approached, she alternated between floating and walking. Her hair, falling to her shoulders in mahogany rivers, seemed to be unaffected by the wind. Her kind almond eyes watched him, welcomed him.

Her entire being radiated warmth. The closer she came, the more the wind fell back, and the warmer Alex felt.

Who are you?

The woman smiled at him as if she could hear his thought.

"Alex," her voice was a whisper, but he could hear it as if it were being spoken directly into his ear. "You know who I am. I'm the Timber Angel. Your Timber Angel."

*

Inside, there was an impressive living room with an L-shaped sectional, a crackling fire, and the TV was playing *It's a Wonderful Life*. Jimmy Stewart was dancing in a gymnasium. A large modern kitchen sat opposite. Two cups of tea were sitting next to the sink.

"Alex!" Paul's voice called from upstairs. Nathan heard the sound of knocking on a door.

"What is going on—" A familiar woman's voice said from the other side of the living room. Julianna's eyes widened at the sight of Nathan. Her voice shook when she asked. "What are you doing here?"

"Alex!" Paul called again.

That's our cue.

To Julianna, Nathan raised a hand. "Hold that thought, would you?"

He dashed up the stairs, taking them two at a time. He charged down the small hallway and came up at a door that Paul was standing beside.

"I can't open it," Paul said, worry heightening his voice. "It's locked."

Nathan squared up to the door and ran his left hand over it. From under his sleeve, he felt the charms scratching his wrist. The door was cold to the touch and a thin layer of frost covered the metal hinges. "It's not locked. It's stuck."

What are you doing?" Paul asked.

"Forcing the issue," Nathan said. He hammered on the door, hard. No response. He glanced up at Paul Ashford and gave a good-natured shrug.

Then he stepped back, braced his legs, and slammed his shoulder into the door. There was a crack before the wood frame splintered easily, and the door fell out of its frame.

"Are you out of your—"

"Bill me," Nathan replied, pushing the door free. It fell to the floor with a thud, and Nathan stomped over it.

His eyes darted quickly over the room, Alex's inner sanctum, but they froze when they came to the figure lying prone in the bed. Alex's face was pale, paler than usual. His eyes were open, forced into a blank stare. *Shit.* It was just like DeMarco.

"Alex!" Paul cried from behind him.

Nathan wasn't paying attention. He was already at Alex's bedside, examining him.

Paul shook Alex by the shoulders. "Wake up!" When Alex didn't respond, his father rounded on Nathan. "What's happening?" A realization dawned on him. "You. You did this."

Nathan couldn't keep the sarcastic snap at bay. "Oh *that* makes perfect sense. Can't possibly have anything to do with your local Angel, right?"

Paul fell silent, and then another shadow appeared in the door frame.

"Alex!" Julianna called. She broke into the room as well, then glared at Nathan. "Do something!"

"I am working on it," Nathan replied with a sharp bite. "Now. Give me room to work."

✳

The woman smiled at Alex, then pointed farther into the field. "Keep going Alex. You'll find what you're looking for. Who you're looking for." She took his hands in hers and wrapped her fingers around the snow globe. "Who that belongs to. He needs it. You understand, don't you?"

Alex understood. Of course he did. It was all so clear now. He pushed forward into the field. Something shifted. Like the Earth turning on an axis, and Alex lost his footing.

From behind him, he heard a sound like a hiss. He turned.

The woman was still there, but a sad, regretful look had crossed her face.

"I think our time is being cut short," she said.

In an instant, she crossed the space between them. Leaned down. And whispered something into his ear.

The words, they brought tears to his eyes, but he couldn't cry. The tears, they just froze on his cheeks.

*

Nathan pulled the silver chain off of his wrist and draped it over Alex's head, tying it off so that it hung like a necklace. He held his breath, waited a moment.

"What are you doing?" one of them asked.

Details like that no longer mattered. Nathan studied Alex's wide open eyes, looking for some sign of life. *Come on.*

Nathan glanced up at them. "Creating interference," he kept his voice steady, but inside he felt his pulse rising, felt his anger growing. *I'm not losing him. Not like this.* "A powerful psychic force has taken hold of Alex. Invaded his mind. Three guesses on what."

"Maybe he's just asleep."

Nathan's voice became a sharp thorn. "Does he look asleep? To either of you?" He turned his ring on his finger. The chain was weak silver, but the ring, his ring was pure. Pure silver was more powerful.

Don't even think about it. You'd be defenseless.

"I need silver," Nathan said. He stood, saw that Julianna was still there. *Good. That was good.* He scooped Julianna's hands into his. No rings, but a mark where one had been. "You've got rings, yes?

Bracelets?"

Her eyes were wide and afraid. "Yes, but not—not here."

Paul glanced at them, his voice trembling, he said, "I know where there's some."

Nathan's voice became a whip. "Then go! Now! Like your son's life depends on it!"

Paul ran out of the room, his footfalls crashing down the stairs. Nathan heard him call to Maddie, telling her to stay in her room.

"Keep her out of here," Nathan told Julianna.

At that moment, she was no mayor. She offered no challenge and left without a word.

Nathan hovered over Alex. "Come on Alex. Don't listen to it." He shot a quick glance at the door, saw that he was alone, then slapped Alex across the face.

Alex's pupils moved.

Nathan took Alex by the shoulders and shook him. The pupils moved a bit more and the eyelids threatened to blink. He lifted the body—for Alex wasn't in residence—and turned it onto the floor. He turned the body back over so that he could see the eyes, but Nathan recoiled as soon as he'd touched Alex's skin. Alex's body had turned cold, bitterly cold, to the touch. To Nathan's horror, crystals of ice had appeared over his fingertips, and a spiderweb of frost had settled into his hair.

Whatever it is, it's fighting back. I'm losing him.

Paul's heavy footfalls stomped back up the stairs.

"I need that silver now!" Nathan shouted.

Paul shoved something into his hand, "Here." It was a silver bracelet with a bouquet of charms attached. Paul noticed Alex's face. His voice turned wet with fear, "No, no."

Nathan tried to put the bracelet on, but it was a woman's bracelet, and Alex's hand didn't fit.

For fuck's sake.

With a shake of his head, Nathan forced the bracelet around the last four fingers of Alex's hand and held it there. *The contact should be enough.*

He pressed his left hand just above Alex's wrist, so that his ring was touching Alex's skin. Nathan shut his eyes and concentrated. He was no true psychic, but he had a glimmer.

In the darkness, a glimmer can be enough.

Alex began to spasm. His back arched and his legs kicked out. He sent the bed frame halfway across the room before Paul managed to hold his legs down. Alex's eyes began to blink. Rapidly. Unceasingly. He made a sucking sound, like trying to breathe through a straw.

"Is he dying?" Paul shouted. "What do we do?"

Nathan shook his head then met Paul's eyes. "You're not going to like this part." *Pain has a power all its own.* He slapped Alex again. Twice. Hard.

Finally, Alex took a great inhale, and fell back to the floor. Paul and Nathan shared a glance then, after a slow nod from Nathan, let up on their pressure. Alex sucked in great breaths of air, then started to cough. His eyes shut, then fluttered again, no longer fixed open, but now seeing them. The storm gray eyes darted between them, then finally, he coughed out a single question:

"W —Why does my face hurt?"

Chapter Nineteen

"You alright?" Nathan asked Alex. They were sitting at the kitchen table, Alex on a banquette and Nathan on the opposing chair. A cup of tea sat in front of Alex in a mug bearing the words *Santa's Favorite*. Julianna had taken the place at one head of the table. Paul was sitting in the seat nearest to her. Every few seconds, his eyes would dart to Alex, as if to check he was still awake. Alex was finding it difficult to concentrate. "Alex," Nathan said again, his voice firmer. "Are you with us?"

Alex's awareness snapped into place. "My face hurts," he said. "Aside from that, I'm fine, I think." The dream was still halfway in his head, like a memory he couldn't quite recall.

Nathan's smile was rueful. "Sorry about that," he replied. "But you weren't leaving us a lot of choice."

Alex looked down at the bracelet squeezed onto his right hand, just above the finger joints. The sight of it clawed at his guts. It was his mother's bracelet. "What happened?" A nervous spark passed around the table. "Guys, what happened?"

"You were asleep," his father said. "At least, I thought you were. You went to bed. You remember?"

Alex shook his head. "Not really. All I remember was being in the square." He looked down into the tea in front of him. "I remember the tree."

"You don't remember walking home?" Nathan asked. He looked troubled. "You're sure?"

Alex tried to remember, tried to fold his memories and force himself back to the square. He shook his head. "No. I don't remember."

Nathan rubbed his hand across his mouth, the silver of his ring twinkling in the light.

"We had to wa—" Paul started.

Nathan raised two fingers from his other hand and Alex's father fell silent.

Alex's throat dried. He had never seen his father silenced like that, not since the hospital.

Nathan leaned forward, his green eyes darting across Alex's face. "Tell us what you remember," he said, his voice as calm as a spring pond. "Take your time. Start from the beginning."

Alex felt his concentration drift again. He shook his head. "Sorry...I don't—"

Nathan reached a hand across the table and took Alex's wrist.

"May I?" Nathan asked.

The touch was warm but firm. Alex was struck by the strength in his fingers and the sureness of his grip, but also by its delicacy; it was like a glass rod connected them, and if Alex struggled, it would break.

Another nervous glance passed between Julianna and Paul. "What are you doing?" Julianna asked. "You're doing something."

Nathan shot her a sideways smile, but his gaze remained focused on Alex. "I'm not doing anything," he said. "It's all Alex. Now, Alex, try again. Slowly. Take it slowly."

This time, the memories came to him as easy as thinking. "I was dreaming, I think. About the town. I was running from something. Or to something. Sorry, I don't really remember."

"That's alright," Nathan said. His voice felt like a whisper, just for Alex. "Just tell me everything you remember."

*

"I'm sorry. That's everything," Alex said.

Not much to go on, Nathan thought.

Alex had no memory of leaving Calbot Square, and Alex's recollection of his dream was vague and far from complete. All he could remember was walking to the Gift Field with one of the snow globes. And a woman dressed in white.

"Come on Alex," Paul said. He put a large arm around his son's shoulder. "That's enough. You should rest."

Nathan started to say something, but a glare from Paul silenced him.

Don't push too hard.

Alex let himself be led away from the table. "Tomorrow," Alex said, turning back to Nathan. "You'll tell me what happened?"

"As far as I understand it," Nathan promised. *More or less.* The two of them went upstairs, leaving Julianna and Nathan alone at the table.

"Will you tell me what happened?" Julianna asked. "Or am I still a suspect?"

"Everyone's a suspect," Nathan replied. "And no, I won't tell you. Because it concerns Alex and I don't know what of himself he's shared with you." He sighed and suddenly felt tired.

Julianna turned earnest, but her voice stayed quiet. "You said it was a...psychic...force," she said.

"I did," Nathan replied. "And because it was, I now shoulder a burden you can't understand."

"Three questions," she pleaded. "That's all I ask. I'll tell you anything you want to know."

Despite himself, despite the thoughts turning around his mind, Nathan managed a smile. He shook his head. "Three questions," he said.

Julianna didn't hesitate. "Do you know who the Angel is? Who did this to him, I mean? Presuming it was the Angel."

Nathan shrugged then pushed himself away from the table. He waited before answering. The question cut more than he thought it would. "No," he said at last. He couldn't keep away the sadness, the worry, that crept into his voice. "I don't know."

She stood as well and came to face him. "I thought knowing is your business."

All Nathan could offer was a sad nod. "Every idea is more fanciful than the last. Each makes no more sense than the last." He noticed Maddie's puzzles, framed along the wall. "It's like I'm looking at two puzzles, at three, at four, all mixed together. The pieces from one might fit another, but the picture, it isn't coming together." He glanced at her. "I still don't know if it's you, to be honest."

Julianna's glare could've nailed a man to the wall. She didn't speak, but she pulled her hand back and, in a flash, slapped Nathan across the face. It hurt, but Nathan was more than accustomed to pain.

"That's for suggesting—again—that I would hurt Alex. Your question," she spat.

Over her shoulder, Nathan spotted a curious alcove of family pictures. He crossed over to it, and noticed Julianna react.

"What are you doing?" she asked. "It's family stuff."

That was an understatement, Nathan realized quickly. The alcove was full of pictures. Framed pictures, picture carousels, and even some photo books were all kept there. In most of them, he spotted the same woman. *Alex's mother.* She was beautiful. In one picture, she wore her mahogany hair short and, judging from her fitness, was more like a marine than a librarian.

Nathan could feel the daggers of Julianna's stare at his back, waiting for him to respond. He no longer cared. The game had changed in ways only Nathan understood.

Nathan's eyes darted to one of the photos. It was one of the more recent ones, judging from Alex's age. It had been taken in a hospital room. Alex was standing at the foot of the bed, facing the camera. There was a smile on his face, but his eyes looked pained. On the supporting table that hovered above the bed, a cake and candles was set. The woman on the bed was present, but she wasn't there.

At least, not all the way.

It was clear by the absent look in her eyes, and in the slackening of her jaw. The hospital gown swallowed her. On the bedside table were a variety of items to make it look like someone productive was in the room. A glasses case, a book, and a purse.

But there was little point in the charade, Nathan thought. Spread all over the table were bits of torn paper, from the book or from a napkin. *Almost like snow.*

At first, he wasn't sure why they would've taken this photo. Why they would've put it on display. But, then he realized it was because the picture had been part of her life, and this was their shrine to her, all of her. In the picture, Alex's mother's wrists had bindings on them.

He picked up the picture, rubbed a finger across the woman's face, then brought it to Julianna. "Why the straps?" Nathan asked at last.

Julianna took the photo, studied it. "You see that paper there." Julianna pointed to the bedside table. "She used to always be trying to give it to you, or anything else on that table, like the book or her glasses. It wasn't a good place for your coffee." Her voice dropped. "Sometimes it hurt her to do it too much. She had a fixation, they said. Something to do with the cancer. She had to be holding something, touching something. Alex couldn't even walk into the room without her wanting to hold his hand."

The detail slapped Nathan harder than Julianna's hand ever could. "You were there?"

"Is that a que—"

"Enough," his voice cracked through the room like a whip. "We're not sparring anymore," Nathan declared, his voice sharpening in an instant. "Whatever the Angel is. It wanted my attention, and it just tried to kill—or at the very least lobotomize—Alex to get it. Well, now it's got it; all of it. I can promise you it will be sorry that it did. Are you going to stand in my way?" Nathan smirked. "And yeah, those were two questions. Are you going to answer them?"

Julianna flared, and Nathan thought she was going to slap him again.

She sighed. "I was there," she said at last. "Anna—Alex's mother —she was a good friend of mine. A very good friend of mine."

"And Paul?"

"We're engaged," Julianna said simply. "I don't expect you to understand. I don't care if you understand."

Nathan's sideways smile returned. "Two lonely hearts can find peace in one another," he said. "Perhaps I understand better than you think."

Julianna's gaze narrowed, but when she spoke, her voice was softer. "Alex isn't happy about it."

"Shocking," Nathan deadpanned.

Julianna laughed, but there was little humor in it.

"Alex told me it was brain cancer."

Julianna pulled back in surprise. "She was diagnosed—I think—a few years before. But when she declined, it was fast. At the end, she wasn't herself."

Nathan nodded, but a thought had taken root. *If she wasn't herself, then who was she?*

"In what way?" he asked.

Julianna replaced the picture into the alcove. "After that was taken," Julianna said, her voice shaking, "a few hours after, she called Alex a 'nasty queer little cocksucker.' In *that* kind of way."

Oh Alex, I'm so sorry.

Nathan winced and his breath caught in his throat.

"She showed that...side...often?"

"Often enough." Julianna replied. "It wasn't her. We all knew —we all know that. But, it's not the sort of thing you forget. For obvious reasons, Maddie wasn't allowed in the room very often. At the end, Anna, she could turn quickly."

"They're sure it was cancer that killed her?"

She turned to him. "Why would you ask that?" She didn't wait for an answer. Her next question was bitten out before Nathan could even think about what to say, "Please, what happened to Alex?"

She cares about him. More than I thought. She was no suspect. She was as afraid as Paul.

Nathan spoke carefully. "I don't know precisely. You must understand, with these things, the more precise—the closer you get —the more dangerous they can become. It can be like cornering a dog. Or stumbling upon a mother bear in her den. What I will tell you is this: a psychic force invaded his mind, forced him to partake in some sort of vision, apparently for my benefit. I don't understand completely."

We do have some thoughts. He raised his hand, showed her his ring.

"Silver protects against many things. It's so prevalent that it's in a lot of folklore and religions. Some you might have heard of—the werewolf's silver bullet, for example—not all of those legends are true, of course, but the principle stands. Silver is a natural insulator against psychic forces. At least, against their ability to invade up here."

Nathan touched a finger to his temple before retrieving a stone out of his pocket floating it in front of her. There was a sharp intake of breath, but to Julianna's credit, she didn't flinch.

"Silver will do nothing to protect me against someone who can do this," Nathan continued. "This force is external. But, against the internal forces, like mind reading, silver is very effective, and the purer it is, the better."

"I bought it for her. As a gift the year we met," Julianna said. "Just the bracelet. She was always showing me a new little trinket one of the kids got her."

Nathan chuckled. "Then I bet it's very pure silver indeed."

Julianna blinked and a sad smile crossed her face. "I didn't know about her allergy, but she kept it and kept adding to it." She sighed. "That's the kind of person she was; if you gave her something, it stayed important."

An allergy to silver, Nathan mused. *In my line, that's a death sentence. You can never be sure what you might catch without an immune system.*

"My ring is pure silver as well." Nathan said. "My chain, not so much. It's enough in a pinch though." His voice darkened. "I can tell you this: the Timber Angel, whoever or whatever it is, thinks it's made a point, but not the one it thinks it's made. Whereas before, I may have stopped. I might have pulled back. But now, I won't stop until I find it. I won't stop. Not until it answers to me."

From the top of the stairs, Paul's voice spoke. It wasn't clear how much he'd heard, but, judging from the furrowed brow, it was probably enough.

"Nathan," he said. "Alex wants to talk to you. He says it can't wait."

Earlier, Nathan hadn't had time to examine Alex's room closely, but now he took his time, ignoring the shattered door that still lay on the floor. It was a young man's room, but one that probably hadn't been touched since high school. A small pile of comics sat on the otherwise tidy desk, the one Nathan had found earlier lay on top of the stack. Professor X's familiar shape was recognizable from across the room. The bed was made despite the commotion earlier, and the sheets were pulled snug and neat. In the center of the bed was a stuffed rabbit in a magician outfit.

"Nice." Nathan picked the rabbit up. It was well-handled but soft. Alex, who had been watching him from a seat in front of the desk, stood to take the toy out of his hands.

"Loopy," Alex said. "The magic rabbit. My mom got him for me at the state fair. Loopy can make stuff happen with his mind, you see."

Alex put him back on the bed.

"Charming," Nathan replied with a grin which died as soon as he noticed the red marks on Alex's cheeks. "You should be resting."

Alex shrugged. "I'm not feeling super tired."

"What is it you wanted to talk to me about? What couldn't wait?"

Alex rolled his eyes, and Nathan noticed another collection of pictures at the end of the room, stuck into the edges of a mirror on top of the dresser. They were all candids of Alex and other people. There were some high school photos, and some selfies of him with another guy about his age. The other guy was Asian and in good shape. One of them looked like it had been taken at a gym, and the look in their eyes looked a bit too romantic for them to be just friends. Nathan smiled and kept scanning.

"That...dream..."

"Don't worry about it," Nathan said. "It was just a dream. You need to rest."

"Bullshit."

"The dream part, yes. The rest part, no," Nathan replied.

Alex closed the distance. "You don't get to tell me that. I deserve to know what's happening."

Nathan glanced away from the pictures. "Maybe I'm trying to protect you."

"Maybe I don't need protection," Alex shot back.

"I don't share your confidence," Nathan replied.

His eyes jumped back to the pictures and came across one of a younger Alex holding an orange cat. Nathan was about to move on, but then he snapped back, back to what he saw in Alex's arms. The orange cat. It looked just like the one he'd seen outside.

"Oh, I didn't know he was yours," Nathan said, pointing at the picture.

"You saw Tolkien?" Alex asked.

Nathan chuckled at the name. *Guess it really is a house of literature professors.*

"Yeah, I've seen him a few times." He checked again. "Same cat. Same little book charm too. At least I think it was. Cute touch, by the way. He's a fast little devil."

Alex's face fell into a concerned frown. "That'd be a neat trick," Alex said.

"Why?"

"Tolkien died Nathan," he replied, his voice quiet. "In my arms, about two years after that photo was taken."

What?

Nathan's voice trembled, "What did you say?"

"Tolkien died," Alex repeated. "He was like twenty-five or something. Are you okay?"

The axis of the world shifted under his feet. Dozens of pieces fell into place. One after another, each one worse than the last.

When someone Projects, they populate. I would've populated as well. Just like them. Just like all of them.

With a shaking hand, Nathan reached inside his jacket, and pulled out the TransAmerica ticket voucher that Ronny had given him. His eyes darted over its face, and his stomach dropped when he came to the route number: 621416. Nathan blinked, and the numbers rearranged: 661124. Sixty-six years. Eleven months. Twenty-four days.

The only message I'd always send myself.

He allowed the ticket to fall to the floor.

With a sharp intake, Nathan began desperately scanning the other pictures, but didn't look at Alex. "You said you needed to see me about something." The intensity crept into his voice. "What was it Alex?"

There were more pictures. Alex running on a track. At his graduation. Standing in front of a car. *Look for the cracks.*

Nathan turned, faced Alex directly, and fired off a cannonball question. "What did you need to tell me?"

Alex stepped back, concerned at Nathan's raised voice. "The woman, in the dream…She said something to me." He shook his head. "I'm not sure exactly, it's hard to remember, but I thought you should know. No, I *needed* to tell you."

It was Nathan's turn to close the distance.

We need to leave Nate. Right now.

Nathan considered running through the open doorway, but— *dammit Nate!*—he had to know.

"What did she say to you?"

Alex seemed unable to speak, unsure of what to say.

"Alex!" Nathan hissed. "Please!"

"I don't understand it—"

"You don't need to," Nathan said. "You're not supposed to."

Pieces are falling. They're tumbling now. Get out Nate.

Nathan brought his hands under his lips then raked them through his hair. He checked his watch, stared at the second hand and waited. It didn't move.

We're in trouble Nate.

Finally, he turned, and once again faced the mirror. What he saw stopped the words in his mouth, froze the breath in his lungs.

In the mirror there lived the hooded statue.

Too late. Much too late.

Nathan swallowed. "Alex. Do you see it?"

Alex's reflection crossed into the mirror, straight through the statue.

Nathan watched as he turned and looked around.

"See what?"

"What did she tell you Alex? I need you to tell me. Right now."

"It was just that—I mean, she said—"

Just then, the vertigo assaulted Nathan. Even as he tried to resist, he felt his will slipping.

Alex's voice was like a pronouncement from the heavens. "She said: 'Tell the little thorn I prefer the direct approach as well.'"

At that, the charms around Nathan's wrist began to rattle and pull. Nathan stumbled forward and fell to his knees. The Slip had full hold of him now, and Nathan brought his full power to resist it, even though he knew it was hopeless. Nathan was aware of Alex standing over him, aware of words he could no longer understand, aware of a touch he could no longer truly feel.

We're not going out like this. Push!

The tide, it receded for a moment. A fire, deep in Nathan's gut, came to life. With a growl, he scrambled with his hands across the floor, and then something took them. It was Alex. Nathan grabbed his shirt, tight.

"It's a trap Alex," he sputtered. The pain, a thousand hot needles, plunged into his brain. "It's not real. The Angel. All of it. It's all just a trap!" Nathan didn't even know if he was speaking words, let alone English.

Dark spots appeared at the side of his vision. Within moments, they clouded his eyesight until all he could see was Alex's horrified face. "You need to focus…for it to work."

Finally, the tide returned, and, this time, there would be no resistance. Nathan had none left to offer.

His vision swam and then turned black. He was aware of falling, but beyond that, all that remained was oblivion.

PART THREE

FRIDAY, DECEMBER 23RD - SATURDAY, DECEMBER 24TH

"When studying such things, one must always account for collateral damage."

The Holding Associate's Handbook

Chapter Twenty

The furnace was a desert. *Or was it the other way around.* Either way, it didn't matter. To Nathan's parched throat and blistered skin, both ways were frustratingly true. They were fifty miles outside of Beatty, Nevada, and well into Death Valley. Marie stood by his side, but, unlike Nathan, she didn't seem to be having trouble with the heat. Together they were watching the taillights of a family's SUV inch farther and farther away. Between them and the road was a red pentagram, and, in its center, was the skeleton of an old bird.

The Shade hadn't gone easily. A patch of dried blood sat in Nathan's hair, and Marie was pale and weak on her feet.

No, not Marie. She shouldn't be here.

A gust of wind kicked up dust which tore at the red pentagram. If this had been fifteen minutes earlier, Nathan would've been concerned for the seal's integrity. But this wasn't fifteen minutes earlier, and the ritual had already been completed. The spirit had been safely removed from the boy. It was trapped in the skeleton while the boy was safely tucked into the back seat of his family car. Within a few hours, they would be back in Las Vegas. A day after that, they'd be back in Minnesota.

"Good day's work," Nathan said.

"Good day's work," Marie agreed. She pointed to the skeleton. "Are you going to get that?"

You didn't say that. Mother Sable did.

The ritual had gone well enough, but he still didn't want to go near the skeleton. Academically, he knew it was safe, or, as safe as these things got.

"I'd rather not," Nathan replied, but he moved towards it regardless. The distance was perhaps twenty feet, but the walk felt like it lasted an hour. A fresh wave of sweat poured down his back and arms. He rubbed his forehead against the sleeve of his so-called moisture-wicking t-shirt.

The bird's dead face was pointed towards the ground. Somehow, that made it easier.

Another blow of wind scratched his face and chipped at the pentagram. The bird's head fell off of the skeleton and clattered to the ground. It stared up at him from the dirt. Something wet slapped against his cheek.

"Nathan," Marie called from behind him. "Try not to panic." She sounded so far away. Too far away. He looked back, and she was standing in the right place, covering her eyes with one hand. Another wet thing hit his cheek. He touched his hand to his face and his fingers came back wet and soaked.

And covered in blood.

"Try not to panic," she said again. But her voice had changed. It had dulled, like the way a vinyl record did when it didn't spin at full speed. Despite Marie's words, a panic gripped Nathan's temples, drilled into them, and flowered into pain.

His legs. Why did his legs hurt?

Because that happens when a car crashes into a ravine.

He fell to his knees for there was no way to stand. His hand touched the hot desert floor, but it wasn't hot at all. Instead it was cold, wet, and smooth. Nathan could taste his heart in the back of his throat. Could taste its tortured beating. He looked at the sky and wanted to scream.

A black hole, cut jaggedly into the sky, hovered in the middle of the sky. Out of it, rain began to pour.

Not the rain. Please, not the rain.

It pelted his face. Frozen rain, the sort that was too thick for summer and too thin for the coldest time of winter.

"The torch. It's yours to carry. The next time we see each other, we'll be swimming through galaxies," Marie's, but not Marie's, voice called. In one moment, it sounded like she was standing right next to him. The next, she could've been calling from the top of the nearest mountain.

Then the sky erupted into Nathan's head. The desert vanished, replaced by groaning metal and drumming rain. In the space where Nathan had traveled to, there was no sight, just an impossible wall of blackness.

There was no sight.

But there was sound.

And there was pain.

Chapter Twenty-One

"Nathan!" Alex shouted. "Wake up!"

Nathan was lying on his back, his face turned upward and watching the ceiling with a blank, endless stare. His face was darkened by a heavy frown and an angry sneer. Is that what I looked like? When the Angel had taken me?

That's what Nathan had said, before his eyes had become glass. It was the Angel. He had sounded so sure, so desperate, and in such terrible pain. At the same time, he'd said something that chilled Alex to his core. Something Alex still didn't understand: It's not real. It's all a trap.

"Alex?" Maddie's voice came from the doorway. Her voice trembled and her eyes were wide. "Is everything okay?"

Alex inhaled sharply. "Yeah, Mads. I'm fine. Everything's going to be fine."

"Is that Nathan? Is he okay?"

"Yeah, he'll be fine," Alex said. He crossed the room and took her arms in his hands. "I need you to go find Dad or Julianna. And stay downstairs until one of us comes to get you. Can you do that for me?"

After a frightened nod, she left the room and before long, her light steps were replaced by his father's heavy footfalls.

Paul cursed when he entered the room. "Not him too?"

Alex looked up at his father. "I don't know what to do. He said it was the Angel, then he just collapsed." It was difficult to focus.

Thoughts weren't arriving like they normally did, leaving his mind barren. "Dad? What should I do?"

With a grim smile, Paul Ashford stepped forward.

"We can try his strategy," he said, rolling up the sleeve of his bathrobe. He was about to slap Nathan when Alex pulled his arm back. "What's wrong?"

"The ring. His ring," Alex said.

He pointed to Nathan's finger where a thin plume of smoke had appeared over the silver ring. There was a sputter and a hiss, not unlike the sound of frying bacon. Alex touched the ring, but immediately pulled his hand back with another curse.

"It's hot," Alex said. "Really hot."

"Should we take it off?" Paul asked.

Alex shook his head. "Nathan said silver is protection, didn't he? Maybe he needs it."

*

Nathan's hands were freezing. So were his cheeks. The feeling returned, and his entire body felt frozen. He woke with a start and almost fell off of the bench.

This isn't good.

He was in Calbot Square, facing the Angel Tree. Precisely as he had been before he'd gone to the Ashford house. Had he actually gone? He took a step forward and felt the snow crunch beneath his feet.

It feels real enough, but then it always does. Nathan checked his watch, and the second hands weren't moving. But then, they hadn't been moving in Alex's room.

So I'm Projecting. What does that get us?

Nathan paced the square. Once he'd completed a circuit, he stepped back onto the street. The heavy snow made it hard to see.

The streets were already coated; so, too, were the lines of parked cars. There were no people, save for himself. There was no sign of life at all, except for the lanterns that hung from the stores and restaurants and homes that ran down Main Street. Their flickering flames were the only source of light. Above and beyond their reach was only inky blackness, for there were no stars and no moon in the sky. The empty street, lit by simple lanterns and surrounded by pitch black, was all there was.

Nathan followed the lanterns down the street. As he passed each one, it blinked out, leaving only one way forward. He had the distinct sense he was being watched, being observed. That was fine by him.

Let them watch.

At the end of the street, where the buildings fell away, the lanterns continued, hanging from stakes set on the sides of the road. They led him off of Main Street and towards one of the bridges. He was being taken to the Gift Field, he realized after a moment.

The river beneath the bridge raged. It was churning and frothing. Steam coiled off the water's surface, so bitterly cold was the surrounding air. Nathan hesitated at the bridge, closed and opened his fists, then stepped onto the stone. Each step he took with care, trying not to slip, and half-expecting the stone to collapse beneath his feet. At the far side of the bridge, Nathan let out a breath he didn't realize he had been holding.

It was then, a burning pain erupted on his index finger. Nathan examined his hand and saw the silver ring on his index finger starting to glow in the night.

"Having some trouble?" he asked aloud, keeping his voice steady despite the pain. "You'll have a hard time breaking into my mind. Harder time removing the ring, as it happens. I've seen to that."

A voice like frost spoke directly into his ears. "I can always remove the hand."

Go ahead and try. Nathan simply shrugged and continued forward.

With each step, the pain in his finger grew worse. *It's a powerful presence, that much is certain. Treading carefully might be our best option.*

"I was told you wanted to speak to me, so what's the hesitation? Too scared to see me face-to-face? Hiding behind whispers and tricks?"

Or we can taunt it. Good plan.

The voice gave no response, so Nathan continued. "Here's one theory," he said as he followed the path around the edge of the forest. "The Timber Angel is a fiction, one you've invented. It's the sweet nectar on the edge of a pitcher plant. Timber's Edge is a psychic construct, a bear trap for psychics. You invite them in, get them good and lost, and they don't realize they're trapped until it's much too late. By then, their minds are jelly."

Nathan crossed the border into the Gift Field, and saw a small shape in the center of the field.

"I take it that's for my benefit? You shouldn't have." As he got close enough to make out the shape of a vase, Nathan realized what he would see. The pain on his finger began to feel as if his ring were made of molten metal. *All part of the plan, I imagine. Pain, after all, can be quite the distraction. All kinds of pain.*

The flower was a white rose and the thorns on its stem were all black. It looked like they'd been painted, but Nathan knew that wasn't the case. He appraised the vase for a moment, and, then, in a flash of deliciously satisfying anger, kicked it deeper into the Gift Field as a thousand shattered pieces. The flower didn't make it as far. This, Nathan crushed under his boot with a single clean step.

"Going back to our theory, it does have its flaws," Nathan called in a clear, strong voice. His fists were in tight balls, but his voice remained steady. "For example, it wouldn't explain what exactly created the construct or what's maintaining it. And, if you were a presence strong enough to create a construct like this, then you would have no need for a fiction like the Timber Angel.

"So here's another theory: Timber's Edge is a shared psychic construct, a place that both gives and takes from the minds that connect to it. Since it has a history, I'd even venture to guess that it's been around for some time. I suspect the construct resonates with like minds and invites them in. But you, the so-called Timber Angel. You are just a parasite. A stalking, pathetic, parasite."

Nathan turned and felt his face turn into a grim smile. There was the hooded figure. In one pale hand, it held a lantern; its skin was mottled and gray. It floated a few feet off of the ground, right at the border of the Gift Field.

You took your time.

Nathan squared up and called to it, "How am I doing so far?"

✳

They tried everything. They slapped him. They pushed him. They poured ice water on his face. They forced him to stand. But nothing changed. Nathan remained a dead weight, totally unconscious. Only his ring seemed to have any life. It remained hot to the touch.

"Maybe there's nothing we can do," Paul suggested. "Maybe it's up to him."

"That's not what you said he did for me. Besides, does that sound like Nathan?" Alex asked. "He's a goddamn know-it-all."

And Nathan had known what was happening. You need to focus for it to work, he had said. It had been the last thing he had said. Probably the most important thing of all. The question was: what did Alex need to focus on?

Alex began searching Nathan's pockets, pulling his hands in and out of the red wine overcoat.

"Alex," Paul said. "What are you doing?"

"Looking for something," Alex replied.

He pulled out the polished stones, the same ones he'd seen floating around Nathan's head. He pulled out a simple flip cell phone—I knew he had one, Alex thought as he put it aside, but the mirror wasn't there.

Without another word, he took off and sprinted down to the guest house. He ran into the bedroom, pulled Nathan's bag onto the bed. Before he could start digging through it, he spotted the mirror sitting on top of the desk, the one Nathan had used to bring them to Anchor. This must be it, Alex thought.

"What...what is that?" Paul asked when Alex returned. While he'd been gone, the only change had been that the skin around Nathan's ring had turned red and blistered.

"It's a—actually, I don't really know," Alex admitted. "But it can help him. At least, I think it can."

Alex rubbed a finger over the surface of the mirror. All he could see was his reflection, precisely as it should have appeared. There was no corridor, no strange sense of vertigo.

"Goddammit," Alex cursed.

His father was staring at him with a look that combined awe and grave concern.

"I've not gone insane," Alex assured him. "Well, I don't think I have."

The English professor returned. "Then what's supposed to happen?"

"It took us somewhere," Alex tried to explain. "Nathan has a friend there. One I think can help him."

Paul's brow furrowed, "Us? Took us? Past tense?"

"He, uh, showed it to me. A few days ago," Alex said sheepishly.

"You sure he did—"

"He didn't drug me," Alex interrupted. "Now, let's try it with Nathan in the mirror. Maybe it needs him to work."

Without waiting for his father's response, Alex lay down on the floor next to Nathan. He held the mirror up, directly above them, just as Nathan had on the couch.

"You just need to focus," Alex whispered. He screwed up his face, tried to clear his mind of any thoughts other than the mirror and Anchor.

He let go of the mirror.

And it floated above them.

"Alex..."

"Dad," Alex said with a confidence he didn't truly feel. "We'll be fine. I promise. Just—keep an eye out."

The corridor appeared in the mirror, just as it had before. Alex—the other Alex—was standing alone. Then came the sense of vertigo, the sense of falling, and Alex found himself standing in the strange corridor staring back through the full length mirror. There he lay, apparently asleep next to Nathan.

At the end of the corridor there was no longer a cloth barrier, but instead a wooden door with a heavy iron lock. Alex didn't waste time thinking. He crossed the corridor quickly to reach the door, but hesitated at the handle. It was then Alex made a fatal mistake. He did what Nathan warned him never to do.

He looked up.

There was no ceiling to the corridor. Instead, where the ceiling might have been, the corridor simply opened to a sort of dark infinity. There were swirling stars and something that might have been a black hole. But, far worse, were the things moving across the darkness. They both did and didn't have a shape. Alex recognized what might have been a head, but it was attached to too many bodies. Or the bodies that should have had arms had other bodies instead. The things, they didn't move, they writhed. They pulsed and they slithered. So foreign were their movements, Alex found it impossible to follow them, let alone understand them.

The longer he looked, the more he found himself unable to look away. Finally, one of them, or one part of them—it was impossible to say—noticed him. There was a flash of purple eyes, hundreds of them, each of them like sharpened teeth. A blinding pain erupted into Alex's head. All thought disappeared, and he found himself lost in a universe of those horrible eyes. Strange sounds, whispers without words, became all he could hear.

It seemed to last forever until a slamming sound silenced the whispers. For a moment, Alex thought he was deaf or even dead. He became aware he was lying on his back. At some point, he had fallen. A familiar face appeared in his view. It was a little girl, one he couldn't place. Her eyes were the color of oil and a twinge of amusement played at her mouth.

"Alex Ashford," she said. "Whatever are you doing in a place like this?"

*

"So which is it?" Nathan asked. "Ghost of Christmas Yet to Come, Death, or the Timber Angel? I have to say, I'm starting to become confused."

The hooded figure maintained its position, but the voice returned to his mind. "Perhaps I am all three, but I am no parasite."

Nathan scoffed. "Nice try. That cryptic shit might work on Alex, but it will not be working on me. When he saw you, he said you took the form of a woman. I've seen you do the same thing."

The hooded figure raised one of its rotting hands to the hood of the robe and pulled it back. Beneath was the same face that Nathan had seen before, the same cruel smile and high cheekbones. Now, however, he recognized it. After all, he'd just seen pictures of her. In those pictures, she had been beautiful, with a kind face and expressive eyes. But the cheekbones were the same, and the shape of the mouth was the same as well.

Alex's mother.

Nathan felt his fingernails press into the palms of his hands. "You hurt two innocents to get to me. Now you're wearing Alex's mother's face. You might come to regret that." Nathan steadied his heart rate, tried to control his burning anger.

The Angel floated towards him, the snow swirling in its wake. "You think Alex is innocent? I've known him all of his life."

Nathan lifted his hand. The ring was glowing like a star on his finger.

"He's not the one trying to break into my mind at this very minute."

The Angel cocked its head and the pain vanished like it had never been there.

"You see?" it said. "I am just trying to protect him. I make no apologies for it, and I never will."

"You've got a funny way of protecting him. If it weren't for me, he'd be just like Mr. DeMarco."

The Angel considered the statement then bowed its head. "I could think of no other way to draw your attention," it conceded.

"I'm supposed to believe you're all peace and goodwill to mankind, is that it?" Nathan sneered at it. "Sorry, I'm just not buying it. What do you really want?"

"I want you to understand," it said.

Nathan felt a needle of doubt. "Understand what?"

"That I'm trying to free him. If you had only one chance to free yourself from an endless prison, would you trust chance? Or in one's good nature? Or would you try force the issue?"

Nathan said nothing. *Desperate times can call for desperate measures.*

"I already know your answer, Nathan Cole. It's written in those crushed petals and that shattered vase. I know that you, of all the beings ever to come to Timber's Edge, can understand."

Nathan ignored the taunt. *There's a bigger question at play.*

"Free from what? From Timber's Edge?" Nathan asked.

The Angel nodded and raised a hand. In a swirl of wind and

snow, the field around them changed. They were standing in the middle of a full size gingerbread village. Cinnamon and nutmeg and clove filled the air, and the taste of sugar and molasses rested on the wind. Icing shingles coated the roofs of each building, and chimneys made of enormous gumdrops somehow spat sweet-smelling smoke into the air. Ghostly people roamed around the village, wearing heavy coats and scarves. They looked like they had stepped out of a history book from the turn of the twentieth century.

The Angel gestured around them. "Yes, free from Timber's Edge. Free from the prison he has built himself."

Timber's Edge. We're Projecting to be here, and if Alex built it, then it's likely a dream. Only one type of mind could build a dreamscape like this. Alex... Why didn't you tell me?

Nathan grimaced. "It's a dream," he said. The words hung between them like frozen glass.

The Timber Angel lowered its head in a slight nod.

"Alex doesn't know what he is, does he?"

The Angel led him around the village, and continued its explanation, "Over the years, I've watched, nothing more than a statue. Unable to touch. Only able to witness. Alex comes every year, and every year he comes closer, but he has never had the courage to reach for the Three Rites."

The Angel's face changed in a glow of light. No longer was it Alex's mother. Now, it wore the unfamiliar form of a man with a hook-shaped nose. A long scar cut down the left side of his face.

Another Angel. Nathan frowned. *Why would there be more than one? Are they all people Alex knew?*

Nathan thought of the snow globes, all the nameplates, but not all the initials were visible. "And who's this?"

"Memories," the Angel replied, the man's voice harsh like a winter storm. "What else is this place but Memories? You know that well enough, don't you?"

"Alex's memories?"

The Angel considered the question, before conceding, "I do not know. As each year passed, I became stronger. More...defined. My thoughts became more clear. I began to be able to alter things, to make small changes, but only this year was I strong enough to make him finally take the Rites on his shoulders. If he will ever escape, if he will ever wake, then Alex needs to complete the Third Rite."

Nathan hesitated before speaking slowly, "If he does, the dream will end. If you're bound to it, then you'll die."

"Yes," The Angel admitted. The man's dark eyes blazed. "But Alex will be free, free to be who he was meant to be, and I will finally be able to fade. He won't need the protection any longer. He won't need Timber's Edge."

Nathan remembered an old cartoon he'd seen as a boy. It was a Disney cartoon featuring Donald Duck's nephews, reliving Christmas Day over and over again.

Too much of any good thing will eventually drive anything mad.

"And that's what Alex is?" Nathan asked. "This year's Angel? He's rather insistent on not being one."

The scene changed again, and now they were walking/floating around a festive winter market. They traveled beneath a red and gold canvas tent, and, at the far end, a small band was playing Christmas songs on fiddles and a piano. Time had changed again. Now, Nathan guessed the ghosts were from just after the Civil War. They were bartering with the vendors, pointing at the crafts, and clapping along with the music.

"Alex is the Timber Angel. However..." the Angel wearing the man's face gave a rueful smile. "He has had some help."

"You rang the bell didn't you?" Nathan said.

The Angel considered the question then nodded.

"How?"

"It took all of my strength so that Alex could hear it. I made it ring from behind the glass, made it sing."

A realization struck Nathan.

That wouldn't have left a stain you lying sack of shit.

"Alex touching it earlier was enough for the connection to stay open," Nathan suggested, struggling to keep his voice level.

It doesn't know. Because Alex doesn't know.

Another piece fell into place, but this one came with more problems, a lot more problems.

The Angel's face changed again. Now it was a teenage girl, with pigtails and teeth too big for her mouth. Once again, Nathan didn't recognize her. The face atop the hooded figure cut a disturbing silhouette and Nathan tried to ignore the gray, mottled skin on the Angel's hands.

"Yes. The touch is all that matters. For the bell, for the tree, for the flame. It is his hand that matters."

"The Third Rite," Nathan said. "What is it exactly? Tell me!"

The Angel, wearing the teenage girl's face, gave him a questioning look. "I would've thought that you would've worked out already."

"Maybe you give me too much credit. You said you want my help. So help."

The Angel considered the statement, and, as it did so, the scene shifted again. They still stood in the middle of the Gift Field, but now it was a graveyard. Rows and rows of graves filled the entire field. The tombstones wore snow on their shoulders like epaulets, and the names carved on their faces were hidden by ice.

"The flame," it said at last. "It is Alex's deepest Well, his Moment of Creation."

Nathan felt his frown harden into rock. Of course it was.

The engine at the center of the dream. To touch one's own Creation, to complete the circle, it is the last step of any psychic awakening, the last step that opens a resonant mind to become more.

"He's too old," Nathan said, defiantly. "He would've awoken a decade ago."

"But he didn't," the Angel replied. "This is the problem that requires correction."

He studied a few of the graves. The gingerbread village had been in a snow globe. So too had the winter market. But the graveyard hadn't been. *This place isn't of an Angel's doing.*

"Why have you taken us here?" Nathan asked.

"To show you fear," it said. They continued down a path of graves until they came across names Nathan recognized. Gloria Armstrong. Julianna Benneteau. Paul Ashford. Madeline Ashford. There was a grave for each of the Brenners, along with one for Marie and even one for DeMarco.

"This is the cost," the Angel said. "If you fail. He must complete the Third Rite."

The young girl's face contorted in pain, and the face suddenly shifted back into the form of Alex's mother. When it spoke, the Angel's voice was strained. "Or they will be nothing more than handfuls of dust."

Nathan's blood froze in its veins. "You'll kill them? You'll kill them all? You can't. They're innocents."

The Angel's voice leveled. It became as unfeeling as iron. "You seek to appeal to my morality, but I have none. To my ethics, but those do not exist. To my humanity, but I am far beyond human. What are they to me Nathan Cole? I care only for Alex, care only for his well-being. He must awaken. He must become whole." The Angel said. "I am willing to do what he is not, and these are the weights on the scale, nothing more. Think of them as your motivation for helping me, for helping Alex."

"I don't respond well to threats," Nathan warned.

The Angel brought them to a final tombstone. It bore the name Nathaniel Hawthorne Cole.

You know an awful lot about me.

Nathan stared at the tombstone before breaking into a bitter laugh. *A step too far friend. Now I've got you.*

He said, "And if you think my life means any more to me than the others, then you are sorely mistaken."

The Angel was unphased, "I brought you here so that you understand. If Alex does not complete the Third Rite, the dream will shatter, and they will all be lost, nothing more than torn threads on the Weave. He must shoulder the dream. Or they will all be lost."

Nathan was horrified.

It's too many minds. If Alex completes the Third Rite, as sure as rain is wet, he will die.

*

Paul Ashford and Julianna Benneteau were sitting on Alex's bedside, watching the two bodies on the ground. Both of them still breathed, but it was a low and steady rhythm, as if both were asleep. Julianna had placed Alex's stuffed rabbit next to him, hoping it might help. She could think of nothing else to do, nothing else to say.

Behind his salt-and-pepper beard, Paul's face was pale. Julianna was faring a bit better; she had made them both cups of tea, but neither had been touched. In an unspoken agreement, they stayed in Alex's room. Julianna had taken Maddie down to the Inn so that Marie could watch her.

Between the two bodies, Alex appeared peaceful, but Nathan's face was scrunched in focus. Sweat coated his forehead, sinking into his blond hair which lay in a sprawled mess across the fake hardwood floor. The ring had stopped smoking, but Paul hadn't allowed Julianna to remove it. He still didn't understand, but he understood the seriousness enough. Silver was protection, and Nathan might still need it.

Julianna placed a delicate hand on Paul's wrist as Alex's face turned suddenly pained. He began to tremble and mutter something.

"Alex," Paul called.

He rose from his place at the end of the bed, shook Alex's shoulders, and repeated his name. Alex gave no obvious sign he could hear, but his face relaxed and he seemed to settle back down. Whatever nightmare seemed to have passed. Paul stood and exhaled deeply. He seemed to notice the tea for the first time and took a long gulp from it.

"I don't understand what's happening," he said. "Nothing's making sense."

"I know," Julianna replied. "This Angel stuff. It seemed so normal to me just yesterday. Another part of our lives. But now, looking at them like this. It's not right. I feel it."

Just then, there came a loud banging from downstairs. It came again and Paul headed towards the door.

Julianna got there first and put a hand on his chest.

"I should get it," he started.

"You should stay here," she replied.

Despite drawing herself to her full height, she still only came up to his shoulder. Regardless, he shrank back.

"But I—"

"If there's a problem," she said, "I'll scream like a banshee and tear their eyes out. Then, you can come running."

Despite everything, Paul managed to laugh. "Like a banshee?"

"I can read too Professor."

For all her bravery upstairs, it vanished as soon as she made it downstairs.

The banging sounded again, right as she stepped into the kitchen. It came from the back door, and she heard a man's voice call. "Hello? Anyone home?"

Then she heard a woman's voice, much more familiar, "Paul?

Julianna?" It was Marie.

Oh, God, Julianna thought, something happened to Maddie.

She pulled open the door and outside, shivering in the cold, stood Marie, Maddie, and a man she didn't recognize. Wait, that wasn't right. She did recognize him. It was the bus driver, the same one who was supposed to have left, but didn't.

"Finally. It's freezing out here," he barked. His voice was angry and frustrated but his eyes were wide with worry. "Now, where is that stupid son-of-a-bitch?"

Chapter Twenty-Two

Anchor had changed since Alex's last visit. Now, it appeared to be a medieval keep, decorated for Christmas. He lay on a bench in a great hall, bedecked with garland and holly. Massive wreaths hung from each wall. Alex sat up and saw a massive log roaring in a hearth, spitting sparks whenever it chose. The table was laden with food, sides of roasted meat, dishes of root vegetables, and bowls of hearty stew. Flagons of brown ale were placed at each seat.

"You are early for the festivities," Anslem said.

He was sitting on a smaller throne next to the larger one. Alex couldn't remember much of his history, but he could remember enough. That was the place of the majordomo, the chamberlain, the one who ran the household. The last time Alex had seen him, the Aegyl had been wearing a beige robe. Now, he wore a simple black tunic and breeches. On his head rested a simple golden coronet.

"What brings you here Alex Ashford?" Anslem asked.

Alex's head ached.

"For help," he managed to say. "For your help. Nathan, he needs your help."

Anslem's face didn't change. His stare remained set on Alex. "He must have told you something to bring you here. What was it?"

"To focus on the mirror. Is that what you mean?"

A girl's voice spoke. It was the Keeper. "That's not what he means," she offered.

She was sitting opposite him and in her lap was one of the dolls, a patchwork creature with three arms and yellow buttons for eyes. Had she been there the entire time?

Anslem inclined his head, as if he agreed with her. "He said—" Alex started, then the thought fell away.

"Take a moment," the Keeper said. "Your mind is still recovering from its shock."

The bedroom returned to him. Nathan, clawing at his shirt, the intensity in his stare, and the words he so desperately said.

"That none of it was real," Alex said at last. "That it was a trap. He was...Nathan...I think he might have been afraid."

Anslem said nothing for a moment.

Then, the Aegyl stood, and vanished into a cloud of sparks.

Alex sighed and shook his head. "I thought you'd understand," he muttered.

From behind him, Anslem's voice almost made him leap across the table, "Walk with me, Alex Ashford. Tell me what has happened."

Alex explained all that he could remember, from their conversation at the tree farm, to his own dream, and then to Nathan forcing him awake. Only when he finished, did he realize the truth of what Nathan had said.

"The message wasn't for me, was it?" Alex asked.

They were walking through a large entry hall lined with Christmas trees. Anslem stopped and fixed him with one of his long, careful stares.

"No," the Aegyl said. "It was not for you. Or, more precisely, it was for you so that you would deliver it to me."

"To you?" Alex asked, confused. "Why do you care about Timber's Edge?"

"I don't," Anslem replied simply.

The Aegyl continued leading him farther down the hall. There were several fireplaces set against the walls. Anslem checked each one in turn, adjusting the wood, sweeping up small piles of ash, and straightening the chairs that sat in front of them. Alex wasn't sure if he was supposed to speak.

But, at the fourth fireplace, Alex's patience finally wore down.

"I'm sorry," he barked, "but Nathan needs help. He might be dying back there! I don't got ti—"

A slight creasing around Anslem's eyes cut him off mid-stride.

"Sorry." Nice job, Alex. Pissing off the…whatever he is.

Without a word, Anslem finished moving the small sofa, then continued to walk.

Alex stayed behind until Anslem said, "Follow me, Alex Ashford. If you still want to help Nathan, that is."

Anslem does everything in his own time, Nathan had explained. And what else had he said? That was right. Time worked differently in Anchor.

"Nathan has shown you a remarkable amount of trust," Anslem said. "Adjusting for his own natural reticence, of course."

"Uh, thanks," Alex said.

The Aegyl stopped in front of what looked like a storage cupboard. Farther down the hall, there came the sounds of clattering pans and sizzling food.

"I cannot say that I understand it," Anslem continued.

Alex felt himself deflate.

Almost to himself, the Aegyl said, "Although there are a great many things about your kind that I do not yet understand."

His eyes flicked around to the hall, lingering a moment too long on the decorations.

"He once explained your kind's practice of gift-giving to me. Quite a long time ago, from your perspective."

"The mirror?" Alex asked. "Was that a gift?"

The stars in Anslem's eyes paused before resuming their motion. "Why would you presume that Alex Ashford?"

Did I insult him again? Alex shrugged. "Just seemed, you know, appropriate."

Anslem nodded, then opened the storage closet. It reminded Alex of a mail-sorting wall in a post office. There were dozens, hundreds, maybe thousands, of rectangular holes. Many were empty, but some had boxes or other small items tucked into them. The room extended higher than the building they were in, and, before Alex's eyes, some of the empty holes filled themselves while some of the occupied ones emptied.

"Our guests," Anslem explained, "sometimes need to store their precious things, in hopes that they might one day hold them again."

He retrieved a small box from one hole that was at the Aegyl's shoulder. How he knew which hole to look for, Alex had no idea. The Aegyl exited the room and showed the box to Alex. It was an old Romeo y Julieta cigar box, covered in scuffs and scratches.

"Cigars?"

"The mirror," Anslem said, ignoring the question, "was not a gift. It is, in Nathan's estimation, a necessary evil. When the stars are in the correct rotation, it can be used as a gateway. Like all mirrors, as it happens. But, unlike most mirrors, Nathan's gateway can be focused."

Alex remembered the corridor, recalled the sheer hungry malevolence from the things that lived there. "The corridor?"

Anslem gave a slight incline of his head. "I have never seen it myself, but that is how it would present, yes. A corridor. A road, a river. A path through a wood. It is not an actual structure, as I'm sure you have so far gathered."

If you say so, Alex thought.

"Rather, it exists only when it is called. It connects two strands of the Weave, binding them, however briefly, through the Betwixt."

"And the...things that live there?" The memory of them made Alex's arms erupt in goose-flesh.

"They and their realm are one and the same. They too are the Betwixt."

Something about the Aegyl's statement turned Alex's stomach. Anslem opened the cigar box, but he kept the contents hidden from Alex. He retrieved something from it, returned the box to the room, and finally closed the door behind him. It sealed with a heavy click, and Alex got the distinct sense that it would only open for Anslem.

"Nathan gave me a gift long ago. And I gave him one in return. It is the custom of your people, that is correct?"

"Yes," Alex replied carefully. "It is."

Anslem nodded. Alex got the sense that he was pleased. More than that, the Aegyl appeared relieved. It was as if the question had been on the creature's mind for some time. The Aegyl opened his hand. In his palm was an item wrapped in black velvet cloth.

Anslem explained, "This was the gift that Nathan gave to me. Take it."

With a nervous hand, Alex scooped it out of Anslem's hand. His fingers briefly touched the Aegyl's skin. It was warm, almost hot to the touch. He wasn't sure why it surprised him. Anslem was no regular person, that much had been made abundantly clear.

He unwrapped the item, Nathan's gift, and found himself confused at what lay beneath the cloth.

"I don't understand," Alex said.

It was a tuning fork, marked with scratches and deformities. Alex doubted it would hold any tune, let alone a clear note.

"No," Anslem replied. "You do not, but that is why Nathan sent you to me. I am to cure you of your ignorance."

It was then Anslem lay a firm hand on Alex's wrist. Before he realized what was happening, Anslem was disappearing into a swirl of sparks, but the sparks weren't contained to the Aegyl. They ran up Alex's arm, hot without being burning, and he felt himself being pulled. He tried to cry out, but the sparks had filled his mouth like a thousand hot, crawling ants; he tried to shout, but the mouth was no longer where it should have been, and Alex couldn't move it.

Finally, the sparks took his eyes, and he saw nothing more than the Aegyl's orange flame.

*

"He can't," Nathan said. "You know he can't. He'll have to come back next year. If he does this, he'll die."

"You will have to help him," the Angel replied.

"Energy is energy," Nathan replied. "He hasn't awoken. He's not strong enough. No mind here is."

The Angel's features didn't change. They were relentlessly blank. "He is stronger than you give him credit for."

It's been lying to us for some reason. Let's see if we can coax it out.

"Then help him," Nathan suggested. "That's what guardians do, isn't it?"

The Angel hovered, silently before him. "I ensured that he could walk the road."

The scene shifted and they were together in a carnival. It was perhaps the late 50's. There was a midway of games, and the smell of popcorn and caramel filled the air. Nathan paced around the ghosts as they played ring toss, clambered aboard rickety rides, and fumbled their way through a house of mirrors.

The Angel watched the ghosts a moment before continuing, "it is the pain in his heart, the weight in his soul, that holds him back."

"It's a matter of energy," Nathan insisted.

The Angel's face turned dark and it hissed, "I won't allow him to run! A cowardly boy, afraid of his own shadow! He is strong enough."

The Angel's voice was turning crazed, and Nathan remembered what Julianna had said. *In the end, Julianna warned us, she could be quick*

255

to change.

The Angel continued, "if you will indulge this disgusting part of his nature, then perhaps you are just as weak as he is. Just as…soft."

Nathan boiled at the word. *Stay focused.*

Through gritted teeth, Nathan spat, "Make no mistake. I am far weaker."

A flash of darkness crossed the Angel's face, a shadow of something, and it filled Nathan with dread.

Little more than a shade. This is bad Nate. Alex is infected. This entire place is infected.

Nathan thought of Ronny, of what had appeared so familiar about him, and of the strange shape on his sleeve. Those three lines, Nathan realized, they weren't smoke. They were flames.

No wonder Ronny is here, no wonder he's been trying to get me to leave. He's sensed the danger, subconsciously. Even when I'm too blind to see it.

"Help him Nathan," the Angel said, its voice had softened, but a calculating cruelty remained in its eyes. "Help him become what he is born to be."

"You set him up. Forced him to start the Rites, put the entire town's expectation on them. You made it fact for every mind here. You kept every mind resonating, pulling more and more people in. Is that why you blitzed DeMarco? Was he rocking the boat too much?"

If the Rites had never begun, we could've just waited it out, but he's part of the narrative now. Like the sun rising in Anchor, expectation and perception can alter this place.

Or they can bring it down like a great house of cards.

"I did what I had—"

"Bullshit!" *Nate! Stay focused!* "You set him up! That way, if the Third Rite didn't happen, the entire shell would collapse. You put all these lives at risk, for what?" Nathan snarled at The Angel, and its form flickered into that of Jake Marley. But it had none of that man's kind warmth.

"So you will not help him?" the Angel asked in Marley's rough gravely voice.

"I won't help him die," Nathan said. "But I can help him in the real world, away from here. I swear it. You help him leave, and I'll find him. I'll help him."

"That is unfortunate," the Angel said.

"Why?" Nathan called, but the answer was in the predatory look that had invaded Marley's face. "Because it's not about helping Alex, is it? Not about him coming into his powers, is it?"

Marley's eyes raked him.

"So," it whispered now. "You will not help him?"

Nate...

"Shut up. Will I help you send him to slaughter?" Nathan asked, the question cracking through the air. He brought himself to his full height. "No. I will not."

"Then you are not part of the solution. I had hoped you would be able to show him the way, but now, I will have to take more direct measures."

The Angel turned its back to him.

"If it's not about helping him, why would you care about the Third Rite?"

The carnival grew louder. The lights grew brighter, the smells more vivid.

It's writing me into it. How is it managing that?

"I leave you here, Nathaniel, here in a prison of your very own."

The words brought sweat to Nathan's forehead. He'd spent far long enough in prisons, and each one had been of his own.

"I'll answer my own question then," Nathan said, a shake creeping into his voice. "Timber's Edge isn't Alex's prison at all, is it?"

Nathan backed away from the Angel, his way out of the field was now blocked by a crowd of very real people. Some of them even seemed to notice him, their eyes curious and disturbed.

It drifted away, once again the hooded figure.

"He will never trust you," Nathan said to its retreating back. "I can help you! Just let them all go first, and I will help you! Let me be leverage enough! I'll help you, I swear it!"

"You would make a tempting host," the Angel replied, "but I must decline. After all this time, I won't deny myself the satisfaction. After all, I'm an old friend of the family, and I know *precisely* where he hurts."

"And his pain will make the juices all the sweeter, is that it, Shade?" Nathan called. "What was that about not being a parasite?"

Nathan's shoulders were knocked by the crowd. The Angel was fading from view.

"Hunters are not parasites," the Shade replied.

"You'll be dooming yourself," Nathan shouted.

It looked over its shoulder, its face obscured by the black hood. When it spoke, directly into Nathan's ear, the voice was full of silky satisfaction, "Then I'll know right where to find you."

A laugh like crinkling foil scratched his mind, and then the Angel faded entirely, leaving Nathan alone, surrounded by a joyous carnival where only ghosts survived.

✳

They were back in the castle's great hall, and Alex spent several seconds running his hands over his body. "That," he said, "was very unpleasant."

Anslem's face didn't react. "As you say Alex Ashford."

The Keeper looked up from the table. "You should be careful Anslem," she warned.

The Aegyl pinned her with a stare.

The Keeper's hands, once toying with her doll's hair, froze.

The Aegyl's quiet voice was as pointed as Alex had ever heard it when he said, "And you should mind your place imp. Keep to your rules and I will keep to mine."

The little girl wilted, and her eyes dropped to the tabletop. "I meant no disrespect," she said. "I just meant that the guests will soon arrive."

Anslem turned his attention to Alex before leading him to a table. He took two of the wine glasses that were sitting in their prepared places and, without looking at them, filled them with water from the jug at the center of the table. Anslem gestured for Alex to sit.

When he spoke, his voice was once again serene, "Nathan's gift. Place it on the table."

Alex put the brass tuning fork on the table. In its base, there was a scratch mark that consisted of three letters: NHC. Alex pointed to the mark, "Nathaniel Hawthorne Cole?"

"Quite so," Anslem replied. He took the tuning fork in his hand. "Nathan has described the process of Projection to you." It wasn't a question. "This is good."

"And if I need a refresher?"

Anslem's eyes paused their motion. "Simply recall those memories and review the details. I will wait."

"Uh," Alex said.

The Keeper chimed in. "Linear time, Anslem. Their memories are sequential." With a predatory smile, she met Alex's eyes and added, "Simplistic."

Thanks, Alex thought.

The Keeper's smile widened and then she nodded slightly.

Unsettled, Alex turned away.

Anslem muttered something. "Did he not explain in Anchor? Here, the memories would not fade."

"He wasn't a guest," she said.

Anslem muttered something else. This time, Alex could hear it. It sounded distinctly like, "Not yet."

"No," Alex said at last. "He told me about Projection in that between place."

"The Betwixt."

"Right. I remember though. He said Projection is when we send our spirits somewhere else?" Alex ended hopefully. The answer was apparently insufficient, for Anslem continued to stare at him. "He said the mirror was how we stay stable here. And that, back home, there's just...meat."

Anslem glanced at the Keeper who returned a skeptical raised eyebrow.

"Sufficient, I suppose," Anslem said. "Nathan is correct. The forced Projection of your essence is a difficult, even traumatizing act. It is the realm of powerful minds, power far beyond that of Nathan. The mirror indeed keeps minds as fragile as yours stable in planes this far from your own. Without it, or without other help, your essence would quickly split."

That didn't sound good.

The Keeper made a flushing sound. "Down the drain," she said. "That's where you go. Like a spoiled custard."

"Another thing to thank Nathan for," Alex grumbled.

To Alex's surprise, the corners of Anslem's mouth twitched. "Quite so. He can be troublesome."

The Aegyl brought the two wine glasses forward.

"Why do you think the mirror brings you here?" Anslem asked. "To Anchor? How do you think the others who come here get here? Present company excluded, of course."

Alex stared into Anslem's eyes, and, for once, the gaze there didn't frighten him. If anything, it seemed kind. Patient. He looked to the wine glasses again and remembered an old trick Grandpa Pat used to do. Unsure precisely of what he was doing, he licked a finger, and ran it around the rim of one of the wine glasses. It started to sing in a clear, steady note. Before long, from a few inches away, the second glass sang as well.

With a gentle hand, Anslem touched Alex's wrist. "Why did you do that, Alex Ashford?"

"That's what it is, isn't it?" Alex asked confidently. "That's what brings us here. Resonance."

Alex remembered the next bit from his music classes. It was why a single guitar string could make the others vibrate. It was why concert halls were designed the way they were.

"Sympathetic vibration," Alex continued. "You're describing acoustics."

"Not bad," the Keeper said. "Dear Nathaniel was a quite a bit slower on the jump."

"I took music classes," Alex replied, smiling sheepishly. "I wasn't very good."

"Likely you were better than you think," the Keeper added.

Anslem placed the tuning fork gently in front of Alex.

"All things touched by Memory, from the smallest ant to reality itself, have what you can think of as a special signature. It extends beyond form, beyond matter. It is woven into their very being, their essence. It is, to use Nathan's parlance, a psychic frequency. They can harmonize, across space, across time, even across the planes." He pointed at the wine glasses. "As you have so aptly demonstrated, a sound of the proper frequency can make these glasses harmonize together. But, so too can a mind. The proper kind of mind."

"Psychics?"

"An incomplete description, but adequate for our purposes," Anslem replied. "There are minds that can feel these frequencies, interact with them, even alter them. Your so-called psychics have minds like this."

"Think of an orchestra," the Keeper added. "You might have your brass section. These might be the ones who can make things move just by thinking. A psychic that can adjust the frequencies themselves might be an expert on several of the instruments, but they're more likely to be the conductor. Able to hear all of the instruments at once. Able to pick out a single out-of-tune instrument and to correct it. All to ensure the audience can understand the music."

Anslem nodded. "Nathan calls them Mindsingers. They bring harmony where there is otherwise chaos. Many of them never realize what they truly are. They simply perform the task naturally, through instinct."

"Or intuition," the Keeper said.

"And that's what Nathan is?" Alex said. It would explain how he always seems to know what I'm thinking.

At this, the Keeper laughed. Even Anslem's mouth twitched. "No," she said. "Nathan is more like a triangle player."

"And not a particularly accomplished one," Anslem added. He gestured to the tuning fork. "This carries Nathan's frequency. He made it while staying here, a long time ago."

He tapped the fork against the table and a bright tone surrounded them.

"Precious metals, imbued with his touch, with his Memory of cutting it, shaping it. It is, in many respects, an echo of who he was when he made it. It will resonate with him, if placed against the gateway through which he was taken."

"The mirror that the Angel took him through?"

Anslem nodded. "The fork is a tether, his tether. It is a reminder of who and what he is. It will give him sufficient purchase to climb his way back."

The Aegyl lifted it and carefully wrapped it back into the velvet cloth.

"Take great care with it," Anslem said. "It is a precious thing he trusts you with."

Alex was confused. He had just met Nathan. "Then, why wouldn't one of you just use it? You know a lot more about this shi —stuff."

Anslem shook his head. "I cannot leave Anchor."

The Keeper shrugged as well, "I'm bound to my Lady's will. Besides, Nathaniel would likely kill me on sight if he saw me holding that."

"Presuming I did not obliterate you first," Anslem added in his smooth voice.

"Wait," Alex interrupted, raising his hands. "Why me?"

"It is a rather simple matter," Anslem replied. "When you two visited together, Nathan asked a favor of me. If you were to return and if you were to need it, he asked that I give it to you. It is, what he calls, an insurance policy."

Alex took the tuning fork, held it carefully in his hands.

Across the table, Anslem leaned a fraction closer. "Now, there is something I need you to do for me."

A nervous flower bloomed in Alex's chest. He didn't like the idea of having to do Anslem a favor. What kind of favor did an Aegyl want? "What...what could I ever do for you?"

Anslem gestured around the great hall. "This. This is like your Christmas celebration, yes?"

"Uh. Not exactly."

The Keeper chuckled.

Anslem leveled a stony gaze at her.

"I mean, it's good," Alex insisted, perhaps too eagerly. "It's just a little...old fashioned."

Anslem brought his fingers together in a steeple. "I see. This celebration is proving more complex than I'd intended. Nathan said I needed trees. Fireplaces. Roasted meats. Something called a yule log."

Anslem gestured at the massive log burning in the largest hearth.

"I think he probably meant a cake," Alex suggested.

Anslem's eyes paused for a moment. "Explain."

"Shouldn't I—"

The Aegyl's eyes came alive in a galaxy of stars. "You may begin."

*

Julianna hadn't been sure what to make of this night, and now that Alex's bedroom had three extra visitors, she was completely lost. The grief and the worry had melted down into a state of shocked confusion. It felt like she was a computer program, merely going through preordained motions, and now all she could do was watch. Except for growing more pale, Alex and Nathan remained unchanged.

Julianna was going to suggest they call a doctor, but then she remembered that there were no doctors in Timber's Edge. And she couldn't even recall the nearest hospital's location. If it wasn't so serious, it might have been funny. The bus driver was leaning over Nathan's body, tapping it with his foot, the way one might tap a dead animal on the side of the road. Marie was straightening things up on Alex's desk, despite never having been in the room, and Paul...Paul was cradling a sleeping Maddie.

"Still alive," the bus driver—Ronny, he'd said his name was— declared. He sounded partly disappointed. He checked Alex as well. "This one's doing better. But that makes sense. He went willingly."

That was enough. "Went where?" Julianna demanded.

Maddie started at the heat in her voice, and Paul shot her a warning look.

Julianna reined herself in. "You seem to know a lot. Start explaining."

With a grunt, Ronny straightened. "Yup. I know some. About as much as this one." He pointed to Nathan's prone body. "But I'm not sure explaining will do you a lot of good. And it might make things a lot worse."

"Try me. I'm the mayor here." As soon as she spoke them, the words sounded so hollow. So ridiculous.

Ronny began to laugh. It was a barking, donkey's laugh. "Yup. That you are. The mayor of Timber's Edge, a lovely little spot. That's to be sure. It's mighty fine."

"That's enough," Paul said quietly.

Ronny's laugh silenced.

"That's my son," Paul continued. "You said you could help."

"Alright," Ronny replied. "Let me ask you all this. Where are you right now?"

Julianna sneered at him. What a stupid question. "Timber's Edge."

"A-huh. And where is that, exactly?"

The question stole her fire. "It's just off the highway. Over the mountain, next to the river. By the forest."

She knew the answer was wrong, but it was the only one she had. When her and Paul's gazes met, both shared the same wide concern.

"And the state? What cities are nearby?" Ronny asked.

Julianna said nothing. She tried to remember, but the information just wasn't there.

"Well, quite the cartographer aren't ya?" Ronny asked, mocking.

Just then, Alex took a mighty breath.

In an instant, Ronny was there next to him. "Now, now son. Take it slow. Nice and slow. You've gone on a deep dive, and you're no expert."

Alex inhaled and exhaled, each breath more stable than the last. His eyes, those deep gray eyes he'd gotten from his mother, darted around the room. They fixed on Ronny.

"That's right. Focus on me. Everyone's here. You got the whole village." The bus driver's mouth stretched into a mischievous grin and he leveled a knowing look at Julianna. "Even the mayor's here."

"Well where the hell else would she be?" Alex coughed out weakly.

Even Julianna had to smile as Alex pushed himself onto his elbows. From out of his pocket, he pulled a small velvet package. Did he have that the entire time?

"Good," Ronny said. "That's good."

Alex shook his head and pinched his eyes, then he stood and unwrapped the package.

"You know what to do with it?" Ronny asked.

"I think so," Alex said. "It's hard to remember."

"Just breathe," Ronny said. "It'll come."

Inside was what looked like an old tuning fork, the sort Julianna hadn't seen since she'd been in school. With his face set, Alex approached the mirror hanging on the wall above his dresser.

"Everyone should step back," he said in a strong voice. "I don't know what this is going to do."

"Listen to him," Ronny said.

Marie, who had been silent, stepped nervously into the doorway.

Paul scooped Maddie into his arms and backed against the window.

Julianna joined them, and Paul put a protective arm over her.

Alex hit the tuning fork against the wall, but no sound came from it. Despite that, Ronny nodded and made a sucking sound with his lips. Alex's forehead knitted in concentration as he placed the tuning fork base-first against the mirror.

At first, nothing happened. Then, the mirror started to change. As if Alex had dropped a pebble into a pond, a single circular ripple extended outward from the tuning fork.

There was silence.

And then the mirror exploded outward in a hail of glass and metal.

Maddie screamed at the noise, and Paul cursed.

Julianna felt a ramrod run down her spine and jammed her nails into Paul's arm.

"Oh my goodness," Marie cried.

Then, there was the sound of a mighty inhale, like an engine shouting for air. A moment passed, and Nathan Cole leaped to his feet from behind the bed.

He stared wildly at each of them in turn, his green eyes studying them. He lingered a moment longer on Ronny.

"You," he said. "Is it real?"

"As real as it has been," Ronny declared.

Finally, Nathan came to Alex, spotted the tuning fork in his hand, and his face split into a wide grin. "Now," he said. "I'm going to go out on a limb and presume you have questions."

Chapter Twenty-Three

They all assembled downstairs in the Ashford family living room. Paul and Julianna sat with Maddie between them. Marie sat opposite, while Alex sat in an armchair. Ronny hovered in the kitchen behind them. Outside the window, the purplish light of morning was showing through the hazy clouds. A few flakes of snow were still falling, but, aside from that, it was totally still.

"It might be a better idea for this to be a grown-up conversation," Nathan suggested to the crowd. He had wrapped his finger in a bandage. It was burned, but it was a pain he could deal with. His silver ring, he'd transplanted to his other hand.

Maddie crossed her arms in protest. "I'm not going anywhere."

"You heard her," Paul said.

Nathan focused on her. "Can you keep a secret? People are going to die if you can't."

Maddie nodded, full of confidence.

He rounded on the rest of them. "Same goes for all of you. Lives are at stake now. Not maybe. Not probably. Assuredly. And if you can't keep a secret, you'll make things a lot worse a lot faster. Somewhere, at the top of a mountain, there's a snowball starting to roll down hill. We need to stay ahead of it for as long as we can. The only way to do that is to work together, with one purpose."

He nodded towards Ronny.

"He doesn't matter," Nathan said with a dismissive wave. "But the rest of you, can you keep a secret?"

Ronny barked a laugh, but the rest of them followed Maddie's lead and nodded in turn.

"Alright. Here goes: Timber's Edge isn't real, at least, not in the way that you think of something being real. It exists, yes, but not as a physical place."

Nathan swept his eyes over them, unable to keep a glimmer of excitement out of his voice.

"The town of Timber's Edge is a communal psychic dream-state."

Nathan let the words disperse through the kitchen and waited for the explosion of protest, of outrage, of denial.

All he received was expectant silence.

So far, so good.

Nathan continued, slowly and clearly. "We've all found it in our own way. Some of us have been brought here. Some of us might have even chosen to come here."

Alex said, "No one gets to choose their dreams."

"Of course you do, you do it all the time," Nathan replied. "All of our dreams are based on our memories. Why do you think you have nightmares after seeing a scary movie? Or dream about being late to *your* college final? Your mind is harmonizing with its own memories while also Projecting itself into a plane just out of sync with your own. All minds—all human minds that is—do this."

"Glossing over that 'human' comment," Julianna interrupted. "I've never gone to Greece, but I dream about Santorini all the time."

"Tell me about it," Paul grumbled.

Honeymoon conversations with her must be a treat.

"You've seen pictures of it," Nathan told her. "Thought about it. Pictured yourself there. I bet you've watched tons of videos on-line from travel bloggers."

Julianna said nothing.

Nathan grinned and continued, "Then you've created a strong enough memory, a strong enough mental picture, for your mind to harmonize, to resonate. That's enough to form a dream shell. As for the little details—the name of the ice cream shop, Paul's much improved physique, Alex missing his flight so he's stranded at home —your mind fills in those blanks to stop you from noticing the obvious truth that you are not really sunbathing on Santorini."

He paced the room, coming to stop in front of the Ashford family Christmas tree. There were already several presents waiting underneath. "These presents," he said, directing his voice to Paul. "You know what's in them?"

Paul concentrated. Nathan could see the strain as he was trying to remember, and the troubled flicker to his eyes when nothing came.

"You think you ought to know. Your mind tells you that, surely you were the one who put them there." Nathan pulled the tag off one covered in bright pink paper. "To Maddie, from Dad," he read.

"You don't remember what you got me for Christmas?" Maddie demanded.

"I—" Paul started, but Nathan cut him off.

"It's not his fault," Nathan told her. He walked the present over to her. "Tell me, what do you want to be in here?"

Maddie reached for the gift, but Nathan kept it away.

"Don't touch it," he said. "Just, whisper it to me."

Nathan crouched, meeting her eyes with his. She whispered, "Grown-up puzzles. The kid ones are too easy."

Still meeting her eye, he passed her the gift. "Open it," he said.

"But it's not Christmas," she protested.

"It's a special case," Nathan replied.

"It's okay Mads," Paul said, his eyes focused on Nathan. "Go ahead."

A nine-year-old, it turned out, only needed to be told once that they were allowed to open a Christmas present early. While she was working on the paper, Nathan crossed back to the adults.

"Grown-up puzzles," Nathan told them in a low voice.

Sure enough, when she tore off the paper, Maddie grinned when she saw a set of thousand piece puzzles, each one of a different vintage train engine.

"Doesn't get more grown up than that," Alex said.

The color had drained out of Paul's face. "How did you know?" he asked.

Nathan shrugged. "Dreams are weird things. By nature, they're paradoxical. They're built on improbability, on impossibility. All the little details come from the dreaming minds; those minds populate the dream. I didn't know. The gift didn't exist until Maddie decided what it was."

His eyes darted to Ronny, and the bus driver smirked back.

"Similar to the route number on a bus ticket," Nathan said.

"I did my bit. Don't blame me for your brain being slow," Ronny called.

Nathan ignored the barb. "Dream-states don't exist until they're called into being. And, no matter how large, they are functionally the same. They're at once powerful and fragile. From the outside, they are impenetrable, but they're flimsy from the inside. It is the core paradox at the center of all dreams, even ones like Timber's Edge. It is why we are all in such terrible danger. Because dreams can collapse. Dream shells, the thin shield that protects our minds when we dream, can shatter like that."

Nathan snapped his fingers.

"All it takes is lucidity. If enough minds recognize the dream, the dream shell will shatter. Just like it does in our normal dreams. An incongruity is a violated expectation. We think something should be one way."

He crossed the room and flicked the light switch, but nothing happened.

"But our observation tells us something different. This tells our mind that things are not what they seem, that our reality isn't really reality."

"It's a quirk of Projection," Alex said, repeating what Nathan had told him.

"What incongruities?" Paul asked. "This is real. I know it is."

"It's harder for you all. You've all been integrated into the dream itself, right into the narrative." Nathan smiled then showed them his ring. "My mind isn't integrated because of my silver. Therefore, I can see the...imperfections."

He met Alex's eyes and grinned, before slipping into Alex's accent.

"'Right quick.' 'Fixing to.' 'The gift, it don't quite exist.' Your accent, it's not quite gone. It slips through here and there. Virginia?"

Alex's face turned bright red.

"I bet you spent a lot of effort at UPenn keeping that clamped down. But this is your childhood home. We should be knee-deep in drawl. Does it look like Virginia out there? To anyone?"

Julianna brought a hand to her mouth. "We couldn't remember what state we're in."

"Exactly," Nathan continued. "There's more. Statues that change face—that's just Monday for me."

"Just what?" Maddie asked, hugging her puzzle.

Nathan waved the question aside. "But you have a ghost cat in your backyard, your general store is stocked with decade old products—and priced to match—no one ever drives out of town, and every guest at the Inn seems to have car trouble."

Nathan was pacing the room, his voice full of energy. "There's a curious lack of cell phones for the 2020's. Christmas paradise and not a single selfie? Snowstorms here, they come and go at will. Time jumps and skips. One moment, it's ten in the morning, the next the sun is going down."

Nathan's eyes darted over each of them in turn.

"All imperfections. All incongruities. All violated expectations. All of them will lead to lucidity. And if that lucidity spreads to the town, then the dream's foundation will break. The dream shell will shatter. The dream has to release us before that happens, we have to wake up."

"If we die, we wake up, right?" Alex asked. "Sounds easy enough. Let's take turns throwing ourselves off the roof."

Ronny barked a laugh. "I like his thinking. Nathan, you first."

Sadness filled Nathan's smile. "It's a bold strategy, but it won't help us here. Mr. DeMarco is our proof of that. For him, the dream was broken. His mind was blitzed, and the stress of that should have woken him up, but his mind had no way to save him, no way to release the dream. Now he longer knows which way is up, so to speak. The plane of dreams is a sort of psychic ocean, and our dream shells are our ships. But there are things that live in the water, things that no human mind can witness."

Nathan noticed a faraway look in Alex's eyes. Alex's lip trembled.

"This is ridiculous," Julianna interrupted. "You can't know this."

"The Betwixt," Alex whispered. The word sucked the air out of the room.

Someone looked up, Nathan realized with dread. Alex was lucky to be alive.

Paul rounded on his son, "What the hell is that?"

Alex simply shook his head, the words seemingly unable to come.

"The Betwixt," Nathan explained, "is the space between planes. If our dream shells shatter, if our ships sink, that's where we end up. Fish food."

"People wake up from dreams all the time," Marie insisted, her voice cracking. "They don't just die."

"That's true," Nathan replied. "Normally, your mind is in control of the dream. It's at the helm, calling the shots. It can decide to release you. It's one of our most primitive defense mechanisms. But, this isn't a normal dream. A normal mind can't project a dream-state, but a psychic one can, and, the more powerful the mind, the more realized the dream. Timber's Edge is one mind's dream, but we're all getting sucked in. It could be something as simple as having been thinking about Christmas shopping. Or falling asleep with the TV playing a Christmas movie. Or a love of fresh mountain air. It doesn't take much for a mind to scent out a dream like Timber's Edge."

Ronny jumped in. "Fresh minds have been arriving constantly, and any psychics that happen to show up will bring even more minds with 'em. It's an ever expanding web. More and more minds will keep arriving."

Alex's voice grew frustrated. "How do we stop them from coming then?"

"We can't, not without risking the logic of the dream," Nathan replied calmly. "Timber's Edge is broadcasting to every sympathetic mind out there. Communal dream states are almost like computer programs. Or the Holodeck on Star Trek. They have narratives. Characters. Settings. In many respects, they're real, breathing things. They just only exist when the psychic mind is projecting them. When the psychic projects them, they act like—"

Nathan searched for the word, before he spotted one of Maddie's puzzles. It showed a black starry night over ocean waves.

"—like a cruise ship open for business. Other minds, when resonating—when harmonizing—with that psychic just right, join these dream-states. They come aboard, become integrated into the narrative. They weave right into the dream. Without insulation from silver, like you all, they don't even know it's happening. At that moment, they're under the dream shell. And, well, I don't have to remind you what happened to the Titanic."

Paul and Julianna and Marie all stared at Nathan like he had two heads, but Alex was staring at the Christmas tree.

"Whose mind is it?" Alex asked, a tremor in his throat.

"Does it matter?" Nathan asked.

Ronny scoffed.

Dammit Ronny.

Alex met Nathan's stare, his gray eyes wide with betrayal. "Bullshit," he said. "I'm not."

"Not what?" Paul asked in a growl.

Nathan drifted to the TV. *A Christmas Carol* was playing again, and young Scrooge was being shown around by the candle-like Ghost of Christmas Past. His eyes flicked up to the picture of Anna in the hospital room.

"All of us carry specters Alex," Nathan said gently. "Some are worse than others. Some minds are different than others."

"No," Alex said.

Nathan's stare was pointed. "The bell Alex, why do you think we're the only ones who can hear it? I have to concentrate, but you don't."

"No," Alex said again. "There's nothing special about me."

"Normal minds can't travel to Anchor, and normal minds can't use this," Nathan said, holding up his tuning fork. "Loopy, your magic rabbit, makes things happen with his mind, doesn't he? I suspect your mother knew, if she wasn't one herself. "

"Wasn't what?" Paul asked harshly.

It's time to put it out there.

"Alex is a psychic," Nathan said.

Alex turned scarlet, his mouth opened then closed again.

Paul hit the table with his fist, his cheeks flushed with anger. He rose to his feet.

Maddie's eyes widened. She dropped the puzzle and whimpered in alarm.

"My son is not the cause of this. He is not some psychic." Paul said, each word punctuated with a finger pointing at Nathan.

Ronny raised an interested eyebrow.

"He's just awakening to his gifts," Nathan replied. "Though, admittedly, your son's timing sucks."

"I've heard enough of this," Paul said. "We nee—"

Julianna placed a hand on her fiance's shoulder. Her hawkish eyes flashed like steel at Nathan.

"Paul. We need to listen to them. He's telling the truth. I've seen things, things like this."

Paul had a full head on her but, in that moment, looked the smaller. "Fine."

"Fine, I'll wake us all up." Alex said, his arms crossed like a petulant teenager.

Ronny's voice broke in. "And how're you going to do that? It's not like there's an off switch." The bus driver was eating a pack of cookies he had found in the pantry. He waved one of the chocolate circles at Alex. "Everyone who's been brought here, well they don't *want* to leave, do they?"

Julianna's face paled. "They want to see what the Angel does, that's what you mean."

Ronny nodded. "We'd have to *force* them out, kicking and screaming, and for each one, you'll put another crack in the shell. The whole thing'll come crashing down before you even get through a quarter of 'em."

"And just who are you again?" Alex bit out the question.

Through a mouthful of chocolate crumbs, Ronny managed to say, "Mind your own business." Ronny swallowed his mouthful. "Very dry. You all got any coffee 'round here?"

"That's why we have to keep it a secret," Paul said.

"Bingo," Ronny replied.

Nathan silenced the driver with a glare. "Yes. Ronny's right. We must not let anyone else know that they're dreaming unless we have absolutely no other choice. That is critical."

Julianna's eyes widened. "I just realized. I have no idea how to be a mayor."

Marie grimaced, "And I have to make breakfast. That was a lot easier yesterday when I knew how to cook."

Nathan nodded. "Your conscious minds are reasserting themselves. We have to try and fake it, so no one notices."

Nathan raised his eyebrows at Paul.

The wide man shrugged. "I actually am a Christmas tree farmer. I took over Alex's grandfather's farm."

Nathan glanced at Alex.

"It's true," Alex said. "I grew up in that house."

"So what do we do?" Marie asked Nathan. "We can't wake up and run away. We can't tell anyone it's a dream. How do we get the dream to release us?"

"That," Nathan said, "is where things get a bit more complicated."

And this is the part where I must be the most convincing I can be.

Or we'll all be dead before we even start.

✳

Birds chirped outside the window, and the pot of coffee had just finished brewing. Alex poured out a cup for each of the adults, each into a different festive mug. Nathan got one featuring a curled up fox, while Alex passed Ronny one in the shape of a reindeer's head. The two of them shared a glance, then switched without a word. Paul and Julianna got a snowman and a Santa mug. When he passed them their coffee, there was a momentary hesitation before they took them. They could barely look him in the eye.

Because I'm psychic apparently.

No, I'm not, Alex thought. All the times he'd gotten his sense of intuition, his sense of instinct, came flooding back to him, from the first time he'd met Patrick to the time he'd spent in Anchor. What had the Keeper said? There's little point in lying to someone like you. Was that what she'd meant?

Alex poured his coffee into a mug the shape of a sweater then made Maddie a cup of cocoa, stirring it into a reindeer mug like Nathan's.

"I got Rudolph," she said to Nathan with a toothy grin. It sounded like a taunt.

Nathan peered down at her, "He's just a showboat anyways."

Alex jumped in, keeping his voice low. "He's you, isn't he? Ronny. He's like old you."

Nathan sipped his coffee. "Luckily no."

Ronny rolled his eyes. "Go float your little rocks you overgrown fairy."

"He's my uhh…muscle," Nathan replied.

Ronny grunted in disgust.

"But he is here because of me. Ronny is my guardian, my mind's defense mechanism."

"Dreamed up straight from the good ol' days," Ronny said with a sardonic smile. "How long've you known?"

"Long enough. You were a bit too eager for us to leave and your memories coincided too neatly with my own." Nathan admitted.

To Alex, Nathan explained, "All psychic minds, connecting to a communal dream, will normally bring two things with them: a palace and a guardian. A ship with which to dock and security to protect it."

"I'm a bouncer for what passes as his pathetic palace," Ronny interjected.

"So you know him?" Alex asked.

"He's been adjusted to fit the context of the dream," Nathan explained. "The Ronny from my memories wasn't called Ronny at all. He was called Brother Flame."

Alex recognized the name from Anchor. "The Keeper, she said

that name."

"Brother Flame was there with me," Nathan confirmed, his eyes darted across Alex's face.

As always, Alex had no idea what he was thinking.

"During my stay, that is. Of course he didn't look like this." To Ronny, he asked. "I imagine you're missing your horns."

"They were my best feature," Ronny said, rubbing a sad hand through his white hair.

His...horns?

"Some guardians are less helpful than others," Nathan replied. "But Ronny is formed from my memories, apparently in the form that my mind thought would be most useful." He shrugged. "Can't win them all."

Marie jumped in before Alex could respond. "DeMarco. He said you were a mechanic."

Ronny laughed at that.

"That pissy S.O.B woke up next to the bus," he said. "And then he made all kinds of assumptions. I didn't bother to correct him. It's not like there is a mechanic, of course. The broken down cars, it's up to the owners to fix, right Nate?"

Nathan ignored him.

"Alex," Nathan said seriously. "You are a psychic. What do you think that means?"

"Enough riddles. Stop babying him, " Ronny barked. Nathan's glare would've given Medusa pause.

The driver turned to Alex, running his glassy eyes over him.

"You've got a palace of your own," Ronny said. "And a guardian of your own."

No, Alex thought. This is all my fault.

"The Angel?" he asked. "It's the Angel isn't it? The one that took you?"

Nathan nodded sadly. "I'm afraid so. And it's worse than that, because you haven't truly awoken, your defenses haven't awoken either. They've become…compromised."

Ronny took a sharp intake of breath, and, for some reason, that filled Alex with more dread than anything.

Nathan silenced the driver with a sharp look, and this time, he stomped without a word to the corner of the living room.

"The Angel, Alex's compromised guardian, thinks it is helping him," Nathan explained to everyone. "At the center of all dreams is a construct, something like an engine. It's what we call the dreamer's individual Moment of Creation. It's a limitless fire, as powerful as the dreamer's potential, and as furious as that dreamer's imagination. The psychic touches it and can create anything. This is the Third Rite. The Angel wants Alex to complete the Third Rite, but, to do so, Alex has to fully awaken first."

"Well what's wrong with that?" Julianna asked. "It saves us all, right?"

"It could," Nathan agreed, but his face was anything but optimistic.

"But," Alex prompted.

"But," Nathan continued with a sigh, "when they do awaken, a psychic mind breaks—just for a moment—like an elastic band snapping before it reestablishes itself. In that moment, just for that moment, there will be no dream at all. The entire weight of the shell will come crashing down onto Alex's shoulders. He would have to support the entire town and all the minds in it."

Nathan shook his head. "Even if it's borne for a single moment, it's still a dreadful weight. I'm latently psychic. If you wanted to put it into a scale, I'm like a beagle. A true psychic, like my mother was, would be, let's see, an elephant maybe. Alex, a nascent psychic, not even out of the cocoon yet, is stronger than me, sure, but not strong enough. And to carry this many minds, all at once? An elephant wouldn't do. A beagle sure as hell wouldn't do. You'd need a giant to do it and survive. It would only be a moment, but it would crush you Alex."

In that moment, everyone would be released. From the prison he was holding them all in.

Paul was unable to look at his son, and Alex immediately understood why. He felt it, deep in his intuition. This was the second death sentence his father had heard in too few years.

"And if he doesn't?" Julianna asked. "If Alex refuses?"

"Then no Third Rite," Nathan said. "Everyone's expectations breaks at once, and the dream shell breaks along with them."

Alex was gripping the back of a chair and hadn't even realized.

"What do I need to do?" he asked.

"No," Paul said. He stared at Nathan. "I don't care about that. What do we do to stop it?"

After another sip of coffee, Nathan nodded. "I have a plan. We want to avoid completing the Third Rite at all costs. Alex, I need you to promise me that no matter what happens, you do nothing, *nothing*, to complete the Third Rite unless I give you permission."

The full weight of Nathan's attention rested on Alex.

"I promise," Alex said. "Why would I?"

"There's only one Angel and six of us. It's going to be looking for leverage, to try force your hand. You have to be strong and deny it. I don't care if it comes after all of us at once. It needs to know that if it touches us, the first thing you'll do is jump in front of the nearest bus. That way, it gets nothing."

Ronny slapped Alex on the arm. "Don't worry son, I'll help you with that."

"What the hell kind of plan is that?" Paul asked through gritted teeth.

Alex felt his anger reverberate through the room. It expanded out of his father like invisible smoke; Alex could almost smell it.

"My son's life is at risk. You tell me what we're going to do. Or so help me—"

Ronny's face twisted in concern, and the look on Nathan's face chilled Alex. A blank stare had replaced his usual excitement. He was weighing something, and Alex was scared of the calculation. As quickly as it had appeared, it was gone.

"To answer your question," he said in a pleasant voice, "it's the kind of plan that keeps us all on the board for as long as possible. As for what we're going to do, we're going to change the owner of the dream. We're going to find a way to make it jump tracks from Alex to another mind."

Alex thought he saw a glimmer of doubt on Nathan's face, but after a blink, it was gone.

"Can that even be done?" Alex asked.

"Presuming I can find a psychic mind strong enough to complete the Third Rite, sure. Until then," Nathan said with a happy smile. "All of us are going to have assignments. We complete them and we go along like nothing's ever happened. Each of us."

The room was silent and uncertain. It was only after a moment that Alex realized something that sent a nervous shock up his spine, "Nathan…"

"It's going to be alright Alex."

"Thanks, but that's not what I mean," he said. He pointed to the kitchen. "Ronny's gone."

Nathan left the Ashford household with Marie. There was no sign of Ronny —*slippery damn fish*—, but Nathan had an idea of where he'd gone.

That went rather well, he thought. *They bought what they needed to.*

He had left the Ashfords and Julianna with their assignments, but hadn't had the chance to do the same with Ronny. A volcano boiled inside of him. He closed and opened his fists, but even the cold air was doing little to calm him.

I should've known. The one I couldn't trust was myself.

They crossed the bridge, and Nathan glanced behind them. The Angel Statue was still there, hooded and faceless. *We have to assume she knows I'm out. On the town, as it were.*

At the boundary to the Inn, just before leaving Marie, Nathan asked, "Are you alright?"

Marie brought a hand to her mouth.

In the early morning light, her rosy skin looked pale. "I don't know. I'm not sure."

"I know," Nathan replied gently. "It's a lot to process."

He put a cautious hand on her shoulder. It was tight and tense.

"You've got a few hours yet," he said. "Get some rest?"

Marie laughed, but there was none of her usual joy. "I can't rest. I'm in the innkeeper after all."

She bustled into the Inn, shutting the door behind her, and leaving Nathan alone in the patio. He closed his fist.

Now, I need to have a word with my driver.

Ronny was where Nathan had expected to find him, standing outside the old, worn down bus, parked near The Pit Stop.

"Well there he is," Ronny declared. "Savior of Timber's Edge. Come to give me my assignment son?"

"Just one question," Nathan said, trying to keep the anger out of his voice. "DeMarco's note. The one he left for Marie, saying he wanted to stay. He didn't write it, did he?"

"Ah," Ronny said. "Nope. That was me."

Nathan glared at him.

The bus driver sidled up against the bus.

"I know what you're thinking," he said.

Nathan opened and closed his fist again. "Oh?"

"You're thinking: he's got strong bladder control. Three days and he's not pissed himself yet. I know you're checkin' on him. Of course.

He's probably projecting within a projection. That sort of thing wrecks ha—"

Nathan crossed the lot, and grabbed the front of Ronny's shirt in a fist. He slammed the old man against the bus with a rough elbow.

Oh dear.

"What am I thinking now? Pray tell," Nathan hissed.

Ronny squirmed beneath him, but Nathan held firm. Ronny was strong, but Nathan was far stronger.

Nathan's voice rose. "Come on! Let's hear it!"

"You're thinking I should've told you."

Nathan loosened, just a bit.

He shouted in the old man's face, "You're damn right you should've told me! You had no right!"

"It's a damn good thing I didn't," Ronny spat back. "If I had, you woulda launched yourself at that thing half-cocked, and now it turns out it's a Psychic Shade! It would've torn you to shreds. It's my job to keep you safe. Even from yourself."

The anger flared again, and Nathan planted a fist into the side of the bus.

"I don't know what sick joke my brain is playing bringing you here—"

Ronny, Flame, squirmed again. "Come on Nathan. Stop pretending to be something different than what you are. I'm the part of you that knows what has to be done—the part of you that knows when you can't win. The part that knows sometimes you have to walk away!"

Nathan let him go then. *We've lost plenty of times before. But that never stopped Her putting us back in the game, bloodied and broken.*

He steadied his breathing. "And that's what you would have me do?"

"Yes! Leave!" Ronny insisted. "Now! Doubly so now that we know what the hell that thing is. I know why you didn't tell 'em.

Why you kept that card to your chest. You want to give 'em hope."

The bus driver pointed to the bus.

"It's only broken down because you want it to be. Get on and your mind will do the rest. You're the only one who can. Your ring protects you enough for that. But that window is closing quick. Once the dream starts to collapse—to really collapse—you'll be brought down with it."

"And leave them all to die?" Nathan asked. "Is that it?"

"Yes! That's it. It's a Shade Nathan," Ronny punctuated the words with a horrible emphasis. "They were dead as soon as they arrived, especially Ale—"

Nathan grabbed his shirt again.

"Go ahead," Ronny snarled. "But I won't lie to you. You know what a Psychic Shade means for him. It's not just an infection. It's terminal."

Nathan let him go again. "Save my own skin?"

Ronny straightened his shirt and laughed. It was a bitter bark. "Oh, because you're the hero now? I recall you runnin' plenty of times before you finally realized what had to be done. When you finally realized the Lady held all the cards, and then what did you do? You played ball, that's what, and I was there by your side. You played Her game. You gave Her what She wanted. And you were damn good at it too."

"Don't remind me."

"You stupid son-of-a-bitch. The hell do you think you brought me here for? The only reason *I'm* here and not that jumped up candlestick is so that I *can* remind you!" Ronny barked at him. "Here, this thing holds all the cards. You're up against a trolley problem son. One life vs the rest of 'em, and, in the end, it's gonna fall on you to make the call.

"But hell, you want to beat the impossible, save 'em all? You know who to go talk to. She'll burn that Shade right out of here. But we both know you won't. Because for all your talk, you won't go back to Her. Yeah, you'll cry and you'll stamp your foot and you'll light candles for 'em, but you know you'll let every single one of them die before you go back to being Her little Black Thorn."

Nathan fumed and squared again, but Ronny put his hands up, trying to calm him.

He's right, isn't he? I'll never go back, no matter the cost. It already cost me everything.

Nathan stepped away from the bus and tried to steady his pounding heart.

When Ronny continued, his voice was softer, "There's no shame in it Nathan. It can't always fall on you to make the impossible choice. You can't always get back into the ring, not when there's another choice. There's no shame in walking away, not when there's nothing you can do."

Slowly, Ronny pointed a finger at Nathan's chest to a spot right above his heart. Right where his tattoo was.

"Sometimes, you just got to take your licks."

"Nothing I can do," Nathan repeated slowly.

Ronny nodded. "That's right."

"You're wrong," Nathan said. "I can always lose."

"Son, that's what I've been sayin'. What the hell does it matter anyway? We need to go. Now."

Nathan shook his head. "I don't think so."

He scratched the spot where his tattoo was.

They don't get to judge you Nate. You don't have to risk it. We have an out. One of these almost killed Mother Sable. Remember Beatty? It took everything in her to banish it.

Nathan whispered, half to himself, "Like you said: one life for the rest of them."

"You are not serious," Ronny said.

"We're going to save him," Nathan said. "That's our job."

"I'm not gonna let you do it."

"Try and stop me," Nathan warned. "Do I have to lobotomize myself? I can do it. Right here, right now."

Nathan met the old man's stare.

"You're not going to stand in my way. We're going to find a way to save him."

It was a command and Ronny knew it.

"Guess I'm not," Ronny, Brother Flame, said at last.

"Cheer up," Nathan said. "We still have Plan A to try."

Ronny scoffed. "You forget I know you ain't got shit."

"I'll come up with something," Nathan said with a confidence he was nowhere near feeling.

Lying to yourself. Literally. That's a new low.

"For starters," Nathan said, "he's not dead."

Ronny blew out his cheeks. "Huh? What are you talking about now?"

"You said DeMarco's body. DeMarco's not dead."

"Now you're just splittin' hairs. He's sure-as-shit not right-as-rain."

"True, but did you even stop to consider why it didn't kill him?"

Nathan thought about Marie's reaction. If he'd been killed, would it really have been any different?

"The Angel had nothing to gain keeping him alive," Nathan said.

There was a glow to Ronny's eyes that brought Nathan back to arenas covered in sand and blood. For a moment, he was Brother Flame again, truly.

Ronny laughed, "Yup. You might have somethin' there. It hesitated."

"Too afraid to alienate Alex," Nathan said. "It needs him. We know what it wants. We can find a way to beat it."

Ronny blew his cheeks out. "You do this, there's no going back. Your window will close."

Nathan ignored him. "If you planted DeMarco's note, then I presume you found him. What happened?"

Ronny's lips made a wet slapping sound. "DeMarco was sitting on the bench, watchin' the snow. As sour as you remember. I figured he was first-in-line to start breaking the dream. I figured I needed to play for time, so I talked to him. He wasn't buying it. The ones without imagination never do. He had the look in his eyes y'know? Then, halfway through my sentence, he just sort of fell over."

"Did what?"

"Just kind of turned all funny, so I carried him back to the Inn. Planted the note so no one would look for him, so the dream wouldn't break down. I would've taken him here to the Palace, but I thought you might see us. Of course you were too busy what with running back to Anslem with your tail between your legs. Besides, I wanted to keep an eye on him."

Nathan stepped back, steadied his heartbeat.

Something had clicked in his mind. "Did you feel anything?"

"My neck's a little bit sore, yeah."

Nathan's eyes flashed. "When DeMarco got blitzed."

Ronny scratched his chin. "No. Can't say that I did. But, it's not like I have nerves. I was lying about the neck. Why?"

Nathan turned his ring on its finger.

"Because I'm not sure DeMarco was the target," Nathan said. "In fact, I'm sure he wasn't. It's too bad you've got no mind to blitz."

He lingered on the bus.

It's only broken down because we want it to be. Well, consider our wants changed.

"Is there anything you need to do to get it ready?" Nathan asked.

Ronny was surprised. "I thought you weren't going?"

"I'm not," Nathan said with a resigned smile. "But that doesn't mean I can't use it. Waste not, after all."

Chapter Twenty-Four

Alex couldn't sleep after Nathan left, so he changed for a run. It may not be real, but the fresh air still did his mind good. He hoped that it would still do the same today. Before he'd left, Nathan had given him his assignment.

"It's the simplest one of all," Nathan had said. "Perform the Second Rite tonight as planned." Then, he'd flashed that annoying grin, and told him to enjoy himself.

Enjoy himself?

As far as Alex was concerned, it felt like he was on death row. He had not wanted to believe Nathan when he'd told him the cost of the Third Rite.

Was that why the dream had made his mother an Angel? As a way of preparing him?

The cancer had taken its time, but it had finally worn her down. She died in January, just after the holidays. She hadn't been able to speak during that holiday, but Alex had always thought she'd been hanging on just so he, Maddie, and their dad wouldn't hold Christmas responsible.

Mom had always had funny ideas about Christmas.

Alex turned Nathan's tuning fork over in his hands. Nathan had given it back, just before he'd left. He didn't say why, but Alex suspected it was because of the Timber Angel—the one that wanted him to perform the Third Rite, the one that wanted him to die. Alex wasn't stupid. Between that man—DeMarco—and what the Angel had done to Nathan himself, Alex realized that he was probably the only person in town that it wouldn't go after, that it couldn't go after. If Nathan's tuning fork was insurance, then it made sense he'd want to keep it in the hands of the only safe person in town.

Downstairs, Alex found his dad and Julianna sitting at the kitchen table. Judging by the way their voices dropped when he entered, he figured they were talking about him. Maddie was nowhere to be seen; she was probably fast asleep somewhere. "Where're you going?" his Dad asked. His voice was light, but Alex could feel the strain in it.

Alex felt himself flush before he could even face his father.

"Just for a run," Alex finally said.

Judging by their faces, he could've said he was going surfing with sharks.

"Are you sure that's a good idea?" Julianna asked.

"You should stay put, son," Paul added.

"It's just a run," Alex said, more testily than he'd intended.

The guilt hit fast. They're just trying to look out for you, he thought. They're scared too. Grow up.

"Sorry," he added. "I can't sleep, and I don't really know what else to do. Nathan says I should enjoy myself, but…"

He trailed off, but Paul cleared his throat. "We've, uh, been talking about that."

"We're not sure we should trust Nathan," Julianna said. "His opinion, that is. He could be wrong."

"Do you really think that?"

Paul opened his hands. "We don't know him, not really. And, now that things are coming back to us, we're starting to think a bit more clearly."

Alex knew the feeling. His own real memories had started returning as well, just as Nathan said they would. He'd grown up in the Virginia mountains, for one. Not Timber's Edge.

Alex pointed this out to them. "Isn't that proof that he knows what he's talking about?"

"That's what I thought when the doctors told me about your mother," Paul said. His voice was quiet, but the admission was like a thunderbolt. "First it was an infection. Then it was cancer. Then a cancer that they'd never seen before. Maybe you don't remember, but they were running tests all the way up until she—"

"I remember," Alex said.

Paul sniffed. "Yeah, sorry. My point is maybe Nathan is running his own tests. You can't tell me you think he's told you everything. He's holding back."

Alex couldn't disagree there.

Paul continued, "I don't know if he's holding back to protect us, or because he doesn't know or because maybe he's involved in all this somehow."

"What?"

"Our point," Julianna emphasized, "is we don't know. But, if all three of us feel there's something he hasn't told us, we should probably pay attention."

"You said he was wrong too," Paul reminded. "About you being, you know."

His father still couldn't say the word, still couldn't admit the impossibility.

"Psychic, yeah. I don't know if I am, but I know this isn't normal."

Alex lifted his hand in the air and concentrated. Snowflakes appeared, misshapen and unclear. It was the first time either of them had seen him do it. Julianna's face turned as white as the snow floating to the floor. Paul simply exhaled, his eyes unable to leave the snowflakes.

Alex went on to explain to their increasingly incredulous faces about Anchor. As best he could, at least.

"Anslem," Alex finished, "he said the tuning fork, Nathan's tether is a valuable thing."

He removed it from his pocket and tapped its edge against his open palm. It was starting to make more sense why Nathan had left it with him. It was more than an insurance policy. It was a show of trust.

"And you trust this Anslem?" Julianna asked.

Alex shrugged. "It's kind of hard not to. He doesn't strike me as the sort of…person…who would lie. And, if he's telling the truth, then this is one of Nathan's most precious possessions. You saw it, it saved his life. If he was trying to hurt us, I don't think he'd leave it with us."

"It's him showing good faith," Paul said quietly. "That's what you mean."

Alex nodded. "Exactly. Trusting him in return doesn't mean we turn off our brains, but, if it's a choice between him and the Angel that trapped him—and me—then it seems to me that he's done a lot more to earn our trust than she has."

Julianna glanced at Paul, the expression on her face unclear. Despite that, Alex knew he'd won her over, at least partly. His father sighed, nodded, and then pushed himself up from the table.

"Alright then," he said. "If we're all agreed, then I suppose Jules, Maddie and I have some work to do."

"You do?"

Julianna jumped in. "Nathan gave us an assignment as well. The three of us. He was specific about that."

"What is it?"

Paul chuckled. "Well, that's the thing, son. He told us we weren't to tell you."

✷

Nathan returned to the Inn to check on DeMarco. There had been no change to the man himself, but he did notice that the flowers in his room had been changed. In the hallway, he could hear guests stirring, starting with Lisa Brenner excitedly asking after the tree lighting that night. When he came downstairs, he found Marie in the kitchen. She was standing in front of the juice mixer and the machine was making a terrible noise. He watched from the doorway for a moment until she, in an exasperated sigh, stepped back into the kitchen.

She noticed him then and gave him a weak smile.

"Problem?" he asked.

Marie wrung her hands, the frustration taking Nathan by surprise.

"I don't know," she said. "I don't know how to work this thing. I remember I did this yesterday, but now? It may as well be like I've never seen it before."

The orange's mangled pulp and skin still sat in the machine.

"It might help if you cut them first," he suggested.

Marie scowled, a look he'd never seen on her before, and bustled around the kitchen until she found a cutting board and a knife. When she had a fresh orange on the board, Nathan saw her hand shaking.

He stepped quickly to her side and placed a hand on top of hers.

"What're you doing?"

Nathan removed the knife from her hand and placed it safely on the board.

"It can be overwhelming, I know," he said quietly. "They're coming back. Your real memories."

"I know that," she snapped.

She caught herself and took a deep breath.

"Sorry. I'm sorry. I don't know what's wrong with me. No, that's not right. I know precisely what's wrong with me: I'm afraid. No, I'm terrified." There was the sound of laughter from upstairs, and

Marie's lip trembled. "They're all at risk aren't they? That, that thing, can hurt them all, can't it?"

Nathan had kept that detail from the wider group.

"Yes," he admitted quietly. "I believe it can. That's why we have to be careful."

"And keep up appearances right?"

"That's right."

"I don't even know where to start with making breakfast, let alone lying to them all. Then I picture them all lying there, like poor DeMarco. And, it's too much. It's just too much."

Yesterday's ginger cake was sitting on a plate on top of the counter. Nathan brought it to the cutting board and cut two slices.

"A wise woman told me," Nathan said. "Cake fixes a lot of problems."

He took a bite. It was dense and sweet and full of spice.

Marie's face was suspicious. "What happened to no room for sweets?"

Nathan shrugged. "Dreams have their advantages," he said. "One of which is that there are no calories."

"I don't know how you do that," she said, shaking her head. The ghost of a smile haunted her lips.

"Mmm?" Nathan asked through a mouthful.

Marie ate a corner of her piece. "Make me trust that everything will be fine. Howard, my husband, he used to be able to do that too."

Used to, Nathan thought with a pang of guilt.

"I live alone now. He passed, last year."

"I'm sorry."

"When I saw you on the floor last night. I thought you were dying. I can't stop seeing it. It reminded me of...it's just too much."

Nathan wanted to say that everything would be fine, that he was fine, but the lie felt dirty to tell.

"You know my son asked me to come see him for the holidays? I didn't really want to. What kind of mother says that? But the travel, the different places..."

"It's overwhelming," Nathan agreed.

"You must think I'm crazy, to be so afraid."

"No," Nathan said. "I don't think that." He wasn't one to pass judgment on anyone's fears.

Marie looked up at him. "I'd like to believe that, but you don't know how different we are. You have your wild life, running around. I wake up. I microwave my oatmeal. I watch television. That's all coming back as well. Then, I remembered my last conversation with Tom."

"Your son?"

She nodded. "I told him that I wouldn't be able to make it. That I had too much to do. You know what he said? He said that it would all be alright. He would fly down just to help me through the airport. Can you imagine that?"

"Sounds like a good son," Nathan said.

Marie smiled weakly.

"A good son with a coward for a mother. I told him no. I insisted. I thought that was the end of it, but then the weeks passed, and I thought I should go. Be brave. He lives in Wisconsin. But then, I went online."

"That's a mistake I try never to make," Nathan said, taking another bite of his cake.

"I read all about the turbulence, about planes getting iced up, about the runways getting frozen. I put that idea far out of my mind. But then, I thought, I could take the bus."

"Hopefully you got a better driver than I did," Nathan said sourly.

Marie's eyes widened, and she looked terrified.

Nathan put a hand on her shoulder. "What is it, Marie? You can tell me."

Footsteps ran up and down the upstairs hallway, and Marie's lower lip trembled.

"When I remembered that, I remembered that I did take the bus. It wasn't so bad, not as frightening as I thought it'd be. The driver, he helped me with my luggage. And, I saw a nice family there. And a young couple. There was a man I didn't like the look of. He didn't look happy to be there. Some sort of businessman, I think."

"Marie…" Nathan said quietly.

"When it came time to get on, I didn't want to sit alone, but I didn't want to bother anyone. So I found a seat next to a nice looking young man. He was asleep against the window, and, I don't know why, but he reminded me of Tom."

It's my fault. I was their lightning rod.

Nathan closed his eyes. He could remember the bus; he had been riding it since Memphis, on his way up north. He could remember waking for a moment as a woman sat next to him.

It had annoyed me.

"It was you, wasn't it?" Marie asked.

All Nathan could do was nod.

All those broken down cars in the mechanic's parking lot came back to Nathan's mind. Guilt dragged his heart into his shoes. They were all his fault, injured minds that had collided with his, and, when he'd fallen into the dream, he'd pulled them all with him. He wasn't much of a psychic, but he was psychic enough for that.

"Did I do this Nathan?" Marie asked in a trembling voice. "Is it my fault? My punishment for being too afraid?"

"You didn't do this," Nathan said. "I can't tell you why these things happen. Just that they do. Bad things happen to good people. Good things happen to bad people. We don't get to choose all of the things that happen to us, but we can pick what we do about them. And then we can make the most out of it."

"How do you do that? Pretend like everything's just fine?"

Tears pooled in her eyes, and the short woman suddenly looked miniature.

"By accepting that it's not," Nathan said with a sad smile. "I do what I can to help where I'm needed. I barely ever have a reason, and I don't always get it right. And sometimes I might not make much of a difference at all. My mother used to say that I've got nice dimples, a curious mind, and two hands. And that it was up to me to decide how I was going to use them."

He showed her his open hands.

"I decided to use them to help, regardless of others' rules, regardless of anyone's creeds, regardless of how much it might hurt. For better or worse, they're all I have left to give. Maybe in three days, this place collapses into dust, and all of us along with it. All I can do is everything I can think of to make sure that doesn't happen. All I can give is everything I am to try stop it from happening. Maybe in three days, time runs out for me. I hope it doesn't, but if it does turn out that my inning is up..." Nathan shrugged. "Then, that's why there's cake."

Marie didn't say anything for a moment, then she wrapped her arms around Nathan's waist.

This is uncomfortable, he thought, but that thought just made his grip tighter.

When she released him, Marie dried the tears from her eyes and nodded up at him.

"So, where do we start?" she asked.

"Keeping up appearances, starting with breakfast," Nathan said.

He took a look around the kitchen; at that point, breakfast was little more than theoretical.

"It's a good thing I know someone who can help," he said, grinning.

He offered his hand to Marie. "I'll walk you down."

At first, Marie recoiled, but then she took a deep breath.

"No matter how much it hurts," she repeated.

She put her small hand in his and let him lead her to the entryway.

"By the way Nathan," Marie said as she pulled on a heavy blue coat, "your mother was right. You do have nice dimples."

And a face for hats, he thought, smiling, as he pulled on the gray beanie he'd purchased what felt like so long ago.

*

The lantern outside the diner was burning bright in the glowing morning. Gloria's was alive with visitors scarfing down their breakfasts before another day in Timber's Edge, but that didn't stop the old chef from calling to Nathan the moment he and Marie walked through the door.

"Got two seats up at the counter for you!"

Marie gave a frightened look around the place, steadied herself, and then led the way to the back of the restaurant. Nathan saw that El was here as well, in his usual place next to the two empty seats. The boy's focus was alternating between the PB&J on his plate and the comic on the counter.

"Now, who do we have here? Another new face?" Gloria asked.

She gave Marie a long, piercing look.

"Pancakes," Gloria said, "sausage—nope, turkey sausage—and two eggs, over hard."

"Marie runs the Inn," Nathan said.

Gloria tapped the counter with her spoon.

"Is that right? Well why're you such a stranger?"

She waved a hand before Marie could answer.

"It doesn't matter none," Gloria said. "Sit, sit. I'll set you up."

"Actually we need some help," Nathan said.

He explained about breakfast.

"I mean," Marie said quietly, "if you're not too busy."

Gloria pursed her lips, then looked around the bustling restaurant.

"This? Please. I used to man the griddle at a Waffle House in downtown Atlanta when I was a young cook. Every day of the week, but twice on Sundays. This is a relaxing stroll."

She called to the back where her massive son was at the line. "Christopher?"

"Yes ma'am."

"Throw me up pancakes, eggs, sausage for ten. Pack it up to go. Throw in some pastries too, hear?"

The deep baritone echoed from the kitchen. "Heard."

"And some turkey sausage."

"Heard."

Gloria turned to them, and Nathan caught a glimpse of a silver loop in her ear.

"There, nothing to it. You take a seat and it'll be up in a minute." To Nathan, she added, "You'll have to get your own coffee today honey."

Before they could thank her, she'd disappeared behind the pass and back into the kitchen. Marie sat at the counter, and Nathan went to get them both cups of coffee.

I'll be into the gallons before today is up. Good thing it's not hitting my actual heart.

He filled two cups, returned to the counter, and found Marie talking with the young boy, El.

"Nathan," she said. "This is my new friend Elliott Patterson."

Elliott looked up at him, the bright gray eyes lighting up in recognition.

"I remember you," he said, "from the library."

"That's right," Nathan replied.

The eyes. They could be the same.

Nathan stuck out a hand, struggling to keep the tremble out of it.

"Let's make it official. I'm Nathan."

"Elliott," the boy replied.

He looked at Nathan's hand and laughed.

"What's funny?"

"Nothing. It's just something grownups do."

"It's polite," Marie pointed out.

She stuck her hand out as well. Elliott shook them both, then laughed again. At what, he didn't say.

"Elliott is waiting for his mother to take him to the tree ceremony."

"We're going to make ornaments first," the boy said, "with the other kids. Everyone gets to put an ornament on the tree after it lights up. But not before."

Nathan met Marie's face. "Of course not."

He toyed with his ring, then pushed up from the counter.

"Excuse me a minute. I need to add something to our order."

He crossed behind the pass and into the kitchen. Gloria was at the griddle, and Christopher, pulverizing eggs in a bowl, was the first to notice him.

"You need something?" he asked. There was a tension to the massive man. *One I'd expect from a guardian.*

Gloria looked up from the rows of sizzling bacon.

"Nathan?" she asked. "Everything alright?"

"Yeah," he replied. "Just had a question."

"You want to help?"

"Not unless you want me to burn the place down," Nathan replied.

Gloria cackled. "Alright, shoot."

She waved to Christopher.

"You get back to that now, I need that batter."

With a final look at Nathan, Christopher went back to the eggs.

He poured what looked like cream into the bowl and added a small fistful of cinnamon.

"You had a question?" Gloria asked.

"Chefs don't normally wear earrings like that," Nathan said. "What're they made of?"

Gloria took a step back from the griddle, retrieved her wooden spoon from its place on the counter, and tapped it against her leg.

She gave Nathan a long, hard look before saying, "Same thing as your ring, I expect."

"How long have you known?"

"Since I first saw you," Gloria replied. "Hard to miss a ring like that, and, those in the know, know."

"You didn't say anything."

Gloria flipped a line of pancakes on the other side of the flat-top. "No, but then people come here all the time. They share what they want. I try not to pry."

Nathan laughed, and Gloria chuckled too.

"Well, I try not to pry about sensitive things," she allowed. "And some people get real sensitive about matters of silver."

No arguments here.

Nathan made a fast decision. "You know where you are?"

The question raised Gloria's eyebrows. "Now that's a weird thing to ask."

"It is," Nathan agreed. "But I'm still asking it."

"If you mean, do I know that I'm dreaming, then yeah. Of course I do. That's what my place is, after all. When I've got the energy for it, I set up shop. Give people a nice place to rest, to relax, y'know? And I make sure they don't forget who they are either. I run a real place too, but, in the real world, you got to worry about profits and rats and wine lists. None of that here. Just good food, the best food you can imagine, and a comfortable chair."

"And as much conversation as you can stand."

Gloria's cackle returned and she banged her spoon again. She slipped the spoon into the front of her apron, and, with a long pair of tongs, pinched the bacon onto a tray. This, she passed to Christopher who began to place the slices onto waiting plates.

"Who's the muscle?"

Christopher glared at him. "Her son."

Gloria patted her son's thick forearm. "He's a marine. My youngest. Should be on his way back to see us for the holidays. I sure do love when I bring him here though."

In the dining room, Nathan remembered seeing a picture of Gloria surrounded by a host of smiling faces. The faces had a lot of similarities, and a lot in common with Gloria herself. All her kids, he guessed. A sudden gust of fear hit him. If he failed to save them, then those faces would all be losing her.

"Why the long face?" she asked.

She already knows. There's no harm in telling her.

Nathan explained quickly about the town and the Angel.

"I'm not sure how to stop it," he said.

"You can't," Gloria said. "Why would you even want to? All dreams end eventually. It's only natural."

"You don't understand. This one's different. Its owner...doesn't have control."

Gloria inhaled a sharp breath. Her voice turned firm, "That's impossible. It can't be this stable. It would be complete chaos. People flying around. People with eight heads. I've seen them. It's not something you forget. I would've felt it."

"I don't understand it either, but I know it's true," Nathan said. "Are you able to carry it?" he asked; the question hung in the kitchen like flypaper.

Gloria shook her head. "There's gotta be hundreds of minds here already," she said. "Not to mention the decades of history. No, Nathan, I'm sorry. I'm just an old chef. I don't think I've ever met anyone who could. Have you?"

Nathan's voice dropped. "I have. But they're very far away, and their help won't come cheap."

"Nathan. If the dream collapses and it doesn't have an owner, then it'll be a disaster."

"Like the Titanic," he said.

She nodded. "The minds like us, we might survive. We can swim. But the others?"

"Yeah," Nathan replied. "That's why I need you to be ready."

"For what?"

"The iceberg."

Nathan peeked through the pass, spotted Marie still talking to Elliott. She was laughing. It was nice to see.

Let her forget for a little bit longer.

Nathan couldn't forget. There wasn't any time. "The kid," he said, "what do you know about him?"

"Elliott?" Gloria shrugged. "Not much. Comes here and waits for his mom to get him."

"You've seen him before? Before Timber's Edge?"

"No, but that's not unusual. He's a nice kid. Polite."

"You've met the mother?"

Gloria was silent for a moment. Christopher beat the batter, but his attention was all on Gloria. He's a guardian all right.

"Come to think of it, no," she said. "I've never met her. He just ups and leaves. Says she's waiting for him. Why?"

"Just wondering how he got here, that's all. He's too young to have brought himself."

"Oh my God," she said, horrified.

Her mouth became a thin line on her face. The laughter lines that brought life to her eyes now made her look a hundred years old.

"Nathan, some of these people, they're here because of me. I brought them."

"I know," he said, his gaze lingering on Marie. "Me, too."

"They may not remember me, but I remember them. I'm responsible."

All Nathan could do was nod sadly. *I know. Me, too.*

Chapter Twenty-Five

Julianna wrote Hartford's name on the paper and marked it with a capital R, just like Nathan had instructed them to.

"I never did like that man," she said.

Hartford, the old collector, had spent most of their visit leering at her. But, there was no lantern in sight, and Hartford certainly remembered enough about the town for him to qualify as an R. Whatever the R meant.

The three of them—Paul, Julianna, and Maddie—moved on down the street, each with their own clipboard. The sisters who ran Lost Then Found Antiques got a P. They had two large lanterns hanging from the front of their building. Paul pointed to a family they hadn't spoken to yet.

"Hello," Julianna said as they approached, putting on her best smile. "I'm the mayor. Julianna Benneteau."

She held up her clipboard.

"I'm just taking down some information. Do you have a few minutes?"

Of course they did, the father said. They were all too happy to help. No, they weren't staying long, but they heard about a tree lighting and thought it'd be fun.

The rest of their conversation became a blur. Julianna had what she needed. The Butterfields got marked with a V.

While they spoke, Maddie disappeared into Timber's Edge Outfitters. A lantern hung from the eaves outside, so she had to go

305

speak to the owners.

After the Butterfields had walked away, Paul asked her, "Any idea what the point of this is?"

"No idea," Julianna replied. "But Nathan said it was important. Besides, it beats sitting around, thinking. Look, here are some more."

They approached a friendly looking older man who was walking his dog, a German Shepherd.

"Hello," she said. "I'm the mayor…"

✳

Microfilm can be a difficult thing to read when you don't have a reader. But, Marley's General Store happened to be well-stocked with flashlights and magnifying glasses. Hartford had even given up a jeweler's loupe after some rigorous bargaining, although the old creep had insisted on calling it dickering. With those, Nathan was able to set up a basic reader in the guest house bedroom. With the lights shut off and the curtains drawn, he was able to use the flashlight to project the image onto the desk by floating the loupe and microfilm together. The magnifying glass from Marley's got him the rest of the way, and he was able to make out the newspaper headlines, along with some detail from the images.

Now, Nathan hoped, there would be something on these he could use.

He emptied the cassettes onto the desk, ran his fingers over them. The rolls were thick, full of pictures. It would take hours to go through them. Thoughts threatened to race, but Nathan silenced them, forcing himself to focus on the film rolls.

Each cassette was organized the same way. Archived memories from Timber's Edge. The first one showed him Sunday, December 25th, 1935. The winter market sat on the desk, captured in pictures and in newspaper articles.

TIMBER'S EDGE GIFT MARKET PROVIDES FREE MEALS TO THE JOBLESS, one headline read.

Another declared MARKET APPEARS OVERNIGHT AT TOWN GREEN.

A picture showed lines of people milling around the stands. Nathan spotted signs for freshly pressed cider, mulled wine, fresh wreaths, and trees. At the back of the tent was an advertisement for a new Oldsmobile 8. He wasn't a car expert, but it certainly had the look of a car from that era. Nathan scanned all of the photos, trying to get some idea of who the Angel was, if the Angel was there at all. As he looked at them, he felt a strange sense of familiarity. If it weren't for the clothes and for the aging of the photograph, similar pictures could've been a hundred feet from where he was sitting.

Some things never change. But they echo.

He moved the film forward.

December 25th, 1968. Another Sunday. SANTA'S WORKSHOP OPEN FOR BUSINESS.

It was the toy factory. Marley's gift. The pictures showed the red train, now full-sized, circling the length of the Gift Field. It was full of children, waving to their families. There, in the conductor's space, was a younger Jake Marley. Lines of wooden tables and conveyors of packages cut through the field. Families were sitting at them, fathers with the hammers, mothers with the screwdrivers, all making their own toys, setting them on the conveyors, and collecting toys other families had made.

He moved the film backwards.

December 25th, 1942. Sunday again. SPRUCE RIVER FREEZES. TOWN ENJOYS A SKATING CHRISTMAS.

Rows of people dressed in heavy coats were ice-skating down the river, and, under the two bridges, fairy lights had been strung. At the Gift Field, tables laden with food and drink gave the town somewhere to rest and to celebrate.

Sunday, December 25th, 1892: CANDY FAIRE COMES TO LIFE!

A chocolate carousel and the gingerbread village appeared at the Gift Field. There were rings of spun sugar, vats of cider, and even a church made from gingerbread. Carolers lined the village streets, and everyone was dressed in their formal best. In the back of the picture, Nathan recognized the hook-faced man. In the picture, he wore a broad smile. The unsettling feeling in his stomach blossomed into an intense clamminess.

He brought back the picture of Jake Marley. He then compared it to the older picture, the one with the hook-faced man. Nathan flipped back and forth between them until he saw what had been unsettling him. The faces in the background weren't all the same, but some were.

Nathan recognized the lady selling roasted nuts in 1892. She had sold him some a few days before.

The family with the Hanukkah tent had been there in 1968.

Imprints, Nathan thought. *For a Psychic Shade, it'd be like a buffet.*

He couldn't turn through the films fast enough. Soon, he turned to another cassette. This time, all he cared about were the newspaper headlines.

Friday, December 23rd, 1950: TOWN CELEBRATES GOOD TIMES, DECORATES TREE.

Friday, December 23rd, 1942: TREE ALIVE WITH LIGHT. TOWN ANGEL ARRIVES.

There was a picture of the teenage girl, placing her hand to the tree.

Tuesday, December 20th, 1942: FIRST SNOW ARRIVES.

A fuzzy picture of snow coating Calbot Square appeared beneath the headline.

Tuesday, December 20th, 1892: HARK! THE ANGEL ARRIVES.

Tuesday, December 20th, 1950: NO SNOW, BUT STILL JOY.

It was the same days. Always the same days.

Nathan frowned at them, at the line of impossibility. He kept scanning. Every year, year after year, every day was the same. December 20th was always on a Tuesday. Saturday was always Christmas Eve. Friday was always the day of the Second Rite and it was always the 23rd. Sunday was always Christmas Day.

No dates on any of the newspapers came before December 20th and none extended beyond the 25th. He brought his hand to his mouth, felt his ring resting against his lower lip. He had noticed it in the archive earlier, but had dismissed it as a possible coincidence.

Like the Ghost of Christmas Present, Timber's Edge had a limited lifespan. Each year, it only existed for six days. No more, no less. In Timber's Edge, Monday simply didn't exist.

Aside from at Marley's. Nathan frowned at the thought. He was pulling on his coat before he even reached the door. *Three days ago, the old man had a case of them.*

∗

The surface of Iron Shoe Pond rippled in a breeze, but the surrounding trees didn't seem to feel it. After a moment spidery cracks of frost appeared on the water's clear surface. Soon, the strain became too much, and Alex had to let go of the Cold Place. The fractals of frost floated for a moment before melting into the clear water, vanishing as if they'd never been there.

Despite the cold, Alex's forehead was covered in sweat. In the cold air, it made him shiver.

Some Timber Angel I am, he thought, shivering in the cold.

He stuck his hands in the pouch pocket of his hoodie to try warm them up, ignoring the feel of Nathan's tuning fork. It's a precious thing he trusts you with, Anslem had said, so Alex didn't intend to leave it out of his sight. Once his hands were warm, he checked the time. Perception alters reality, and he didn't want to lose a minute.

He needed all the time he could get. It reminded him of cramming for exams in college, watching the minutes tick by during all-nighters, knowing that, no matter how prepared he was, the time was going to come when he'd have to take the test.

He tried not to think about what would happen if he wasn't ready for this one.

"But then I don't even know what ready is," Alex said to the pond.

It was a lie he didn't even believe any more. For he remembered the snow globes in the archive, and he remembered the feeling of walking up to the Gift Field on Christmas morning. He knew what an Angel's power was, what it could be.

He was sitting on the stone bench with the town at his back. Nathan had told him to rest, to try and relax. Alex's part was coming later, Nathan had said. Alex took the tuning fork out of the pouch pocket and examined it. It would be nothing for him to throw it in the pond, or fling it off of the overlook, and Nathan would never be able to find it again.

Did he really trust Alex that much?

Alex tried to focus on the pond again. This time, he couldn't even get the frost to appear before his head split open in pain. He kicked the snow in frustration. It felt like when he was rehabbing his leg. The muscle just couldn't do what he needed it to.

Thoughts of Nathan returned. He seemed so certain about Alex, about his being a psychic—and, if his time with Anslem was any indication, maybe even a so-called Mindsinger. Nathan had been so certain that Alex had started to believe it himself.

After all, there had been signs. Ones he'd tried to ignore. His peculiar sense of intuition, of being able to read people, his natural instinct to know how rooms of people were feeling were all gifts, but none of them amounted to being psychic.

An image of a red train came into his mind, and Alex tried to push it away without any luck. That had been the first time he'd had the feeling that he knew what someone was thinking. He had only been eight, and it hadn't been pleasant.

Around him, the wind picked up again, and Alex, finally cold enough, stood to leave. What he saw locked his jaw and tensed every muscle in his body.

Things had changed. The trees around the pond had grown thicker, more full. They looked almost wild. In the spaces between them, a strange white fog rolled in.

Alex turned to face the town and then felt his stomach plummet into his shoes.

Timber's Edge was gone, replaced by a thick white shroud. It was almost as if he was trapped in the middle of a swirling gray storm cloud. Most troubling of all, of course, was the fact that Alex couldn't make out the trail that led back down from the overlook. The fog had already arrived to block his path.

Trapping him at every turn.

The fog enclosed the pond. The water's surface began to harden, to freeze. Within moments, it was solid ice.

From out of the fog at the far end of the pond, a shape emerged. It was a woman. She wore a sleeveless white gown, the color of the freshest snow. Her long brown hair was styled in the way Alex remembered, before the cancer had fully taken hold, and her smile was wide and pleasant.

"Alex," she said in a kind voice. "I thought it was time we talked."

Alex stared at her, the initial shock being replaced by an anger that could've boiled an ocean. He only had two words to say to her —the thing that was choosing to use his mother's face.

"Fuck off."

＊

Marley was nowhere to be found when Nathan entered the general store later that morning. He was the only customer in the store, and, except for the model train puttering around the ceiling, it was nearly silent.

"Mr. Marley?" Nathan called.

A voice shouted something from deeper within.

At the back of the store, Nathan climbed a thin staircase led up to a landing that Marley had converted into a workshop-slash-office, albeit one in dire need of a filing system. Papers sat everywhere. In stacks. Paper-clipped. In loose sheets. They covered almost every surface, save for a desk that ran the length of the far wall.

"Mr. Cole," Jake Marley said, looking up from his desk. "Come round, come round. Just trying to get this finished before tonight. My eyes aren't what they used to be."

A pair of glasses was perched on the end of his nose. He was working on painting something. A Christmas ornament, Nathan noticed as he crossed around the desk.

"You and the IRS are going to get along real well," Nathan remarked.

"I know where it all is." Marley grinned. "What can I do for you? More cat treats?"

"Information," Nathan said. Despite his attempts, urgency had bitten into his voice. "About a snow globe."

The chair creaked as Marley leaned back.

"Information huh?"

"Yeah. Case of the Mondays," Nathan said.

Marley scoffed.

"How much do you remember about it?" Nathan asked. "About that year? Your year? J. M. It's you, isn't it?"

"Well this is a rare treat. No one's asked me about that in a long time," Marley said. He stared at Nathan like they'd never met. "I doubt what I know would mean much to you."

"Try me," Nathan said.

Marley coughed a laugh. "That's not what I meant. What I'm trying to say is that Jacob Marley and I are two very different people. He left. I didn't. I doubt I'd even recognize him if I saw him. If he's still alive, that is."

"You don't seem to mind," Nathan pointed out.

"Why would I mind?"

"Some might say you've been trapped here."

Marley's laugh boomed through the workshop. "Let me show you something."

He crossed the room and retrieved a heavy, leather bound photo album from what was almost another dimension. The shopkeeper balanced the book on top of a stack of papers before gesturing him over.

"These were taken back when the store first opened. It wasn't always here, you know? The town, it grows with each year, with each Angel Year. All Angels leave something of themselves behind, you see. My grand-pap. He opened it, left it behind after his Rite."

Their Memory will forever remain in Timber's Edge. It's like we thought, they're imprinting here.

"He was an Angel?"

"That's right," Marley replied. "This is a relatively young chain. Grand-pap's—oh that had to be thirty Angels strong. It's easy to pass it through family. Grand-pap passed it to—" Marley scratched his chin. "—You know, I don't recall precisely. His assistant, I think."

"He passed it?" Nathan asked. "Like a cold?"

"It's not a sickness," Marley replied. "But the Angel has to pass it on, yeah. That's the last part of the Third Rite. That's how this all ends. Even if they pass it on to nobody, they still need to let it go, to put it down."

"Can the Angel be changed?"

"No," Marley said. "Not until the Rites are over, but you don't need to worry. They're perfectly safe. They couldn't be chosen otherwise."

I don't share your confidence Mr. Marley. Not when a Psychic Shade has put itself into the works.

Marley leaned across the desk to study Nathan.

"You're not the Timber Angel. What is this to you?" he asked. "You look like someone's walking on your grave."

Nathan considered telling him about the Angel, the rogue Angel, but decided against it. Marley, after all, might choose Timber's Edge over the visitors.

If he tries to take matters in his own hands, he could kill us all.

"Just curiosity," Nathan replied. "The bell tower is yours. It's what you added." It wasn't a question.

Marley grinned. "Not bad eh? Before me, it was just a bell. But I gave it a proper home."

The model train made its way up to the workshop and promptly fell of its track. The shopkeeper pushed himself up from his desk.

"Gah. It's always doing that."

Nathan chuckled, but he couldn't keep his eyes off of the train. The red engine kept trying to move, despite being turned on its side.

If it's derailed, the trolley won't move at all.

While the engine struggled there, helpless against the fake hill it was stuck against, thoughts began to strike like lightning.

"It could work," Nathan muttered. "Alex won't be happy. But it could work."

The timing will have to be perfect. And we'll need all the lifeboats.

"You say something Mr. Cole?" Marley asked.

"Come to think of it," Nathan said, "I could use some supplies as well."

Marley was focused on resetting the train. "Supplies? Go ahead and take a look around. I'll be down in a minute."

"Well, that's kind of the thing," Nathan said. "I'm going to be a little short this time."

That got Marley's attention. The shopkeeper peered at him from over the miniature tracks.

Marley clucked his tongue, then said, "What the hell? It's the spirit of the season. Besides, it's not like the money's real anyhow."

Nathan left Marley's ten minutes later with two heavy bags. One was full of the souvenir bell towers while the other was weighed down by compact mirrors from Marley's rather sad cosmetics section. He was about to head back to the guest house when he spotted Hartford's Curiosities across the street. The case of jewelry reflected the morning light.

Nathan checked his watch and frowned. It was already later than he'd wanted it to be, and he had a lot more stops to make if he was going to be ready. Nathan crossed the street. He was in the market for silver. The purer, the better. He hoped Hartford wasn't in the mood for "dickering" but then he thought better of it.

It's not like the money's real anyhow.

✽

Nathan had warned him. He had told Alex, told all of them, about how the Angel could use other faces. That didn't make it less unnerving when his mother's face, when her eyes, widened in disapproval.

"That doesn't sound like my son."

"I'm not your son."

The Angel sighed. "You speak with his words, but you're not Nathan. You may not believe this, but I am your mother. At least, I'm the part of her she left behind."

"She didn't leave anything behind. She was never here!"

The Angel's face fell with sympathy.

"Every Angel leaves part of themselves behind, their best part," she said. "The part that harmonizes with the holidays, with feelings of love and family and joy. That's what I am."

"Except you're trying to kill me," Alex's voice was full of force. "This is just a dream. My dream. There is no part of her left here. All you are is my Ronny."

"Is that what you believe? All your memories here, so easily discarded?"

The Angel walked, barefoot, across the icy pond.

"It's alright Alex. He can be very convincing, and his story has a certain logic to it. That's because a lot of it is based on truths. Half truths, twisted to fit his theory."

"I believe him," Alex said, waving the words like a torch.

"Then you would've told him the truth about the first time you came here," the Angel said. "You've been running from it, afraid to tell Nathan, because you know it will poke a small hole in his theory, isn't that right?"

He did remember Timber's Edge. Christmas morning, receiving his gift, as clear as any memory. And he remembered who gave it to him that year. He'd held it back; the one piece that had still been his.

Alex grit his teeth. "It doesn't mean you're not trying to hurt me."

"I am not trying to hurt you Alex," the Angel said. "I have no intention of ever causing you pain."

"Nathan says the Third Rite will kill me, that you want me to do it."

"He's lying," the Angel said, simply. "Nathan doesn't think you're strong enough sweetheart. He told you right to your face."

Alex felt the tuning fork resting in his sweatshirt.

"You've already tried to kill me," Alex said.

A flash of disappointment crossed her face.

"You were never in danger. But I needed to lure Nathan to you. He's a danger. To you. To what you could be. I tried to trap him to keep him away from you. I'm sorry that I had to resort to such a measure. Nathan Cole means well, but he doesn't understand. He's scared of the power here. Why shouldn't he be? He's spent so long dealing with evil and spirits and all kinds of darkness that he no longer sees light when it's shining in his face. He's afraid that there can be something genuinely good and joyful. Because, then what's the point of him?"

"You don't know him."

"Neither do you," she replied simply. "He told you what you are. What this place can do for you."

Alex said nothing.

"Did he even bother to tell you how he was going to help you achieve it? Or was he content to let you remain asleep at the wheel?"

"I—I don't know." Nathan hadn't said anything.

"Is this place really the nightmare he'd have you believe? Look around you Alex. Is there one sad face? One person in pain? This is a place of joy. No wonder someone like Nathan Cole can't understand it. His life is one of pain. He was a prisoner for almost seventy years. How could he ever understand it here?" How did she know that? Did Nathan tell her?

Alex had no answer. Was it possible that Nathan's perspective was leading him to see things in the worst possible light?

"All I want is for you to become what you were born to be," the Angel continued. "Your memory would live here along with us. You can come visit again and again. You and I, we can actually get the time back that was stolen. We can live here, in Timber's Edge, for as long as we like."

"This is your dream Alex, and you know why? Because it was given to you."

Alex tried to fight the memory back. No. It wasn't real. It didn't really happen!

"I gave it to you," she said.

The Angel raised a hand and the surface of the pond shifted.

Shapes appeared out of the ice, a living ice sculpture. There was the tree. There were the presents. There was a young, eight-year-old Alex, and there was his mother, standing over him. The sculpture even wore her heavy jacket, the one lined with fake fur. The one she liked to say made her look like a Bond villain.

Alex tried. He tried to look away, to ignore it. But he couldn't, because he remembered it as well.

"That's it," she said.

The memory brought sweat to his forehead. He was watching it both ways. The first, acted out in the ice before him, but the second, was in his own mind. They had just opened the presents. Alex had run his hands all over the books, the thick, handsome volumes. They were the sort of things a grownup had, the sort of books his mom had in her library.

When she'd asked him to put them down, it had been hard, but he'd done as he'd been told. He tried to listen to his mother. After all, it was just the two of them.

The Angel's voice, his mother's voice, filled in the line. "There's something I want to give you, Alex. Something special."

"Something special?" he asked. He was talking, but his voice felt lighter, younger.

Mom had taken his hand. In both past and present, there was a sudden, stinging bite of cold, and Alex drew his hand back.

"Why'd you do that?" he asked. "That hurt."

"Does it still hurt?"

No, it didn't. Actually, he felt strong, like he could fly.

Like he could do anything.

Just like his mom.

The ice sculptures shattered, and Alex fell to his knees. The smell of frozen earth and sweat invaded his nose. It forced him back, pushed the memories away. The Angel studied him from the center of the pond. The fog around them began to fade.

"You see?" the Angel asked. "She gave you Timber's Edge. All those years ago. You've just refused to take it. This time, you can finally take up your place, give Maddie what your mother gave you."

Alex flushed, but he already felt changed.

"This is your dream, not his, " the Angel said, crossing her arms. "It's up to you. If you're not ready, I won't interfere any more."

Her smile was patient and understanding.

"After all, there's always next year."

She turned and stepped away, into the fog and out of sight.

Alex wasn't sure how long he watched after her. Behind him, Timber's Edge had returned. The sun was moving lower. It was already late in the afternoon. He had time to try again. He focused again on the surface of the pond, tried again to reach that Cold Place he'd come to know. This time, it flooded into him, as if the kink in a hose had been freed. Alex staggered at the surprise; the sensation was unlike anything he'd felt. It wasn't cold at all. Instead, it was the opposite. It was warm, almost joyful.

Fingers of frost reached across the pond, freezing it inch-by-inch. With a shocked smile, Alex took a nervous step on its surface. It held his weight easily. He pushed his mind out farther and reached into the air around him. Before long, a healthy breeze shook the trees, and fresh powder spiraled around him. Within moments, he felt the weight of the snow on his shoulders.

But there was one thing he could no longer feel, and that was the cold.

Chapter Twenty-Six

There was a knock at the door, and Nathan was surprised to find Julianna standing outside the guest house. The day had turned dark since he'd been studying the microfilm, and the temperature had plummeted. Julianna had clearly come down directly from the house. She had her arms wrapped around her body, and had neglected to wear a heavy jacket.

"Come in," Nathan said. "You'll catch a cold."

"Can we even catch cold here?" Julianna asked, but she came inside regardless.

Nathan caught her running her eyes around the place. He wondered if she even knew that she'd done it.

"Can I get you anything?"

Nathan had already opened a beer, but, now that he knew it wasn't real, it wasn't able to do much to his senses.

Julianna eyed the bottle on the counter. "Got another one of those?" she asked.

Nathan got her one from the fridge, twisted the top off with his shirt, and handed it to her. She thanked him and, in exchange, she passed him a small stack of paper.

"This feels very cloak and dagger," she said as Nathan flipped through them.

Perfect. Exactly what we need.

"There is an element of secrecy required," Nathan agreed.

"You going to tell us what any of it means?"

"When it's safe," Nathan promised. "Compartmentalization is critical. We're dealing with a mind-reader. The less you know, the safer you are."

He held up his burned finger as a reminder.

"Unless you want to take it on as well," he said darkly.

Julianna showed her own hand in response. She was wearing her engagement ring. It was a plain silver band.

"We told Maddie," she explained. "So I could wear it. It's the only silver I had besides Anna's bracelet. We gave that to Maddie, just in case."

"I figured you'd be a gold and diamonds sort of woman."

She chuckled. "Guess you don't know everything then. I'm allergic. And I'm not marrying Paul for diamonds."

"Anna was allergic to silver. You're allergic to gold. Paul knows how to pick the metallurgically disinclined."

Nathan appreciated they were taking precautions, but he also knew that they were largely symbolic.

"The silver will protect you, but only from an external force trying to push its way in. Don't think for a second they will protect you from a psychic hammer being dropped on your head."

"I understand."

She sipped the beer, and winced in distaste.

"Blame Alex," Nathan said. He took a sip of his own.

After he'd swallowed, he continued, "Since you're here, I have another little job for you. Wait here."

He retreated to the bedroom and retrieved one of the bags he'd taken from Marley's. He'd consolidated several of the bell tower models and cosmetic mirrors in this bag while leaving the other bag for himself.

As he was leaving the bedroom, Julianna caught a glimpse inside. Her eyes focused on the desk like a laser.

"Are those...from the archive?" Her expression withered. "You stole them?"

"Stealing implies that I don't intend to return them," Nathan pointed out. "Besides, they're not even real."

"When you took them," she said icily, "did you know about the dream?"

"Not exactly. I had suspicions."

"So you thought they were real and you still took them."

Nathan shrugged. "I still intended to put them back, but I needed to study them in private."

Her hawkish eyes bore into him.

"It'd be a lot easier to trust you," she said, "if you didn't do untrustworthy things."

"Noted," Nathan deadpanned. "The next time I steal something, I'll run it by you first."

"Did you even find anything?"

"Compartamental—"

"Just shut up. I don't want to hear it."

Nathan grinned then placed the bag in front of her.

"What is this?" she asked.

"Phase two," he said. "I need you to place these around town."

He gave her back the papers. He'd already gotten what he'd needed from them.

"One of each. In every shop, tent, household that you marked with a P."

"How am I supposed to do that?" Julianna asked.

"With your mayoral gifts," Nathan said. "Otherwise, I'd do it myself. Say it's something for the Angel or for the town or because of a local ordinance. I don't care. Just make sure they're there before tomorrow night."

"Fine. Consider it done," she said, taking a long drink from her beer.

"Don't tell Alex," he warned.

"I know," she said. "Compartmentalization."

She finished her beer then turned to leave, but Nathan stopped her.

"It's not a two-way street," he said suddenly.

The mayor of Timber's Edge sighed. "What?"

"Compartmentalization," Nathan said. "Psychics are very good at it, even from themselves. They have to be. Take Ronny. He's part of my mind. The part that needs to protect me. Sometimes, in order to do that, he needs to lie to me. He needs to know everything I know, but I can't know everything he knows. He can't lie to me otherwise."

"Is that significant?"

"You tell me," Nathan said.

Julianna sipped her beer and her eyes studied a spot behind Nathan's head. There it was, the glimmer of understanding.

Nathan smiled.

Her eyes narrowed. "You're telling me this. Only me?"

"Yes."

"Why?"

Nathan met her gaze and didn't let it go. "I'm working on the trust deficit."

Before she could answer, there was another knock at the door. Whoever it was didn't wait for one of them to open it, and it swung open to show Alex in the doorway. His glance jumped between them, noting the beers in both of their hands. His eyes lingered on the ring on Julianna's finger.

"I don't know what's worse," he said, "you two not getting along or you two getting along."

Julianna laughed. "We're a long way from getting along."

She closed the souvenir bag tightly.

Good, good.

To Alex, she asked, "Everything alright? You've been gone a

while."

"Yeah, just clearing my head."

Nathan didn't buy it.

Judging from the tightening around Julianna's mouth, she didn't either.

"You mind if I have a word with Nathan?" Alex asked.

"I'm popular today," Nathan commented cheerily.

Julianna scowled at him.

"Don't take too long. We have to go soon."

She left the guest house, and the door shut with a heavy click.

Alex rubbed his hands together. "Uh, I wanted to give this back to you, before I forget."

He pulled the tuning fork out of the pouch in his sweatshirt and put it on the counter.

Interesting timing, Nathan thought.

There was a change to him, Nathan realized. A sureness in his eyes, a newfound confidence.

Something's changed.

"Thanks," Nathan replied. "I was wondering where that'd gotten to."

"I was wondering," Alex said, "why a tuning fork?"

Nathan picked it up from the counter and weighed it in his hand. He didn't have to hit it to know precisely what it sounded like, didn't have to run his finger down it to know each bump and scratch.

"It's pretty simple," Nathan said. "We're the sum of our memories, do you agree?"

"I guess," Alex replied.

"We have memories that are solely our own. No one else can ever know them, ever understand them because they weren't there. One of my most powerful memories, one I'll never forget, was my first night at The Holding. I was taken to a room—I say room, but it was more of a broom closet—and there was a cot and a small dresser and a bathroom."

The room appeared in his mind's eye, as clear as it was when he first saw it. Nathan couldn't keep the smile off of his face. It hadn't just been his first room but his first real home.

"I remember every second of that first night," Nathan said. "It was just me, all by myself. Those memories exist only here," he pointed to his head. "How I felt, what I did that day, when I woke up, all of that is unique to me. Exists only within me. We all have memories like that."

Alex leaned against the counter. "When my dad married my mom," he said. "I got ready by myself. My first tux. I won't forget it."

Nathan leveled a long stare at Alex. *How didn't I consider that?* The thought pressed in the back of his mind, leaving a thumbprint of dread.

"Right, that's exactly right," Nathan said slowly, half to himself.

He brightened and tapped the tuning fork against his palm.

"My tether is much the same way. This was given to me my first night in Anchor. The Lady offered me my choice, and I agreed to—to serve, and then I was given this."

"By Anslem?"

"That's right" Nathan replied. "Anslem is Anchor's steward, bound by its rules and forbidden from interfering with our service. He's both ruler and prisoner. Once I agreed to serve, I became a resident, a prisoner, like Anslem. You've been there. Anchor can be a hard place to navigate. It's folded upon itself over and over again. The tuning forks were like—well, like lanterns I guess. They guided us to our cells."

Pity swam in Alex's eyes and Nathan laughed.

"It's not the note itself that matters. But this fork sang to me every day for seventy years, calling me from my cell, guiding me back. Each day I would spend in my cell, I would make changes to it. I'd scratch it, carve it, shape it. All by myself. Only ever by myself."

"But why?" Alex asked.

Nathan appraised him. "To keep me sane, Alex. Anchor's in constant flux, constantly resetting itself or changing. While in service, even I reset. My tether was the only part of Anchor that I could control. This, and my body. Anslem helped me with that. He's quite the tattoo artist."

"Anslem gave you your tattoo?"

"Tattoos," Nathan corrected. "A new one every day. I never told him what they meant, but he guessed eventually. His first attempts were, to put it nicely, butchery. But he got the hang of it, somewhere around the third year."

Nathan slipped the tuning fork into his pocket. "If ever I drift too far or too deep, the tether can bring me back, provided enough of my mind remains to hear it."

"It gives you purchase," Alex said.

"Something like that."

From his pocket, Nathan tossed Alex a small box.

"Think fast," Nathan said.

Alex opened it then frowned. "A necklace?"

"It's silver," Nathan said. "Psychics should always wear silver. At least one piece on their person. Hartford didn't have much great stuff, but that's not too bad."

"I'm not—"

Nathan held up a hand. "Humor me? Even if I'm wrong, and you're not psychic, then it will still offer protection against those who are."

Alex nodded, and a small smile crept into his mouth. "Thanks," he said. "Does it even matter if it's not real?"

Nathan frowned at him. "What makes you think it's not real?"

Alex laughed. "We're dreaming, aren't we?"

"Precious metals, particularly those touched with Memory,

they're special. They transit through the planes. It's one of the reasons things like the Holy Grail or Excalibur hold such power in our legends," Nathan explained.

He picked up his tuning fork for emphasis.

"Like my ring. Or this. There's only one of any of them, in all the planes. Items slip away all the time. Sometimes they're lost. Sometimes they fall through the cracks. Sometimes they're pulled away. Sometimes, they're placed where they can cause trouble. This is, in fact, why The Holding exists in the first place."

Alex crossed his arms. "The people you work for?"

"Once upon a time, but not anymore. Now, we're more like two independent parties. The Holding, however, remains one of the most secure vaults in our plane, on our world, for so-called touched items."

Among other things.

Nathan's throat was dry, so he drank his beer.

"I should go get ready," Alex said. His cheeks had turned red. "It's a big day."

He opened the door and stepped out into the night.

Nathan followed him outside, grabbing the bag of cat treats he'd been keeping near the door.

"Before you go. You know, there are good things about dreams," Nathan said.

Alex turned, his eyebrows raised.

"You can eat whatever you want," Nathan continued. "No calories, at least for our flesh back home. You can see amazing things, and sometimes, old friends can come back to visit."

Before Nathan could even open the bag, Tolkien, not the ghost cat, but the memory cat came bounding through the grass. The orange cat glanced at Nathan, then turned expectantly to Alex.

"Tolkien!" Alex called with a laugh.

Despite the cold and the damp, he dropped to his knees, and

Tolkien rubbed himself against Alex's legs.

"Aww it is him. He feels exactly the same," Alex said, his voice full of wonder.

The cat meowed, and Nathan threw him a treat.

Alex sat back on his haunches and looked up at Nathan, a wide grin on his face.

"He was a Christmas gift to me, you know? My mom got him for me. This year, I asked my Dad if I could get Maddie a kitten for Christmas, like how Tolkien was for me," he added, looking almost like a kid again himself.

Alex cradled the cat's face between his hands and then bundled Tolkien into his arms. The cat curled with content and purred loudly. Alex met Nathan's eyes and shook his head.

"For all your insanity, Nathan, I've got to admit, you do have your moments."

*

Tolkien followed Alex back up the yard, and, as soon as the back door opened, the cat darted inside.

Paul's voice boomed. "What the hell? Was that a cat?"

"It's Tolkien," Alex replied. To Paul's confused frown, Alex simply shrugged. "Something dreamy, according to Nathan."

Alex's head was swimming with new perception. Whereas before he had a sense of how someone was feeling, now there was almost a cloud curling off of them—everyone except Nathan, that was.

Paul scowled. "As if things couldn't get any worse," he said. "That little menace tore through my favorite chair."

He watched as the cat disappeared up the stairs, then turned to Alex.

"We were getting worried."

"Just clearing my head," Alex replied. "Where're the other two?"

"Getting ready," Paul said. "Jules pointed out that if we're going to keep up appearances, we should all look the part."

His father had dressed in a button-down shirt and a pair of slacks, more the professor than the tree farmer.

"Guess I should get ready as well," Alex said.

As he headed upstairs, he heard, no, he felt, something in his father shift.

What is it now? Alex wanted to ask, but the look on his father's face kept the question to himself. What Alex had come to think of as the smoke darkened.

"Ah," Paul began. "I know this hasn't been the easiest time for you, with me and Julianna and the engagement. Every time we seem to get close to talking about it, something comes up. Now we've got this on our plates, and, if we are trusting Nathan, then that means we're trusting what he says might happen."

There was a sudden crack in his voice and the smoke shimmered.

"Maybe I should've said this a long time ago. No, that's not right. I definitely should have said this a long time ago."

"It's alright."

I already know, Alex thought.

"No, it's not. You've finished school and you're going out in the world now. I don't care if you're an Angel or a psychic or a goddamn unicorn. You're my son and, wherever I am, you'll always have a home."

Alex felt the doubt in his father's voice, saw it in the shimmering of the smoke that surrounded him. There's something he's not telling me, but Alex knew what it was. It was the inevitable question of what would happen if Julianna happened to disagree. Torn between his new wife and his grown son, it didn't take a psychic to tell where his father would land.

And Alex happened to be a psychic. Like his mother before him.

"Thanks Dad," he replied, dazed. "I'll remember that."

Upstairs, Alex pulled off his sweatshirt and started the shower in his bathroom. He had to avoid the broken glass on the floor, and it was hard to look at the mirror. It was glowing like a spotlight. He was able to retrieve his clothes from the closet.

As he waited for the water to heat up—you'd think a dream would have instant hot water—he ignored the ache building in his head. He shut his eyes to avoid the glow from the mirror, but all that did was cause the tolling of the bell to grow louder.

Alex pulled off the rest of his clothes and stepped into the shower. The hot water pelted him, and the sound of the spray managed to block out some of the bell. Standing there, under the hot water, Alex suddenly felt very alone. The throbbing in his head made his eyes water, and soon tears were streaming down his face. His hands shook as he tried to stop crying, but he couldn't.

So the tears continued to fall, mixing with the water, until together both ran down the drain.

*

Nathan returned to the Ashford house just as they were all getting ready to leave. They had dressed up, Julianna in a dark gray suit, Paul in a blue checkered dress-shirt and slacks, and Maddie in an expensive green dress and leggings. Nathan, for his part, didn't have much in the way of formal attire, so he simply wore his burgundy overcoat, his darkest pair of jeans, and a stiff gray button-down shirt.

"Figured I'd walk over with you," Nathan said.

"You want anything?" Julianna asked. She held a glass of red wine between her fingers. "I won't make a habit out of it," she said with a thin smile.

"Whatever you're having, thanks," Nathan replied. "I figure it's probably the best in the house."

Despite the awkwardness, Paul laughed. "We're just waiting on Alex," he said.

A silence descended on them as it became clear what they were really waiting for. Tonight, Alex was going to offer himself up as a sacrificial lamb, and, though Nathan had no intention of letting him go through with the Third Rite, none of the others even wanted him to get this close to it.

I can't blame them. Better to avoid the cliff altogether.

Julianna gave him a glass of the full-bodied red wine. It was good, full of flavor, and deliciously dry. While they waited, Julianna finished her glass and poured herself another. Nathan took to examining the family photos, more closely this time than he had before. After all, the Angel had given him something new to look for. Or rather, the absence of something to look for.

The higher shelves were stocked with plenty of Paul and Anna together. Several of these also featured a teenage Alex, lanky and with a mop of black hair. Maddie appeared on the lower shelves. First, as a small bundle in Anna's arms, but then there were pictures of all of them in parks, on vacation, during holidays. There were none of Alex as a baby.

It's in the blank spaces, truth reveals itself.

Nathan sipped his wine, but struggled to stop his hand from shaking.

The lower shelves were more sparse, and they had a few of Paul and Julianna, and a few more of Paul, Julianna, and Maddie together. Alex was less frequent in these, but he appeared every now and then. This was the Alex Nathan had come to know, lean without being skinny, and seasoned without losing his youthfulness.

In several of the pictures, Alex wore something bearing the UPenn logo. Just after Mother Sable had died, Nathan had visited the campus with a request to track down one of Ben Franklin's old chess sets. He'd not been able to recover it, but he'd found plenty of ghosts roaming the place.

I wonder if Alex and I crossed paths. Or maybe it was before his time.

As if sensing his thoughts, Alex came downstairs, dressed in a dark blue suit with a white button-down and no-tie. His hair looked professionally messy. He wore a watch with a leather strap, and, around his neck, Nathan saw the top of the necklace he'd given him minutes before.

Alex glanced at Nathan when he stopped to pull on a pair of black dress shoes.

"What?" he asked.

"Looking sharp," Nathan noted.

"Just figured I should look the part."

"What's looking sharp?" Maddie asked.

"Something my mother used to say," Nathan replied.

Julianna crossed her arms. "How often did she used to say it to you?"

Nathan laughed. "Less as time went on," he admitted. "But the road does that to you."

As they walked out of the house, Paul and Julianna leading, Maddie behind them, and Alex and Nathan bringing up the rear, Alex whispered to him, "You do alright."

There it is again. That confidence.

"I try," Nathan replied.

Alex bit his lower lip. "Nathan. I—"

"You'll come out of this alright," Nathan promised.

Wearing a relaxed smile, he clapped Alex on the shoulder.

"We're just playing for time. I'm not going to let anything happen to you."

Presuming, of course, that I'm not already too late.

Chapter Twenty-Seven

They collected Marie on their way. There was a brief tremble to her lip, but no hesitation to her step. Together, they walked onto the street, turning towards Calbot Square. The Ashfords, Julianna, and Marie all shared the same forced, firm look to their faces.

Their eyes, so firmly set, could have been made from glass. Around them, the crowd swelled and surged. The street was full of joking and laughter, but it stood no chance at penetrating the cloud around them.

Calbot Square started filling up just as the black night fully set in. The vendor tents had multiplied since the First Snow, both in number and in the extravagance of their design. The bell tower wasn't about to be outdone, however. It had found time to acquire a wreath for each of its eight faces along with twinkling Christmas lights. A small line of carolers waited at the entry to the field, singing "Away in a Manger."

Nathan was no longer having any of it. The lines had been drawn now, between him and the Angel. For all the wonder, all the holiday spirit, to him, he may as well have been participating in a procession of the damned.

The smell of fresh popcorn drew his attention to a table. Children of all ages sat and were making popcorn garlands. Nathan watched while one of the children finished their piece, and then ran, no sprinted, up to their parents who stood near the town tree.

Another table was full of ornaments being painted. A third

featured boughs of holly being wrapped into small wreaths that could be ornaments themselves. Nathan spotted Elliott sitting at a table, sticking something that looked like wood together.

But the tree remained bare, and it would remain that way until it was lit. Nathan ran his eyes over the groups closest to the tree. They had a hungry look to their eyes, one of expectation and anticipation.

They want to be first, he realized. But for the life of him, he couldn't understand why.

Once they reached the center of the square, Julianna and the Ashfords began their nervous march to the dais while Nathan stayed behind. Marie drifted off to look at some of the ornaments, and Nathan felt a surge of pride.

It's a difficult thing to face your own fears. Go kick experience in the teeth, Marie.

Mayor Benneteau took the podium a few minutes before the lighting was scheduled. She began to speak, but her voice quivered. She looked back at Paul, cleared her throat, and managed to steady herself.

A small wave of nervous excitement had found its way inside Nathan's gut. He'd never been to a tree lighting before, not if you didn't count plugging in an artificial tree in the back of a camper van. Nathan had expected to see a massive, garish lever or switch to turn on the lights, and was quite disappointed that he could see nothing of the sort.

"So, Timber's Edge," the mayor was saying. "This is a special tree this year. We. We all know why that is."

Her voice grew higher and higher. Even nervous, Julianna Benneteau was a natural speaker, and she appeared to have the excited crowd close to cheering.

Nathan wondered what she did in the real world, and had a strange sense of guilt that he hadn't even bothered to ask her. He missed what she'd said, but whatever it was caused the crowd to break into applause.

The crowd's clapping died down, and then Mayor Benneteau continued, "Yes, it is a beautiful tree. As it is every year."

Again, she gave Paul a pointed look. The farmer took the meaning and blushed. The crowd cheered.

"But we have to thank something else as well. Our—" her voice dropped for a moment, "—our special benefactor is here tonight."

Nathan scanned the crowd. Each face wore the same excited expression, the same wide-eyes, the same partially open mouth. He was struck by the sea of similar faces.

When he looked up at the small dais, Alex's face was set.

It made Nathan twist his ring. The charms on his wrist began to shake, began to rattle, as Alex took in the crowd's expression. There was color in his cheeks, but not from embarrassment, not from discomfort, but from resolve.

Julianna began to count.

*

Julianna started at the number twenty, and the crowd followed.

With each number, Alex took another step closer towards the tree. When the crowd realized he was the Timber Angel, they cheered even louder. They pushed themselves out of the way to make room for him, as if he were some prophet delivering them a miracle. In a terrible way, he was. But it was a miracle of no true value.

It was just Christmas lights on a tree. That was all.

When finally the count made it to zero and he reached the tree, there was the briefest moment of stillness, of silence, of an entire town holding its breath. Alex was holding his breath as well. He took a deep breath, felt the Cold Place swell up within him, and felt the aching twitch behind his eye. He held his breath. It was only a few seconds, but it felt so much longer. In the crowd, he saw Nathan watching him, his face tight with concern.

Alex placed his palm on the tree's trunk, right on the rough bark.

For a moment, nothing happened. He felt the town waver around him, felt their doubt wash over him.

Then, the trunk opened to him the way that the ground opened up for rain. It hungered for him, and instinct took over. The skin on his arm rippled with goose-flesh, and, one at a time, each hair stood on end. He focused all of his attention on the tree, and Alex poured the Cold Place into it.

The tree shimmered then burst into light. It began at the point he was touching, but spread quickly and fiercely. The ends of the branches each took on a light of their own, as if they'd been strung with tiny LEDs. The lights spiraled around the tree, each one finding their respective tip and resting there. They spread up and down the tree, and the crowd collectively gasped. Finally, the stream of fairy lights reached the top of the tree, where it coalesced into an orb of clear, white light.

The crowd exploded, but Alex barely heard them. His eyes had been taken by something else. In the distance, high in the mountains, there was another light shining like a spotlight back at the town. He knew that spot. He knew it very well. He ran there every morning.

The light came from Iron Shoe Point.

*

Once Alex stepped away, the crowd surged forward. Despite the cramped space, it all remained orderly, if energetic.

Not a fight in sight, Nathan thought.

The children hung their ornaments first. Garlands of popcorn, brightly painted balls, and wreaths of fresh holly all found homes on the tree's branches. The adults came next. Many of them, Nathan saw, had brought their own ornaments. There were novelty ones and old picture frames, souvenirs from theme parks and cities.

Marley lingered over his choice, but eventually hung the red and gold ornament he'd been painting somewhere near the middle of the tree.

Maddie eventually approached the tree and hung an ornament of her own. It was a simple silver snow angel.

Fitting.

Nathan had noticed the light on the mountain as well. Although it wasn't as bright as it was when Alex had first touched the tree, it was still shining bright enough to be seen.

The next brick in the road, he thought.

He still didn't know precisely where it was, but Alex had recognized it; Nathan was sure of that.

Nathan's charms shook, and pulled behind him.

Before he could turn, a voice called, "You're not hanging anything."

There, sitting on the bench, was the Shade. It was still wearing the face of Alex's mother.

"Shame on you," it said. "It's tradition to hang an ornament."

Nathan said nothing, but his lip curled.

"Oh come now Nathan," it chided. "I could turn your brain to soup if I wanted to."

"Do it then," he replied.

For a moment, the Shade appraised him. "Tempting, but it wouldn't do much for Alex's trust, would it?"

It was worth a try.

"I suppose not."

He stepped closer to the bench and tried to ignore the desire to throttle it then and there.

It would be so easy.

The thought made his stomach clench.

"It is interesting," it said. "You could have told them what I really am, but you chose not to. What am I to make of that?"

"Maybe I don't want to ruin their Christmas by telling them you hollowed out their mother."

"Anna was an interesting soul. A real fighter," the Shade said. "But, sadly, lacking in true pain."

"What do you want?" Nathan asked. It felt like bargaining with a spider.

"I think you're saving that little fact. For insurance. Perhaps to turn Alex against me."

"You didn't answer my question."

The Shade smiled. It was a smile that would've struck fear into a crocodile.

"I have nothing to hide," it said at last. "I wanted to see how my pupil got along."

So that's where he was. Alex…

"I thought as much," Nathan said.

"What's a mother to do?"

"His mother? And here I thought you were just an evil bitch."

"Mom!" Elliott's voice called out from the crowd.

The boy was talking directly to the Shade.

Not the boy. No. No! NO!

Nathan's feet felt like they'd been dipped in concrete. The dream was supposed to only be keyed to Alex.

Who told us that?

The thought brought Nathan's mind grinding to a halt.

The boy was holding an ornament in his hands. Like Maddie's, it too was a simple ornament. But, unlike her metal one, Elliott's was made from wood and it was in the shape of an angel.

"Can I hang it now?" Elliott asked.

"Let him go," Nathan whispered.

To Nathan's disgust, the Shade called back, "Go ahead. But don't push! And say thank you!"

Then, it dropped its voice, "You're going to want to watch this part."

We have to stop him. This'll ruin everything.

Nathan started after the boy, but the Shade continued, "I don't have to tell you what happens to the others if you try to interfere, do I?"

Nathan froze and glared at it. His fists were already clenched, ready to beat it to death or die trying.

Live to fight another day Nate. We can't help them if we're drooling into a cup.

"You really are an evil bitch."

"Now, Nathan. Language," the Shade chided.

Elliott ran up to the tree, and, as his mother had asked, waited his turn. Then, he stepped up to the tree, found a free branch, and hung his ornament.

"Such a polite boy," it said.

He stepped away, and, with a wide smile on his face, reached out and patted the tree on the trunk.

Saying thank you, Nathan thought, in horror.

It was only a moment, only an instant, but Nathan didn't miss it. His stomach dropped and he felt a brutal shock in his hands.

The lights on the tree shimmered. And the light on the mountain glowed just a bit brighter.

"What have you done?" Nathan asked, his voice taking on a murderous edge. "Tell me, now, what did you do?"

"Mr. Cole, I'm disappointed," the Shade said, its voice dripping with sweetness. "You didn't think you were the only one with an insurance policy did you?"

Chapter Twenty-Eight

The doorway to Anchor opened up to a cobblestone street, coated with slush and ice. Horse-drawn carriages clopped down the street, their drivers cracking whips and calling for passersby to move out of the way. They spoke with British accents, and Nathan, who had never crossed an ocean outside of his mind, wondered if he was in London. The streets smelled of smoke, but also of wet stone and horses.

Across the street was an immaculate series of row homes. They were made of dark stone cast golden by the surrounding street lamps. Bay windows looked out onto the streets, and, within, Nathan could make out decorated Christmas trees and wrapped presents. Ornate facades coated the outside of the buildings, full of stone carvings of creatures that not even Nathan recognized. Above the buildings, tall towers looked down like giants watching the streets below.

Curious, Nathan crossed the street and knocked on the door of the center row home. The knocker was as ornate as the rest of the building. It was carved in the shape of a creature that reminded Nathan of Cerberus except where Hades' three-headed beast had been a dog, this one was a sort of lion. After a moment, the door opened, and an older man stood in the entryway. Around his neck hung a brass tuning fork on a chain.

"May I help you?" he asked.

Nathan recognized him. He had been sitting in Anchor back when it had been a chalet. Judging by the look on the man's face, he clearly didn't recognize Nathan.

How long has it been for you, friend?

"I'm here to see Anslem," Nathan said.

"Are you expected?"

"I'm always expected," Nathan replied.

The man considered the statement before stepping aside.

"I'll inform the master that you're here. Come in. Make yourself at home. I'm sure he will find you."

Now Anslem's gone too far, Nathan thought.

He stepped inside a warm reception area. A square wooden staircase curled up the building. Nathan peeked up, and saw that the staircase had no end. It simply kept climbing. To his right, there was a drawing room, full of people, human and others alike. They were playing some sort of party game. A dining room to his left was in the middle of a formal dinner. The massive table, long enough to host a state banquet, carried dozens of turkeys, several roasts of beef, and every variety of vegetable imaginable. There were platters of assorted breads, entire jugs of gravy, and even trays of some sort of popover that Nathan didn't recognize but immediately wanted.

Now, he's really gone too far.

Near the end of the table, the Keeper sat at a smaller table by herself. Her dolls, as they normally did, surrounded her. For once, it was her he was looking for. She met Nathan's eyes as soon as he walked in, so, with a reluctant sigh, he crossed the length of the room.

"He's gone too far, hasn't he, Dear Nathaniel?" the Keeper asked.

"You could've reigned him in."

"I did," she said. "You should have seen the castle."

Nathan chuckled. Alex had told him about his visit to the yuletide fortress.

"This is your fault, you know," she said.

"All I did was tell him about Christmas."

The Keeper tutted. "You know how he is with something new."

She toyed with one of the doll's hair.

"You're alone this time."

"Just dropping something off," Nathan replied.

"Of course. Can't have something like that floating around," the Keeper replied. "And Alex? How is he?"

"Coming to terms," Nathan said.

At least, I think he is.

Nathan had to swallow before continuing, "Thank you. For what you did for him."

"I did nothing."

"You helped explain. Helped him understand."

The Keeper waved a hand. "He would've understood without us. His mind is powerful and he has a natural touch, but his development is wanting. How has he come that far without knowing himself? It is, troubling, is it not?"

Tell me something I don't know.

"Regardless," she continued, "with a mind like that, he should be wearing his silver."

"With any luck, he'll start. Assuming I can get him out of this mess."

The Keeper's strange, lifeless eyes, ran over Nathan's face.

"Nathaniel, I do hope you're planning something that will lead you back to Her. We have so missed you."

Just then, Nathan noticed a small arched door behind her. It was painted purple and black, and its frame was coiled with moving stone serpents. Ever since Elliott became involved, Nathan had been unable to keep the door out of his mind.

There it is. The way out that will save everyone. No risk, all reward. It would be a simple deal. By the Lady's power, I could save them all.

Even myself, given time.

Given pain.

Given death.

Given whatever energy I have left.

But what would he become at the end? If again, he served as her Black Thorn. If again, he soaked his hands in blood and sand and filth for Her, would he even recognize himself? If again, he butchered for Her amusement, would there ever really be a way back?

Live to fight another day Nate. We can live to fight another day.

What would be the point? Even if he could save everyone else, even if he could escape on his own lifeboat, Alex and Elliott would both be dead.

That was too heavy a weight to carry. He'd find a way, even if he had to make himself an Angel. Even if he had to carry this dream himself.

This is more than just losing, Nate. We'd go down with the ship.

If that was true, then the Shade would come with us.

So be it. I would never have guessed that Christmas would be the thing to finally take us out.

Finally, his heart full and his mind resolved, Nathan laughed. It was a deep, hearty thing. "Don't count on it," he told the Keeper. "But you can tell Brother Flame something for me."

"Oh? He will be pleased to hear it, I'm sure."

"Tell him, I've not forgotten his most important lesson, and that it may well have saved my soul."

The Keeper said nothing but simply inclined her head.

When she looked up, she said, "Ah, there is Anslem. Be warned, he will have you try one of the 'puddins.'"

"What exactly is a 'puddin'?"

The Keeper sniffed before saying, "It is the yellow thing."

She pointed to the nearest tray of popovers. At that moment, Anslem appeared next to them in a shower of sparks. He was wearing a formal black tailcoat, complete with a white vest and a deep, green waistcoat. A sprig of holly sat in place of a boutonnière.

"I apologize for my delay, Nathan Cole of The Holding," Anslem said. "I have been occupied."

"I can see that," Nathan said.

Together they drifted away from the Keeper, and stopped by the table.

"Have one of these," Anslem said. "They are called Yorkshire Puddings. I have learned they are a staple at these gatherings of yours."

Nathan tried one of the curious puffy breads. It was flaky and melted in his mouth. It tasted a bit like a savory pancake, and it wasn't long before he'd chewed through the rest of it.

Through a full mouth, Nathan asked, "Gatherings of mine?"

The stars in Anslem's eyes swirled. He was clearly pleased with himself. "Yes. Alex Ashford told me that a hallmark of the Christmas feast is a dinner with friends and family. You neglected that detail when you were telling me about trees and yule logs and religious iconography."

"I thought you wanted a history," Nathan said, half to himself.

Anslem, apparently, didn't hear. "These gatherings, then. This is why such days are so important to your kind?"

Nathan looked along the table. It was true. The guests sitting there were all enjoying themselves, even a set of Vael looked like they were happy.

Not an easy thing for them.

"I would say this captures it," Nathan said.

"Ah excellent," Anslem said. "This, then, is familiar to you?"

"Not exactly."

Anslem froze, and Nathan winced; he may as well have slapped the Aegyl.

"It's not familiar to me because I didn't live in this time. Or in this style. It's about two hundred years or so out of date."

"Only two hundred," Anslem said. "I am growing closer."

Nathan had to laugh. "Yes, my friend. You're growing closer. But why are you doing this?"

Anslem studied the table, considering the question. "So that I can understand," he replied.

"Christmas, I know."

"No. Your kind, Nate. Your perspective," Anslem replied. "The meaning of a day. For one such as me, that is a foreign concept. I confess, it still eludes me."

Nathan began to understand.

"The meaning of a day," he repeated. "It's in the anticipation. You spend all year looking forward to it, but it's always gone too soon. However, in the moment, when you're opening that first gift, or cutting the first slice of turkey, or watching the first scene of your favorite movie, it feels like it can last forever. The moments stretch on. Fleeting and infinite at the same time."

Nathan thought of sitting across a campfire from Mother Sable, a can of Spaghettios (with turkey meatballs) in his hand and a spoon in the other. She was singing Christmas carols in her strong, husky voice while a blanket of stars rested overhead. He thought of when they had played Monopoly at the meeting table at The Holding, and he'd flipped the board because she had bankrupted him for the third time in a row. Nathan had been finding tiny red hotels all the way until February.

Nathan smiled when he continued, "My kind are not always aware when they create memories. We don't always pay enough attention to good times, but we spend plenty of time wishing we had. Days like Christmas, I think they tend to make my kind stop. They make us pay attention, just for a little while."

Anslem bowed his head.

When he spoke, sadness touched his smooth voice, "I think I am coming to understand better Nathan. Thank you."

Nathan held out his tuning fork, wrapped once again in its black velvet. "For your safekeeping."

Anslem took it but didn't look at it. Instead, he studied Nathan's face until Nathan had to look away. "What is it?"

"Do be careful my dear friend," Anslem said. "I would hate for this to be the last time we see each other."

He had never spoken like that before, and it caught Nathan's voice in his throat. He swallowed, nervously, before asking, "I thought you don't have firsts and lasts?"

Anslem nodded. "This is so. I see all the eventualities, all at once, and only when fate has cast its lot, do I know which echo is true. I never know if you will return. But I hope for it, every time."

Nathan grinned. "Me, too Anslem. Me, too."

He was about to leave, but thought of something.

"In my cigar box, if you want to truly understand Christmas, there's a picture in there that might help. Feel free to look at it."

I don't suspect I'll be needing it.

"I will do so."

"And tinsel. You've gotta get some tinsel. Monopoly and tinsel, Anslem. At the end of the day, that's what Christmas is about."

✳

Alex had been concerned when he'd found Nathan on the couch, unresponsive, but then he'd noticed the mirror on the coffee table. He'd turned to leave then, but then decided it was better to stand guard. Just in case.

Nathan stirred just as Alex finished a beer. He was glassy-eyed for a moment, but then his eyes darted to Alex.

He jolted the rest of the way awake. "Is everything alright? Did something happen?" The questions were quick and sharp like rifle shots.

Alex raised a calming hand. "No. I just wanted to talk. I found you Slipping and figured I'd wait. I hope that's alright."

Alex passed him a beer.

Nathan sighed and took it.

"It's not considered great etiquette," he said. "What can I do for you?"

"How's Anslem?"

"Same as ever," Nathan replied. "Actually, he's made Anchor quite Dickensian."

"Dickensian?"

"It means—" Nathan stopped, and waited, but Alex said nothing.

"I've got no idea, dick," Alex admitted, laughing.

"Well, he made it look like Charles Dickens' front room at Christmas. I thought you had English professors for parents?"

"It doesn't mean I know all the words," Alex said.

He wished he had something else to say, something to keep this part from coming out, but he could think of nothing.

"I, uh, didn't see you after the Second Rite," Alex said.

"Yeah," Nathan said. "Sorry. The Angel paid me a visit and— well, things have changed. I've had to come up with a new plan."

"The Third Rite's tomorrow," Alex said. "I can do it Nathan. It won't hurt me."

Alex tried to make his voice sincere, confident. He knew what to do now, knew that Nathan was wrong.

Nathan's face looked crushed. "I thought you might say that. In fact, I've been afraid of it."

Alex was confused. "Afraid of what?"

"She's lying to you Alex. You have to trust me," he said.

"You don't understand."

"She showed you something, didn't she? Some memory you've been keeping locked away? From me? Something you don't even let yourself think about?"

Alex stepped back. "How…how did you know that?"

"Because psychics awaken when they're much younger," Nathan said quietly. "Somewhere, along the way, you built a wall in your mind, repressing your powers. I don't know why you did, but it's the only thing that fits. She wants you to break that wall right now. But, she doesn't want what's best for you. She wants what's best for her."

"You can't know that!"

Nathan's smile was sad. "You have to trust me, Alex. The engine of this dream is beyond anything I've seen. Something that only a full psychic should be able to touch, let alone bear. The Third Rite doesn't kill the one who performs it, but that doesn't mean it won't kill you."

Nathan looked pained when he continued, "You aren't strong enough Alex. You haven't woken up to your powers yet. The Third Rite will force you to shoulder the entire dream and every mind connected to it. It would overwhelm you. It would burn through your mind."

Alex's hands turned clammy and his voice stuck in his throat. "What are you saying?"

"The Angel has set it up, don't you see?" Nathan lifted his hands. "It wants you to perform the Third Rite, to bring that wall down. To force the issue, it's put every other mind at risk. It's a trolley problem."

Alex was familiar with it. A trolley is running down a track, hurtling towards a group of people. There's a lever which will switch the track, sending the trolley down another path. But, in that path, there is a single person.

Nathan sat back, and, all of a sudden, looked very tired. "Who am I to pick?"

"It's not up to you."

Nathan laughed, but it was a pale copy of his usual humor. "Of course it is. As it turns out, the trolley problem isn't that complicated. All you need to do is derail it. The solution is simple: I put myself in the path of the trolley, don't you see?"

Alex felt his eyes water. *No Nathan. There's another way.*

"I'm not going to let you."

"It's been after me all along. I could've walked away."

Nathan's eyes dropped. It was like he couldn't bear to face Alex.

"But I could never resist saving you. I was always its endgame. It's a parasite, Alex. It feeds off of Memory, off of painful Memory, and I am likely the largest living Memory it has ever encountered."

✳

Alex's face was pained.

I am sorry Alex, but there is no other way.

"You said you're not strong enough," Alex said. "You said it yourself. You'll die."

"Yes, I will die. And I imagine it will be quite unpleasant. It's alright. I've died before." Nathan replied. "But my Memory will be transplanted here. I won't have long, but I'll have enough time to release the dream."

What's one more lie? The dream will collapse for good and me along with it.

"You don't get to make that choice for me. You're. You're better —"

"No Alex," Nathan's voice stabbed like a knife. "I. Am. Not."

It's time he knew, time these illusions he has about me are shattered, once and for all.

He stood, pulled aside his tank-top so that his tattoo was fully visible. ξϛ ια κδ. Just as he had before, with a finger, he moved between the three sets.

"Years, months, days. Sixty-six years, eleven months, twenty-four days. A total of twenty-four thousand, four hundred, and forty-eight days. That's how long I served Her."

Nathan's rubbed a hand over his mouth. The words weren't easy to find.

"There are other things than Timber Angels and psychics. Far worse things."

"The Betwixt?" Alex asked.

"Yes," Nathan said after a moment. "Infinite entities. Creatures that live outside of any plane, but who want nothing more than to join them. For them, reality is just a toy. For the Lady and others like Her. Anchor is somewhere where the walls are thinner, where, when the rotation is right, they can even reach. They prowl through Anchor, offering a choice. Others may make you a king. Or save your wife from cancer. Or maybe even reincarnate you. But the Lady, She deals in second chances. "

"She tricked you?" Alex asked. "She must have tricked you."

"No," Nathan's voice was steady, "I knew what I was doing. There's no need for a being like that, like Her, to lie. It would be like you or I lying to an ant. Or Anslem lying to a child. A deception like that is beneath them. You get an invitation. And you make the request. There is just the request and there is simply the Price. If the Betwixt listens, if one of them chooses you to enter into their service, then there will be an offer. And a deal will be struck."

"But why?" Alex asked. "Why would you make a deal like tha—"

"Because I killed my mother," Nathan said.

There was no hesitation, no flicker of a question, no shadow of a doubt. The words carried the terrible, final weight of a fact.

Alex couldn't bear to look at him.

No surprises there.

"I was driving," Nathan said, his voice turning thick and wet despite his best efforts, "I sent us off the road. We crashed into a ravine, sinking into the mud, drowning in the rain. Just before I lost consciousness, I felt her die. That was my last living Memory. The last part of my story was killing my mother."

Nathan wiped his face and the sad smile returned.

"For me, the deal was simple," he said. "The Lady offered me time enough back to save my mother. Second chances. All I had to do, my Price, was to fight and to kill. What she gave me were second chances, and I used them. She called me her Black Thorn. I was a gladiator, Alex, for lack of a better word. A pit fighter. An animal."

"But why?" Alex hesitated at his place in the living room.

Nathan couldn't tell if he wanted to run or come closer.

"Why?" Nathan had to laugh. "For fun. For amusement. To take our greatest torment and to turn it against ourselves. To force ourselves to revel in it, and, make no mistake, I did. To see which one of us can do it the best, and—make no mistake—I was the best. They want the Memories, and there's no Memory more valuable than that born from pain. I fought because there was no better way to hurt me. No other shame that would cut me deeper. Forcing me to fight. To break bone. To tear, to rip, to slash, and to cut. To kill. With no other purpose than the act itself. Every day."

"Sixty-six years, eleven months, and twenty-four days. Twenty-four thousand, four hundred, and forty-eight lives. And, in return? She sent me back, time and time again. Five minutes. Then ten. Then twelve. Each extra minute, soon each extra second, costing more than the one before. Eventually, I couldn't pay it anymore. Eventually, I—"

Nathan swallowed and his hands trembled.

The next words were wet with emotion.

"I gave up," he said at last. "I let her die."

AND IT WAS A MISTAKE!

Nathan wiped his tears against his shirt and hands and took a deep breath. He approached Alex, stood close enough that he could feel Alex's warmth.

"That's why it has to be me, Alex. A choice between the two of us is no choice at all. You, and the things you're going to be able to do, they will be incredible. You can hear the music that connects all of us. You can't control it yet, you can't adjust it, but soon you will be able to. You will be able to help people in ways that you can't even imagine. If you can keep your nerve. If you can be better than I am. One day, the whole world will hear the song you can sing."

Alex didn't move. It didn't seem he was able to.

That's good. It'll make this easier.

Oh Alex. I am so sorry, but plans have changed.

"Nathan, I—" Alex couldn't find words.

And nothing can be left to chance.

Nathan reached out, and with all the speed of the Black Thorn, kicked Alex's legs from under him; all Alex could do was grunt. Nathan pulled Alex down, turned his body around, and then wrapped his powerful arms around Alex's thin neck.

Alex squirmed, kicked, but the fight was already over.

All that was left was the waiting.

"This is the difficult part, I'm afraid," Nathan said.

He applied pressure, the perfect amount.

Within seconds, he felt Alex grow slack beneath him.

Within a minute, it was over.

Nathan checked Alex's pulse then exhaled deeply. Nathan's heart rate was firing in a machine-gun pulse and he felt sick.

A minute passed and the door opened. Ronny strode in, took one look at the body on the floor, then said to Nathan, "Well, I must say, I didn't think you'd have it in you."

Chapter Twenty-Nine

The sun hadn't risen when Nathan strode into Calbot Square. The tree, full of decorations, was still full of light, and the lantern nearby was burning brightly with a merry flame. This early on Christmas Eve, the square was empty.

That suits me fine, Nathan thought.

He crossed quickly over to the library, and tried the front door, but, unsurprisingly, it was locked. If he had time, he could've picked it, but time was something he was in short supply of. Nathan continued around the building, until he came to the Archive's windows. Here he stopped, took a quick look around to confirm that no one had suddenly come into view, and took his river stones out of his pocket.

It was simple enough to send them through the windows; each pane shattered easily, and, soon there was space enough for him to climb through. He used his jacket to protect his hands, and vaulted into the Archive, suddenly glad that Mayor Benneteau hadn't bothered with an alarm system.

It's Christmas paradise, after all. Breaking and entering isn't exactly common. Besides, they don't even have a sheriff here.

He started to move through the room, but quickly froze. The snow globes in the center of the room were still snowing, except it was no longer gentle. Inside each, there was now a blizzard, storming and writhing, blocking any view of the displays within. A frown set into Nathan's forehead and he continued through the room, towards the angel's bell. It sat in its locked display case, but that was another simple matter for stones and an application of speed. Once that case was smashed, and the bell lay exposed, Nathan took it into his hands. It felt heavier than he expected, denser than it should have been.

Memory can carry weight, and this thing has Memory to spare.

With a set mouth, he turned the bell so that he could read the inscription once again.

So much for not getting involved, he thought.

Then, with a sigh, Nathan rang the bell. He had hoped for an electric shock, or pins and needles, or at least a mysterious gust of wind, but nothing came. Not even a whisper.

"Hmph," Nathan scowled. "Anticlimactic."

He thought of Alex, of the snow he'd been able to summon, and then turned his palm upwards. Nathan concentrated, as hard as he could, but nothing came. Not even a single solitary snowflake.

"Well, that is troubling," he said.

We've missed something, Nathan thought.

The dream was supposed to be keyed to Alex. That's what Marley had said, that the Angel couldn't be changed. In the mirror, the Shade had said the same thing, not that a single one of its words could be trusted.

Nathan stared at the bell in his hand, stared closely at the stain on the leather strap. It was dark blue, almost purple, and it was sticky.

It confirmed something else. There was another person who could have performed the First Rite, but only one other. He'd been there. Reading his comics and eating a sandwich. A PB&J. Nathan cast his mind carefully over his memory of the boy. It was the same sandwich that Gloria had made for him. Grape jelly.

It was him Nate. Elliott rang the bell. There's only one reason the Shade would keep it hidden.

Nathan wanted to vomit. How could he have missed it? How could he have put them all in so much danger?

The eyes. They could have been the same.

Nathan dropped the bell to the ground and desperately grabbed at the snow globe that showed the Christmas tree and presents.

How old had Alex said he'd been? Eight.

Nathan rubbed a cautious finger over the nameplate as if it could burn him. A.P.

Alex's words from the night before came thundering back.

"It was the day my dad married my mom..."

Paul Ashford had given his name to Alex. Alex wasn't born Alex Ashford at all.

Pat's Tree Farm, where Alex had been raised. The sign had been too large for the letters. They'd fallen off, worn with time. Alex had called his grandfather, his maternal grandfather, Grandpa Pat.

"Everyone in town just called him Pat." Pat wasn't his first name. It was his last name.

That made his daughter, Alex's mother, Anna Patterson.

"Oh I am so blind," Nathan whispered.

Nathan's hands began to shake. "I've killed us all."

The hell you have. Work the damn problem.

The graveyard, Nathan remembered. Elliott had been missing, just like Alex. What had the Angel said? It wanted to show me fear.

In handfuls of dust, Nate.

Anna had been reaching out. Whatever part of her that was left, ingrained in the Angel, it was still trying to help, trying to send him a message.

A message from across The Waste Land.

The memory struck him like a fist. He'd had the name wrong all along. It wasn't Elliott. It was Eliot. After T.S. Eliot. Precisely the sort of person a Professor of English Literature might name her son after.

The Angel could've fed everything to Eliot. The Shade had invaded

Alex's defenses, had twisted itself into his guardian, so it knew everything he knew. It knew where to find the key, knew when the library was empty.

Now he understood why. The Shade had been telling the truth about one thing. It was trapped, trapped inside Alex, trapped behind the repressed wall keeping his psychic gifts at bay.

All to make Alex whole. All so that it can be free, free to devour him.

Nathan stared at the snow globes, at all the stored Memories of the Angels that came before. A smile twisted its way into his face.

"Plan C," Nathan said. "It's time to make a trade."

The Shade would kill him as surely as it would kill Alex, but Nathan's longer Memory would take much longer to burn through.

It could be long enough.

Did it help?

If he could hold on long enough, it did, but first the Titanic has to hit the iceberg. First, we have to evacuate these minds.

He turned his attention to the snow globes. He took the one marked J. M, the one that showed the toy factory and Santa's village, and weighed it in his hands. Then, he dropped it unceremoniously onto the ground where it shattered into a wet storm of glass.

"It's a start," Nathan whispered, half to the empty room, half to himself.

✳

"And what's this?" Gloria asked Julianna. She eyed the bell tower figurine with a sideways glance.

"A souvenir, to commemorate the Angel year," Julianna replied. "We're hoping everyone will put them up today."

"Uh-huh," the old chef replied. "Well, I suppose it's handsome enough. And I know just where to put it." She crossed the restaurant and placed it on the hostess stand. "There. Now everyone will see it."

"There's something else," Julianna said. She placed the mirror next to the toy.

This, like everyone else that morning, Gloria frowned at. "I don't need a mirror, Ms. Mayor."

"Humor me. It's, uh, a tradition."

"Uh-huh," Gloria said again. "Is lying a tradition as well?"

She leaned closer.

"This got anything to do with a certain blond, green-eyed menace?"

The answer stunned Julianna. Nathan Cole always showed up when she least expected it.

"It does," Julianna replied.

"Good enough for me," Gloria replied. "And if anyone gives you trouble, you tell them I put them up with bells on. Tell 'em if they refuse, they won't get another crumb out of me either. That should get a few of the holdouts on your side."

Once again, Julianna was shocked by the loyalty Nathan had managed to cultivate. "I will," she said. "Thank you."

The door to the restaurant opened and Denise the librarian entered. "Denise," Gloria said. "Happy Christmas Eve darling."

Denise's face was snow white. "Hello," she said in a shaky whisper.

"Everything alright?" Julianna asked. Immediately, her mind jumped to Alex, to Paul, to Maddie.

"Yes," Denise said. "Well no. Something terrible's happened."

"What? What's happened?"

"The Archive," Denise said. "It's all gone. Everything."

"Gone?" Gloria asked.

Denise nodded. "It's been destroyed."

*

Alex woke to a gentle rattling and the smell of old diesel. He was blindfolded and his hands were tied to his sides. He had been attached to something that felt like a chair. At first, he was struck by a coil of fear, of disorientation, then he remembered Nathan putting him in a chokehold.

Alex fumed in the chair. He can't believe Nathan had tricked him. Worse than that, he'd knocked Alex out as easily as breathing. Alex felt blood running to his cheeks.

"Hey!" he shouted. "Nathan! Somebody help!"

"Pipe down," came a rough, familiar voice. "I'm comin'." There was a squeal and Alex felt himself being pushed forward. Whatever was attaching him to the chair wouldn't let him move far. He was moving. Heavy footsteps stomped closer to him.

"I can't take the blindfold off," the voice said.

Alex recognized it now. Ronny, the bus driver.

"I figure you've probably already worked out enough."

"Worked what out?" Alex shouted. "What the hell is going on?"

"Calm down, calm down," Ronny replied from above him. Alex could smell tobacco.

"Are you... are you smoking?"

"When this day's up, I'm as good as dead son. You're damn right I'm smokin'."

Ronny coughed.

"You want one?"

"No!" Alex shouted again. "I don't want one. I want you to let me go!"

"Can't do that son. Doctor's orders."

"Doc—Nathan?"

"Yup," Ronny replied.

Alex thrashed against the chair. Nathan—that son of a bitch!

Above him, Ronny laughed like a donkey.

"That was about my response when he told me his master plan. I can't keep track of exactly what plan this is. Plan C I think we're onto. But he gave me strict orders, and here we are."

"What orders?"

"To keep you safe and to keep you quiet. I'm battin' .500 right now."

Alex struggled against the chair, but he was completely immobilized.

"What did you do to me?" he demanded.

"Why don't you tell me?" Ronny said. There was a laugh in his voice.

"Did you—am I duct-taped to a chair? Did Nathan tell you to duct-tape me to a chair?"

Ronny chuckled. "Well, I confess I took some artistic license."

*

Breakfast at the Inn for Christmas Eve was as busy as Nathan had seen it. There were more than just the regular guests. It seemed every guest had made at least three friends since the day before. The voices around the table were quiet however, almost hushed. News about the Archive must have gotten out. The buffet spread was fully stocked as well. On his way through to the kitchen, Nathan stole some sort of cream pastry and ate half of it with a single bite.

"The end of the low-carb diet?" Marie asked when she saw him.

"Incoming oblivion tends to have that effect." Nathan's smile was grim, his face set and serious. There was none of his regular humor. "Besides, no calories in dreams. These are good."

"Gloria sent her son over," Marie explained. "I wasn't even expecting him, but I'm glad that he showed up. All these people—I wasn't expecting them."

Through a mouthful of cream of pastry, Nathan said, "How's

DeMarco?"

"No change," Marie said sadly. "Paul was here a few minutes ago. He stopped here looking for you. He knows Alex is missing."

Nathan figured as much. "And what did you tell them?"

"The truth. That I hadn't seen him, that I didn't know where he was." Marie looked nervously at Nathan.

"Good," he replied. "That's good." He finished the pastry. "I'll go see them." A moment of silence hung between them. It was goodbye, and it was likely their last one. "Be careful Marie. She might come for you," Nathan said. He checked his watch, "She would've heard by now."

"I know. You told me. I'm going to Gloria's as soon as everyone's finished here."

Nathan's voice sharpened. "No, you can't go there."

"Why?"

"Because Gloria needs to be protected. Stay in the park. Somewhere public with lots of people. It'll slow her down."

Marie's lip trembled. "If she catches me, will it hurt?"

Nathan considered lying. He thought of telling her it would be just like falling asleep, but he couldn't bring himself to. It was one lie too many, one told to a woman who deserved the truth. "It will. But only for a moment."

After stopping to flip the bird to the Angel statue and her fake lantern, Nathan crossed the Ashford yard in large sweeping steps. Morning was already fading fast. With Alex out of the picture, the day wasn't going to last, and he had one last assignment for Paul Ashford.

There was no hesitation from Paul when Nathan knocked on the door.

"Alex is missing," he said as soon as he opened the door. His face was pale and worried.

"When did you last see him?"

"Last night," Paul said. "At the square. Is it her? That thing? Did it take him again?"

Nathan raised a calming hand. "Don't worry. Even if it did, it needs him alive. And in a specific place at a specific time." Nathan explained how the Angel had prepped Alex for the Second Rite. "I imagine she's doing something similar now."

Maddie was sitting at the kitchen table. Her unfinished puzzle sat in front of her, but she wasn't placing any pieces.

The front door opened, and Julianna's familiar footfalls echoed her arrival. She saw Nathan standing in the kitchen and nodded to him.

"It's done," she said.

"Good," Nathan said. "You've saved a lot of lives."

"But the archive. It's been destroyed."

"That's unfortunate."

Julianna sighed. "Is there *any* chance that it wasn't you?"

Nathan shrugged.

"Jesus Christ Nathan!"

Paul growled. "You lying son of a bitch. You know where he is, don't you?"

The growl turned into a shout, and a thick vein in his forehead seemed close to bursting. Maddie's face had become frozen in fear at her father's rage.

Julianna crossed the room and held the girl's shoulders.

"It's so easy for you, isn't it?" Paul spat. "To lie and play us all for fools. To not tell us a damn thing when it's Alex's life on the line!"

Nathan didn't rise to the challenge. Now that he completely understood, the situation had become simple. He would do what was necessary to save their lives, even if that meant steamrolling through each and every one of them. There was no more room for emotion. It was time to do the job.

"You're right Paul. Alex's life is on the line. I have lied. I have played you. But you're very wrong about it being easy," Nathan said quietly, but firmly.

The admission cooled Paul's anger, if only for a breath. Nathan stared the tree farmer directly in the eye. His green eyes burned with a terrible fire. For, in that moment, he was the Black Thorn again. The arena may have changed, but he was every bit as dangerous and every bit as intimidating.

For all Paul's anger, Alex's father shrank.

"Now, sit down," Nathan Cole said. "I'll tell you everything. I'll tell you the story of Alex Ashford."

Chapter Thirty

Nathan paced in front of the family pictures until he found the one he needed. It was the one of Anna, Alex's mother, on what was to be her last birthday. He placed it down on the table in front of them. Maddie glanced into her lap.

"Some of this will be difficult for her to hear," Nathan said.

Before Maddie could speak, Paul cut in, "She's staying. No more secrets."

The man was still fuming, and Nathan couldn't blame him.

Where to begin?

Where else? At the beginning.

"I've lied," Nathan said.

"We know," Paul growled.

Nathan allowed himself a smile. "I do it all the time, you know? In my line of work, it's sort of a necessity. I deal with things you can't touch but that can touch you back. Lying can make that a whole lot easier for people to understand. Except, every now and then, I come across a place like this. Here, the lines are blurred. Here, regular people like you, get to see things with a touch of magic."

Paul tried to stand up again, but Julianna stopped him.

"Please, get to the point," she said.

"Where are the wedding pictures?" Nathan asked.

"What?" Paul said. "The what?"

Nathan raised a hand.

"Never mind them. Plan A," Nathan said. "Do you remember

what it was? I told you all."

"Change the owner of the dream," Paul said, "to save Alex."

Julianna's glare was full of disdain. "It was a lie, wasn't it?"

"It wasn't a lie," Nathan replied, "but it was never a viable strategy. I needed *it* to think that was the plan."

"Why did you have to lie about that?" Paul asked. "It seems the same sort of shit you've been saying all this time."

Julianna answered. "Because of the guardian. The Angel."

Paul's look of surprise made his face burst to life.

She continued, "Everything Alex knows, it knows. Compartmentalization."

Very good, Madam Mayor.

"Compartmentalization," Nathan declared. "Julianna is right. This is the only reason Alex is still alive. Every plan I've given him about how we might win, on what I might do: they were all lies. I needed it to think I was still trying to beat it, that I was still trying to save everyone."

"But, why?" Julianna asked.

"Interference," Nathan replied. "For all of you. The Timber Angel, the thing that's trying to get Alex to perform the Rites, the thing that trapped me in its mirror, is no Angel at all. It's not a guardian either, but it's in his head like one. It's an infection. A conscious, scheming, living infection. And, like any infection, all it wants is to feed and to spread."

Nathan pointed to the picture of Anna in the hospital bed.

"Tell me how you think she died," Nathan said.

"How I *think* my wife died?" Paul's question was biting. "Well let me think, since I was there and you weren't, she died of brain cancer Nathan."

"No," Nathan replied. "I'm afraid she didn't."

Paul lifted his hands. "This is ridiculous. You weren't there."

"Paul—" Julianna said.

"No Jules. We need to find Alex. Wherever this bastard took him."

He tried to get up, but a firm hand from Julianna kept him at the table.

"Did they ever show you the cancer?" Nathan asked quietly.

Paul's voice stammered. "Wha—how did you know?"

"They never did, did they? What did the doctors tell you? Perhaps the scan wasn't strong enough? That the tumor was hidden somewhere? Maybe if they did an exploratory surgery, they might be able to find it, but it wouldn't make a difference."

"You can't…you can't know that."

"They're called Psychic Shades," Nathan said.

"What the hell is a Shade?" Paul asked.

Nathan placed a finger on the picture, right under Anna's face. "Creatures that do that."

"You've known all along," Julianna said. "That's why you've been compartmentalizing everything. You knew this thing was a Psychic Shade or whatever you call it. That it was never some sort of Angel."

"Yes," Nathan admitted. "Ever since returning from the graveyard, I've known Alex was infected."

Paul ran his hands through his beard. His eyes were watery and afraid.

"You're saying Alex has caught a psychic…bug?"

"It's a bit worse than that. Psychic Shades are cruel creatures," Nathan explained. "Psychic minds are valuable. Their Memory is more vivid, more potent, and painful memories are the most potent of them all. A Psychic Shade feeds on this Memory, making their subjects relive their worst moments over and over. If they have it their way, they'll do it under a bridge somewhere. I've encountered one once before, with my own mother. It was in a boy outside of Vegas. We saved him. Barely. Banishing it almost killed my mother."

"But what does it want?" Paul asked.

"To feed," Nathan said simply.

Maddie's eyes filled with terrified tears.

"To keep feeding until the subject's mind is broken," Nathan continued. "Eventually, there will be nothing left. Only the Shade. The subject's mind finally snaps in something called a Psychic Schism. It's the moment when the infection finally takes over. This is the moment when the Shade acquires a new, most pressing need."

Julianna looked sick, and Paul was unable to look away from the picture in front of them.

"The need to spread," Nathan said. "And so the cycle goes. Feeding and spreading, mind to mind, for centuries."

Paul shook his head. "How? How did he get…infected…at all?"

I'm sorry Paul. This will be hard for you.

"To understand that," Nathan said, pacing the room, "you need to understand the sort of mind your wife had, the sort of mind Alex has. For all their strengths, psychic minds are also very fragile. Unprotected, they can be like open doors. It's why silver is so very important, and, Anna, she was allergic."

"Oh, God," Julianna gasped.

"I don't believe this," Paul said. "She died from cancer." But even that sounded weaker than it ever had.

"I lied about this dream being Alex's. It's not. It never has been. It's a living dream. John Calbot's living dream."

Nathan removed the snow globe from his pocket. It was the last one left, the one with J.C. on its nameplate. It showed a quaint Timber's Edge.

"'We must see the world as we want it to be, and not be simply content with it as it is.' Who was he? I don't know for sure. Perhaps he truly was a pioneering settler with a dream, or maybe he was something more. Connecting to a place like this will expose a mind to all sorts of influences. Think about getting on a plane during flu season. You're sure to catch something. If Anna had even the slightest damage, or the slightest weakness—it's like someone immunodeficient catching a cold."

A look of disgust turned Julianna's face dark. "That's what you think killed her?"

"I don't think, I know. It confirmed it for me itself. In its mirror, it said that it has been with Alex for a long time. And," Nathan gave a heavy sigh, "was a friend of the family."

"You knew all this time?" Paul asked. His voice was outraged, but there was no focus to it. "And you didn't tell us? You lied to us about Anna? How da—"

"Yes," Nathan interrupted. The word cut like a scalpel. "Because I can't worry about the ones who are already gone. I had to focus on how to save the ones still living. So I lied. And I'd lie again if it meant an improvement to the odds."

Paul wrapped his arms around his daughter. Maddie wasn't crying yet, but her chin was trembling with fear.

Nathan's attention turned to Julianna, and he pointed to the picture of Anna in the hospital bed.

"I'll ask again. Why did she need the straps?"

"I told you," she said. "Anna kept trying to give us things."

Paul, in a quiet, horrified voice, said, "No. It was only Alex. She would only do it when Alex was in the room, and she'd fight to get to him. Eventually, she needed the straps for him to even be in the room with her. And, in the end, she would say the most horrible things to him. I had to stop him going in, from seeing her like that. That was it, wasn't it? The Shade."

Mr. Ashford's face turned stony.

How long did you have to spend with the thing eating your wife from the inside?

Nathan nodded. "Yes. The straps presented a problem. It couldn't pass itself on, but Shades are clever hunters. Alex told me about the last day you were all together. Your last Christmas."

Paul's tears fell freely now that he understood.

"It was January," he said. "Anna had rallied. She was herself again. The doctors warned us it couldn't last, but it was a miracle, and she asked me to bring the kids by. To have one last Christmas morning."

"I'm sorry," Nathan said. "Truly I am. Your wife—Anna—she didn't come back."

"We exchanged gifts," Paul whispered. "And Alex he gave her—"

Paul broke off, unable to continue. Julianna put an arm on his shoulder, but her eyes were inflated by tears as well.

"That was when the infection spread. When the Shade passed on. You couldn't have known," Nathan said quietly. "Sometimes, bad things simply happen."

*

"What if I told you that this thing was trying to eat you?" Ronny asked.

"The Angel?" Alex asked. "I'd tell you I know you're wrong. I can handle the Third Rite."

"It ain't no Angel, and this isn't about the Third Rite," Ronny replied. "It's coming for you, so it can bring you somewhere."

"Iron Shoe Point," Alex said. "That's where the Third Rite is."

He was still blindfolded, but they hadn't moved for some time. That had been the pattern so far. They would move for a while, then stop for a while. With each stop, the ache in his head was growing worse, and the tolling of the bell was growing louder. He had to get to Iron Shoe. Had to complete the Third Rite.

"When it comes for you," Ronny said, "you're going to have to buy time. Do you understand?"

"Where are you even taking me?" Alex asked.

"Do you understand what I'm telling you?"

Alex exhaled. "I have to buy time."

"That's right. As much as you can."

"Fine, now where are you taking me?"

"Well, I can't tell you that son," Ronny replied, "it's a secret."

"I don't understand," Alex said. "Nathan wants to complete the Third Rite and kill himself? Why?"

Ronny scoffed. "Well if I had it my way, he would've left all of you to die. But, he's a foolish dreamer. And foolish dreamers don't ever listen to sense. Even if it comes from themselves."

Alex wasn't going to let Nathan die for him, just because he thought Alex wasn't strong enough. Alex would prove him wrong. In the end, Alex would be the one to save him.

"Don't you worry though. I'll let you go as soon as I get the word."

"From Nathan?"

"Who else?" Alex heard a sucking sound as Ronny inhaled. "Well, that is a problem, isn't it?"

"What?" Alex called. "What's happened?"

"Inclement weather," Ronny said, his voice suddenly serious.

Something was no longer going to plan, Alex thought.

"Very inclement weather."

*

"How do we stop it?" Maddie piped in. "How do we help Alex?"

Nathan stared into her face, into her electric blue eyes.

"We use what John Calbot left us and we give the Shade precisely what it wants," he said. "John Calbot wanted others to experience this place and was apparently powerful enough to keep the dream running in his absence. That's what the Timber Angels are. They're carrying his baton, much like Christmas traditions are passed generation to generation. Each one, imprinting itself upon the dream, and each one passing it along in chains. Every now and then, the chain breaks, and Timber's Edge falls dormant."

Thanks Mr. Marley.

"But, someone will eventually resonate with it, and bring it back. What Alex has been trying to keep from us—and from himself, at least until the Shade got involved—was that his mother brought him here before. He's the next link in the chain. Anna was the Timber Angel. She completed the Rites and then passed Timber's Edge to Alex. The dream is keyed to him, and to him alone."

"But the bell didn't work for him," Julianna said.

"He tried, but it didn't work," Paul added.

Nathan nodded. "Because here Alex is not a psychic at all. In the real world, his powers are repressed behind a wall inside his own mind. There's a fault line running directly through Alex's mind, separating his regular self from the part of him that remembers his powers. But no wall is perfect. For Alex, his powers have been bleeding through."

Nathan offered them all a guilty smile.

"I'm afraid Alex has, more or less, been reading your minds for years without ever acknowledging it. To him, it's likely a sense of intuition or instinct. But it's more than that. Intuition is good guess work, but Alex doesn't guess—he knows."

Paul and Julianna both shifted together.

"He asked us about our relationship before anyone could have possibly known," Julianna said. "He simply made a comment about how we 'looked good' together."

"He knew about the engagement ring," Paul confirmed. "He didn't confront me or shout. He just said 'I hope she knows she's lucky.'"

Nathan's heart sank for Alex, for how long he'd been suffering in silence.

"He told me once that I was very hard read." Nathan held up his silver ring. "I believe it's why he finds me interesting. I'm an unknown in a world that's an open book to him."

Julianna held up a hand. "Hold on, what do you mean he isn't a psychic here? You've been telling us nonstop that he's psychic."

"He is," Nathan replied. "My mother used to say, psychics are always of two minds about things. Here, in Timber's Edge, that's a literal truth. Alex's mind is split. One part, Alex Ashford, is the son you know. The other part is the psychic part. The part that's been holding the Shade at bay. The part that knows precisely what Alex is."

"You're saying Alex doesn't know what he's doing?"

"I'm saying there is another Alex here. He's always waiting for his mom. Like there's no one else in the world for him. He's fond of PB&J with grape jelly, comic books, and lives up at Pat's Tree Farm. There's another Alex here. He's an eight-year-old boy with gray eyes, called Eliot Patterson."

Julianna snorted. "The kid in the library?"

"He's the kid I keep seeing around. Eliot," Paul said, lingering on the name, breathing it. "He looks just like Alex did at that age."

"Alexander Eliot Ashford-Patterson," Nathan said. "Your late wife was a fan of T.S. Eliot."

"One of her favorites," Paul whispered.

"Patterson was her maiden name. Alex was born Alexander Eliot Patterson, and, at some point when he was eight or nine, his mother brought him to a place called Timber's Edge. They spent the holidays here. I understand a good time was had by all," Nathan said.

Paul couldn't lift his stunned gaze from the table. "Alex, he used to talk about it. I met his mother the following spring." he said. "I thought all of his stories...I thought it was just a kid's fantasy."

"One must wonder what Anna thought," Nathan said. "Apparently you passed the test."

Paul chuckled. Julianna took his hand in hers.

"I've met Eliot a few times," Nathan continued. "The Shade helped him ring the bell, but didn't notice when he left a stain on the strap.

He even completed the Second Rite just after Alex did. This morning, I tried an experiment and tried to perform the First Rite myself. I couldn't, because only the keyed Timber Angel can."

"What are you saying?" Julianna asked.

"That Alex, our Alex, isn't really keyed here. Not completely. He doesn't have a palace at all. Eliot does. Alex doesn't have a lantern like all the other psychics in town. The statue down at the edge of the lawn isn't his. It belongs to the Shade that's hunting him. The real lantern, Eliot's lantern, will be up at the farm. The Angel has been working both of them all along. It needs both of them."

Nathan continued, "Alex isn't aware of Eliot. It had to stay that way. On that point, the Shade and I agree. He's never met him. It's not that Alex can't see him. It's that he won't see him. It's a whopping paradox that he's even here, the sort of thing that will set alarm bells off in Alex's head. If they meet, if they really meet, Alex's repression will end. He won't be able to ignore his memories, his gifts, any longer."

"What's wrong with that?" Julianna asked. "Alex will be strong enough for the Third Rite then."

"No," Nathan replied. "Now, this is critical, the Three Rites are not rituals, and they're not fun holiday traditions."

Julianna put a hand on her shoulder. "If they're not traditions, what are they?"

"They're tests. Specifically, tests to ensure that the mind that is touching the Third Rite, that is touching that powerful psychic power source, is strong enough to handle it. The town itself provides support, I suspect, but not nearly enough for Alex. His psychic powers are chaotic, untapped, but they're there. Consciously, I doubt he's been aware of them, but here—here they're waking up. He thinks he's strong enough."

Maddie looked at her dad. "Is Alex going to be able to complete the Third Rite then?"

"No," Nathan said sharply. "No, he must not. The Shade wasn't lying about everything. It wants Alex to complete the Third Rite, to finish awakening. What it wants, above all else, is for Alex to recognize Eliot and to become whole. It's been starving, trapped behind that part of Alex's mind. Because then, and only then, can it escape its prison and finish eating him."

Maddie's tears finally started to fall. Paul wrapped his arms around his daughter.

"Once they join together, Alex will be complete, yes, but he will also be flooded by the Shade's presence. Without any defenses, Alex will Schism immediately. He'll die if we can't stop it."

"Nathan," Paul said, his dry voice cracking like old mud. "What do we do? Please. Just tell me what I need to do."

In the distance, there was a rumble of thunder.

"We do the same thing we did for the town, the same thing he did for me. We find Alex a tether. Now, I'll ask again. Where are the wedding pictures?"

✱

Nathan stormed across the room again and came to the photo alcove. He turned directly to Paul, waving a hand over the pictures.

The absence. It's in the absence we see the truth.

"See anything missing?" Nathan called. "Where are the wedding pictures? Or any pictures of Alex as a child?"

"We populate dreams from our real Memories," Nathan's voice cut through the room. "These are yours, your family's. Alex took your name when you married Anna."

"Proudest moment of my life," Paul said.

"Then where're the pictures? No wedding photos? Photos of everything else, but no pictures of your wedding? In your house, right now, in the real world. Where are they?"

Paul looked stunned. "I put them away. I wasn't sure—"

A look of fury crossed Julianna's face. "Paul! How could you?"

"I didn't think anyone would notice. I thought it was a fresh start. I didn't want you to feel...lesser. Alex didn't—"

Nathan's anger erupted, "Alex didn't need you to say anything! He dreamed himself into a guest house!"

The room inhaled and Maddie squirmed under Nathan's raised voice.

Nathan open and closed his fists, steadying himself.

"Remember," Nathan continued, "Alex can't pull thoughts out of your heads. But he knows what you're thinking. To him, it's written on your faces, written in the strengths of your convictions. Reading minds, it's like being able to detect belief. To Alex, you probably appeared as unflinching as iron."

"Not if he'd asked," Paul said. "Not if either of them had asked."

"Alex's powers are spilling out. They have been for some time. Be glad Alex—he—has a good heart. He could have manipulated the two of you to hate each other, could have driven you apart as easily as breathing. If you think I can be manipulative, you should see an immoral psychic at work. You might recall Joseph McCarthy."

And 1933 comes to mind.

Paul put a hand to his mouth. "We spoke yesterday. Just before the tree lighting. I tried to talk to him about all these changes. I told him he'd always have a home with me, and it was like...like he just looked right through me. With the engagement, I wasn't sure he'd even wanted to see us any longer. Why couldn't he just ask me?"

Nathan caught a picture in the alcove. It was one of Alex standing in front of a beat-up car. Alex wore a wide grin and looked to be about sixteen.

"Because Alex is frustratingly sure of himself," Nathan said simply. "He's so relentlessly pigheaded that I've had to step in to stop him from performing the Third Rite—you know, that thing that'll kill him. Forget asking for help, Alex won't unless he has no other choice. I took him to an alternate dimension and he barely blinked an eye. You tell him he's trapped in a psychic dream, his first reaction is to throw everyone off the roof."

Nathan swept his eyes over them.

"Alex is also alone," he said. "He loses his mother, the only one who actually understands what he is. He loses his friends. They've all moved on. His sister is growing up, so fast that even Christmas is starting to lose its wonder. He loses his room, his dream town. Then, finally, assuredly, he loses his home."

Nathan met Paul's eyes, drilled into them.

"He loses his father, the only one who actually chose him. To Alex, these are all certainties. To Alex, this is his last chance, his last Christmas with all of you. Where else would he turn to but the scene of his best Christmas memory?"

The room darkened, and Nathan's stomach sank.

The Shade's started the Third Rite. If it doesn't have Alex, then it's used Eliot. *It won't be enough.*

Quickly, Nathan crossed the length of the house and stepped outside the front door. The sky had darkened, and his heart sank. It wasn't evening yet. A glance at his watch confirmed that it wasn't. Even so, the temperature had dropped considerably and the air felt tight. Then he turned, and saw it. Coming over the mountains and stretching across the length of the sky, was a terrible black cloud.

Iceberg.

Crackles of lightning burst within it, and, even at this distance, he could see a pounding stream of snow being hurled against the mountainside.

"Oh, my God," Paul said from his side.

"We're running out of time," Nathan said.

He went back inside and joined them at the table again.

"It's our iceberg," Nathan declared.

"Wasn't the plan to avoid hitting it?" Julianna asked.

"Afraid not," Nathan said.

Julianna rubbed her eyes. "Did you tell the truth about anything?"

Nathan had to smile.

"It's a strateg...strategic loss," Maddie whispered.

Not bad, kid. You are paying attention.

"Maddie's quite right. The most likely outcome was always going to be us losing, so the best strategy was to prepare for our Titanic to hit the iceberg. The Shade controlled all the variables, all of the leverage. Except for me. I was the unknown, so I kept it looking at me. While Alex's mind was telling the Shade all the ways I was hoping to win, I had you all getting us ready to lose, had you all getting ready to evacuate. If we can't shoulder all of the minds at once, then I figured we should work on getting rid of the minds. I couldn't get this town ready on my own, and I had to trust that none of you would tell him."

The house shook under the rumble of thunder, and Alex's sister wailed in fear. Julianna pulled the girl close to her, but the older woman was barely able to keep her own lip from trembling.

There was another rumble of thunder. Nathan looked between Paul and Julianna.

"One more assignment for each of you. One of you needs to take me to the Patterson Farm. We need to try find Alex's tether. The other, needs to go house-to-house, door-to-door, and get everyone you can to shelter wherever there is a lantern. Do you understand me? The Ps. All the houses, all the shops, with Ps."

"P is for psychic," Maddie whispered. The tears had stopped for now.

Nathan nodded. "V for Visitor. P for Psychic. Don't worry about the residents. They're part of Timber's Edge itself. We need to get the visitors into the psychic palaces. All of them. Gloria, Marie, Ronny, they all know this."

The first howl of wind roared.

"We're about to hit the iceberg. For the regular minds, the palaces are their life rafts. If I can't stop the dream from collapsing, then at least you'll stand a chance. Full disclosure: You will have one hell of a headache."

His green eyes blazed over them, his company of fellow fools.

"Now, which one of you is the better driver?"

Chapter Thirty-One

"Alex is with Ronny," Nathan explained. "He's being driven around, kept from the Shade for as long as possible."

Presuming Ronny's playing ball.

"A diversion?" Paul asked.

"More like playing for time," Nathan said. "Every second counts. The longer we keep the Shade distracted, the less time it has to come after us. Now that the pretense is done, it won't hesitate to remove us from the board."

In response, Paul slammed his foot farther down. The engine roared as Paul pushed the truck up the hill towards the tree farm.

"Why the picture?" Paul asked. "Why's it matter?"

"Because it's one of his strongest, most personal memories. It should be a perfect tether," Nathan explained. "It's the fault line. That was the day he became Alex Ashford-Patterson. It should work for him like my tuning fork. If the Schism starts, it might be able to hold him together."

"Might?"

Nathan grimaced. "It's not an exact science. Better to prevent it from starting at all."

"And how're you going to do that?" Paul took a turn far faster than Nathan would've wanted.

"The Shade has gone to great lengths to keep Alex and Eliot separated until the right moment, the last moment. It requires a complete, whole mind to perform the Third Rite. The weight of the dream is too great; this storm is the dream collapsing. The engine has stalled because the Shade has likely tried to use Eliot alone. I know it doesn't have Alex, not yet. But once it does, it'll combine them together. But, what it won't have, is a way to spread."

"That doesn't sound like an endgame," Paul said.

"No," Nathan replied. "That's because it isn't. Once I have one of them. I'll have leverage. Then I can give it what it wants."

There was a sharp inhale from Paul. "You?"

"Regardless of if the Schism starts, that thing is still in him. Once we abandon ship, I'll be the only mind here that can draw it out. I'm too nice a prize, and, I've thought of a way to sweeten the pot."

Paul hesitated, but he managed to ask the question. "And will you do it?"

"To save him? In a heartbeat."

Around them, the clouds finally opened, and blankets of snow began falling from the sky. It was gray and spotty like old pigeon feathers. Quickly the heavy powder had covered the windshield. The wipers did what they could, but the snow smeared across the glass. Visibility quickly dropped, and Paul threw on the high beams.

"Is this the Shade?"

"That and something I sped along when I destroyed the Archive."

"Why the hell did you do that then?"

"To leave this thing no shelter," Nathan said, his tone deadly. "The memories of all the past Angels are there. Imprints. Echoes of their minds. It would be enough for it to survive on. It's been wearing their faces and desecrating them all. I gave it a chance. It didn't take it. This thing is dying, here and now."

Paul grunted his approval.

"That's what I want to hear."

*

"What's going on?" Alex asked as the bus seemed to slide around another turn.

"Can't keep her steady," Ronny replied.

Another voice whispered to Alex: "Don't worry. I'm here."

Before he could say anything, Ronny called out.

"Ah shit!"

There was a terrible crash and the bus came to an abrupt stop. Thanks to his restraints, Alex wasn't hurt, but he could hear Ronny groaning from somewhere ahead of him.

"Ronny!" Alex called. "Are you alright?"

The bus driver didn't answer, but in reply, Alex heard the wrenching sound of metal being forced open. Then, he heard his mother's voice. It had none of the kindness that he remembered. Instead, it sounded cruel and cutting.

"You shouldn't have kept him from me," she said.

In his mind, Alex flashed back to the hospital room. It was the last time he'd heard her sound like that. The memory made his blood run cold.

"Leave him alone!" Alex called.

The Angel either didn't hear him or didn't care.

The next thing he heard was a cry of pain from Ronny.

"I wish I was really here," Ronny gasped. "I'd beat you up and down this bus, honey."

There came a shaking, pounding sound.

"You really are dumb," the bus driver grunted. "You think you stand a chance. He's got your number girlie. Now, let's get on with it."

"I missed you the first time. But, this time, I'll try something more direct."

There was a wet, choking sound, and then Alex heard Ronny say no more. He could hear nothing except for the wind and the thunder.

Then, all of a sudden, an icy cold hand was pulling the blindfold off of his face.

He looked up and saw his mother's face.

"That's alright," she said. "I've got you. Now, can you walk? We need to hurry if we're going to save the town."

She was smiling at him, but that's not what Alex paid attention to.

He was too busy staring at the spatters of blood across her cheek.

*

They pulled into the tree farm just as the storm began to throw gusts of wind across the property. Branches and twigs and pine needles flew through the air. As they headed towards the farmhouse, Nathan saw the farmhand, Jonesy, come out from the barn. He waved at them with frantic hands.

"Go!" Nathan said. "Get him in the truck and we'll drop you both off. I'll find the tether!"

While Paul sprinted over to the barn, Nathan ran up to the farmhouse. The door was locked. Without hesitation, he kicked the door in. It flew off of its hinges, spraying splinters of wood inside the house. The inside of the house was bare aside from a few pieces of ancient furniture. It smelled like dust and mildew.

Are we sure this is the place? No one's been here for a long time.

Nathan moved through the house, keeping an eye out for anything that looked like family heirlooms.

He got to the kitchen. It was a simple, single line of laminate counter tops. A window looked out onto a backyard. At the back of the yard, Nathan saw a collapsed shed and what looked like a cellar hole. In the center of the backyard, there was a stake, and, hanging from the stake, was a simple lantern.

"It's the right place," Nathan said.

He returned to the living room and headed up the narrow

staircase. The steps creaked beneath his weight. Halfway to the second floor, however, Nathan felt a blinding pain in his head.

He doubled over and lost his footing.

Iron Shoe, the word came in a pained growl.

It was then his vision cut out, and he fell forward into the staircase, slamming his knee into one of the rough wooden steps. The pain subsided down to a dull roar, and his vision finally swam back into focus.

Ronny, he thought. *The Shade found him.*

Nathan pushed himself up the stairs, and, like a weaving drunk, felt his way down the hallway. He recovered enough to push open a bedroom door, and found himself in a young boy's bedroom.

There was a small bed, decorated with a solar system blanket. A corkboard hung from the wall opposite; push pins pressed pictures into the board. Nathan scanned them. Eliot's face looked back at him, but now Nathan saw him for what he was. A young Alex, not even ten years old. There was one of him with his mother. Alex was sitting on a red train decorated for the holidays. Anna beamed next to him. Another was of him and a wide, older man Nathan assumed was Grandpa Pat. They stood in front of a large Christmas tree, a seven or eight year old Alex holding a bow saw the same height that he was.

Nathan scanned and scanned, but couldn't find the picture he thought would be here. Paul appeared in the doorway.

"It's not here," Nathan said.

He slammed his fist down on the child's desk.

"Damn it! It has to be here!"

Nathan put another fist into the desk then pushed himself away.

Paul stepped into the room and joined Nathan in looking at the pictures. It was as if he'd never seen them before.

How long has it been since he'd seen them? Since he'd seen Alex like that?

Paul's eyes were full of emotion, and he ran a hand through his beard. He shook his head.

"I never sat him down and told him," Alex's father said. "I thought he needed space, but I let him suffer alone. I let him miss her alone." Paul broke down completely then. "If I had just…would this be happening? Tell me Nathan, could I have changed it?"

Nathan's anger with himself was boiling, and the pain from what had happened to Ronny still burned in his mind.

"I don't know," Nathan said harshly. "Maybe. Maybe not. It doesn't matter now."

Paul was running his eyes across the pictures, unpinning a few so that he could bring them closer to his face. Every now and then, the tall tree farmer's shoulders shook.

After a moment, Nathan could no longer watch. He turned, spun around the room, and then his heart leaped into his throat. A silver picture frame, sitting on the bedside table.

The last thing he'd see before going to bed. The first thing he'd see when he woke up.

Nathan stepped carefully over to it, and scooped it into his hands.

Alex had worn a black tuxedo that day, tailored to fit a young boy, but it matched Paul's almost precisely, down to the white rose boutonnières, the silver cuff-links, and the pearl buttons. Alex's dark hair was combed and cut short, his gray eyes bright with laughter, and his smile wide and proud. Paul beamed next to him, and, at the larger man's side, was the newly minted Anna Ashford, one hand around her husband's waist, and one hand over her son's shoulder. Her radiant smile gave the impression that it was all she could do to keep from laughing along with her son.

Nathan took the picture over to Paul who took the photo and cradled it in his hands. It was as if he'd seen it for the first time.

"Alexander Eliot Ashford-Patterson, the day he became whole," Nathan declared.

His voice firmed and his brow set in a serious line.

"Now, it's my job to see that he stays that way."

✳

They walked slowly and deliberately up the trail towards Iron Shoe Point. Their way was lit by fairy lights that shone from the tips of the trees. Despite the blizzard roaring through town, the woods were quiet. Somehow, The Angel was able to keep them insulated from the storm.

"It's of my making, after all," she explained.

Alex didn't even need to ask the question.

Her voice tinged with impatience. "Now, we have to hurry. The dream is collapsing. Nathan has done a very dangerous, very stupid thing."

A vision of Ronny's body, hunched over the bus' steering wheel, came back to Alex, and he felt nauseous.

"I had no choice," the Angel replied. "They kidnapped you Alex. Nathan is willing to destroy everything just to keep it from you, and to keep you from me."

"That's not true," he said. "I don't believe it."

The Angel responded only with a disappointed scowl. They continued up the trail. Despite Alex having run on it every day, it had never looked more foreign to him. Even the trees seemed to coil away from them.

Then Alex stopped. He had to buy time. That was what Ronny had told him.

The Angel's scowl became ferocious.

"Keep moving, Alex," she hissed. "If we wait too long, the entire town will be lost along with everyone in it. Is that what you want?"

"Maybe it's not that bad."

"Look around you, you silly, selfish boy," she said.

Despite the smile on her face, Alex winced at the tone. It hummed between his ears a song of horrible cruelty.

"Don't you believe your eyes?" she asked. "We either perform the Rite or we die. Your sister. Your father. Even sweet little Nathan. All will die. All because you're too afraid. What would Nathan do? He would try, wouldn't he?"

Alex hesitated. He wondered what Nathan might have said, but that was stupid. He wasn't Nathan Cole. He was Alex Ashford and he could see no other way. He kept walking.

They reached Iron Shoe just as night had fully fallen, but the lake was well lit by lights in each of the trees. They were fairy lights, like the ones that had guided them here, like the ones that had appeared on the town tree. Each tree was full of the little sparks, and Alex thought they might be watching him.

At the end of the lake, in the center of the stone gazebo, now sat a torch alight with a deep orange flame. It was curled and shaped like a cornucopia. Between the pillars of the gazebo lay pairs of stone wings, inlaid with pointed silver feathers.

"They will let you pass, Alex," the Angel said. "All you need to do is lay your hand upon them. And then the Third Rite will sit in your hands."

She put a hand to his back. It felt like being guided by an ice sculpture.

"Go. Now. Hurry."

Alex stepped forward, but his legs were shaking. A terrible disquiet gripped his chest as he approached the gazebo, even though he'd spent plenty of time beneath it. Of course, it didn't have wings then. Finally, he came to one set of the wings. The pointed silver feathers looked like knives.

Writing had appeared on the gazebo's crown.

Here Only Shall the Timber Angel Pass.

Nathan's words echoed in his head: "You'll die, Alex."

Alex straightened his back and set his gaze. No, Nathan, Alex thought. I can do this.

With a single hand, he reached out and touched the wing closest to him.

＊

The truck screamed as it hurtled down Main Street. Sometime on their way down the mountain, it had turned to night, and the storm continued to throw sheets of snow in their path. Nathan saw no one else on their way.

Good, Julianna must have gotten them into shelter.

The lantern outside Gloria's was burning brightly, despite the howling wind, so too was the one outside the Timber's Edge Outfitters. In the distance, he could see the dots of lanterns from a few of the houses. There weren't many; Nathan hoped that there were enough.

Paul brought the truck to a shuddering stop outside Gloria's. Jonesy hopped out of the truck and rushed inside. Then it was Paul's turn, but he hesitated.

Why am I not surprised?

Nathan pushed out the passenger side door and ran around to the driver's side.

"Paul!" he shouted as he pulled open the driver's door. "Come on. There isn't time!"

Alex's father shook his head. "I can't leave him Nathan. I can't leave Alex!"

"You will die if you stay here! Not maybe. Not possibly. In there, you have a chance!"

"I can help you!" Paul cried.

"No!" Nathan shouted.

The wind screamed, sending the lanterns and shop signs swinging and slapping.

Nathan had to shout as loud as he could to be heard. "You'll be giving it what it wants. Leverage! Don't let it do to Alex what it did to Anna. Trust me!"

"Damn it! I'm his father!"

"You're Maddie's father too!"

Nathan grabbed Paul's arm and shook him.

"I'm not letting him go. If it costs me my life, I will bring your son back. You have my word!"

From his place behind the wheel, Paul glared down at him, his blue eyes desperate, pleading, but full of fire. Finally, he unbuckled his seat belt and got out of the truck.

Nathan got behind the wheel, but before he could close the door, Paul put his hand in the way.

"Bring him back to me Nathan. Please."

Nathan nodded and Paul moved his hand.

"Get inside. Hurry!"

With a final look at the truck and at Nathan, Paul turned and ran inside the diner. Nathan slammed the door, insulating the cab from the howling wind. His hands were shaking as he gripped the wheel.

You haven't driven in seventy years Nate.

"Really didn't need that reminder," Nathan growled.

This is not a good idea.

He put the truck in drive and brought it around in a u-turn.

"Like riding a bike," he said as he put his pedal down on the accelerator.

Nathan pushed the truck up Main Street, stopping only once he got to Calbot Square. As quickly as he could, he got out, and sprinted to the lantern in the center of town. The wind whipped at his face and the hail cut at his hands, but he didn't stop until he could press his hands to the glass. The lantern was dead. There was little more than a tiny flame at its core.

Time to finish the job.

Nathan pulled his river stones out of his pocket and started to float them. Immediately, they caught the wind.

"Son of a bitch!" he growled.

He tried again, but he wasn't able to control them in the blizzard. Protecting his face, he spun desperately to look for some way to break the glass. His eyes landed on the black iron fence, and the Ashford truck just beyond.

This won't end well.

"Oh, shut up!" Nathan shouted to the wind.

He rushed back to the truck, slammed it in gear, then gunned it towards the fence. With a horrendous crash, the giant truck cut through the fence in a sparking burst of metal. Nathan was hurled around the cab, but he managed to keep control enough to steer the truck directly towards the lantern.

The lantern exploded into glass and twisted iron, and, as it did, the entire ground seemed to shake. Nathan turned the truck and pushed it through the hole he'd made. It leaped into Main Street, and Nathan struggled to keep the great vehicle from going straight into the building opposite. The brakes shrieked at him, and the tires slipped on the icy road, but finally the truck stopped.

Nathan allowed himself a single shuddering breath.

"Like riding a bike," he said again, his voice shaking.

His eyes darted down what was left of Main Street. With the lantern broken, the buildings had all gone dark. All the lanterns had vanished. Gone were the signs for Gloria's and the Timber's Edge Outfitters. The neon green frog for the ice cream shop had hopped away and Marley's General Store was just an empty shell.

Nathan put the truck in gear and headed towards the trail access road, the engine now rattling and clunking.

Around him, the town of Timber's Edge was dead, and not even the ghosts were making a sound.

Chapter Thirty-Two

The trail access road was narrow and barely paved. The truck clipped trees and branches as Nathan tried to keep it on the road. It was like he was back on the Oregon back roads, Mother Sable at his side, just before the accident.

That's a thought we really don't need.

Against the snow and the hail, the headlights were barely able to show him the road, and the wipers stood little chance in keeping the windshield clear. On his wrist, the charms were rattling, and Nathan was scouring the treeline, looking for an entry to the trail.

The access road ended in a circular turnaround, and Nathan threw the truck into park. He grabbed the flashlight he'd bought at Marley's, along with the souvenir clock tower. These he shoved into his pockets. Finally, he took one last item, another souvenir, but this one had been from the Archive. It was one of the snow globes. The last snow globe, the one belonging to J.C.

So much for Calbot's Dream.

He pushed the truck door open, and the wind immediately shoved it back shut. Nathan had to push with his shoulder to wrench it open. When he finally did, a fist of snow and hail punched him. The cold was brutal, enough to suck the air out of his lungs.

Outside the truck, he scoured the trail-heads, trying to find one that would lead him to Iron Shoe. Finally, he stared down at his charms. The wind had caught them, making them rattle like wind chimes in a hurricane. It was impossible to get a good bearing. He

389

turned in a slow circle, and then, there it was. The angel charm, made from the bough of the town tree, was pulling in a direction against the wind.

With the beam from his flashlight, Nathan followed the line to a path that disappeared into the woods.

We won't have time to double back.

"It's the best we've got," Nathan said.

In reply, the blizzard crackled with lightning and screamed another sheet of snow.

Then let's move, Nate. Before there's no path left.

Nathan took off at a dead sprint and cast himself into the trees.

＊

The response was immediate; with a grinding sound, the stone wings pulled up and back, exposing the center of the gazebo along with the pedestal and the burning torch that sat upon it. Alex stepped forward, about to take the torch into his hands when his eyes fell upon something that the stone wings had blocked from view.

Alex recoiled at the sight of it. Lying on the floor of the gazebo, just at the base of the pedestal, was a child's body.

"What?" Alex asked. "Are you okay?"

The child didn't move.

Alex turned around, faced back to the other side of the lake, where the Angel had been just a moment before.

It was gone.

"Alex," his mother's voice said from behind him. The Angel had moved. She was now drifting at the edge of the gazebo, her face smooth and impassive. "You've done it."

"Yeah, but who is that?" he asked.

"The one who came before," the Angel replied. "He was here a few hours before you. My first charge."

"Your…first?"

"He wasn't strong enough," the Angel said sadly. "The Angels let him pass, but he wasn't strong enough to bear the torch. The dream started collapsing. It's unfortunate."

The Angel floated closer to the gazebo, closer to the boy.

"Get away from him," he said. "Leave him alone."

Although he didn't want to leave the child like that, Alex stepped back from the torch, away from the Angel.

"As you wish," the Angel said. "I wish him no harm. He's my child. Like you, I would never lay a hand on him. I won't leave either of you. Not when I've put so much effort into you."

She drifted away.

"Step closer," she said. "Look at him."

No, Alex thought. Turn. Run.

Despite himself, Alex stepped forward.

"Alex!" Nathan's voice cut through the clearing. "Don't!"

The Angel seethed at the voice, "Him, I will lay a hand on."

Alex turned and there he was. His shoulders were covered in snow, his face was cut and marked, and his coat was ripped in several places. Against the black night, Nathan Cole's eyes shone brighter than any of the twinkling lights. They were like emeralds, angry and aflame.

The Angel regarded the intruder with disgust. Her face twisted. It paled and lost its color. Where there was pale, pink skin, now there was only cold gray flesh.

"Let them go," Nathan said. "Now!"

Nathan's jaw was set, his stare ancient and furious. There was no laughter in his eyes. No trace of the joy that Alex had come to recognize, none of the sparking curiosity. In their place, there was only the terrible calculation, the same one Alex had seen before, the same one that frightened him.

"Are you here to make me an offer Nathan?" The Angel's voice danced with delight and mockery.

"An offer?" Nathan whispered. "There was a time when I would never have made you one. In that time, I would've already broken you. I would've already shattered you. I would've already torn you apart, scrap by scrap, thread by thread. It's fortunate. That time has passed. So, yes. I will make you an offer. One offer, and it's this: Leave. Now."

The Angel's face turned. The smile disappeared, and doubt lingered in its eyes. A silent moment stretched until finally the Angel, in its voice like frozen steel, said, "I decline."

With its hand, it cut across the air, and an arc of ice soared through the clearing.

Nathan dived out of the way, and the ice shattered against the trees behind him.

The Angel raised its hand again, but this time Alex grabbed it and pulled it down.

With a glare at him, the Angel easily pulled the hand free and sent a powerful backhand across Alex's face. It felt like he'd been hit by a hand of metal armor. A sharp pain cut through his cheeks, and he tasted blood. The force of the hit spun Alex to the ground, at the border of the gazebo.

Nathan was sprinting down the clearing, and Alex watched as the Angel advanced upon him.

Just then, he heard a voice behind him.

It was the voice of a little boy. "Mister," he said, afraid and trembling.

"Alex! Don't!" Nathan's voice cracked with desperation.

"I don't know where I am. Can you help me?"

Alex pulled himself towards the boy. The boy had a swollen lip and a bruise across his face, and his gray eyes were wide with fear.

I know that face, Alex thought. From somewhere.

He'd seen him around town.

"ALEX!" Nathan called again.

Alex looked up, saw Nathan taking cover behind one of the trees.

The Angel was hurling bolts of ice at him. One after another, sharp and deadly. They cracked into the tree, sending wood splinters across the clearing and onto the surface of the frigid lake.

Around them, the blizzard had finally broken into the clearing, kicking up snow and ice from around the clearing.

"Can you help take me home?" the boy asked. "Please?"

Alex climbed to his knees, then approached the boy. The Angel turned to face the gazebo, and Alex saw it then for what it truly was. The face was no longer like his mother. It was and it wasn't. It was twisted and misshapen, as if shadows had leaked from its empty eyes.

It smiled a horrible smile, and then sent a new icicle directly at Alex.

Directly at the boy.

"Don't touch him!" Nathan cried out, his voice dulled by the wind.

But it was too late.

Alex wrapped the boy into his arms and faced his back towards the incoming bolt of ice. He waited for the impact, expected it to pierce through him, but he felt nothing. Alex stood and looked around. The bolt had simply exploded into diamond dust around him.

The Angel's smile was full of a terrible triumph.

Alex caught a glimpse of Nathan. His face was cloaked in sweat, but his eyes—for once, they were afraid.

"What?" Alex asked.

He remembered the boy, turned back to where he had been.

The boy looked up at him. His cheeks were flushed red and his gray eyes, the color of a thundercloud, were full of confusion. Alex recognized the face.

It was the same one he'd seen in the mirror growing up.

With the thought came the pain, the one that had been building in his head. Now, it came again, blinding into his skull. Alex cried out, screamed out, cast his hand to his forehead. His eyes filled with water, blurring his vision. But he was able to make out the boy, the Alex from so long ago. He had become wreathed in light and was fading from view. The light was being pulled from the boy in streams, and each stream had an anchor in Alex.

Stream and stream again cast into him, each one like a molten rod through his body.

Alex found the Angel's face.

She smiled at him, and said, "Alex, my dear, I did say I would never do anything to hurt you. I never said I'd stop you from hurting yourself."

✻

Alex! Damn it!

Nathan watched as Eliot vanished into Alex. He melted into him like butter at the bottom of a pan, and, within moments Eliot was gone. Alex cried out again, clasped his hand to his forehead. *The schism. It's starting.* Nathan tried to move towards him, but the Shade's moldy voice cut through the clearing.

"No! You will stay!"

An arc of icicles appeared over the Shade. With a hand, it pointed two at Nathan and two at Alex.

"Nathan..." Alex trailed off. He gasped, fell to the ground, and then started to convulse. His body contorted and writhed, and the only sounds Alex made were grunts of pain and moans of despair.

"Let me help him! Please!"

"It didn't take much to put out your fire, did it?" The Shade asked.

Nathan said nothing, and the Shade laughed.

Enough. We have to act! Now!

"Congratulations," Nathan said.

Alex spasmed on the ground, and Nathan felt bile rise in the back of his throat.

"You've got him," Nathan said. "Your prize."

"And it's thanks to you, I know that he's a Mindsinger."

"What happens next?" Nathan called.

The Shade's laugh died. "Next? Next I feast."

"It'll be a short feast," Nathan remarked. "His mind is already unraveling."

As if in agreement, Alex's body shook like an electric current was running through it.

"What happens next?"

The Shade stared at him from across the clearing.

"You're a clever boy," it said.

Nathan raised a finger. "Oh, right. You think I'm going to take you out of here."

"If you want to live, you will."

Nathan laughed. "I told you. If you think my life means more to me than his does, you've got another thing coming. If I woke up with you in my mind, the first thing I'd do is remove you. With a twelve-gauge shotgun."

The Shade said nothing.

"You could wake Alex up, I suppose. But his family will never touch him, not after their experience with you." A merciless smile crept onto Nathan's face. "You probably shouldn't have eaten their mother."

The Shade advanced across the clearing, its robes scenting the air like a coil of snakes.

"You won't get a choice," it hissed at him. "You will take me out of here."

"Don't you get it?" Nathan called. "You'll die. No matter what happens, you die. You'll get Alex. You'll even get me. But after that, nothing."

Nathan pulled the snow globe out of his pocket and held it up for the Shade to see.

"And what is this?" it asked.

It's me. Derailing a trolley.

"It's another option," Nathan said. "Timber's Edge is a living psychic construct. 'And forever shall their memory remain in Timber's Edge.' The snow globes are those memories. Backups of Timber's Edge. The living memory of the town."

Nathan advanced on The Shade, striding past the icicles.

"Any time someone thinks about Christmas, they'll find their way here. It's better than that though. It's a filter. Only powerful psychics can connect to the Third Rite itself. If you could hunt here, you'd be guaranteed quality."

"Quality," The Shade finished. "Only the best, the strongest, the purest minds. Their fruit fattened, their juices sweetened, unable to escape."

Nathan pointed at the torch. "In his state, Alex will never survive it. I could do it for you. I can be your conductor. Pass from Alex to me, then from me to the dream. You'd only be able to touch it for seconds, for moments."

"But a moment is all I would need," the Shade said.

"Let Alex go," Nathan said. "If not, I destroy the dream for good."

Nathan held the snow globe up at it.

"This is the last memory of Timber's Edge," Nathan called. "I've already destroyed the rest. If I destroy this, then Timber's Edge will fade. Its fire will burn out."

The Shade raised a hand, and immediately Alex lifted into the air.

"I have another offer."

Alex began clawing at his throat.

It's killing him.

"Let him go!" Nathan roared. "Or I'll destroy it."

"Give me the globe," the Shade said. "Or I will pull Alex apart right in front of you. One piece at a time. I will make his last moments agony."

The Shade floated Alex over the lake. Alex cried out, his eyes bulging with shock.

Last bluff called. Time to lose.

The Shade laughed. It sounded like the smashing of glass.

"We were always headed here, did you know that Nathan? Do you know how I know that? Because Alex knows it."

Alex kicked his legs, his cheeks had turned a deep shade of purple.

"Take me!" Nathan cried. "You can have the dream! Hunt here to your heart's content. I don't care. Just let Alex go."

"Nathan," Alex managed to choke. "Don't…"

"Why?" the Shade asked. "Why would you die for him?"

Nathan refused to look at Alex, refused to look anywhere but at the Shade's sinking face.

"I'd die for any of them," Nathan said. "But none more than him."

"What a novelty you are—a member of The Holding with an *attachment*."

"Senior associate, actually," Nathan deadpanned. "Not to be a stickler."

"Marvelous. Simply marvelous," the Shade sent the words slithering. It inclined its head. "I accept your offer."

Nathan removed his ring. He approached the Shade, weighed the globe in his hand, and, with a heavy sigh of defeat, placed it into the creature's waiting grasp.

With its free hand, the Shade traced a finger down Nathan's cheek. It felt like wet leaves.

"I will sow your memories here and feed upon them. Together, you and I will peel you apart."

Then the Shade grasped Nathan's cheek, and moved its hand down to Nathan's throat.

Nathan had to talk around the tightness holding his neck. "Alex. Leave him."

A revolting presence slithered into his mind. Each touch sent another horrible icepick into his brain.

"It's done."

Finally, the Shade settled itself like a filthy spider. Nathan could feel it plucking the strings of his thoughts, sending waves of nauseating pain cascading over his mind.

His vision swam out, but Nathan reached out and broke his fall against the gazebo.

"Now now, you won't last long. Bring me my fire. Just a moment, and this will all be over."

Nathan reached out and grasped the torch. The fire, the pure psychic energy, burst into his mind in a blinding flash. It was too much. Too much to bear.

Nathan shouted but couldn't hear if he made a sound.

Just a moment.

Around them, the clearing began to change. Massive black brambles began to claw their way from behind the trees, each one coated in thorns as hard and dark as obsidian.

"What?" the Shade laughed with sick glee. *"What are you, Nathan Cole? What are you, really?"*

I...I don't know.

The brambles continued to wind their way around the lake, but the fire was already too much for Nathan's mind. He felt his consciousness slipping, felt his mind fade into the river of pure energy.

Hold on, Nate. Just a bit longer.

Then, the Shade touched the river. It began to melt into it.

Nathan felt the sickening wetness ooze out of his mind.

"Just a moment. One's all I need."

Now, Nate! Now!

"Yeah," Nathan said. "One's all I need too."

While one hand had been holding the torch, his other one had been in the pocket with his river stones. Now, he focused on them with the full force of his concentration. They shot out of his hand, three bullets of stone, straight into the snow globe. The globe may have contained the remaining Memory of Timber's Edge, but it was also glass.

The stones tore through the snow globe, and it exploded in the Shade's open hand.

There was a strangled cry.

Nathan shoved himself away from the Shade, slamming his ring back on its finger.

With a surprised hiss, the Shade immediately recoiled, hunting for Nathan's mind, but he held up his hand.

"One way trip," Nathan shouted.

He dropped the torch, dropped Calbot's Moment of Creation, right to the ground.

It clattered to the gazebo's stone floor, sending sparks of flame hissing into the snow.

The Shade, already trapped in the Moment, but now with nothing to sustain itself, burst into flames. It screamed as the flames took over.

"I am ancient!" it called. "I am the devourer of minds!"

The flames caught, licked up its robes with a staggering quickness.

"You wanted the fire," Nathan said. "Now enjoy it."

The Shade seethed at him, cursed him, swore at him. The flames crept into its hood, wrapped its head like an immolating crown. Finally, the flames ate into the screaming thing. It writhed and twisted, unable to stop the fire. Within seconds, the Shade was gone, left as nothing more than ash floating in the wind.

The instant the Shade died, its hold on Alex released, and Alex fell directly into the frigid lake below. The water's smooth surface exploded with the impact.

Nathan threw off his jacket and sprinted towards the lake. Without a pause, he leaped into the water after Alex.

The icy water knocked the breath out of him, but Alex hadn't sunk far.

Nathan kicked his legs straight down. Around him, the lake and ice and the night all reflected colors and shapes, like a mirror full of a thousand phantoms.

Nathan ignored them, and kept pushing. He wrapped his arms around Alex's shoulders, and then reversed course. With all his strength, he kicked and kicked until finally they broke the surface. Nathan pulled Alex on shore, then, shivering from the swim, shook Alex.

"Come on!" Nathan cried. His voice was hoarse. "Come on!"

Alex didn't respond. Nathan checked his breathing, but there was none.

We might be—

"No!" Nathan's growl was savage. "I'm not letting go of him."

Nathan sprinted to where he'd thrown his jacket, then returned to Alex's body. He wrapped the jacket around Alex.

"Come on, this should help you get warm."

From the jacket's pocket, he retrieved the picture he'd found at the Patterson Farm. He pressed it against Alex's chest.

"There. I found it. Your tether. To bring you back."

He shook Alex again and again, but the body refused to respond.

"Damn it Alex," Nathan cried again. His voice broke. "Please!"

It was there, by the shore of the lake at Iron Shoe Point, on the edge of a crumbling dream, and in the first minutes of Christmas Day, that Alex Ashford died.

Part Four

Sunday, December 25th

"Above all, never become involved, even if it costs lives. It is only at distance we can observe. It is only from arm's length we can learn. It is only through impartiality we can issue judgment. This is our foundational law, and it must be obeyed above all others."

The Holding Associate's Handbook

Chapter Thirty-Three

Nathan hung his head between his knees and struggled to keep from screaming out. His fists were clenched into tight balls, but there was nothing he could do with them. All his anger, all his fruitless, impotent rage, it amounted to nothing. All of his so-called intelligence, it had led him to ruin.

Alex's body didn't stir. He continued to stare lifelessly up at the sky. Nathan dared to look at the body, but then looked away just as quickly. With a sigh, Nathan ran a hand through his blond hair. It was matted and wet from his dive into the lake. A few strands pinched when they got caught in his ring.

The ring.

Nathan bit through a breath, then turned back to Alex. Nathan threw the silver chain off of his wrist, pulled the ring off of his index finger, and then undid the chain of Alex's necklace.

No silver. No boundary now.

Nathan sat Alex up into a seated position, then, making sure both of their hands were on Alex's picture, he placed his forehead against Alex's.

"Come on, Alex," Nathan whispered. "I can't restart this thing on my own."

He shut his eyes, stilled his mind, tried to shut out anything that wasn't Alex.

Nathan lost the sounds of the water, the howl of the wind and the feeling of cold. He forgot Timber's Edge, and Christmas Day became a distant memory. Nathan dived deeper. He threw away his own breathing, discarded his own heartbeat.

Then, he heard the bell, the low tolling of the bell that had been ringing since the First Rite. He directed all of his mind towards it, and hoped, desperately hoped, that, somewhere, Alex could hear it as well.

Nathan felt his mind wax, felt it stretch and peel, and then came the familiar vertigo.

Finally, he was falling.

Falling, falling, falling.

Through a reality of darkness where the only existence was the sound of the tolling bell.

*

The raindrops were the first thing he felt. Acrid smoke filled his nostrils, coughing him into consciousness. Nathan woke, face-to-face with a broken windshield, the deflated ruin of an airbag, and the twisted remnants of a tree. Beyond the tree was a sheer mountainside, and, towards the top, Nathan could see the gap in the roadside boundary. The car had turned, had flipped as it crashed its way down the mountain.

How am I here?

Nathan put a hand to his head, felt the crunch of glass in his hair. He was sitting in the passenger seat, and from his left, he heard something move. He tried to turn his head, but flinched at the pain. The thing moved again. But this time Nathan forced his head to move all the way.

In the driver's seat, bloodied and battered, sat Alex Ashford. His left eye was swollen shut, but his right eye was awake and, as far as Nathan could tell, responsive.

That's a start.

"Alex," Nathan's voice scratched out. "Can you hear me?"

Alex's mouth opened and closed, but any words were formless.

"It's alright. You're probably wondering where we are," Nathan said. He wasn't sure why he was talking.

It wasn't even clear that Alex could understand him.

"It's familiar to me. I hope it isn't to you. That would be a remarkable coincidence. You see, I'll never forget this view."

Nathan stared up at the road above.

"I'll never remember what happened up there, but this, this I'll never forget."

Alex made another strange sound.

"Yeah. This is my memory. I've tried to Slip in your head. My mind is giving you stability. My memories are giving you something to hold on to. I'm anchored to you now. Where you go, I go. The Shade's gone—the Angel, as far you're concerned. I gave it what it wanted. I let it win."

Nathan allowed himself a small smile.

"I had to lose after all. I just made sure everything was ready. I broke the connection to the other minds—sorry about your truck by the way—they should all be in palaces, hopefully floating back to life. Your family. They should be safe. So, Timber's Edge was empty. It was just us and the Shade. Enough for me to carry, just for a little bit. With you dead, the Shade needed a way out. I gave it one. It passed from you to me, then from me to the town. Before it could finish, I broke the last of the town's Memory. No more backups. There it was, stuck with one hand in the cookie jar, and no way to take it out. A Moment of Creation...it burnt through it like tissue paper."

Nathan chuckled, but his chest hurt.

"It's the first Moment of Creation I've ever seen, for the record." Nathan's voice turned wistful. "Anslem would want to hear about it. Except I don't think that's going to happen."

From his side, Alex's voice rasped, "Has anyone ever told you that you talk too much?"

The pain in his neck was worth it to see Alex's good eye looking at him.

"It has come up," Nathan replied.

"It hurts," Alex said.

"I know."

"I know you know," Alex replied, raising his arm enough to gesture towards his head.

"I'm psychic," he said. "This is your memory."

"Yeah," Nathan replied.

"Of the car accident." Alex's voice drifted out.

"Stay with me Alex. This was the car accident."

"Sorry. Why?"

Nathan heard the painful swallow, and suddenly his own throat felt dry as well.

"You said. Driving."

"Why are you driving?" Nathan asked. "Why not me?"

"Y—" Alex gave up on the word and just nodded.

"It's your mind. I'm just visiting."

From the top of the mountain, a flash of light appeared. It was a spotlight, passing through the trees. As it passed over them, it blinded Nathan. It swept back and forth, but finally, it stayed on the car, filling it with light, but forcing Nathan to shut his eyes.

Then, he heard shouts around him.

He opened his eyes and the car was gone. In its place, he was now sitting on a stone bench looking onto a circular arena. A purplish night sat in the sky above, lit by two massive moons. The crowd, faces of all sorts and colors, was cheering the fight happening in front of them.

On his right, a creature with a face full of horns, was shaking one of its five fists.

From his left, Alex asked, "This is another one of your memories?"

This is a greatest hits of bad days.

Nathan had been here before, of course.

"Yeah," Nathan said. "This is my memory. One of twenty-four thousand, four hundred, and forty-eight memories."

Despite everything, he couldn't help but feel the weight of shame slump his shoulders forward.

"You're looking at the Black Thorn."

*

The Black Thorn darted around his opponent. It reminded Alex of The Lizard from Spider-man, except its scales were the color of sandstone, and its arms were shorter; its thick neck twisted and darted like a snake. With a mouth full of jagged teeth, it snapped at the Black Thorn, but was never able to make contact. As the two of them danced around each other, sand kicked up, coating both of them in clouds of dust.

Alex couldn't look away. The version of Nathan, the one in the arena with a lizard-creature, had his hair cut short. He wore a simple garment, made of black, flowing cloth. There was a silvery gauntlet on his hand that extended up his forearm. It cut off before his elbow. The lizard-creature struck again, and this time, the Black Thorn blocked it with the gauntlet. He cried out in pain as the creature's teeth sank into his arm.

"That had to hurt," Alex said.

Nathan wasn't smiling. "It was part of the plan."

Alex then saw why.

With the lizard-creature's mouth locked on the gauntlet, the Black Thorn was then able to use his other hand to grab the back of the lizard-creature's head. He prevented it from disengaging, and then he twisted his body, pulling his opponent off balance.

The monster was taken by surprise. One of its knees fell forward, into the sand.

The Black Thorn didn't hesitate.

Using his free hand, he shoved the lizard-creature's head into the ground.

There was an audible, sickening crack that echoed throughout the arena.

When the lizard-creature raised its head a fraction, it left a pool of blood weeping into the sand; it was too dark to be human.

The Black Thorn was able to free his gauntleted hand, but a lash from his opponent's tail, sent him rolling into the sand.

With a savage roar, the lizard-creature spun its head around, spraying the sand with broken teeth and streams of blood.

The Black Thorn lowered his shoulder and charged like a furious bull. The lizard-creature wasn't ready for the assault, and they fell again, rolling to the sand.

This time, its opponent was on top of it, smashing downwards with his gauntlet, over and over again, each subsequent hit painting the gauntlet a deeper and deeper shade of red.

Alex couldn't bear to watch, but he couldn't close his ears to the endless crunch of metal on bone.

Nathan was staring, transfixed at the scene. He blinked, slowly, methodically, and there was a sad curl to the corners of his mouth. As it continued, as each pounding blow hammered out, Nathan winced, and his eyes filled with tears until there was a steady trail running down each cheek.

But he never looked away, not once.

Finally, it was over.

Alex glanced at the arena and saw the Black Thorn stalking to the sides; from his angle, Alex caught a glimpse of the familiar green eyes, but there was none of the humor he'd come to know. As far as Alex could tell, there wasn't even life in them. All that Alex could make out was that calculating stare, the one that made him tremble.

In the center of the arena, the lizard-creature's body lay in a pile.

"For nothing," Nathan muttered, shaking his head. "All for nothing."

He wiped his eyes with his hand and breathed to steady his voice.

Alex wasn't sure what to say. He could feel the pain curling off of him in clouds of black dust, could hear the shame in every careful breath.

"You had to fight monsters a lot?"

Nathan's glare was furious.

"Monster?" he scowled. "Whoever said she was a monster?"

She, Alex winced.

"She was a fighter. That day, there was only one monster down there."

Nathan sighed. As if on time, the Black Thorn's eyes darted up to the crowd. For a moment, it seemed like the two Nathans recognized each other.

"She may have been brought back, but I never saw her again. For all intents and purposes, I killed her that day, and I left her body there. Right there. To rot in the sand."

"Brought...brought back?"

"You didn't think I won every time, do you?"

Nathan's wet laugh tightened Alex's stomach.

"Sorry, to disappoint you," he continued, "I had my share of losses, but The Lady wasn't about to little thing like death get in the way of Her fun."

"Why did you bring us here?" Alex asked.

Nathan shrugged. "I didn't. You did. Resonance brought us here. Your gift is to sense the frequencies around you, Mindsinger."

Nathan let the word hang in the air. For once, Alex didn't correct him, didn't deny it.

"There are all kinds of pain Alex. And all kinds of shame."

Nathan retrieved something out of the pocket of his jeans. Carefully, he placed it in the space between them.

Alex refused to look down. He knew what he would see.

"That's quite rude, you know," Nathan chided quietly.

Blood rushed to Alex's cheeks. "Sorry, I—"

"It's alright," Nathan said. "My mother used to tell me that reading minds is a difficult business, a fool's errand. For everything you see, every thought that is clear, there are hundreds of little details that you miss. It's the first step to losing your humanity, the first step on the road to madness. Psychics, she liked to say, are of two minds about everything. Even when it comes to interpreting thoughts."

"I don't want this Nathan."

"I know, but it's yours. You populated Marley's store with it. It was in your pictures at your house. It's time you took it back."

Alex hung his head, and finally picked up the item Nathan had placed between them.

It was, as he thought, a toy red train engine. Golden letters were stenciled on the sides: The Christmas Express.

✳

All of a sudden, they were sitting at a square table in a mall food court. The boy sat next to Alex, and Nathan sat across from the younger Alex. The last chair was empty. Each of them had a container of Japanese stir-fry in front of them. As if this were the most normal thing in the world, Nathan started eating.

"What?" he asked to Alex's face. "I'm hungry. They're not bad either."

Alex was as well, but when he tried to eat the food, he found he couldn't. It was this place.

"I...I don't want to be here," Alex said.

The toy still sat in his hand, but Alex didn't want to look at it.

Not now that he knew; not now that he remembered.

"Where is here?" Nathan said. He asked the boy. "Eliot?"

The boy shrugged. "The mall."

Nathan pointed a chopstick at Alex. "The mall. Why're we here?"

Alex turned to Eliot, to himself.

"We always come here before Christmas. For shopping." The boy's voice was a sing-song whisper.

That was right. Alex's mother used to take them to the mall for Christmas shopping. It was a long drive. They made a day out of it.

"Just to get some things for everyone," Alex said. "Like Grandpa."

"And then we'll do lunch…" Eliot said.

"…Like a pair of professional shoppers," Alex finished.

The pain, the horrible pressure, came back and he cradled his head in his hands. It felt like his eyes were going to explode.

"I don't remember."

"Give it time," Nathan said. "Have a noodle."

Eliot pushed his food forward.

"I want to ride the train," Eliot declared. "We always ride the train."

The train? It was a red train, Alex knew, but, beyond that, he knew nothing. It would be done up for Christmas.

No. He didn't know anything about it.

"No," Alex said. "I don't want to ride it right now."

Eliot scowled at him, the spots in his cheeks turning red.

"You came here to shop," Nathan prompted.

"Yeah. Me and my mom. She'd take me everywhere back then. There was nothing special about it."

Nathan considered the statement.

"I'm not lying," Alex said hotly.

"I never said you were," Nathan replied.

"You—"

"Thought it?" Nathan asked.

Alex fell silent.

"I always think people are lying. But, context, Alex. I don't think you're lying, but I think you're seeing things as you want them to be, not as they were."

Alex flushed, but said nothing.

The food court around them changed. The light grew darker, and the food on the table vanished, just as Nathan was about to take another bite.

He tossed down the chopstick and it clattered to the table. "Typical," Nathan said, crossing his arms.

Eliot was gone. The chair scraped against the smooth floors as Alex looked around for him.

"Eliot!" Alex called as a dreadful stone plummeted in his stomach.

Alex stood, ran his eyes over the teenagers going in and out of the clothing stores and the families waiting in line to meet Santa. The food court was on the second level. Alex finally caught Eliot standing on an escalator, one hand on the moving railing.

Alex rushed across to the escalator, pushing gently through the crowd of shoppers.

Nathan followed, studying Eliot and Alex as if he were a wildlife photographer.

"Are you going to help me?" Alex called back to him.

"You seem to have it handled," Nathan replied evenly.

Alex excused himself down the escalator, brushing up against bags of shopping and their annoyed owners.

Nathan kept to the second level, striding quickly to keep his eyes on Eliot.

In the sea of adults, Alex lost track of him.

But from up ahead, he heard a tinny speaker call out, "All aboard!"

The line of shops opened into a round spur. At its center towered the mall's Christmas tree. Jumbo-sized and plastic-looking decorations stuck out of the tree at odd angles. At its base was a simple picture station, and, running in a loop around the tree and out about the spur, was a narrow-gauge track.

The only one in the state, Alex remembered.

It's why we came here. It was an attraction, like the mall itself. There were even railroad crossing stations for pedestrians.

The train itself was made to look like a vintage steam train. It had a red engine and four wagons. For Christmas, it was decorated with ropes of garland and lengths of tinsel. A large wreath hung from the fake smokebox door. There was no operator and the cab had a seat for one.

That seat on the ride was the best one. It was the one Alex always wanted.

He spotted Eliot, standing in line. He was one of the larger kids in the line, but Alex remembered that he didn't mind. He liked the ride.

It wasn't Christmas without a ride on the train, and he didn't think that would ever stop. After all, if adults could ride with the little kids, then why shouldn't he be able to ride at any age he wanted?

Alex couldn't help but smile when he watched Eliot count out his quarters. It was $1.25 for a ride. Eliot paid, and then clambered aboard the train. Although he himself had no memory of this particular ride, he'd ridden the train enough times to know how excited Eliot was. The boy got the seat in the front, right in the cab.

"All aboard!" the speaker called out again.

The train lurched out of the station. It made its way around the spur, playing an instrumental version of "O Christmas Tree!" as it puttered down its track.

Eliot wore a dumb grin on his face. He wasn't crying out or cheering like a real little kid, but he was clearly enjoying himself.

Then, right as the train passed the miniature railroad crossing,

Alex felt it. It was like a wave of, something, passing over him. Suddenly, he felt cold and his stomach wanted to cramp.

The train kept moving. It had almost completed its loop when Alex felt another wave. He caught a glimpse of Eliot's face in the cab.

The boy's smile was gone, and now his brow was furrowed in concentration and confusion.

Alex felt a sudden lurch of fear and he headed towards Eliot. Before he made it half the distance, the cab was bathed in a hazy glow, a golden static. Like a flash of lightning, the glow exploded before disappearing. Alex covered his eyes, but no one else noticed the glow.

Even Nathan, from his place on the second level, was watching with an unchanged expression.

In a sudden burst of speed, the train jumped forward. Alex saw the front of the train lift, just barely, and half of the engine hopped out of the tracks. With a grinding screech, it tipped to a diagonal angle without falling all the way over.

The kids on the train cried out in shock, but it was Eliot's surprised shout that chilled Alex's blood. He got a glimpse of the cab, saw Eliot hunched over, one hand to his forehead.

"Eliot!" Alex called.

At the sound of his name, Eliot looked up and saw Alex. The boy smiled and waved as if to say everything was alright, but then he turned rigid. It was like he'd stepped into an electric current.

It passed, but then it happened again.

Now, he spasmed. Unable to control his hands or his head, Eliot shook rapidly, as if he were being electrocuted over and over.

Something appeared around the cab, and, at first, Alex thought it was the same glow as before, but this was different. This was a dark cloud, made up of what looked like thousands of spider hairs.

Eliot gave a dramatic, final spasm, and the cloud around the cab exploded outward. The hairs, now like darkly glowing needles, fired across the crowd.

Alex got a face full of them. The force of the impact sent him falling backwards, towards the mall floor.

But he never hit the ground. Instead, in the moment he should have, Alex appeared standing next to Nathan, looking down at the scene from the second level.

"Watch," Nathan said quietly.

Below, there was a commotion around the train track. The red engine still sat askew, out of its tracks. Someone had been hurt.

"It's Eliot. We have to get down there."

Nathan grabbed Alex's arm.

"Watch," he said. "You need to see it."

There was a gap in the crowd and, lying on the floor, was a woman. Her long, mahogany hair pooled around her and her eyes were staring blankly up. Bags of shopping had spilled around her, tipping new jeans, small boxes, and shirts all around her.

Mom, Alex thought. It's my mom.

Someone in the crowd shouted. It was Eliot.

"That's my mom!" The boy's terrified scream carried clearly through the stunned mall.

The crowd didn't know what to do.

Eliot found a gap and pushed through, but an older woman abandoned her husband to hold him back by his shoulders. Eliot stood over his mother, and, after a few terrible seconds, she twitched. Then she blinked and began to move, slowly at first. Then she was sitting up, and Eliot leaped into her arms.

The older woman wasn't able to stop him this time, but that seemed alright.

Alex watched as Anna Patterson thanked the woman. They talked for a bit, but it was clear there was no lasting damage.

Alex could hear her voice carry through the room. "Just feeling a little faint. I'm fine now."

At the words, Alex sniffed.

"She wasn't fine, was she?" Alex asked.

Nathan put a hand on Alex's shoulder. The grip was tight, but kind. The answer rang clearly in his mind: no, she wasn't fine. There was no misinterpretation this time. No context he was missing.

"What happe—what did I do to her?"

"A psychic normally awakens in periods of heightened emotion. Good or bad, it doesn't matter," Nathan said. He paused before continuing. "But, they're accessing their gifts for the first time. They don't have complete control. They're sort of like nerves firing for the first time, reaching out, desperate to find a connection, something to help give them stability. Naturally, they latch on to the nearest psychic mind they can find. It doesn't take much. A latent psychic would be able to provide the necessary stability. The mature psychic doesn't even normally feel it."

"You awoke, right there," Nathan said. "The excitement. The time of year. The surprise. Even leaving your mother alone. For a kid, it all contributed to your heightened emotional state. Your powers triggered and you were unable to control them."

"It was like something was in my eye. Behind my eye. In my head. I had to get it out." Alex remembered the sensation; he felt it now. It was like he had discovered that he'd had a third arm all along, but it was weak, terribly weak.

"Regular minds wouldn't have felt anything—at most a passing malaise. For any psychic mind, it feels like a toddler tantrum. But, for an *unprotected* psychic mind, one not wearing any silver and one not prepared..." Nathan sighed sadly. "That can leave damage. And damage can get infected. Given enough time, any infection can become deadly."

The Shade. Alex felt the floor drop away. All that was holding him up was a single hand on a railing.

"It's my fault," Alex said. "I killed her."

Nathan turned Alex so that they were face to face.

"No, Alex," Nathan said, his voice hot and serious. "You were a child."

"It's my fault she's dead. My fault she's gone!"

"You had no choice. Alex, you couldn't help it! She had no way to know, either. But look at Eliot's face."

The boy was staring at Anna with wide, concerned eyes, even as she stroked his hair.

"You knew something had shifted. You felt that you hurt her, and you did what almost all young boys do. You pretended it never happened."

Sure enough, Alex watched as the switch flipped on Eliot's face. The concern disappeared from his eyes, and, in a moment, he was smiling again.

"You sealed that power away, but nature, it won't be denied. It began to leak out, in your heightened sense of intuition and in your resonance with people and places like Timber's Edge. Once the Shade transferred to you, it set to work trying to break down your wall. The more your gifts began to leak out, the stronger the Shade became. Until finally, it was able to exert enough control to try and break free."

It felt like he'd been punched in the gut.

Nathan's voice was gentle. "Sometimes, Alex, bad things—they just happen."

Nathan pointed down to the floor of the mall. The train had been reset on its tracks, and Eliot was now sitting next to Anna in the second wagon.

They were both smiling, and Anna had her arm around her son as the Christmas Express took them on a tour around the mall.

"But, sometimes, good things—they happen as well."

Chapter Thirty-Four

It was freezing when Nathan woke by the banks of the lake. He had no idea how long he'd been under, but the storm had done its damage. A coat of snow fell off of him when he stood, and the town was hidden behind a white fog. *It may as well not be there at all*, Nathan thought.

There was no sign of the Shade. Whatever remnant it had left behind had long since been buried by snow.

Good riddance, Nathan thought.

He checked Alex for signs of life. He was breathing in shallow breaths, but he was breathing, and that was a marked improvement. Over at the gazebo, Nathan saw the torch lying where it had fallen. He jogged over to it, his shivering making it hard to stay in a straight line. The torch was still smoldering with orange whispers of embers.

Nathan hesitated over it, unsure what touching it again would do to him.

"Let me," Alex called. He was standing with Nathan's coat still pulled around him. Alex shivered as well, so much so that he needed both hands to pick up the torch. In his hands, the embers' glow brightened, but no flame came.

"It's weird." Alex's voice shook in the cold. "It's like, I can feel that it needs something from me, but I don't know what. It's warm though, so that's good."

"Good for the one who can hold it," Nathan said.

"What do we do?" Alex asked.

"Check your pocket," Nathan replied.

With a frown, Alex put his hand in the coat pocket and pulled out the picture.

"I don't understand," he said, rubbing a finger over it.

"Your tether," Nathan said. "It's what let me bring you back."

Alex's face fell.

"I couldn't remember where it went," he said.

"Now check your other pocket," Nathan said.

Alex pulled out the small souvenir bell and compact mirror.

"We can save the town with these?"

Nathan grinned and shivered all over. "Provided we don't freeze first. Of course, I've never tethered a town before."

Nathan took the bell from Alex and placed it on the pedestal at the center of the gazebo. He put the compact mirror next to it.

"Now," Nathan said, "let's hope someone out there is listening. There's one of these in every psychic palace that was in Timber's Edge, and mirrors are gateways, particularly when you happen to know someone like me. Resonance, Alex. Remember?"

Alex nodded as he understood what it was Nathan needed him to do.

"Just concentrate," Nathan urged him. "Picture all of them in all those buildings. Concentrate and pull."

Alex steeled himself. With the smoldering torch in one hand, Alex rang the bell with the other. The high, twinkling note rang clearly through the gazebo, and across Iron Shoe Point. It traveled across the surface of the lake, pulling ripples across the water's surface.

The note died away, swallowed by the icy white fog.

Alex's shoulders slumped forward.

"Sorry," he said. "I guess I'm not strong enough."

"Again," Nathan said. "Try again."

Alex screwed his eyes shut.

Come on. Just like you did for me. Trust your instincts.

Alex rang the bell, but, this time, the note didn't fade away. Alex's brow furrowed in concentration, and the note kept ringing, just as it had ever since the First Rite.

It's like he's holding it here.

Alex rang the bell again. The chime surrounding them grew louder.

Then from somewhere beyond the white fog, the same note answered.

Nathan's smile grew, as another note came back, like a twinkling star.

There came another. And another. As one palace answered, the others rang out in unison. Soon, Iron Shoe Point was awash in the sounds of the bells.

The torch in Alex's hand burst to life, and Alex couldn't help but shout.

"Time for your Third Rite," Nathan said with a grin.

Smiling widely, Alex shut his eyes and screwed his face up in concentration. Sweat erupted down his forehead, and the flame in the torch turned white with heat.

I told you Alex, the song you will sing, it'll be a good one.

Alex's eyes snapped open, and he grinned at Nathan.

Nathan Cole ran down the length of Iron Shoe Point, stopping short at the overlook. Just as he did, the white fog rolled on and the blizzard cleared. There, nestled down in the valley, each rooftop covered in a blanket of fresh unspoiled snow, lay Timber's Edge. He counted the buildings.

All lifeboats accounted for, Nathan thought with a proud smile.

At the edge of town, where the Gift Field was supposed to be, something was different. In place of the field was now what looked like an opaque, crystal ball.

Not crystal. Ice.

"Made some changes?" Nathan asked when Alex joined him.

Alex had placed the torch back on its pedestal and was now looking over the town. His eyes lingered on the massive dome of ice and a satisfied smile played at his mouth.

"The Angel is supposed to give a gift," Alex said. "And it is Christmas Day, after all."

"In that case," Nathan said. "Give me my coat back. I'm fucking freezing."

✳

By the time they made it back to town, familiar faces filled the streets. The visitors that had arrived over the past week were examining the town. Almost all of them were amazed at the lack of damage the storm had caused.

"It was the weirdest thing," Nathan overheard one of them, a college-aged girl say. "It felt like the longest night of my life, and, that wind, it was something else, but then it was gone."

An older man agreed with her. "We were holed up at Gloria's," he said. "It was one hell of a storm. They'll be talking about that here for years!"

Nathan and Alex shared a glance, and then both shook their heads. Once again, they were both wearing their silver, but there were some thoughts you didn't need to be psychic to read.

They returned to the Inn, and Marie wrapped them both in her arms. Her eyes looked every bit like merrily burning coal.

"Nathan," she cried. "I'm so glad you're alright."

"Me, too," he said.

"And Alex. What happened?"

Nathan smiled down at her.

"Complicated dream stuff," he said. "But it's all settled now."

Marie laughed.

To Alex, she said, "I appreciate you coming to see me, but you really should go home. Your family's worried sick. I think Paul almost paced a hole into Gloria's floors."

"There's something I have to do first," Alex said. "And it can't wait."

DeMarco's room hadn't changed since Nathan had last been inside it. Alex looked down at DeMarco and frowned.

"He... I don't know. Chaotic," Alex said.

"Can you help him?" Nathan asked.

Alex stepped forward and held the man's wrist. He closed his eyes and his eyebrows knitted together. Nathan saw his grip tighten on DeMarco's wrist, but then Alex let it go.

When he stepped back, Alex was panting and a sheen of sweat shone on his forehead. "There," he said, then shrugged. "I think."

Nathan grabbed DeMarco's wrist. The pulse was stronger than before. He checked the eyes, and the pupils rolled around. Eventually they landed on Nathan's.

"I've had...I've had the strangest dream," DeMarco said. "Haven't I?"

"Mr. DeMarco," Nathan said with a smile. "Welcome back."

Nathan left Alex at the guest house to go change, so Alex crossed the rest of the way up to the house on his own. He entered through the back door, and the three of them were there waiting for him. Maddie dashed up to him first, wrapping herself around his waist like an nine-year old anchor. Paul hugged him tight enough to knock the air out of his lungs, but Julianna stood back.

Alex gestured for her to join them.

"Nathan told me to tell you: you were a good helper," Alex said.

She scoffed and shook her head, but she was smiling.

"I hate him. I really think I do."

Paul pulled her into their embrace and the Ashford-Patterson-Benneteau family stood together in the kitchen. Alex felt the love, the warmth, and the kindness interchanging between them, harmonizing together in a beautiful chorus. Words may not have been needed, but Nathan's words rang in his ear, and Alex said, "I love you all."

Afterwards, they changed into pajamas and spent Christmas morning by the tree. They had no gifts to give, but that didn't seem to matter. Somewhere, they had slipped away. When Nathan knocked on the door a few minutes later, he'd changed into a black long sleeve shirt and a fresh pair of jeans. He still wore his burgundy overcoat though now it was ripped in several places.

His eyes darted over the scene, of all of them in their pajamas, drinking hot chocolate, and he looked suddenly uncomfortable.

"Ah," he said. "I thought you were all—never mind, I'll come back later."

"Nathan," Paul said with a grin and a shake of his head. "Shut up and take a seat. I'll get you a mug."

Chapter Thirty-Five

"Something's up at the field," Nathan heard one voice say.

"What is it?" another asked.

"Is that it? Is that the Gift?"

"What are they going to do? We can't get in."

The questions continued on and on. As per tradition, the Gift Fair was scheduled to open at noon, but that didn't stop a crowd from gathering at the ice dome throughout the morning.

After a morning drinking hot chocolate and explaining most of what happened up at Iron Shoe Point, Nathan walked alongside the Ashford family down to the Gift Field. Marie, Gloria, and Christopher joined them as they passed. Their small crowd joined a larger group and, pretty soon, it became clear that the entire town had turned out. The crowd was so thick that they couldn't get through—at least until people saw Alex was with them.

"It's him," someone said.

"The Angel," a bewildered man said.

He was right to look bewildered. And he wasn't the only one. Once they got close enough to see the gift, even Nathan was stunned by the dome's size. Julianna's eyes turned into saucers when she saw the Gift, and Maddie was tugging on Paul's sleeve and pointing.

Alex had encased the entire Gift Field in a massive sphere of opaque ice.

"I'm surprised it's still standing," Alex murmured to Nathan once they reached the front of the line.

"Sure, you are," Nathan replied with a shake of his head. "How much longer are you going to keep them waiting?"

Alex gave a sheepish smile. "You'll find the seventh Timber Angel is quite punctual. The fair opens at noon, remember."

Precisely at noon, a great ripping sound tore through the air. Someone in the crowd screamed, but then someone else pointed at the sphere.

Nathan recognized Marley's voice. "It's cracking!" he called.

A massive crack appeared in the side of the sphere. Before all of their eyes, the crack traveled until it had spread the entire height of the sphere. There was another ripping sound, and a shimmer ran over the sphere's surface.

Nathan dared a look at Alex and saw that his eyes were tight with concentration. One of his hands was balled into a fist, and he bit his lower lip, but there was also a gleam of triumph in his thunderhead eyes.

A crashing sound came and the sphere began to collapse. But, instead of collapsing to the ground, it collapsed upwards and outwards. The shards of ice exploded but turned into harmless vapor within moments. The fragments hung in the air like tiny flecks of diamond, surrounding the freshly revealed Gift.

Where the sphere had been now stood an enormous castle made purely of ice. It sat towards the back of the field such that an already assembled midway ran through its gates. Alex hadn't stopped there. An ice-skating rink ran the length of the field, and there was an ice maze in the castle gardens. Running around the perimeter of the field was an unmanned miniature railroad.

Carved from crystal ice, it was designed to look like a steam train, except, instead of hot steam, it expelled cool water vapor. The train made a circuit around the field, and even made stops at two stations.

"The Christmas Express" Nathan whispered with a point to the train. "Nice touch."

"I made some improvements," Alex said. "Mads, I told you I'd help with your puzzle. What do you think of Castle Angel?"

Maddie was beside herself and almost pulled Alex's arm out of its socket in her demand to see everything, and Alex had included a lot to see. There was nothing that took her focus more than the train.

"Alex," she cried. "Look. It's The Christmas Express. Like the one we used to go on at the mall. You remember?"

"Yeah, Mads, of course I remember," Alex replied with a laugh.

He looked down at her, then crouched so that he was at her eye level. "Say, you want to take a ride?"

*

The day at the fair passed quickly as good days spent in good company always do. It passed so quickly that Nathan couldn't believe it when he noticed the light starting to fade. It turned out, Alex had considered that as well, for as the day grew darker, the castle grew brighter and brighter. Once the daylight had vanished, the castle looked like it was made of nothing but Christmas lights. As the night deepened, Nathan noticed people beginning to leave, but no one walked out of the field. They were simply there one moment and gone the next.

It's starting. The day is almost done.

As the crowd thinned, Alex caught Nathan's eye. He was playing with Maddie at one of the midway games. They shared a sad glance.

He understands as well.

"Quite the show," Gloria said. "He offered it to me, you know? Alex."

"Tough act to follow," Nathan said.

The old chef cackled. "It's why I turned him down. I think one of the Outfitter girls is going to keep it going, but, between us old cynics, she's not Angel material."

"Someone will come along," Nathan replied. "So long as the Memory gets passed, another Angel will show up eventually."

Gloria handed him something. It was a silver spoon, engraved with the name Gloria's.

"Something for my regulars," she said. "Don't be a stranger Nathan Cole. Any time you get lonely out there, you come by. Remember, the coffee's always fresh. Besides, you got to meet the rest of the family."

"I'll remember. Thanks."

With that, Gloria put her arm into Christopher's and together they walked through the gates of Castle Angel and out of Timber's Edge.

Safe travels.

Nathan nodded, then took a wrapped leather bundle from the worn duffel bag at his feet. Inside it, like archeologist's tools, he had a few tuning forks, a rosary, and even a wickedly-sharp letter opener. He tucked the spoon next to it before replacing the bundle back in his jacket.

Across the castle grounds, he spotted Marie sitting alone, admiring the castle. She was one of the last.

"Enjoying the view?" Nathan asked.

Marie looked surprised to see him. Her lip trembled.

"Oh, hey Nathan," she said. "Take a seat."

He sat next to her, and they watched the castle in silence together. The Brenners were riding the train, but they vanished before they got back to the station.

"It's not going to hurt," Nathan said gently.

Marie nodded. "I'm not going to remember, am I? Because I'm not like you."

Nathan considered the question. "You have dreams you remember, don't you? The good ones? The really good ones—those we remember."

"Is this a good one?" Marie asked.

Nathan took her hand and gave it a comforting squeeze. "I don't think it was too bad."

Marie rested her other hand on top of his. She smiled at him. "No, I suppose it wasn't."

"Besides," Nathan said. "I'll be right there with you. And it's a long way to Wisconsin. I can fill you in on anything you might forget."

"I thought you were heading to Chicago," she said.

Marie rested her head on his arm.

"I go where I'm needed," Nathan said simply.

*

Soon only the residents, Nathan, and Alex's family remained. Night had fully fallen. The moon hung in the air, full and glowing. Alex talked with his family at a spot under the castle gates. Paul, Julianna, and Maddie spotted Nathan and raised their hands to him. Nathan waved back.

Goodbye, he thought as they passed under the gates.

The residents faded as well, leaving just the two of them at the castle.

"I guess it's time," Alex said, "for the last step."

Alex gave Nathan a sad smile, then shrugged. Castle Angel and the grounds of the Gift Field began to fold, started to twist. A wind blew across the field and pulled icy fragments off of the castle. Piece by piece, the ice vanished into dust, caught by the wind until, soon, there was nothing left of Alex's Third Rite save for a small item in the middle of the Gift Field.

Together they left to collect it.

"Will I see you again?" Alex asked as they approached the center of the field.

"Me? I'm like gum stuck to your shoe, Alex Ashford. You'll never quite scrape me off."

Alex laughed. "Merry Christmas Nathan Cole."

"Call me Nate," Nathan said. "My friends, they call me Nate."

Alex glanced at him, and there were tears in his eyes. "I don't want this to be the last time we see each other, Nate"

Nathan wore another one of his easy smiles. "Dreams are funny things, Alex, especially psychic ones. They're memories that we might forget, up until the moment we need to remember them again. Any time you need to see me, just remember that. Remember this place. And you'll find me."

They reached the center of the field. Nestled perfectly into the snow was a perfect sphere of glass.

It was a snow globe, set into a brass base, and, within the globe was an ice castle.

At its base was a small inscription: A. A.

Chapter Thirty-Six

Anchor had changed again. Nathan felt it even before he had crossed the corridor's boundary. It was no longer a Victorian door or the flap of a desert tent. It wasn't even a pathway to a mountainside chalet or a medieval keep. Now, it was just an ordinary door, the sort of simple wood paneled door that appeared in houses all over the country. Beyond the door, Anchor had transformed. Instead of a Victorian street, Nathan stepped into a comfortable, but massive living room. High carpet ran throughout the floors, and the sunken living room housed a trilogy of Christmas trees. Tinsel ran along the ceiling, looped around the stairwells and even somehow found its way into the open concept kitchen. Outside the window, snow was falling in steady sheets and the pale glow of morning was peeking above the horizon.

Anslem, for once, was sitting. He was in a comfortable leather armchair, facing a merrily crackling fire. The Aegyl wore a red festive sweater, complete with a stitched reindeer on its front.

"The hour is late Nate," the Aegyl called. "You will have to pay for succor."

"Pretty sure I've got an account."

At this, Anslem made a curious sound, somewhere to be a grunt and a strangled laugh. "Come, sit by the fire. I have come to find it most diverting."

Nathan sat on a matching sofa, but he kept his eyes on Anslem. "I like what you've done with the place. It's very… Christmasy."

"Do you really think so?" Anslem asked. "I believe you were correct. The tinsel. It has made all the difference."

"Timber's Edge, Anslem. I think it was a living Moment of Creation. It ate through the Shade, but left me alive. Unbound to any mind."

"Really? Fascinating," Anslem replied, his gaze remaining on the fireplace.

"That was Calbot's dream, after all."

Anslem's head turned. "What did you say?"

"Timber's Edge. It was made by a man called John Calbot. Why?"

"Calbot." Anslem repeated the word. "That is a name I have not heard for some time. Yes, that makes the matter of Timber's Edge much more clear."

"You've heard of him?" Nathan's heart leaped into his throat.

Was Calbot an Aegyl? The kind of mind required to make Timber's Edge would have had to be powerful.

Anslem returned to the fire, saying only, "I have heard of a great many beings Nathan Cole of The Holding."

Nathan knew him well enough to know that he would say no more on the subject.

Seeing they were alone, Nathan had to ask, "Why are you doing this? Christmas? It's not the sort of thing an Aegyl troubles themselves with."

"As I told you before, perspective."

"I know that, but Anslem, what do you mean?"

"As you know, I experience time differently than you do. At times, all of the folds and variations can be overwhelming. I have never questioned that experience. It is my nature, after all, to see my reality in that way. After you left to go find your Angel, I considered your perception, what it must be like for you. For each effect to be preceded by a cause. For each cause to lead directly to an effect. How do you know what to do? How do you know which choices are optimal? The weight of those decisions. They must be exhausting."

"At times, they can be."

Anslem nodded. "I thought as much. In many ways, each day here is like the birth of a new universe. Nothing that happens this day will affect the next, not in any way you might consider material at least. Each day here I am born anew to serve my purpose. There is little—outside of our friendship—that ties me from one day to the next. From one cause to its effect. Perhaps one day I will find a way to leave. To see the universes as you do."

"Anslem..."

"Ah, forgive me. I digress. I considered what it must have been like for you to be here. I placed myself here, studying the fire. Studying the turning of the days. I then realized how much of your time, your linear time, was stolen from you. And then I saw the failure of my understanding."

"It's not your fault."

Anslem did not look away from the fire. "You measure your lifespan in years. An Aegyl measures theirs in eternities. But, in both of our planes, a day is a day. The difference is that, for your kind, a day can carry consequence. It carries the promise of change. Sitting here, amongst your time, I saw all of your important days unfolded before me. The days that marked your birth. The days that marked your mother's birth. Your rituals. All your days of promise."

Nathan felt a cloud form in his brain. It reminded him of his first conversations with the Aegyl.

"You asked why I was doing this," Anslem continued. "The reason is simple. Because, it is beyond my power to return that stolen time to you. My friend, I wanted to give you another one of those days. And, before the night returns, I wanted to experience the promise of one of those days the way that you might."

Anslem faced him, and, with the entire galaxy swirling in his friend's eyes, Nathan felt his own eyes swim.

Nathan sniffed once and managed to keep the wetness out of his voice. "On Christmas morning, it's customary to exchange gifts."

"Ah." Anslem reached next to the arm of the chair and retrieved a meticulously wrapped package. The paper was green, almost the exact shade of Nathan's eyes.

"You will never lose time again, my friend." Anslem said solemnly.

Inside was a new pocket watch, complete with dials and gears that Nathan couldn't guess the purpose of. The hands on the watch's surface moved. It was two minutes past seven o'clock in the morning.

A tear escaped, and, as it ran down his cheek, Nathan rubbed his thumb over the watch's surface. Its chain was made from silver.

"It is unbreakable, of course," Anslem said. "I know how clumsy your kind can be."

Nathan laughed. The sound of it surprised him.

He pulled off his old watch, the one given to him upon ascendancy at The Holding, the mark of his station, and passed it to Anslem. The Aegyl weighed it in his hand.

"It's a promise Anslem," Nathan explained. "One day, I'll find a way. To help you leave. I'll take you to a place where those hands move."

The stars in Anslem's eyes stopped in their tracks.

Did I insult him?

"A promise to an Aegyl," Anslem whispered. "It can be a binding thing. Are you certain?"

With a grin and a laugh, Nathan strapped the watch to his friend's wrist. The edges of the Aegyl's lips twitched upwards, and the stars in his eyes began to dance.

"Looks better on you anyway," Nathan said.

He looked around the room, bedecked with trees and boxes of presents.

"Now, which one has the Monopoly? It's been a hot minute since I've flipped a board."

The Aegyl's eyes sang. From beside his armchair, he produced another box. "This, I found quite challenging to acquire."

Shaking his head, Nathan opened it. Inside was a vintage 1935 Monopoly board game.

"This is the game you referred to, is it not? I have studied the rules and determined an optimal strategy. I intend to—"

"Anslem," Nathan said. "Keep that part to yourself." He opened the board game's box and ran his hand over the neatly organized pieces. "Now, what piece do you want?"

Anslem raised a decisive finger. "It will be the thimble."

"The thimble?"

Nathan rolled his eyes as he set the board up on the coffee table between them.

"Rookie mistake. You need the battleship, every time."

Gloria's was quiet this particular night, and when Nathan had Slipped in, there had been plenty of choices of places to sit. He came every now and then, when dreams of his time as the Black Thorn were keeping him from sleep. The coffee was fresh, the calories nonexistent, and the food fantastic.

What more could we hope for?

Tonight, Gloria had summed him up with a look.

"Christopher," she called when he walked in from a nondescript street. "Meatloaf. Glazed carrots. Mashed po—nope, French fries."

She banged her spoon.

"Whew boy. You *are* lucky you don't got to work it off. I swear, next time you'll just ask me for bacon grease in a mug."

"Is that an option?" Nathan asked.

How she does that even despite my silver, I'll never understand.

"How's the family?" he asked.

"Spread all over, like usual." She cackled. "Pie's good tonight, if I do say so myself. My daughter-in-law made it. She makes a good pie. It's not great yet, but we'll get her there."

Gloria nodded her head over to the coffee shop side of the restaurant where a pretty young girl with a cascade of ring curls waved at Nathan.

Nathan grabbed himself a cup of coffee then took a seat up at the counter, right under the picture of Gloria and her sons. He studied the picture, trying to figure out which son the daughter-in-law belonged to.

When Gloria came out from behind the pass with a plate laden with food, he guessed, "She's married to Rocky, isn't she?"

"You mean Gemma?" Gloria laughed. "Christ boy. Rocky don't go in for the ladies. Thought you were supposed to be a detective?"

"I'm not a detective," Nathan replied. "Just a problem solver."

"Uh-huh, and I always paid taxes on all my tips."

Nathan laughed.

Gloria fixed him with a long stare, "You're coming by a lot."

"Is that a problem?"

She shook her head. "Never. I just wonder how you get on when I'm closed up."

"I stay busy," Nathan said. "Places to go. Things to detect."

He played with a fry on his plate.

"I don't suppose—"

"Not yet, Nate. But that doesn't mean anything. You know how it is."

"Everything in its place and everything in its time," Nathan said.

Gloria rested a hand on his before returning to the kitchen.

Alone at the counter, Nathan ate his food slowly, one careful bite at a time. The fries were thin and crispy, and they soaked the brown gravy up like a sponge. In his zero plane, Nathan may have kept a careful diet, but all gloves were off here.

Pie. Pie sounds good.

The door opened with a ring of a bell, and out of habit, Nathan checked behind him. His easy smile came to his face as the newcomer walked up to the counter.

He wore a pair of blue jeans and a simple black t-shirt. Over the shirt, a silver chain was visible. His black hair was cut shorter, and a small silver stud was pierced in one ear. After grabbing his own cup of coffee, he took the seat at the counter next to Nathan.

The storm gray eyes hadn't changed. They met Nathan's own.

"You look familiar," Alex Ashford said with a smile. "I feel like we've met before."

"I don't know," Nathan said. "I tend to get around. Help jog my memory. If we've met, where did we leave off?"

Alex chuckled. "I can't remember exactly. But I do get the sense that you're the type to steal beers and never replace them."

Nathan rolled his eyes.

"Tell you what," Nathan said. "I hear the pie's good here. Call it even?"

Alex grinned.

"Yeah. Pie sounds good. Pie sounds really good."

AUTHOR NOTE & ACKNOWLEDGMENTS

Each year, when January 1st rolls around, I normally sit myself down and make resolutions. I've done this since high school. Sometimes I'll write them out. Other times, I'll just tell them to myself. They're never too exciting; on this score, I like to keep things simple.

For well over two decades, high on the list—right at the top, in fact—has been *Release First Book.*

If you're reading this note now, then that's one thing I can finally check off.

That's why the biggest thank-you goes to you, the readers who gave this story a chance. If you enjoyed it, I hope you'll consider leaving a review wherever your voice is best heard. For an independent author, these make a big difference.

If you really liked it, feel free to shout. If you didn't like it as much, feel free to whisper.

You might wonder: why Christmas for the first book? The simple answer is timing. When I started this book in December 2023, I decided to get an early start on my annual resolution. The holidays are a naturally charged season—full of imagery, the changing times, and yes, magic—so I found myself interested in making a holiday myth of my own.

Besides, if Christmas was good enough for Dickens to write a ghost story, then I figured it'd be plenty good enough for mine.

As for what's next…well, Nathan has plenty of detecting still to do, and Alex has plenty he still needs to learn. I imagine I'll catch up with them soon enough.

If the idea is good, then in short order, we might be having a similar conversation to this one.

I, for one, am looking forward to it.

To Brett, whose patience and support were unwavering, thanks for going down this particular rabbit hole with me.

To my Dad, I don't think either of us thought you'd be the first one to read my first book, but I'm glad you were.

To my family, thanks for all your support.

To my editor, George, thanks for your efforts. You helped turn a rough draft into a finished book. Every reader who holds this story owes you a debt.

Dallas, Texas
October, 2025

ABOUT THE AUTHOR

Ethan M. Strowd is an author based in Dallas, Texas. After a career in the corporate world, he now writes full-time. Inspired by the speculative and the mysterious, he does his best to accurately write down the ideas he makes up, no matter what world they're from or what world they might explore.

You can learn more and join his newsletter for early access to new releases and behind-the-scenes notes at ethanmstrowd.com